D1459263

MURDER
IN MIDWINTER

LESLEY COOKMAN

First published by Accent Press Ltd – 2007

This edition printed 2012

ISBN 9781908262820

Printed and bound by CPI Group (UK) Ltd, Croydon, CR0 4YY

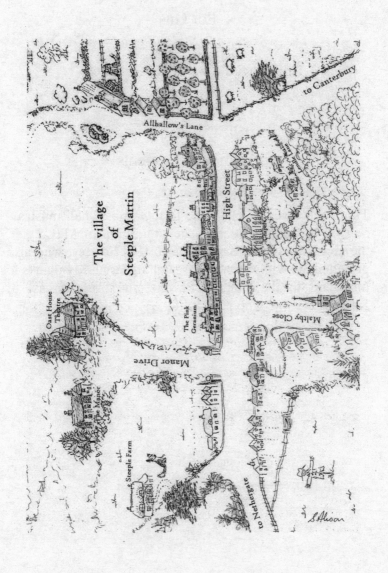

The village of
Steeple Martin

to Canterbury

Allhallow's Lane

High Street

Malthy Close

Oast House
Theatre

The Pink
Geranium

Pub

Manor Drive

The Manor

Steeple Farm

to Nethergate

S Alison

For Gus

Acknowledgements

This book owes its existence to my "music hall musical" *Summer Season,* written at the suggestion of Max Tyler, the archivist for the British Music Hall Society, who also provided me with valuable research material. My thanks to him, and to the Lindley Players, the original cast of *Summer Season,* who gave it life.

WHO'S WHO IN THE LIBBY SARJEANT SERIES

Libby Sarjeant
Former actor, sometime artist, resident of 17, Allhallow's Lane, Steeple Martin. Owner of Sidney the cat.

Fran Castle
Also former actor, occasional psychic, and owner of Balzac the cat.

Ben Wilde
Owner of The Manor Farm and the Oast House Theatre.

Guy Wolfe
Artist and owner of a shop and gallery in Harbour Street, Nethergate.

Peter Parker
Ben's cousin. Free-lance journalist, part-owner of The Pink Geranium restaurant and partner of Harry Price.

Harry Price
Chef and co-owner of The Pink Geranium and Peter Parker's partner.

Hetty Wilde
Ben's mother. Lives at The Manor.

Greg Wilde
Hetty's husband and Ben's father.

DCI Ian Connell
Local policeman.

Adam Sarjeant
Libby's youngest son. Works with garden designer Mog, mainly at Creekmarsh.

Lewis Osbourne-Walker
TV gardener and handy-man who owns Creekmarsh.

Sophie Wolfe
Guy's daughter. Lives above the gallery.

Flo Carpenter
Hetty's oldest friend.

Lenny Fisher
Hetty's brother. Lives with Flo Carpenter.

Ali and Ahmed
Owners of the Eight-til-late in the village.

Jane Baker
Chief Reporter for the *Nethergate Mercury*. Mother to Imogen.

Terry Baker
Jane's husband and father of Imogen.

Joe, Nella and Owen
Of Cattlegreen Nurseries.

DCI Don Murray
Of Canterbury Police.

Amanda George
Novelist, known as Rosie

Chapter One

'BLOODY AWFUL, AREN'T THEY?' muttered Peter Parker, as Libby Sarjeant returned to her seat in the auditorium to pick up her script and basket, having dismissed the cast of *Jack and the Beanstalk* after a fairly dismal rehearsal.

'No worse than they were for *The Hop Pickers*. They'll be all right.' Libby crossed her fingers.

'Sure we haven't bitten off more than we can chew?' Peter wound a scarf round his neck as they went into the foyer.

'Oh, I expect so. After all, we don't do things by halves, do we?' Libby went to switch off the lights. 'Our first play, written by you in a theatre owned by your family and converted by your cousin Ben was somewhat marred by a murder, so in a spirit of reckless abandon, we decide to do a pantomime, also written by you, with musicians we've never worked with and an inexperienced cast.'

Peter held the glass doors open for her. 'Piece of cake,' he grinned.

'Not, of course, to mention the fact that in amongst all this we have Christmas and your wedding.'

'Civil Partnership, dearie,' he corrected.

'Same thing. How's it going, anyway?'

'Nothing to it.' Peter shrugged. 'Harry's doing it all.'

Libby raised an eyebrow and said nothing.

The pub, in the middle of the village High Street, had appeared on many postcards and calendars. With its hanging baskets now filled with seasonal holly, the windows shining like golden nuggets in the darkness, Libby decided it would make a great Christmas card. Inside, the fire was roaring, and several members of the cast were herded together in the smaller of the two bars. Harry, Peter's intended and owner of The Pink Geranium, still in chef's trousers but with a fleece jacket instead of his whites, waved a pint in their direction.

'Hello, dear hearts,' he said. 'What are you having?'

'Lager, please,' said Libby. 'You're early, aren't you?'

'He shouldn't be working at all,' said Peter. 'Monday's usually his day off.'

'Oh, yes. Why is he, then?'

'Christmas party. Special booking. Loads of them between now and the big day.'

Harry handed them both glasses. 'Need all the dosh we can get for *our* big day, dear,' he said.

Libby changed the subject. 'Anyone seen Fran?'

'She's in London seeing to the house sale,' said Harry. 'She popped in this morning on her way out.'

'Good, because she forgot to tell me she was going and I was without a Baroness at the rehearsal tonight.'

'Where's young Ben, then?' asked Harry, making a dive for a table that had just become free.

'He said he'd meet us here,' said Libby. 'He popped in to see his Mum.'

'Uncle Greg's not too well again,' said Peter. 'I just hope he doesn't get worse before Christmas.'

'So do I.' Libby looked gloomy.

'Because you might lose your wicked Baron?' said Harry mischievously.

'No!' Libby was indignant. 'Because it's awful to lose someone at any time of year, but Christmas is worse, somehow.'

'Ey-up,' said Harry suddenly. 'Don't look now, but guess who's just come in?'

'Who?' said Libby, turning round immediately. 'Blimey!'

'Who is it?' Peter craned round her to see.

'It's that Inspector, you know, Connell.'

'He's still after Fran,' said Harry with glee.

'He's not after Fran,' said Libby, although she was by no means sure. Inspector Connell had been involved in a recent murder investigation during which he had met both Libby and Fran, and afterwards had showed a marked predilection for Fran's company.

Peter snorted.

'Good evening, Mrs Sarjeant.'

Libby looked up at the tall, dark man looming over the table. 'Good evening, Inspector Connell,' she said. 'I'm afraid Fran isn't here. She's in London.'

'I know. I spoke to her this morning.'

'Oh.' Libby was taken aback.

'Just wanted to say hello.' He nodded affably round the table. 'I'll see you before the trial, I expect.'

'Oh, God, another trial,' moaned Libby, as he moved away to join a group of people on the other side of the fireplace. 'Never had anything to do with the police in my life and now I've got two trials to go to. In less than a year!'

'Well, you could have stayed out of the last one,' said Peter, reasonably. 'You didn't have to get involved.'

'But it was Fran. She needed me.'

'Well, it obviously wasn't Fran he was here for tonight,' said Harry, still staring at the imposing back of Inspector Connell. 'I wonder why she called him this morning?'

'We're supposed to keep the police informed if we go anywhere,' explained Libby. 'In case they need us for more questions or anything.'

'Is that normal?' asked Peter. 'Or just because Connell's interested in Fran?'

'Oh, I don't know,' said Libby. 'Stop badgering.'

'Is Fran still after that cottage in Nethergate?' said Harry, still watching Connell.

Peter followed his gaze. 'Hoy. Eyes right, love.'

'I was just wondering if it was him or Guy she wanted to be in Nethergate for,' said Harry, patting Peter's hand.

'Why should it be either?' Libby finished her lager. 'She just wants to buy the cottage back that should have been hers. I don't blame her, either. It's a gorgeous location.'

'But unhappy memories, I would have thought,' said Peter.

'Not any more. She seems to have exorcised those. She just remembers the holidays. Happy memories.'

'She certainly seems to have honed her – what do you call them – psychic powers? Doesn't she?' said Harry.

'Because she needed to use them,' said Libby. 'She's not so frightened of them now, although she still doesn't trust them properly.'

'And what about your idea of a detective agency?' grinned Harry.

'Your idea, you mean. You were the one who started it.' Libby grinned back. 'I still think it's a great idea.'

'Libby, don't be daft,' said Peter. 'You said yourself, the police always get there before you do.'

'Ah, but not always the same way. And anyway, there are bound to be little matters which wouldn't interest the police, like finding out about houses –'

'Fran does that already, for Goodall and Smythe,' put in Harry.

'No, things about houses people already own. Or things they've lost. Oh, I don't know. There must be loads.'

'Well, let Fran get settled before you go involving her in hare-brained schemes,' said Peter. 'As you so rightly said earlier on, there's a lot going on at the moment. She's trying to sell the London house, buy the Nethergate cottage and be the Baroness in our panto.'

Libby felt a hand on her shoulder. 'And just where *was* my Baroness tonight?'

She looked up and smiled, thrilled to find her solar plexus quivering at the sight of her beloved, even though they'd now been together for several months and she should be used to it.

'What-ho, Ben,' said Harry. 'Are you buying?'

'All right, but I still want to know where Fran was,' said Ben, giving his cousin Peter a friendly clap on the shoulder. Libby explained about Fran while she went with him to the bar.

'She forgot,' she said, 'she's got a lot on her mind.'

'And I don't think Guy's helping,' said Ben, handing her two glasses.

'Guy? Why? He's really keen, although I'm not sure about her,' said Libby, weaving through bodies towards their table. Guy Wolfe had also been peripherally involved in the recent investigation and had almost managed to appoint himself Fran's significant other. But not quite.

'Too keen, and a bit jealous.'

'Oh, yes.' Libby nodded towards the group by the fireplace. 'Inspector Connell.'

Ben looked surprised. 'What's he doing here?'

'Meeting friends, by the look of things,' said Harry, accepting his drink. 'Nothing to do with Fran, apparently.'

Ben looked at Libby.

'True. He knew she'd gone to London.'

'Ah.'

'You wait till tomorrow,' muttered Libby. 'She's got some explaining to do.'

'It's her own business, Lib,' said Ben, gently.

'Not if it affects my pantomime,' said Libby, 'then it's mine.'

Later, as Ben and Libby walked back to her cottage in Allhallow's Lane, he returned to the subject.

'Aren't you and Fran getting on so well any more?'

Libby looked at him, surprised. 'Of course we are. Why?'

'You seemed a bit put out with her.'

'Only because she's been holding out on me. I don't call that friendly.'

'You said she forgot the rehearsal.'

'That's what Harry said. I think she talks to him more than she does to me.' Libby sounded grumpy.

'See, you're not getting on so well.' Ben dug her in the ribs.

'Well, *I* thought we were. She obviously doesn't.'

They turned into Allhallow's Lane. The lilac and cherry trees overhanging the old brick wall on the left poked bare branches at their hair and scraped eerily on the wall.

'Do you remember when I first asked if you wanted me to see you home?' said Ben, squeezing Libby's arm.

'And I said no. And then regretted it.'

'Did you?' Ben turned to look at her. 'Oh, good.'

She smiled at him. 'Yes,' she said.

Libby was drinking tea at the kitchen table the following morning when the phone rang.

'It's me,' said Fran. 'I'm so sorry about last night. I meant to get back in time, but I got held up and my mobile ran out of charge.'

'OK.' Libby took the phone back into the kitchen with her and turfed Sidney, her overfed silver tabby, off her chair. 'I thought you were staying up there overnight.'

'How did you know I'd gone?'

'Harry told me.'

'Oh, I see. Well, I'm sorry. I didn't get home until after midnight.'

'How did you get back from the station?'

'Taxi.' There was no mistaking the triumph in Fran's voice. 'You just cannot imagine the joy of being able to afford a taxi.'

'Oh, I can,' said Libby, who couldn't.

'Anyway, the house is sold – more or less –'

'To those developers?'

'Yes. Well, once I found out about what had happened there I didn't want to keep it. So now all I've got to do is sort out the Nethergate cottage and I'll be done.'

'Oh, yes,' said Libby, remembering, 'that Inspector Connell turned up at the pub last night.'

There was a short silence. 'Did he?' said Fran eventually.

'It's all right, he wasn't there to see you,' said Libby, slightly maliciously. 'He was meeting friends.'

'Oh.'

'But he said you'd called him that morning.'

'No. He called me. To say he was meeting friends in the pub and if I was around could he buy me a drink.'

'I thought you'd rung him.'

'Why would I do that?'

'I don't know,' said Libby, exasperated. 'I thought you were keeping something from me.'

'A secret affair with Inspector Connell?' Fran laughed.

'He's quite attractive.'

'I know. So's Guy.'

'Who's acting like a terrier with a bone, I gather?'

'Who says?'

'Ben. I don't know how he knew, though.'

'Libby, you live in a small rural community. Even I know how gossip spreads in a place like this.'

'Really? Well, can you tell me? Because I can never work it out.'

Fran laughed. 'Come off it. You're one of the nosiest people I know.'

Libby sniffed. 'I find out things. So do you.' She paused. 'Harry was asking about the detective agency last night.'

Fran sighed. 'Oh, Libby, be serious. Do you really want to go through all the complications of setting up a business? Trying to get clients? Just because we've been involved in a couple of murders by accident?'

'Don't trivialise them!'

'I'm not, but it's very different being involved because you actually *are* involved to barging into an investigation.'

'I wasn't thinking of doing that,' said Libby indignantly. 'It was more lost items, or – or well, what you do already, but not for estate agents.'

'Well, it's not on, whatever it is,' said Fran. 'Now, would you like to come to lunch and I'll tell you about the house progress and everything?'

'Great,' said Libby, cheering up. 'I'll bring a bottle. What time?'

Chapter Two

ROBERT GRIMSHAW OF GRIMSHAW and Taylor came round a teak desk that had been the height of furnishing fashion in the sixties. Bella thought that he had probably got stuck in the same time warp.

'Mrs Morleigh. So pleased to meet you. Do sit down. Tea? Or coffee?'

'Er –' said Bella.

'Tray of tea, please.' Robert Grimshaw addressed the secretary hovering by the door without looking at her and went back to his chair behind his desk. 'Now,' he said, opening a buff folder. 'I expect all this came as a bit of a shock to you?'

'You could say that.' Bella smiled, trying to relax her tense shoulders and sit more comfortably in the low slung chair.

'It surprised me, as well, and I knew Miss Alexander.' Robert Grimshaw surveyed Bella over his clasped hands. 'You have a look of her, you know.'

'I do?' Bella was obscurely pleased.

'Remarkably well preserved lady for her age. Ninety-two, she was, you know.'

'Ninety-two? My father would have been eighty-eight this year.'

'That would be Bertram, Miss Alexander's half brother.' Robert Grimshaw looked up as the door opened to admit the secretary struggling under the weight of a laden tea tray. Bella had to fight with herself not to get up and help while Robert Grimshaw merely watched benignly, tutting when a little tea trickled out of the spout.

'Will you be mother?' He leaned towards her archly. Bella tried to avoid the pale eyes which swept her lasciviously as, gritting her teeth, she levered herself to the edge of the chair and poured tea into two pale green cups.

'So.' Robert Grimshaw sat back in his chair and sipped his tea appreciatively, his expression as he looked over the rim of the cup still faintly salacious. Bella, unused to such admiration, felt uncomfortable.

'Let's fill you in a bit. How much do you know about your Aunt Maria?'

'Nothing at all. I didn't even know she existed.' Bella considered leaning back in her chair and decided against it as the tea in her cup threatened to transfer itself to her saucer.

'But you knew your grandmother?'

'Hardly. She died a year after I was born. My father didn't talk about her much.'

'I gather he left home very early and went to work in the city.' Robert Grimshaw referred to something in the buff folder.

'As soon as he could, I think.' Bella replaced her cup on the tray and edged surreptitiously back in to the chair. There was no beating it, she decided, as she collapsed backwards.

'You know your grandmother's name?'

'Dorinda? My maiden name was Durbridge, so presumably she was Dorinda Durbridge.'

'No, she never was.' Robert Grimshaw looked pleased by Bella's surprise. 'She was Dorinda Alexander. She never married. Your father took his father's name – in fact, he was registered as Durbridge on his birth certificate.'

Bella thought for a moment. 'So who was my grandfather?'

'A gentleman called Daniel Durbridge. I don't have much information about him, I'm afraid.'

'So my grandmother was a bit of a girl?'

Robert Grimshaw sighed. 'Well – yes. But there is quite a story to all this. I don't know all of it, but I expect Maria will have told you.'

'Maria? Oh, my aunt. But she hasn't told me anything. I've just said – I never met her.'

'No, but she left some documents to be passed on to you, and I would assume she will have written you a letter. She wrote one for your father, but she destroyed it when he died.'

'How did she know about us?' Bella had forgotten about the uncomfortable chair.

'She kept track of both Bertram and you.'

'Did he know about her?'

'Oh, yes. They both lived here. But he left home and she stayed here to run the theatre.'

'Theatre? What theatre?'

'The Alexandria.' He frowned. 'I did tell you in the letter.'

'No, you just said my aunt had left me property including March Cottage.'

'Oh.' He picked up what was obviously a copy of the letter and tutted. 'Dear me. Well, she has also left you the Alexandria. I could never understand why she didn't sell it, myself.'

Stunned, Bella gaped at him. 'Do you mean to say –' she gasped, when she could speak, 'that I own a *theatre*?'

'Well, yes. Except that it's virtually derelict.'

'Where is it?'

'At the western end of the bay. It looks out over the sea – quite a pretty spot, actually. But it's been boarded up for years. It was used for storage for a long time – various people used to rent it.'

'Could it be restored?' Bella's mind was leaping ahead.

Robert Grimshaw looked bewildered. 'Restored? What for?'

'To use as a theatre, of course. There isn't one here, is there?'

'Well, no. There's the Carlton Pavilion – they have entertainment, but –'

'Well, there you are then! Every seaside town needs a live theatre!' Bella pushed herself out of the chair and it banged loudly on the floor, affronted.

'Good heavens! You can't mean that you'd want to do that? It closed because of lack of interest. You'd never keep it going.'

'Well, I can look in to it, can't I? When did it close?'

'Years ago. In the fifties, I think. She could have sold the site for quite a lot then – and even more in the eighties. I intended to get it on the market for you as soon as possible. I even had it valued.' Robert Grimshaw looked extremely put out.

'Well, I'm sorry.' Bella sat down again and the chair hit her behind the knees. 'I love the theatre you see. Perhaps I got a bit carried away.'

'Yes.' He looked at her warily. 'Well. I am to give you the keys of both properties, her deed box which contains the documents I mentioned, and arrange an advance on her bank

10

account. Probate won't take long, but in the meantime, you cannot sell anything of hers, or draw on her bank. If you'll give me details of your bank, I will make the necessary arrangements.'

Bella was beginning to feel shell-shocked. 'Bank account? I didn't know anything about that.'

'Well, you are Miss Alexander's sole legatee.' He looked at her as though she was half-witted. 'Obviously you would inherit her bank account. Not that there's much in it,' he added, as an afterthought.

It was another twenty minutes before Bella came out into the autumn sunshine clutching a folder of documents and feeling dazed. Her first thought was to phone home and share the incredible news, until she remembered that Andrew would be at work and the children at school. Not, she realised, that Andrew was going to be overjoyed anyway, having only been interested in the re-sale value of her inheritance in the first place. She walked slowly along the narrow High Street until she found a cafe that had remained open after the end of the summer season, where she could while away the hour or so until she reconvened with Robert Grimshaw, who was going to take her to see March Cottage.

'Is this it?'

Visions of a whitewashed cottage with roses climbing over the door and into the thatch disappeared. Bella sat in Mr Grimshaw's car and stared at the row of red brick cottages, their front doors opening straight on to the narrow street. The third one from the right had "March Cottage" on the planked wooden door in uncompromisingly plain metal letters. Both door and letters were painted the sort of green she remembered from her childhood, neither emerald nor bottle nor apple, but reminiscent of grim school buildings.

'Yes, this is it.' Robert Grimshaw got out of the car and politely came to open the passenger door for her. 'Very desirable property, this. Second homes, you know.'

Bella did know, and had always despised second home owners who plucked the best properties from the mouths – figuratively speaking – of the local people. Now, it seemed, she was one herself. She followed Mr Grimshaw to the door, which he opened with a struggle, the door sticking in the frame as if reluctant to let them inside.

'A bit musty,' he said cheerfully, as he led the way in to the sitting room and put a hand to the light switch. 'Oh, dear. Electricity's not on. I'll see to it, if you like.'

Bella nodded absently, taking in the over-furnished room, the high-backed wooden chairs with their patchwork cushions either side of what looked like a genuine range, the tables laden with small ornaments and photographs on lace covers stiff, now, with dust and neglect. Her eyes went to the window, hung with lace curtains under worn velvet, and despite the lowering grey clouds which had begun to gather over the sea since lunchtime, her spirits lifted.

'How soon could we get the electricity on?' she asked, turning back to Robert Grimshaw, who was running a bony finger along the top of a doorframe.

'Oh, a day or so. Why – not thinking of staying here, are you?' He laughed heartily.

'Well, yes, actually.' Bella hadn't known that, but it was quite obvious that she was. 'After all, whatever I do with the cottage, it will need cleaning up, won't it? Would it be all right if I stayed here? I mean, with probate and everything?'

'No problem – but are you sure? I mean, it's not exactly up to date, is it?' He was looking at her as though she'd suddenly grown an extra head.

'Well, I'll soon find out, won't I?' Bella smiled at him and held out her hand. 'May I have the keys, now? I don't want to hold you up any longer.'

'Don't you want me to drive you back? I thought I could take you to the station – save you a taxi.' His expression told her that he was fast having his first impression of her confirmed – she was batty.

'No, thank you, Mr Grimshaw. I've taken up far too much of your time already.' Bella smiled sweetly at him again.

Clearing his throat and going faintly pink, Robert Grimshaw edged a little closer. 'Ah – no trouble at all, I assure you. Matter of fact, I was going to suggest a spot of tea –'

'No, no. I shall be fine – really.' Bella, the smile solidifying on her face. 'May I have the keys?'

He handed her a large bunch of keys with a buff label attached. 'The keys to the other building are there, as well. I don't advise you going inside it, though. It could be dangerous.'

'I'll be careful.' Bella moved towards the door, hoping he would take the hint.

'Call the office in the morning and I'll be able to tell you about the gas and electricity.' He sighed and stooped to go out of the door. 'Good luck, Mrs Morleigh.'

Bella watched him drive down to the end of the little street and went back inside. She was conscious of a rising sense of excitement as she explored the cottage. Despite Robert Grimshaw's gloomy predictions, it was in very good order. The range, when inspected, still contained grey ash and half-burnt wood, so, clearly, it had been functioning until Maria died, and in the two bedrooms at the top of the enclosed staircase, modern, slimline storage heaters had been installed. Both these rooms contained old metal bedsteads, whether or not they were brass Bella couldn't tell, both made up with white linen sheets, blankets and hand-crocheted bedspreads. A thick sage green carpet covered the whole of the upper floor and continued down the stairs, where it gave way to polished floorboards and rugs in the front room and a step down on to the stone flags of the kitchen. Here, an old wire-fronted cabinet and a huge dresser provided the storage, while an ancient cream Rayburn proved to be the only cooking source. The deep Butler sink was crackle-glazed but clean, except where the cold tap had dripped over the months and left a raindrop-shaped stain. Through a door on one side of the sink was a lobby with a door to the garden and a variety of baskets and old boots, newspapers and flowerpots, and the door to the bathroom. Bella stopped in surprise.

The bathroom had been fitted very recently. Pristine white fittings had their full complement of aids for the disabled, the flooring was soft cork tiles and a top of the range electronic shower had been fitted over the bath, which had a pull out seat at the other end. Over the sink stood one or two little bottles and a tube of Steradent tablets.

A sudden thump against the frosted window and a dark shape appeared. Bella jumped, her heart racing. The shape patted the glass. 'Miaow,' it said, faintly. Bella backed out of the bathroom and struggled with the bolts on the back door. When she eventually won, she had barely pulled the door open a crack before a fluffy black cat with a distinguished white shirt front had pushed its way in and started winding itself around her legs.

'Well, hello.' Bella bent down and stroked the long fur. 'And who might you be?'

The cat walked away from her hand and straight to the Rayburn, where it began sniffing round the floor. It turned to look at Bella, then went into the sitting room, jumped on to one of the wooden chairs and began to wash.

Bella watched it for a moment. It must know the house well, but it obviously didn't belong here, or it would have starved in the four months since Maria died. And this cat was by no means starving.

She settled down in the chair opposite the cat, picked up the buff folder and leant towards the window to catch the light. Mr Grimshaw had opened the deed box in her presence and, sure enough it had revealed a letter addressed to "My niece, Arabella Durbridge."

'That was why we had a bit of trouble tracing you,' Robert Grimshaw had explained. 'We assumed that was your name now – she didn't leave any indication that you had married.'

Funny names, thought Bella as she slit open the long brown envelope. Glamorous names. Maria, Dorinda, Arabella. She had never questioned her own name before, other than to wish it belonged to somebody else when she was a child.

"My dear Arabella," the letter began. "No doubt you will already know that you have inherited my house and the Alexandria Theatre by the time you read this letter. I expect this came as a shock to you, as I am quite certain you did not know of my existence. I do not know if my half-brother Bertram ever told his wife, but I think it unlikely as he did not even invite our mother to his wedding."

Bella looked up from the spidery writing and met the green eyes of the cat, who had stopped washing to stare at her.

'I never knew that,' she said, and returned to her reading.

"Doubtless Bertram had his own valid reasons," the letter went on, "but it distressed her very much. She had returned here to live with me when he first left home, and, as I'm sure you know, she died a year after you were born. She made me promise that I would not embarrass either Bertram or you by getting in touch and I have respected her wishes. Bertram was ashamed of his mother, I am proud of her. I believe his father, Daniel Durbridge, whose name you bear, had been in touch with him, and whether this had a bearing on his feelings towards our mother, I shall never know. Durbridge was an unpleasant man, out for all he could get. In fact, at one point he tried to gain control of the Alexandria from my mother by underhand means, but I am afraid he underestimated me. I have no idea how you will feel, but I will tell you her story."

Bella edged the chair a little nearer to the window and tried to get comfortable. She was cold, and dying for a cup of tea, but something told her she should read Maria's letter in Maria's house. The cat jumped down, yawned elegantly and came to put its paws on her knees.

'Come on, then,' said Bella and moved to accommodate it. It settled down, purring, sending warm vibrations through her thighs as she resumed reading.

"My mother, Dorinda Alexander, was a governess. She was the youngest daughter of a middle-class tradesman and his wife, who in her turn was the daughter of a brewery owner. Dorinda was sent to Mr & Mrs Shepherd, friends of her parents, to look after their daughter Julia, while their sons were away at school. Every summer, as was the custom in those days, the family took a house here at the seaside. The staff came with them, while the boys joined them when their school closed for the holidays, when Dorinda would have charge of all three children, and Mr Earnest would come down for as long as he could in August.

"In the summer of 1903, the family were living here when Dorinda met a young man called Peter Prince, who was with a troupe of Pierrots called Will's Wanderers. The relationship was highly irregular, especially as it became more intimate. Naturally enough, it was discovered and she was turned off. She could not go home to her parents, but luckily the young man, who, you will have guessed, was my father, did not desert her, and they moved in to digs together. Dorinda, who could play the piano and sing very well, was incorporated in to the troupe – one of the first women known to have performed with Pierrots – and they obtained a piano on wheels for her to play. At the end of the season, Dorinda advertised private French and piano lessons and Peter took any jobs he could. During that winter they were able to rent this cottage.

"During the season of 1904, Dorinda became the leader of a new troupe called the Silver Serenaders, so called because their costumes, which, instead of being white, were made of a silvery material. Eventually they were given their own 'pitch', of which after a couple of years, Dorinda bought the freehold and built the Alexandria Theatre. She was an extremely successful woman and a wonderful mother. I was born in March 1914, and Peter Prince went to join the army later that year. She never saw him again. She and I stayed here in this cottage, which she eventually bought.

"The Silver Serenaders became The Alexandrians and were as well known in this part of the country as Will Catlin's Royal Pierrots in Scarborough. Eventually, the Alexandria stayed open all year and attracted some of the top Music Hall artistes. My mother would go to London during the winter to see their acts and bring them down here the following summer. She was also somewhat of a personality among the literary set, several of whom professed to be in love with her.

"During the war The Alexandrians became an all female troupe, but towards the end of the war, when my mother went up to London, she met a popular singer and comedian called Daniel Durbridge whom she persuaded to join us. Unfortunately, by the time she discovered she was pregnant, she had also discovered that he was already married. Bertram was born just after Armistice Day in 1918, Daniel left his wife and persuaded my mother to join him, leaving Bertram and myself in the care of one of the women in the troupe. Together, they went to South Africa and then toured Ceylon, but when they returned, Daniel went back to his wife. I wanted her to come back here, as The Alexandrians were still running the theatre, but my mother wanted to try her luck in London and sent for Bertram to join her. Unfortunately, she wasn't successful, and in 1932, when Bertram left school, he left home as well, so she returned here. We continued to run the Alexandria until her last illness in 1952, after which I used to lease it for the summer season to small companies for summer repertory. By the beginning of the sixties, that sort of thing was dying out and I closed the theatre.

"What you intend to do with the building, I do not know. It has been used as warehousing for various businesses in the town, but as far as I know, the seating and the stage are still there. Robert Grimshaw has tried to persuade me to sell it time after time – the site alone being worth a considerable amount of money – but I have a good deal of affection for the old place and I like to go and sit on the park bench opposite and remember. I hope you will do the same. For some reason, my mother thought, when you were born, that you would be the one to carry on the family tradition, but as far as I know, you are not in the profession and I have no idea whether you would have any interest in it. If you wish to sell the Alexandria, I hope you will, but please make sure that all the programmes and costumes that I have kept are housed properly, as I cannot help but feel they will be of great interest to historians, particularly local and theatrical.

"It is interesting that your father should have chosen a name so similar to mine and our mother's for you. Perhaps he still retained some family feeling for us, after all.

"I hope my bequest will be of some help to you, my dear Arabella, and I regret that we did not meet during my lifetime.

"Your affectionate aunt,

"Maria May Alexander."

It was dated five years previously.

Bella sat staring out of the window for a long time until the cat recalled her attention by changing position and kneading her knees through her jeans.

'Ow! Stop that,' she said, giving it a gentle push and standing up. It stretched and promptly jumped back on to the other chair.

'Well, you obviously knew Maria.' Bella told it. 'What a pity you can't talk.' She sighed. 'But you can't stay here. I've got to go. Come on.'

After she had put the protesting cat out of the back door, she refolded the letter and replaced it in its envelope before taking a final look round. Outside, she stepped back to have a good look at March Cottage and its six neighbours, all of which looked in good repair and quite attractive, now she came to think of it. The street, Pedlar's Row, was only the length of the terrace of cottages and on the opposite side consisted of a high stone wall, over which hung variegated foliage suggesting a large and well tended garden behind. The village, all twisting lanes and a couple of small shops, which were now a high class delicatessen and off licence respectively, had a pub, The Red Lion, which hid round the corner of the high wall and Bella went inside.

There was no one in the dark, flag-stoned bar, except a large, middle-aged man behind the counter.

'Can I help you?'

'I wondered if you had the number of a local taxi firm?' asked Bella.

'Over there,' he said, waving a hand towards the end of the bar and retiring behind his newspaper.

Bella dialled the number of the taxi service on her mobile and told them where to pick her up. She had ten minutes to wait, so decided to risk a half of lager instead of the longed for cup of tea.

'I don't suppose you knew Miss Alexander who lived round the corner in Pedlar's Row?' she asked as the landlord handed over her change.

'Maria? I should say.' He grinned. 'Here, you're not her niece, are you?'

'Yes.' Bella stared at him.

He laughed. 'Lor' bless yer! She was always telling us that she was leaving her house to her niece. And the theatre, of course. "She doesn't know, yet," she'd say. "It'll be a nice surprise for her." I'll bet it was, too.'

'It certainly was.' Bella took a sip of lager, surprised at how different it tasted in the middle of the afternoon. 'So she used to come in here, did she?'

'Oh, yes, reg'lar as clockwork, every evening about seven o'clock, she'd come in for her brandy. Then off she'd toddle about eight. Till last winter, of course.' He looked gloomy. 'The missus realised she 'adn't been in and popped round. Lucky we knew about the spare key, or she could 'ave died then and there. Still, we got 'er to 'ospital all right. Not that she liked it there.'

He looked up at Bella, a pained expression on his face. 'We

wanted to call you, but she wouldn't tell us how to get hold of you, so we couldn't. She said you didn't know about her.'

'That's right, I didn't. I can't believe that I've gone all through my life not knowing I had an aunt.' Bella shook her head and swallowed some more lager. 'By the way, do you know anything about a black and white cat who must live near here? He came into the cottage with me.'

'That's Balzac. He was her cat. 'Er next door's been lookin' after 'im – except I don't think she allows 'im inside.'

'Oh, I see. Shame I can't take him back with me.' Bella finished her lager as she heard the taxi draw up outside. 'I'll be down again, soon, so I'll call in again. Thanks.'

'Pleasure.' The landlord nodded. 'Nice to meet you.'

She hesitated. 'I suppose –' she began slowly, 'you don't let rooms?'

The landlord shook his head. 'No, love, sorry. Was you not goin' to stay in the cottage?'

'I'm not sure yet. Not to start with, anyway.'

'I tell you where you could stay – over at Steeple Martin. There's a nice little pub there – three rooms, I think they've got. Good food by all accounts.'

'Is it far?'

'About two miles. Reason I suggested Steeple Martin is they've got a theatre there. In a converted oast house. Woman over there runs it. Might know something about Maria's theatre.'

'Well, thank you Mr, er –'

'Felton. Just call me George.'

'George.' Bella smiled. 'Thanks again.'

'Do you know the old theatre, the Alexandria?' Bella asked, as the taxi drove back into the town, into tree-lined streets with shining pavements, battered by the rain which had started while Bella was in the pub and was building itself up in to a positive downpour.

'Yeah. Why, do you want to go there?' The taxi driver didn't look at her.

'Will it take us out of our way?'

'It's the other end of town, but it don't matter to me.'

'All right, then, yes please.' Bella sat back and peered out of the window as the taxi turned and began to go back to the old part of town.

'There.' The taxi driver pulled in to the side of the road and put on his hand brake.

The Alexandria stood alone, facing a small ornamental garden, the cliff and the sea to its right, the town ahead of it and to its left. It reminded Bella of a miniature pier pavilion that had been marooned, its pointed glass cupola smashed, the front boarded up behind important looking pillars. The pillars and the boards had been the recipients of the usual graffiti and fly posting, the whole looking gloomy and forlorn under the grey clouds and persistent rain.

'Thank you,' said Bella, sitting back in her seat. 'I'll go on to the station, now.'

Two hours later she fitted her key in the lock and bent down to pick up the parcel of fish and chips.

'Mum.' Tony was there, enfolding her in a bony hug. 'What have you got there?'

'Chips.' Amanda sniffed as she poked her head over his shoulder to give her mother a kiss. 'Great.'

'Let your mother get in, now.' Andrew's voice was avuncular, tolerant, someone playing a part. Bella winced. The children parted like the Red Sea and he loomed towards her.

'Good journey?' He planted a dry kiss on her lips. 'You needn't have bothered with fish and chips. We've eaten.'

'Well, I haven't,' snapped Bella and bent wearily to pick up her holdall, no one else having thought to relieve her of it.

'Here, Mum, I'll take that.' Tony grabbed the greasy parcel and bore it off towards the kitchen. 'Did you get some for us?'

'Yes.' Bella dumped her holdall on the kitchen floor and pulled out a chair. 'I'm whacked.'

'Shall I put the food out?' Amanda lounged through the doorway, chewing idly on the end of her school tie.

'Yes, please, darling. And could you put the kettle on?'

Andrew pulled out another chair and sat down opposite her at the table. 'So, tell me. How did it go?'

'All right. I saw the cottage. March Cottage, it's called, in Pedlar's Row, Heronsbourne. I also found out she's left me a derelict theatre. So I found out where that was, too – is, rather. It hasn't been used for years, but it's still there.'

'Come now.' Andrew was big, bluff and superior. She could see him stopping himself from saying "little woman" and patting her on the hand – or the head. 'A theatre? Prime real estate, would it be? And your father knew nothing about it?'

'I don't honestly know. I suppose so, but he never mentioned it to me, or to mum. I didn't know until the will, you know that.'

'I think it's exciting.' Tony put a plate of fish and chips in front of her, tastefully decorated with bits of greaseproof paper. She peeled them off.

'Can I have some?' Amanda was hovering over the open parcel on the draining board. 'Go on about the theatre.'

'Well, there isn't much more to tell.' Bella chewed a mouthful of fish and extracted a bone. 'It's there, although I didn't see inside it, it's mine, and I don't suppose there would be a problem if I wanted to re-establish it as a theatre. About the licence and all that.'

She became aware of the silence as she finished the next mouthful and looked up. Tony and Amanda were studiously avoiding Andrew's set face.

'Re-establish it?' he asked finally. 'What do you mean?'

Bella didn't actually know what she meant. It had just come out.

'Er, well – re-open it. You know.' She returned to the rapidly cooling fish. She didn't want to discuss the Alexandria now.

'No, I don't know.' Andrew pushed his chair back and stood up. 'I thought the whole idea was to see what the cottage was like in order to sell it – see if we could realise some capital on it.'

Amanda leaned between them and put down a mug of tea. 'We'll be in the front room, Mum,' she said tactfully, and vanished.

Bella pushed her plate away and pulled her tea towards her, recognising the inevitable. There was to be a row – decreed by Andrew.

'I don't think I ever said that.' She refused to meet his eyes. 'I just said I wanted to go and find it.'

'Yes – but I assumed you'd sell the cottage. And this

theatre –' he gave it undue emphasis '– I mean – what on earth would you do with a derelict building in Kent? You couldn't live there.'

'Not in the theatre, no.'

'What *are* you talking about, Bella? You're not seriously suggesting we move there, are you? What on earth *for*?'

'I don't know.' Bella was exasperated. 'I haven't really thought about it yet.' She stood up. 'I've only just got in, for heaven's sake.'

Andrew stood back, glowering at her. 'We'll talk about it later, then. After you've unpacked.'

'I'm not going to unpack just yet.' Bella swept past him, ignoring his thunderstruck expression. 'I can't be bothered.'

'Where are you going? What about the plates?'

'You can do them, if you like. Or I'll do them in the morning. It doesn't matter.' She steeled herself against the barrage of words that was sure to come – but surprisingly, didn't. Round One to me, she thought, and wandered in to the front room to talk to the children.

It was much later, in bed, when Andrew returned to the subject. Bella didn't mind, because if she annoyed him he wouldn't pester her.

'So what's all this about a little theatre, then?' She could hear the indulgent smile in his voice.

'All what?' she asked, turning a blank face towards him. She watched the twitch of annoyance, quickly smoothed away, as he settled his naked body more comfortably under the duvet, turned slightly towards her.

'Well, opening it. That's what you said, didn't you? Or did you mean you would hand it over to the local council to run?'

'I don't know, Andrew. I haven't thought it through, yet, as I told you. All I could think about on the train home was that I owned a theatre. That is very exciting, you know, especially for someone like me.'

He turned heavily on to his back.

'What do you want to do, then? Run an am-dram group down there, or something?' He clasped his hands behind his head irritably. Out of the way there, thought Bella with satisfaction.

'Hardly,' she said out loud. 'That's difficult enough here. I couldn't do it down there. No,' she said, turning her back on him and switching off her bedside light. 'It would be professional.'

The silence that followed this remark – which had surprised Bella quite as much as it had surprised Andrew – went on for so long that Bella began to get worried. Could people have silent heart attacks? she wondered.

'I don't understand you.' Andrew's voice was tight. 'Are you saying you *will* lease it to the council after all?'

'I don't … *think* so,' said Bella, slowly. 'I think I'd like to look in to running it myself.'

'But how?' Andrew came nearer to a screech than he ever had in his life. 'You couldn't run it from here.'

'No.' Bella was thoughtful. 'But I could commute.'

'You don't know what you're talking about. For a start, where would the money come from? You can't set up a venture like that without working capital – and I certainly haven't got any to spare. This family takes up every penny and more, as you know.'

I know, thought Bella. You're always telling me.

'So, tell me. Where would you get the money?' He raised himself up on his elbow to lean over her and she buried her head more firmly in the pillow.

'I don't know, Andrew, I've told you. I've got to think about it. Just leave me be.'

'When you've thought about it, you'll see I'm right.' He reached a hand down and patted her shoulder. 'Impossible to live there or do anything with the theatre. Far better to sell them both. Cottage in the country, great as a second home, and where's the theatre?'

'On the seafront,' said Bella tiredly.

'There you are,' he said. 'Brilliant. Get it valued. We might even be able to get a little place in Spain, or somewhere. Bulgaria's supposed to be nice, isn't it? And much cheaper.'

Oh, yes, thought Bella. It would have to be much cheaper.

'I'll think about it,' said Bella. 'I can't do anything until probate's granted anyway, and I'd like to find out a bit more about my aunt and my grandmother before I let everything go.'

He threw himself over with his back to her and yanked the duvet away from her shoulders.

'Well, do let me know what you've decided, won't you?' he muttered, and let out a gusty, disapproving sigh.

Bella was up before Andrew in the morning, cutting sandwiches for the children when he came into the kitchen tying his conservative blue and red striped tie.

'Tea?' he asked, riffling through the pile of post on the table. Bella gritted her teeth and pushed a mug of tea across the kitchen table before turning back to the bread. 'Do you want an egg? I'm doing one for Tony.'

'No, thanks. I was up a pound or two yesterday at the club.'

Bella glowered sideways at his stocky but well-toned figure. 'Bloody squash,' she muttered under her breath. Andrew didn't hear and retuned the radio to Radio Four.

'Oh, Dad.' Amanda slouched in to the kitchen. 'Do we have to listen to that rubbish?'

'Better than your rubbish.' He sat down and poured himself a bowl of health-conscious cereal. Amanda regarded it with dislike.

'Here are your sandwiches, Manda.' Bella handed them over. 'Sorry they're a bit thick.'

Amanda shrugged. ''Salright. Can I have some money for the way home?'

'Money?' Andrew looked up. 'What for?'

'They always have some extra pocket money on Fridays.' Bella scrabbled in her bag for her purse. 'They always have. You know that.'

'I do not.' Andrew chased the last soggy flake round his bowl and Amanda sighed theatrically and raised her eyes to the ceiling. Bella handed over some money and went to the kitchen door.

'Tony. Are you dressed yet? And have you got your rugby gear?'

'Yes.' An impatient and muffled reply came from the bathroom, followed quickly by size ten feet coming down the stairs two at a time.

'Sandwiches?' He grabbed them from the table and thrust them in to an already bulging sports bag. 'I'll be late tonight, Mum, I'm going to Danny's after rugger.'

'No "Please may I?" I suppose?' Andrew stood up with a

teeth grating scrape of his chair.

'He is seventeen, Andrew.' Bella found some more money and gave it to Tony. 'Get your coat on, Manda.'

'Hang on.' Andrew slid his arms in to his suit jacket and smoothed down his hair. 'I'll give you both a lift to the bus stop.' He went into the hall to pick up his briefcase and Bella and the children exchanged surprised glances.

'Come on, then,' he called from the front door. 'See you later, Bel.'

Bella was mildly astonished when her daughter came up and gave her a hug.

'We missed you, Mum,' she whispered.

When they had gone, Bella sat down at the table with a fresh mug of tea feeling as though she had shrivelled up like a prune. All the fight had gone out of her and Andrew had completely forgotten about her minor rebellion of the previous evening. Pointless, really, wasn't it? She giggled. How absurd it sounded now, in the cold light of day in her own kitchen. Why had she thought she could do it? She couldn't even plan a holiday without Andrew's help, so why had she thought she was capable of such a gargantuan undertaking as the restoration and re-opening of a theatre?

She rested her chin in her hands and gazed out at the grey morning. The truth was that she hadn't thought about it, it had just popped out last night in response to Andrew's obvious disapproval. When she thought about it logically, of course she couldn't de-camp to Kent leaving the children here with Andrew, who was so palpably out of his depth with them.

But she thought about it all morning while she got dressed, cleared up the kitchen and tried to tidy away all the evidence of two days away from home. She talked to herself as she wiped round the washbasin, collected damp towels and fished socks out of the waste bin and collected magazines and papers in the sitting room.

After raiding the fridge at lunchtime and coming up with nothing but a lettuce and some cold potatoes, she decided to go early to the supermarket. The inside of her ancient Fiat was like a fridge until the dodgy heating system turned it into a blast furnace bringing her out in an uncomfortable film of perspiration which the open window did nothing to combat. By the time she had collected her trolley and pushed it in to the air conditioned bliss of the supermarket her hair was sticking limply to her forehead and the back of her neck and she was scared to lift her arms and reveal possible dark patches. Shopping was very difficult if you could only take things from below shoulder height.

'Bella.'

'Oh, hi, Viv.' Bella wrenched her trolley to a halt and surreptitiously wiped her damp top lip.

'You look hot.' Viv, an acquaintance from Bella's amateur drama society, squinted up from under a cloud of dark hair which surrounded an unseasonably tanned and painted face, sharply pointed like a snooty weasel. Heavy gold chains clanked painfully against protruding collar bones and wrists, but she never seemed to either notice or get bruised.

'I am hot. And bothered.'

'So, did you go down to Kent?' She fixed Bella with a beady brown eye.

'Yes, I did. Got back yesterday.'

'Golly.' The other woman's eyes widened even further than normal. 'I never thought old Andy'd let you go.'

'What do you mean? Let me go? It wasn't up to him.'

'Rubbish. He treats you like one of the children – *and* you let him. I must admit I was surprised when you said you were going.'

'Well, I went. And I'm going back.'

'Back? When?'

'I don't know when.' She stared at the contents of her trolley. 'In fact, I don't quite know what I'm going to do at all, but I'm definitely going. I've been left a derelict theatre.'

'What?'

'I didn't actually go inside, but I know where it is. I want to open it up.'

'Open it?' Excitement swept across Viv's sharp features. 'As a theatre?'

'Yes. If I can find out how to go about it.'

'Fantastic. Will you take us down there? I mean the Monday Players.'

'Oh, Viv, I couldn't.' Bella shook her head. 'I don't know how to go about it all – really.'

'But what does Andrew say about it all? I bet he's mad.'

Bella sighed. 'Yes, he is. He can't understand why I want to do it. He thought I should sell the site for "us" to get some capital out of it. And he doesn't want me swanning off to Kent every five minutes.'

'I don't suppose the children do, either,' the other woman nodded sagely, 'not if it means them being left with Andrew.'

'No.' Bella sighed again. 'I thought it would be all right. After all, Tony's seventeen and Amanda's nearly sixteen, but they missed me.'

'So how would they cope? I can't see them being over-enamoured of moving to Kent.'

'Oh, no, there's no question of that.' Bella realised that she was lying and rushed on. 'I'll just have to commute until I see what's going to happen.'

'Well, I don't know how. You haven't got any money and Andrew won't fund you.'

'Something'll work out.' Bella made to push her trolley further on. 'See if it doesn't.'

Viv couldn't refrain from a final valedictory comment. 'It'll work out in the divorce courts if you're not careful,' she said. 'Mark my words.'

Chapter Three

FRAN OPENED THE DOOR to the flat with her phone in the other hand.

'Yes,' she was saying, 'of course, but I don't see why ...?'

Libby followed her up the stairs.

'All right, I suppose so.' Fran frowned. 'Give me her number. No, she can't have mine. And I don't know why you think I can help her, anyway.' She waved Libby towards a bottle on the table. 'All right. Yes, I'll let you know. Goodbye.' She switched off the phone and looked at Libby. 'That was Inspector Connell,' she said.

'Really?' Libby put her own bottle down next to Fran's. 'Which wine?'

'Don't mind,' said Fran. 'You'll never guess what he wanted.'

'To ask you out?'

'Don't be daft, Lib. Didn't you hear my side of the conversation?'

'Something about giving someone your number.'

'Exactly. Pour me a glass and I'll tell you all.'

Libby poured two glasses and sat on the window sill. 'Go on then.'

'Apparently, Inspector Connell has suggested I can help some woman who's just found a body.'

'What?' Libby's mouth dropped open.

'This woman's inherited a theatre or something. In Nethergate.'

'In Nethergate? I didn't know there was a theatre in Nethergate. There's the Carlton Pavilion, of course.'

'No, it's disused. I think I remember it on the seafront.'

'Oh!' Libby's face lit up. 'Of course. The Alexandria! They used to have summer shows there, revues and things. I believe it had been going since the First World War. Not sure of the details, but I remember being taken to see shows there.'

'That's it.' Fran nodded. 'Well, this woman's inherited it.'

'Lucky bugger,' said Libby.

'It's derelict apparently, so I assume it's going on the market. Should fetch a good price. Anyway, when she was looking over it this woman found a body.'

'And Inspector Connell wants you to help?' asked Libby, excited. 'See! I told you we could do it.'

'No, no, Lib. She wants to know about the theatre and her relatives. She didn't know anything about them.'

'So what made Connell suggest you?'

Fran shrugged. 'Connections with local theatre? Keep me out of trouble? I don't know.'

'An excuse to keep in touch with you?'

'Oh, do stop, Libby,' said Fran. 'You were just like this with Guy. Stop match-making.'

'I only want you to be as happy as I am,' said Libby, climbing off the window sill.

'I am happy. Deliriously. I've suddenly come into money and the loveliest cottage in the world – almost.'

'And some new clothes,' said Libby. 'Did you get those in London?'

Fran stared self-consciously down at her new jeans and jumper. 'Yes. I thought I ought to get a bit more up-to-date.'

'Very nice too,' said Libby. 'Wish I could.'

'You couldn't change your look, though, could you?' Fran went into the kitchen.

'That's probably because of where I shop.' Libby followed her. 'Can I carry anything?'

'Salad,' said Fran, handing it to her. 'And I take it you mean charity shops?'

'Of course,' grinned Libby. 'I couldn't possibly desert them.'

'There are some lovely clothes of your kind, now,' said Fran sitting down at the table and passing Libby a plate of something savoury.

'Very expensive,' said Libby. 'I get the same effect for next to nothing. I mean, look at my cape.'

They both turned and looked at the slightly moth-eaten blue

blanket hanging on Fran's coat hook.

'That'd cost a fortune these days.' Libby helped herself to salad. 'Now, back to this woman. Who is she?'

'A Bella Morleigh.' Fran pulled a piece of paper towards her. 'A London number. That's all I know.'

'So she isn't local.'

'Doesn't look like it.'

'Exciting, isn't it?' Libby looked up at her friend, her eyes sparkling. 'This is just what I was suggesting.'

'This is pure coincidence, Libby, and, forgive me for saying it, nothing to do with you.'

Libby gasped. 'Fran! How could you? You *can't* keep me out of it.'

Fran shifted in her chair, looking down at her plate. 'Well, I'll tell you about it, of course, but –'

Libby looked at her through narrowed eyes. 'Oh, I get it. Connell warned me off, did he?'

'Sort of,' said Fran, looking uncomfortable.

'Keep that meddling bitch out of it, I suppose?' said Libby.

'Something like that.' Fran looked even more uncomfortable.

Libby laughed. 'Oh, don't look so bad, Fran. After all, if it hadn't been for my meddling we wouldn't have got very far last time, would we?'

'I know.' Fran sat up straight, looking happier. 'But I think he wants me to report back to him, so we'll have to keep you low profile.' She raised an eyebrow. 'If possible.'

'Now why,' said Libby, resting her chin on her hand, 'does he want you to report back to him? Does he suspect this woman of something?'

'If he did, he would be questioning her, not turning her over to me.'

'Must be he thinks something in her background is a clue, then,' said Libby. 'I told you he was more intelligent than Inspector Murray.'

'Inspector Murray at least believed in me,' said Fran. 'It was only right at the end that Connell had to give in.'

'Fancies you,' said Libby. 'I keep saying.'

'I know you do, and I wish you'd stop. And I'm going out with Guy tonight, anyway.'

'Good,' said Libby, 'I like Guy. So tell me, when are you going to ring this woman?'

'This afternoon? Then perhaps I can arrange for us to meet her.'

'Aha! So you do want me in on it?' Libby was triumphant.

'As long as you don't interrupt,' said Fran, 'I suppose so.'

But when Fran dialled Bella Morleigh's number later that afternoon, all she heard was a rather pompous male voice asking her to leave a message. She did so, being deliberately vague, and said she would call again. She was surprised, therefore, to receive a call from a breathless woman while she was getting ready to go out with Guy.

'Mrs Castle?' asked the woman. 'I'm Bella Morleigh. You rang earlier.'

'But I didn't leave my number,' said Fran.

'You happened to be the last caller, so I dialled 1471,' explained Bella Morleigh. 'I hope you don't mind.'

'No, of course not,' said Fran, cursing herself. 'So, how can I help you?'

'Um, well,' said the voice dropping to almost a whisper, 'it would be better if I could meet you. Would that be possible?'

'Where?' asked Fran, not wanting to commit herself to yet another trip to London.

'I'll be down on Thursday. Could I come and see you? Or meet you somewhere?'

'Are you staying in Nethergate?' said Fran.

'I was recommended to a pub in somewhere called Steeple Martin.'

'Right,' said Fran slowly, with a grin. 'Call me when you get down here and we'll decide what to do.'

'Thank you so much,' whispered Bella. 'Oh – I must go now. I'll speak to you on Thursday.'

Well, thought Fran, as she switched off the phone. What's she afraid of?

Guy Wolfe picked her up half an hour later, and on the way to their newly favoured out-of-the-way pub for dinner, Fran told him about Bella Morleigh and Inspector Connell's strange request.

'Fancies you,' he said, echoing Libby.

'Oh, not you, too,' said Fran, 'of course he doesn't.'

'Wouldn't blame him,' said Guy looking at her briefly, teeth sparkling above his neat goatee beard.

'Well, it isn't that. And this Bella person sounded scared of something. No, not scared exactly, nervous.'

'Well, if she's mixed up in a murder, no wonder. Weren't you nervous back in the summer?'

'Of course I was, but I don't think it was that. It was something about where she was.'

'At home?'

'Yes. Her husband? Why would she be scared of him knowing she was speaking to me? How odd.'

Their meal was a success. The pub, just outside a village on the other side of Canterbury, was in danger of turning itself into a gastro-pub, but just managing to stop short. Guy was a popular guest and had even persuaded the owners to hang some of his work. Fran noticed two of Libby's efforts in an alcove, which pleased her, as they were views from the window of her soon-to-be cottage. She sighed with pleasure, reflecting once more on the astonishing coincidence that had brought about this change in her fortunes.

'Well,' said Guy, when she mentioned this over their starters, 'it didn't really, did it? The contents of your uncle's will would have come out whatever else happened, and you would have ended up in the same position. The only coincidence was your old Auntie being down here after Ben had brought you down to help Lib and Pete and the theatre.' He frowned. 'Yes, that's right. Convoluted, but right.'

'I suppose so. But I wouldn't have found the cottage, would I?'

He leaned across and patted her hand. 'Or me,' he said.

'So what do you know about the Alexandria?' asked Fran, as they drove slowly home through narrow, high-hedged lanes.

'It's never been a theatre since I've been in Nethergate. It's been a carpet warehouse, and at one point a venue for raves, but mostly it's been shut up and falling into complete disrepair.'

'Would it be possible to restore?'

'Ooo, now.' Guy tutted. 'I couldn't say. I wouldn't attempt it, although it's got a beautiful cupola worth rescuing, but not much else.'

'What about inside?'

'No idea. I would imagine a large empty space if it was used as a warehouse.'

'Pity,' said Fran.

Guy, as usual, left her after a cup of coffee in the flat, reiterating his impatience for her to move into Coastguard Cottage, which was only a few yards from his own gallery and flat. This was the only drawback as far as Fran was concerned, as she was still unsure of the importance of her relationship with Guy. She liked him, even fancied him, somewhat unusual in her experience, but having been alone for such a long time the thought of having someone permanently in her life was slightly scary. She realised how lucky she was; she and Libby had had many conversations in the recent past about the difficulties facing middle-aged women wanting relationships with men, and now she actually had someone interested in her. Two, if everyone else was right and Inspector Connell had his eye on her. She was dubious about this, as he was quite obviously younger than she was, but it was flattering.

Wednesday was a quiet day. Fran and Libby met in the butchers and Fran told Libby about her phone call from Bella Morleigh.

'So you're seeing her tomorrow. During the day?'

'Well, yes. We're rehearsing tomorrow evening, aren't we?'

'Yes, we are, but I could jiggle things around a bit.'

'No,' said Fran, 'Ben would be cross. He wasn't pleased because I wasn't there on Monday.'

'Well, tough. But I'd obviously prefer you to be there.'

'Well I'm going to see her in the afternoon I hope. I thought I might ask Harry if he'd open in the afternoon for tea.'

'Like we did for Nurse Redding?' Libby smiled at the memory. 'He does a lovely tea.'

'Do you think he would?'

'Sure he would. Let's go and ask him now,' said Libby, picking up her parcel of stewing steak and bidding a cheerful farewell to Bob the butcher. 'See you tonight, Bob.'

'Which one's he?' asked Fran as they walked along the High Street towards The Pink Geranium, over which was Fran's flat.

'One of the funny men, stoopid.'

'I know that,' said Fran, 'I meant, which one of the double act.'

'Oh, sorry. Bob's Smashitt and Baz is Grabbum.'

'You could have kept their real names,' laughed Fran.

'Bob and Baz. Yes we could.' They stopped outside The Pink Geranium. 'In you go.'

Harry was open every day for lunch in December, The Pink Geranium being one of the most highly thought of vegetarian restaurants in the area. Donna, his waitress, was already taking orders from a large and noisy party in the corner. Harry, luckily, was standing behind the till looking resigned before going into the kitchen to produce his masterpieces.

'Hello, dear hearts,' he said. 'Come to cheer me up?'

'No, to ask you a favour,' said Libby, smiling winsomely. She hoped.

'Ah.' Harry looked nervous. 'Will I like it?'

'No.' Fran took over. 'I wondered if you'd do me a tea tomorrow like you did for Libby in the summer.'

'Oh?' Now Harry looked interested. 'Not another case, surely?'

'Well –' Fran looked at Libby, '– just someone who wants to talk to me.'

'Oh, go on then. Carrot cake and banana bread again?'

'Yes please,' said Fran smiling happily. 'Thanks, Harry.'

'No probs. Let me know what time,' said Harry. 'Right, here we go.' He nodded towards the party in the corner. 'Izzy wizzy, let's get busy.' He disappeared into the kitchen.

'He's too young to know "Izzy wizzy let's get busy",' said Libby.

'Repeats,' said Fran. 'Anyway, Sooty came back when he was a child, didn't he?'

'Suppose so.' Libby followed Fran outside. 'I must go and see what they're doing at the theatre. I'll see you there tonight.'

Peter was chewing the end of a pencil and staring blankly at the stage when Libby arrived that evening.

'What's up?' she said, unwinding a scarf and throwing off the blue cape.

'I'm trying to fill that space we've got now you've cut one of the songs,' he said. 'Might have to be a standard. A money gag, or something.'

'Not the busy bee joke,' said Libby. 'I can't stand it when they blow water all over each other.'

'No, all right, I'll use one of the others.' He sat up and rubbed his hands together. 'Have we got a full complement tonight?'

'I think so, but you can never be sure,' said Libby. 'I must get myself a production assistant one of these days to check up on things.'

The cast arrived in dribs and drabs and eventually the rehearsal got under way. Libby noted that Bob the butcher and his on-stage partner, Baz the undertaker, were shaping up to be a very good double act, and Tom, playing Dame Trot, was better than many of the professional Dames she'd seen. Mind you, she thought, he ought to be after all the years he'd been playing it in the society from which Libby had purloined several on and off stage members for the new company at The Oast House Theatre.

It was when the Fairy Queen tripped over her fairy helpers for the third time that Libby decided to call a halt.

'If you can't manage that run on we'll think of something different,' she said with a tired sigh. 'Meanwhile, let's have a tea break.'

Outside the auditorium in the foyer bar, the cast were queuing at the coffee machine.

'I hear you and Fran have got another case?' Ben handed Libby a hot chocolate and pushed her into one of the little white-painted iron chairs.

'No, we haven't.' Libby took a sip and pulled a face. 'And who told you?'

'Pete. He got it from Harry.'

'Can't keep anything to yourself in this place,' said Libby.

'Would you have told me?'

'Of course. Anyway, it's nothing to do with us personally. This came via Inspector Connell. Someone's found a body.'

'Oh, come on!' Ben threw his head back and laughed. 'He's not asked for your help to find a murderer?'

'No,' said Libby, irritated. 'He's asked Fran's help on behalf of the woman who found the body.'

'Why?'

'I don't know. I'll probably know tomorrow.' Libby stood up and picked up her mug. 'I'm going back. Drag the others through as soon as you can.'

Fran and Libby had no chance to do more than say goodnight to one another after the ritual drink in the pub, and Libby was uncharacteristically reserved with Ben when they went back to Allhallow's Lane.

'What's up?' he asked after she'd served him with a glass of the whisky he'd bought her.

'Nothing.' She took her own glass to the creaky cane sofa and put it down before giving the fire a good poke.

'Come on, Lib, don't try and pull the wool over my eyes.' Ben sat down in the armchair and shifted his feet to avoid Sidney, who gave him a look.

'I don't know what you mean,' Libby curled her feet under her and looked longingly at the packet of cigarettes on the table beside her.

'Go on, have one,' said Ben. 'You know I don't mind. Then you can tell me what I've done.'

'You haven't done anything,' said Libby, lighting the cigarette with relish.

Ben looked at her in silence for a long moment. 'I know what it is,' he said. 'You thought I was making fun of you.'

Libby looked at the fire.

'I knew it. Well, I'm sorry, I didn't mean to. Tell me all about it.'

'I don't actually know any more than I told you,' said Libby. 'This woman's inherited a theatre and she found a body. I think Fran said she wants to find out about the relations who left her the theatre.'

'She doesn't know them?'

'I suppose not. I've told you, that's all I know.'

'And Harry's giving you all tea tomorrow?'

'Oh, you know that, too, do you?'

'I told you, Pete told me. Harry tells him everything.'

'Yes, I know,' said Libby.

Ben stood up, stepped delicately across Sidney and moved

Libby's feet before squeezing onto the sofa. 'Now I've apologised, be nice to me,' he said.

Libby smiled reluctantly. 'How nice?' she said.

'Oh, this'll do to begin with,' said Ben, and kissed her.

Bella Morleigh phoned Fran the following morning and Fran invited her to tea at The Pink Geranium.

'Is three o'clock all right?' she asked.

'I think so. I have to go and see my solicitor and then I can take a taxi.'

'Is he in Nethergate? That'll be an expensive taxi ride. It's a long way.'

'The solicitor will advance me money from the estate,' said Bella, 'he told me he would. And I've got to find out if the cottage is habitable. He was arranging to have the services switched on.'

'Right,' said Fran. 'Well, we'll see you around three?'

'We?' said Bella, sounding apprehensive.

'My colleague, Libby Sarjeant,' said Fran airily, 'see you later.'

When she phoned Libby she warned her that Bella might baulk at her presence, but Libby was confident. 'I'm the down-to-earth one,' she said, 'she'll trust me.'

Fran wasn't so sure, but nevertheless arranged to meet Libby just before three in The Pink Geranium.

Harry had set their favourite table with a cloth, cups and plates of carrot cake and banana bread.

'Kettle's on the boil,' he said, turning the door sign to open. 'Shout when you're ready.'

'Well, here goes,' said Libby, as he went back to the kitchen. 'There's a taxi pulling up now.'

They both watched as Bella Morleigh paid the driver. She looked to be around their own age, middle-fifties, although, in Libby's opinion, she could have been at least ten years older, judging by her clothes. True, she was wearing jeans, but they looked more like slacks made in imitation denim, and her shoes were sensible and worn with white socks. Fran caught Libby's eye and frowned. 'Don't say a word,' she said as the door opened. 'Bella? Come and sit down. I'm Fran and this is Libby.'

Bella sat down with a nervous smile.

'I'll ask Harry for the tea,' said Libby, with rare tact. 'Tea for you Bella? Or coffee?'

'Oh, tea, please.' Bella cleared her throat.

'Right,' said Libby, and made off towards the kitchen.

'So.' Fran sat back and looked at Bella. 'Inspector Connell recommended you speak to me.'

'Yes.' Bella was obviously ill-at-ease.

'Why, exactly?'

Bella's fingers played jerkily with the strap of handbag. 'I – I'm not sure.'

'You wanted to speak to me, though, or you wouldn't have phoned and arranged to meet me.'

'Yes.' Bella looked up as Libby came back to the table. Fran made a face.

'Tell us how we can help you,' said Libby, leaning forward and smiling warmly. 'Fran's awfully good at finding things out, you know.'

Fran hid a smile. Libby was good at this, when she managed not to be too outspoken.

'Well,' began Bella, 'it all began with a letter from a solicitor in Nethergate, a Robert Grimshaw. Do you know him?'

Libby and Fran shook their heads.

Bella went on to recount her visit to Nethergate and March Cottage, and the surprising letter from Maria Alexander. Harry brought the tea.

'So then,' she went on, as Libby poured tea, 'the following day I just couldn't forget it, so after Andr– after the children had gone to school and I'd done the shopping, I just rushed off to the station and came down again. This time, I went straight to the theatre.' She paused, looking down into her cup. 'At first, I couldn't get in, the locks and padlocks were so rusted, but eventually I found a door at the back where the lock turned easily.'

'Had it been oiled recently?' asked Libby.

'That's what the police asked. I don't know, but I think they thought it had.'

'So when it opened, what happened?' asked Fran.

'I pushed it open, and oh, the smell!' Bella wrinkled her

38

nose. 'I was in some sort of passage, and it was dark. I could see rubbish ahead of me, but it didn't look as though I'd get very far. I just took a step or so inside, to see if I could see any more, and that was when I saw it.'

Libby and Fran waited.

'I thought it was more rubbish at first, old clothes, or something, and – and then I realised.' She took a deep breath. 'I sort of backed out and after a bit I found my mobile and rang the police.'

'Horrible for you,' said Libby. 'Drink your tea.'

'What happened next?' asked Fran.

'Well, I rang Mr Grimshaw after the police got there, and he took me to the police station to make a statement. After that, the Inspector suggested I talk to you.'

'Why?' asked Fran.

'Because I inherited the theatre and I didn't even know I had an aunt to inherit from. He thought you might help me find out about the family.' Bella looked up and Fran saw the appeal in her eyes. 'I don't know how, though.'

'Fran can sometimes sense things about places, you see,' said Libby, when it looked as though Fran had no intention of answering. 'She works for a big London estate agents who ask her to go and look at places and find out if any murders have been committed there, that sort of thing.'

'Then you can help,' Bella said slowly.

'Well, only in a way,' said Fran, 'and you already know a murder's been committed at your theatre.'

'But Aunt Maria left me the cottage, too. She and Dorinda – her mother – lived there almost all their lives. Could you come there?'

Libby looked at Fran. 'A good start, Fran,' she said. 'Are there any of their things still there, Bella?'

'Oh, yes,' said Bella, 'and somewhere there's a collection of memorabilia and costumes. Maria told me in the letter she left. I don't know where, exactly, but she wouldn't have left it in the theatre, so perhaps it's in the loft at the cottage.'

'Fantastic,' said Libby. 'When shall we come?'

'I'm moving into the cottage tomorrow morning. Mr Grimshaw says the electricity will be on then. I've got to give it a thorough cleaning, but I'm looking forward to it.'

'So where are you staying tonight? You're not going back to London again, are you?' said Fran.

'No, I'm staying at the pub – here, actually,' said Bella with a smile.

'Oh, well, that's good,' said Libby, 'because we both live here.'

'Yes, George at the pub in Heronsbourne mentioned you when I asked about rooms,' said Bella. 'He said you ran the theatre here.'

'Well, I'm involved,' said Libby, modestly. 'Coincidence, then, George mentioning me, wasn't it?'

Bella nodded and finished her tea. 'Do you know him?'

'Vaguely. Nice pub, if I remember.'

'He said you might know something about the Alexandria.'

'Not really. Fran and I both remember it being active when we were children. I was taken to summer shows there when I was on holiday. It was a lovely little theatre.' She smiled reminiscently. 'I remember coming out at the end of the evening on to the promenade, with all the coloured lights strung between the lamp-posts, and walking along to the other end to where we used to stay. It was all so exciting.'

'My father never took me to a theatre,' said Bella. 'Or even a cinema. Looking back on it, we had nothing to do with any sort of entertainment. He would never have variety or music shows on the television either.'

Libby cut a slice of banana bread and handed it to her. 'That really is sad. Have you made up for it since?'

'Oh, I love the theatre,' said Bella. 'I belong to an amateur company near where I live in London. I don't act, or anything, you understand, but I help out backstage wherever I can.'

'Then I can see two reasons why Inspector Connell recommended you talk to Fran,' said Libby. 'One because we've done investigations together before and he knows about our involvement with theatre, and two, because of Fran's psychic abilities.'

'Is that what they are?' said Bella, looking slightly scared.

'I don't honestly know,' said Fran, 'but whatever they are, they've had some success, even with the police.'

Bella nodded, and turned her attention to the banana bread.

'So, you're staying here tonight?' said Libby. 'Where are you eating?'

'Oh, I hadn't thought,' said Bella. 'Does the pub do food?'

'Hang on a minute. Harry,' Libby called, turning towards the kitchen, where she could see Harry hovering in the doorway. 'Have you got room for us to eat early tonight?'

'How many?' Harry emerged.

'Fran?' said Libby.

'Yes, sure.'

'Bella? Do you like vegetarian food?'

'Oh – yes,' said Bella.

'Three,' said Libby.

'OK. You might be squeezed into the corner. About six-thirty?'

'Great,' said Libby. 'All right with you, Bella?'

'Yes, thank you,' said Bella, looking bewildered.

'And then, if you wanted to, you could come to our panto rehearsal with us.' Libby beamed round the table.

Bella beamed back. 'I'd love that,' she said.

Chapter Four

THEY SAW BELLA INTO the pub and left her to it.

'What was she going to say?' said Fran. 'When she said "after and – after the children had gone to school". After and what?'

'Don't know.' Libby frowned. 'She's obviously younger than we are if she's got school-age children. Perhaps they don't know anything about all this.'

'Why wouldn't she tell them? And what's she done with them now? She can't have left them all on their own.'

'Her husband must be at home. Perhaps that's who she hasn't told.'

'Well, she must have told him she's coming here, or he'd have put out a missing person call. Very odd,' said Fran.

'As odd as being left a house and a theatre by someone you didn't know existed,' said Libby, looking thoughtful.

'That's not her fault,' said Fran.

'What did you make of her?' asked Libby.

'I couldn't sense anything wrong with her, if that's what you mean,' said Fran, 'but she's dreadfully nervous.'

'Finding a body couldn't have helped,' said Libby. 'You and I haven't even done that.'

'You did.'

'Not a new one.'

'Are we going to the house with her tomorrow?' said Fran, putting her key into the lock.

'To help her scrub and polish? I thought we'd offer,' said Libby, with a grin.

'Yes, I thought you would,' said Fran, grinning back. 'See you at six-thirty.'

Bella, looking a lot more relaxed than she had in the afternoon, and wearing a long black skirt and matching jumper

42

which looked much more up to date than her previous outfit, joined them at just after half-past six and gratefully accepted a glass of red wine.

'Fran and I seem to spend a lot of our time eating and drinking,' explained Libby. 'We exchange most of our best ideas over food and drink.'

Bella smiled. 'What better way is there?' she said.

'So, who have you got at home?' Libby went on.

Bella jumped visibly.

'You said children,' prompted Fran.

'Anthony and Amanda,' said Bella.

'At school?'

'Tony's doing A levels and Manda's doing GCSEs.'

'Ours are all older than that,' said Libby. 'Fran's even got grandchildren.'

'I started a bit late,' said Bella. 'Andrew and I didn't meet until I was over thirty.'

'Well, that's the way of it, now, isn't it?' said Libby. 'They all start late. So what do yours think about this theatre business?'

'The children were excited at first. But I haven't really talked to them much about it since – well, since the murder.'

'And your husband?'

'Andrew – well, he – er – he's not really into theatre.' Bella buried her face in her wine glass and Libby and Fran exchanged looks.

'Ready to order, ladies?' Harry appeared beside them with pad and pencil at the ready. 'I hate to hurry you, but I have the hungry hordes descending in about an hour.'

'Oh, right, sorry, Harry.' Libby handed Bella a menu. 'We'll be a minute while we tell Bella what's best.' She smiled winningly. Harry scowled.

During the meal, Libby and Fran told Bella about the Oast House Theatre and their own involvement, only lightly touching on the murder that had brought them together. Bella, however, picked up on it.

'So you've been involved with a murder enquiry before?' she said, her eyes going from one to the other.

Fran looked at Libby and shrugged.

'Er – two, actually,' said Libby.

'Two?' Bella gasped.

'Complete coincidence,' said Fran.

'I don't believe it.' Bella slowly shook her head. 'That doesn't happen in real life.'

'I know, that's what we thought,' said Libby. 'I just hate those books where some innocent member of the public just keeps falling over murders, don't you?'

'Well,' said Bella, 'you've just fallen over another one, haven't you?'

'Not at all,' said Fran. 'Inspector Connell put us in touch. That's quite different.'

'Did he do it because you've – er – been involved?'

'I think it was because of Fran's peculiar abilities,' grinned Libby.

'Who are you calling peculiar?' said Fran.

'Peculiar in the Oxford dictionary definition,' said Libby.

'Oh,' said Fran.

'So those were the investigations you mentioned this afternoon,' said Bella. 'I thought you meant family investigations – you know, like genealogy searches.'

'Well, funnily enough,' said Libby, chasing her last morsel of refried beans round the plate, 'they have been family investigations, haven't they, Fran?'

'Both of them,' agreed Fran, 'so I suppose it makes us qualified to look into yours.' She looked at her watch. 'Hadn't you better get going, Lib? You need to be at the theatre before I do.'

Libby stood up. 'Let me know what I owe you later,' she said. 'See you later, Bella.'

'She seems nice,' said Bella, watching Libby struggle through the door in a flurry of basket and cape.

'She is. A bit impulsive at times, but a good friend.' Fran waved at Donna and asked for the bill. 'Do you mind if we go now? I don't want to be late. I missed a rehearsal on Monday.'

Bella obediently pushed back her chair and picked up her handbag. 'Can I take care of the bill?' she asked tentatively. 'I really appreciate what you're doing for me.'

'We haven't done anything yet,' said Fran, 'but if you insist. My turn next.'

'How far is the theatre?' asked Bella, as they left The Pink Geranium.

'Just up there,' said Fran, indicating the drive to The Manor, now resplendent with its swinging sign, carved locally.

'The Oast House Theatre,' read Bella. 'Wow. Aren't you lucky?'

'I am. It was Peter Parker and his cousin Ben Wilde who had the idea a couple of years ago, apparently. The oast house was standing empty and belonged to Ben's family, and as Ben's an architect, they decided to turn it into a theatre. Then Peter, who's a journalist, wrote a play about some events that happened in the family during the war, and they got Libby in to direct it, as she'd been a professional once.'

'What a story,' said Bella, as they approached the Oast House Theatre.

Fran smiled wryly and glanced sideways. 'You don't know the half of it,' she said.

'Oh?'

'Libby'll probably tell you eventually,' said Fran, holding open the glass doors to the foyer. 'Come on in.'

Libby was on stage talking to the set designer with much waving of hands. Peter was sitting on the side of the stage looking broody. Fran introduced Bella.

'Do you mind if she watches the rehearsal?' she asked.

'Up to Lib,' said Peter. 'I don't mind.'

'Is that the one who wrote the first play?' Bella asked in a whisper as Fran settled her in a seat towards the back of the auditorium.

'And this pantomime, yes. He's Harry's partner.'

'Harry?' Bella's eyes widened. 'Harry at the restaurant?'

'Yes.' Fran paused in the act of taking off her coat. 'You're not shocked, are you?'

'No.' Bella looked doubtful. 'But he's so handsome.' She put her hand to her mouth. 'Oh, you did mean what I thought you meant, didn't you? He isn't his business partner?'

Fran laughed. 'No, you were right first time,' she said. 'But in fact, I believe Peter did buy the restaurant for Harry, so he probably is his business partner as well. Now I must go and see what I'm supposed to be doing tonight.'

Libby was now marshalling her troops into vaguely cohesive lumps at each side of the stage. 'Where's that bloody choreographer?' she muttered under her breath.

'Behind you!' shouted the chorus.

'Oh,' said Libby.

The choreographer, a sneering young man with all the experience of a West End musical flop behind him, lifted his chin as high as it would go and swept on to the stage. Libby shrugged and went back to her seat in the auditorium.

'Right,' she said. 'Everybody ready? Ben? Fran? Are you there?'

'Here,' came the muffled voices.

'Off we go, then,' said Libby, and the rehearsal started.

Apart from the cow falling over itself and the Fairy Queen falling over her helpers, it went reasonably well. Bella was enthusiastic when Libby called for a tea break.

'We've never done pantomime at my society in London. I always assumed it would be too hard to do.'

'It is,' said Libby, 'and when I was in the professional theatre, the thought of amateur pantomime made me cringe. Some of it still does, but when they're done well they can be better than pro panto. But hard work, and you can't tell people off because they're doing it for nothing.'

'Oh, you should hear our resident director in London,' said Bella. 'He tells people off all the time.'

'Don't they walk out on him?'

'Yes,' said Bella and pulled a wry face. 'All the time.'

'But I suppose you've a big catchment area so you can get replacements?'

'Well, I suppose so,' said Bella, looking doubtful again. Libby eyed her thoughtfully. They were going to have to toughen Mrs Morleigh up.

Later, in the pub, Bella sat with her mouth slightly open and a dazed expression on her face as she listened to the conversations being conducted across, around and over her. Libby squeezed in beside her.

'Difficult being in with a load of people you've never met before, isn't it?' she said. 'Fran was like that only a couple of months ago.'

'Was she?' Bella looked surprised. 'She looks as though she's been here for years.'

'It's knowing the right people,' said Libby, looking smug. 'Like me. Oh, I don't mean knowing me,' she amended, seeing Bella's raised eyebrows, 'I mean, Peter and Harry found me my cottage, so I knew people straight away.'

'And did you know Ben, too?' asked Bella, who'd noticed the signs of togetherness between Libby and Ben.

'Yes, I knew him, too, but I've got to know him much better since I moved here.' She felt herself blushing and looked up to meet Ben's amused gaze. 'He always makes me do that,' she muttered.

Bella sighed. 'You have been lucky,' she said.

Libby looked at her, frowning. Unhappy marriage, definitely, she thought.

'Well, so have you, haven't you?' she said. 'Being left a cottage, and a theatre! How exciting.'

'And a body,' said Bella, 'but yes, it is exciting. Except that I shall probably have to sell the theatre as it's virtually derelict, but it's a good site, so the land will be worth quite a bit.'

'Don't you want to keep the theatre?' asked Libby. 'I would.'

'Yes, I do – did, rather. The body was a bit off-putting, but Mr Grimshaw said it was too far gone to rescue anyway, and there would be no market for that sort of entertainment.'

'Hmm.' Libby took a sip of her drink. 'Well, we can look into that after Fran's found out about your family, can't we?'

'Can we?' Bella was startled again, and obviously coming to the conclusion that these were very strange people.

Fran had worked her way towards them.

'OK, Bella?' she said.

'Yes, thank you,' said Bella, standing up, 'but I'm a bit tired, so I think I'll go up to my room, now.'

'OK,' said Libby, also standing. 'What time tomorrow? We'll pick you up, won't we Fran?'

They agreed on ten o'clock, and Bella slipped through the press of people towards the staircase.

'Timid little rabbit, isn't she?' said Peter, coming up behind them.

'Just a bit put off by all us loudmouths,' said Libby. 'This is enough to daunt anyone.'

'And she's had a couple of shocks during the last week,' said Fran. 'She's probably quite different once you get to know her.'

'Well, we'll soon find out,' said Libby.

The following morning, when Libby drew up outside the pub in Romeo the Renault, Fran and Bella were standing outside, Bella back in her middle-aged jeans and zip-up jacket. What must her husband be like, thought Libby, as she leant over and unlocked the passenger door. Fran ushered Bella into the front seat and climbed into the back herself.'

'This is all we've got in the way of transport at the moment,' she said, 'but I'll be getting a car any day now.'

'Will you?' said Libby. 'That's news to me.'

'I can't keep on borrowing Romeo, can I?' said Fran. 'And I can afford it, now.'

'Fran's just come into money,' Libby told Bella.

'Libby,' Fran protested.

'Well, you have. No sense in lying about it,' said Libby. 'Now, Bella, where exactly are we going? Heronsbourne, you said, didn't you?'

It didn't take long to get to March Cottage, which looked to be the same age and vernacular as 17 Allhallow's Lane. Libby parked outside and they all climbed out. Bella had two large plastic carrier bags.

'Cleaning stuff,' she explained, when she saw Libby looking. 'I don't know what's there.'

Inside, they found that the electricity had been switched on and the storage heaters in the bedrooms were throwing out a decent amount of heat. Libby, with her expertise in lighting open fires and Rayburns, offered to have a go at the range, while Fran and Bella tackled the kitchen.

A loud bang on the window alerted Bella to the presence of Balzac, who walked in and allowed himself to be admired, before sitting hopefully beside the sink, gazing thoughtfully into the middle distance.

'Good job I bought a tin of cat food,' said Bella. 'I must see about a cat flap. And I must go and see the woman who's been feeding him to ask her to carry on.'

'You're not going to live down here permanently, then,' said Libby from the front room.

'No, well, I can't really, with the children still at school and everything,' said Bella. 'I thought, just weekends, maybe.'

'What does your husband think about it?' asked Fran.

Bella didn't answer straight away, and Libby and Fran exchanged looks.

'He wants me to sell them both,' said Bella eventually.

'Doesn't he like the idea of a weekend cottage?' said Libby.

'Not this one,' said Bella, with a little laugh. 'I think he was thinking more of an apartment in Spain.'

'Has he seen it?' asked Fran.

'No,' said Bella. 'He's been rather busy at work, so he couldn't get the time off.'

'But you could?'

'Well, I only work the occasional shift in a local shop,' said Bella, colouring faintly, 'so it wasn't difficult.'

'Hard work, shops,' said Libby, lifting a soot-covered hand and brushing rusty hair off her brow.

'You look like a clown,' said Fran. 'Bella, does that electric kettle work? We could have some tea, couldn't we?'

After Libby had managed to get a fire going in the range and Fran and Bella had found cups for the tea Bella had remembered to bring with her, thanks to an early morning visit to the eight-til-late in Steeple Martin, they all sat down in Aunt Maria's front room.

'This was where she lived with your grandmother, was it?' asked Libby. 'But your father didn't?'

'As far as I can work out from the letter,' said Bella, taking it out of her handbag and riffling through the pages, 'he lived here while my grandmother was abroad, but I *think* he went to live with her in London when she returned. When he left home, Dorinda returned here, and they lived together for the rest of their lives.'

'Dorinda was your grandmother, right?' asked Fran.

'Yes. What I don't know is who else was here when Dorinda was abroad. Maria and my father were too young to be left alone. She says –' Bella found the relevant passage '– in the care of someone in the troupe. But I don't know whether they were in this cottage or somewhere else.'

'That doesn't really matter, does it?' said Fran. 'It's Dorinda and Maria you want to know about.'

'Well, yes. I mean, Maria's told me most of it. I just want to know if they were happy, or if there's anything – something – in the past I ought to know.'

'Just like Goodall and Smythe, in fact,' said Libby, patting her lap and accepting Balzac into it.

'Yes,' said Fran, 'but I'm still not sure why Inspector Connell should have suggested you ask me about it.'

'No,' said Bella slowly, 'I don't really, either.'

Libby snorted. 'Honestly, you two. Fran, I thought you'd be able to see that. He thinks the body in the theatre might have something to do with Bella's family.'

'But how could it?' Bella looked horrified. 'There's been no one left of my family – except me, and no one knew about me – for years.'

'And Auntie Maria,' said Libby.

'She wouldn't have murdered anyone,' said Bella.

'How do you know?' said Fran. 'You didn't even know she existed until last week.'

'Oh.' Bella looked into the fire, and Balzac jumped from Libby's lap on to hers. 'So that's it,' she said, absentmindedly stroking his head.

Fran and Libby looked at each other.

'Well, we think we know why Inspector Connell wanted you to see me,' said Fran, 'but why did *you* want to see me?'

'Well, as I said yesterday, Dorinda and Maria lived here, and she says in her letter there are some things from the theatre somewhere that she would like kept. They could be here.'

'Is that all?' asked Fran.

Bella's colour deepened. 'I – I – I just wanted to know –' She stopped.

'Anything Fran could tell you.' Libby nodded. 'I understand, even if she doesn't.' She stood up. 'Come on, let's go and see if we can find any of this memorabilia.'

'Programmes and costumes, she says,' said Bella, following Libby up the stairs.

'Wow,' said Libby. 'I wonder how the costumes have stood

up.'

'Crumbling probably,' said Fran, bringing up the rear, with Balzac padding alongside, plumy black tail waving curiously.

They searched both bedrooms without finding anything more exciting than some costume jewellery, and a few pieces of what Libby said was probably the real stuff. Two old fur coats hung in one of the wardrobes, but nothing that suggested the theatre.

'There's very little here at all,' said Fran, looking round her with arms akimbo. 'It's as if she cleared everything out.'

'Yes?' Libby sat on the edge of a bed. 'Is that what it feels like?'

Fran nodded, looking round. 'Empty. And yet she and her mother lived here for what – eighty years?'

'All her life, except I still don't think she can have lived here while her mother was abroad,' said Bella. 'She must have lived with one of the families in the troupe.'

'Still, she was here for most of the time. Hasn't she left any sort of – I don't know – imprint?' said Libby.

'Oh, yes, there's a feeling of something, but almost disinfected. There's more downstairs than there is up here.'

'What sort of thing?' said Bella eagerly.

'Oh, just – normal, really,' said Fran, assuming her uncomfortable expression, which Libby now knew to mean Fran couldn't, or didn't want to, put something into words.

'How about the loft, then?' said Libby.

'I don't know whether we can get into it,' said Bella, 'and it's difficult to get at.'

'Which means,' said Libby, gazing up at the small hatch over the equally small landing, 'that if we can't get into it, the odds are that neither could Auntie Maria.'

'Ladder,' said Fran. 'There must be a ladder somewhere.'

'I'll go and look outside,' said Bella. 'I haven't looked in the garden yet.'

Libby and Fran watched her clatter down the stairs.

'She's a lot more cheerful now than she was when she first arrived,' said Libby.

'She's at home here,' said Fran. 'She's not happy in London.'

'But it sounds as though she's always lived there,' said

51

Libby.

'Doesn't mean to say she's always been happy, does it?'

'Is it her husband?'

'I think so,' said Fran, 'and my guess is she won't leave him because of the children.'

'Do you think –' began Libby, then stopped as a crashing sound heralded Bella's reappearance, looking flushed and triumphant.

'Ladder,' she panted. 'There's a brick-built shed thing in the garden that one of the keys unlocked. It's quite a new ladder.'

It was, quite a shiny aluminium ladder, which only just fitted on to the tiny landing. Bella went up, with Libby and Fran holding on tightly, and pushed hard at the loft hatch, which finally gave way, releasing a cloud of dust.

'Can't see anything,' said Bella, coughing. 'There's no light except for a few cracks in the tiles. The loft floor's insulated, but I can't see any boarding.'

'There won't be anything up there, then,' said Fran. 'You can't put things in an un-boarded loft.'

Bella climbed back down the ladder, which they carried back downstairs and out to the shed.

'What a great building,' said Libby.

It was part of the original building and had obviously housed the coal shed at one time, while the outside privy, to which the doorway opening could still be traced, had now been turned into the bathroom, with access from the inside. Libby guessed that the current kitchen, which was quite large, had once been the dining room, while the lobby had been the scullery.

'Well, this is where the stuff will be,' said Fran, pulling wide the door. 'See?'

'Of course,' breathed Bella, stepping inside.

'Light switch,' said Libby, finding one.

They all gasped.

Along the opposite wall to the door were a series of what looked like cabin trunks, each labelled, on the end wall a workmanlike set of metal shelving containing box files and a filing cabinet, and along the wall beside the door, a white worktop with a computer and printer.

'Good God!' said Libby. 'Didn't you see this when you

found the ladder?'

'I didn't switch on the light, and the ladder was just inside the door. I can't believe it,' said Bella. 'Robert Grimshaw didn't say anything about this.'

'I don't suppose he knew,' said Fran. 'Come on, let's see what she used her computer for.'

'It might be password protected,' said Libby, airing her fairly newly-found knowledge.

'Unlikely,' said Fran. 'No one else came in here.'

'How do we know? She might have had loads of friends,' said Libby.

'No,' said Fran. 'Only her.'

Bella looked at the computer as if it might bite. 'You do it,' she said to Fran. 'I'm not very good with computers.'

Fran sat in front of the monitor and found the switch. It hummed softly into life and within seconds presented them with a screen full of folders.

'There,' said Fran.

Bella sat down on a trunk with a bump. 'I can't take all this in,' she said. 'What does it all mean?'

'By the look of it, she was cataloguing what she'd got here,' said Fran. 'Yes, look, this folder's labelled 1920s.'

'Do you want to open it?' Libby asked Bella. 'It's your Aunt, after all.'

'Go on,' said Bella. 'I don't want to.'

The folder, when opened, contained details of programmes, costumes, names and letters.

'They'll all be in those box files, I expect,' said Libby, going to the shelves. 'They might tell you where Maria and your father spent that time when Dorinda was abroad, if that's what you want to know.'

'Show me what to do, Fran,' said Bella, getting up and going over to peer at the screen. 'Then perhaps if I find the right date I can find the right file.'

Fran gave Bella a quick lesson in how to start up the computer and how to open the folders.

'Now I know, I can go through it later,' said Bella. 'It's too cold to stay out here now. I'll have to find a heater.'

'There's an electric radiator over here, said Libby. 'Shall I switch it on?'

'OK – yes.' Bella came over to have a look. 'She must have spent a lot of time here.'

'Yes, and after she wrote that letter to you,' said Fran. 'When was it dated?'

'Five years ago.'

'She wanted to get things in order for you,' said Fran. 'I expect she intended to write again and tell you all about it.'

Bella nodded. 'It doesn't help Inspector Connell, though, does it?'

'No, not on the surface. But you don't know what you might turn up,' said Fran. 'I'm sure there's something.'

'Sure sure?' said Libby. 'Or hope sure?'

Fran smiled. 'I can feel something, but I'm not certain what it is. If Bella comes across anything in all this that she feels might be useful, I'll have a go at it.'

Bella, under Fran's guidance, closed down the computer, turned off the light but left the radiator on.

'I'll come out here later, when I'm feeling stronger,' she said, as she led the way back inside March Cottage. 'I'm a bit shell-shocked at the moment.'

'I can imagine,' said Fran. 'I've had that sort of experience myself.'

'But you can't feel anything that might help me in here?'

'It feels a contented sort of home,' said Fran guardedly. 'I'll have to think about it. Tell you what,' she stopped in the act of putting on her coat, 'can you give me something of Maria's? It might help.'

'Something? Do you mean the letter? Because –'

'No, not the letter. That's too personal.' Fran looked round the room and lit on a framed photograph. 'What about that? Do you know who it is?'

Bella picked it up. 'No,' she said. 'I hadn't noticed it.' She turned it to the light. 'It could be Maria or Dorinda, couldn't it?'

'May I see?' asked Libby. 'Well, it's obviously 1920s, and Maria wouldn't be grown up by then, would she? And these women are definitely grown up.'

'Dorinda, then? But which one is she?' asked Bella.

'That one,' said Fran, indicating the tallest figure in the

photograph, a laughing woman wearing a cloche hat.

Bella stared. 'How do you … oh.'

Fran smiled. 'Don't know if I'll get anything from it, but we can but hope,' she said.

'Right,' said Libby. 'Now, is there anything you want us to do before we go, Bella?'

'No, thanks, you've been wonderful,' said Bella. 'Can I ring you if I need to?'

'Of course,' said Fran, 'and you might give Inspector Connell a ring, too.'

'Do I have to tell him what we've found?'

'I think you must,' said Libby. 'They always find things out in the end, and the quicker you get to the bottom of your murder, even if none of this matters, the better. Then you can get on with sorting out the theatre, can't you?'

Chapter Five

'I NEARLY SAID "GET on with sorting out your life",' said Libby, as they drove out of Heronsbourne, 'but she hasn't admitted there's anything wrong with her life, has she?'

'Not yet,' said Fran, 'give her time.'

'So what did you get in there? Anything?'

'I'm not sure.' Fran stroked the photograph, which she held on her lap. 'I'll think about it.'

'That means you did.' Libby stopped at a T-junction. 'Do we want to go home, or shall we go and see Guy?'

'Nethergate. I'd like to have a look at the theatre.'

'Oh,' said Libby, sending her a sidelong glance, 'not Guy, then?'

Fran grinned. 'Oh, I daresay we could fit him in as well.'

Libby drove the other way along the promenade from Guy's gallery and the cottage Fran hoped would soon be hers. The Alexandria stood, forlorn and wind-battered, a blue-and-white police tape fluttering around it like absurd bunting.

'There's a policeman there,' said Libby. 'He won't let you through.'

'I just want to have a look,' said Fran, and got out of the car.

She crossed the road towards the theatre, pulling her sensible navy coat closer against the wind that whipped over the top of the cliff. The other end of the promenade dipped down to the same level as the beach, and Fran could see lights swinging outside The Sloop on the end of the Hard. Here, though, high up on the cliff top, there were no lights, just an abandoned building with a sinister secret. Fran felt her heart thump in her chest and a familiar blackness descending on her. Scared, she grabbed the railings along the cliff edge and closed her eyes.

'Mrs Castle?'

She looked up, her heart rate returning to normal.

'Inspector Connell,' she said, relieved to hear her voice steady.

'Have you met Mrs Morleigh yet?'

'We've just come from her cottage,' said Fran.

'We?' said Inspector Connell, his dark brows beetling together over his deep set eyes.

'Yes, Inspector,' Fran sighed. 'Surely you didn't expect me to see Mrs Morleigh without Mrs Sarjeant?'

'But I told you –'

'Told me, Inspector? I thought I was doing you a favour.'

There was a moment when Fran sensed a struggle within him.

'I'm sorry. Of course. Mrs Sarjeant's been – ah – a great help in the past, hasn't she?'

Fran smiled. 'To me, she has,' she said. 'And no, we've found out nothing that might help you so far. Mrs Morleigh knows nothing of her aunt or her grandmother, and we found little at the cottage to help us.' Despite what she'd said to Bella, Fran felt it better at the moment to conceal the photograph. Inspector Connell was in just the mood to impound it as evidence.

'This is where she found the body?'

'Yes.' Connell turned and looked at the side door, where the constable stood on guard. 'Did you want to see?'

'What?' gasped Fran.

'I thought it might help you.'

Was he teasing? Fran surveyed him warily. He looked quite serious.

'The body's not there, is it?'

'No, of course not. SOCOs been all over it, but there's so much rubbish in there we're going to have to clear it all out and have another go.'

'Can you get in the front door?'

'Not at the moment. We'll manage to open it up once we're inside properly. Well? Do you want to see?'

'Just from the door, then,' said Fran, aware of a nasty liquefying feeling in the pit of her stomach.

At the door, all she could see was a dark passage and piles of rubbish that appeared to have been pushed to either side. Her stomach was definitely unhappy, now, and her breathing was distinctly uneven.

'All right, Mrs Castle?' asked Inspector Connell, taking her elbow and peering down into her face.

'Not really.' She attempted a smile and broke away from him. 'I think I'd better go.'

'Did you – er –'

'Get anything? No. Just great discomfort.' Fran smiled again, feeling better now she was away from that door. 'Can you tell me how old the body was?'

'How old?' Inspector Connell looked bewildered.

'I mean – how long had it been there? Was it a new body?'

'I see. Oh, yes. Very recent.' His tone was guarded. 'Why did you want to know?'

'I thought it might help.' Fran shrugged. 'Sorry not to have been more use, but I shall be seeing Mrs Morleigh again, and we'll try and find something in her aunt's past that might have a bearing. Although, looking at this place, surely it's more likely to have been a tramp squatting here, isn't it?'

'And why would he be murdered?' asked Inspector Connell. 'And by whom?'

'So why,' said Libby, as they drove off towards the other end of the promenade and Harbour Street, 'didn't you ask him how the body died?'

'He wasn't being very forthcoming about the age of the body, so I don't think he would have welcomed any more questions,' said Fran.

'Well, I think it's a cheek,' said Libby, pulling up in the car park of The Swan with a screech of brakes. 'He asks for your help and then won't tell you anything.'

'He didn't actually ask for my help, did he, Lib? He just suggested that Bella talked to me.'

'In case you could find anything out for him, yes.' Libby got out of the car and locked it. 'Shall we ring Guy and ask him to meet us here, or do you want to walk down to the shop?'

'I want to have a look at the cottage. You stay here, if you like,' said Fran. 'Give Guy a ring.'

Libby watched her friend stride off along the harbour wall,

her coat pulled tight around her, sleek dark hair swinging slightly with every step. Libby sighed. Why wasn't she neat and groomed like Fran? She looked down at the blue cape and the long denim skirt and sighed again. No hope really.

She went to sit at the bar after ringing Guy on her mobile.

'Yes,' he said, 'I can see her coming. I'll go and join her.'

But five minutes later he came in alone.

'She wanted to be alone,' he said, giving Libby a quizzical look. 'What have you two been up to?'

'Fran'll tell you. She told you about that woman, didn't she? Bella Morleigh? Well, we've been with her. And I think she wanted to commune with her cottage. I do hope she doesn't go into hibernation once she's moved in there.'

But after another few minutes, Fran joined them.

'I can't get in,' she said. 'It isn't mine yet. And even though the owners aren't there, they've got to clear it out. I don't know when they're going to do that. It must be difficult for them, not living down here.'

'Oh, they'll get a removals company to pack everything up and put it into storage, I should think,' said Guy. 'That way, they can sort things out at their leisure.'

'Storage is very expensive, though, isn't?' said Libby. 'I couldn't afford it.'

'If they can afford a second home, they can afford storage,' said Guy. 'Now what are we eating?'

By tacit consent the subjects of Bella Morleigh and the murder were avoided, although Fran was very quiet. Libby chattered away about the pantomime, Peter and Harry's civil partnership celebrations and Christmas. Guy told them about his new line of Christmas cards, which included one of Libby's wintry sea scenes, much to her delight, and his daughter Sophie's sudden decision to go to university.

'What does she want to do?' asked Libby.

'History of Art, would you believe,' said Guy. 'She'll be lording it over me when she comes back.'

'You should be pleased she wants to follow in your footsteps,' said Libby. 'Don't you think so, Fran?'

'What?' said Fran.

Libby repeated the last part of the conversation.

'What will you do for help in the shop?' asked Fran.

'Well, you could help out, couldn't you?' said Guy. 'You'll only be along the road.'

'Gee, thanks,' said Fran. 'Cheap labour.'

'Of course not. I'd pay you.'

'Maybe now and then,' said Fran, 'in an emergency.'

'She'll be busy investigating things, anyway,' said Libby.

'Oh, Libby, shut up about it. Just because it's happened once …'

'It might happen again,' said Libby, 'you never know.'

Guy looked from one to the other, amused. 'This from the woman who didn't want to play Miss Marple,' he said.

Libby sniffed and returned to her soup.

After arranging to see Guy over the weekend, Fran suggested she and Libby should get back to Steeple Martin. 'I've got a couple of calls to make,' she explained.

Libby looked dubious, but agreed and gave Guy a kiss goodbye.

Fran continued to say very little on the journey back to Steeple Martin. Libby decided to leave her to it, hoping that she would tell all when they reached home. Fran, however, climbed out of the car, thanked Libby for the lift and disappeared straight upstairs to her flat.

Disgruntled, Libby sat for a while in the car, wondering what to do. There was no rehearsal that night, so she had no preparation to do, she and Ben had made no arrangement to see each other, although she was fairly sure they would, and the afternoon stretched emptily ahead.

A tap on the passenger window startled her.

'Looking for a good time, dearie?' Harry grinned at her.

Libby wound down the window. 'Yes, actually. Got anything in mind?'

'Do you want to come and look at our wedding venue with me? I've got a few details to finalise.'

'Are you sure? Shouldn't Pete be with you?'

'He's in London. Anyway, I told you, he's leaving most of it to me.'

'OK, then, I'd love to. Do you want to go in my car?'

Harry wrinkled his nose. 'No, thank you. I value my image.

You go home and I'll come and pick you up.'

Fifteen minutes later they were on their way.

'Have you ever been to Anderson Place?' asked Harry, as they left Steeple Martin in the opposite direction to Nethergate.

'No, although I've always meant to. I should have taken the children there when they were young but I never got around to it.'

'It's beautiful. I can't believe they had a vacancy for us at such short notice.'

'Perhaps because it's near Christmas?' suggested Libby, as the car began to climb a steep lane between high hedges.

'No, Christmas is very popular for weddings,' said Harry. 'I think they must have had a cancellation. They only offered us the one date.'

'Is this it?' said Libby as a pair of huge gateposts appeared on their right. 'It's not very far, is it?'

'That's what so good about it,' said Harry. 'Right on our own doorstep.'

He drove between the gateposts and up a wide drive bordered with enormous trees. Libby, not the best horticulturist in the world, had no idea what they were, as they hadn't even got their leaves on, but naked as they were, they were still impressive.

The drive opened out on to a wide forecourt. Discreet signposts pointed to "Shop", "Visitor's Car Park" and "Spa", while the building itself sported a colonnaded entrance approached by sweeping twin staircases.

'Wow!' said Libby. 'Are you going to lose your glass slipper on those steps?'

'Funny you should say that. They filmed a telly Cinders here, apparently. Out you get.'

'But it says the car park's round there,' said Libby.

'Only for open days or functions,' said Harry, holding the door for her. 'Come on, there's only so long I can go on being a gent.'

He led the way up the stone steps, which did indeed look like something in a fairy tale. Inside the huge double doors, all was gold and cream, but somehow understated, which couldn't be said for the girl who came towards them with a welcoming smile on her iridescent pink lips.

'Hi,' she said, her stripy pink and red hair nodding towards them Medusa-like.

'Hi,' said Libby nervously.

'Hi, Mel,' said Harry, leaning forward to plant a kiss somewhere between the nose and eyebrow rings. 'This is Libby. She's our bridesmaid.'

'Pleased to meet you,' giggled Mel, holding out her hand. 'He's a case, isn't he?'

'Oh, yes,' said Libby, not realising her offer of attendant had been taken seriously. 'Am I?'

'We said, didn't we. I think you're actually sort of best woman. You know, holding the rings. What normally happens, Mel?'

'Oh, well, it depends on the couple. Anything goes really. Long as the celebrant is happy.' Mel was leading them down a corridor lit by amazing chandeliers and lined with superior-looking console tables. She made a sudden left turn and ushered them into a tiny office labelled "Melanie Phelps, Events". Libby viewed the spiky stripes with more respect.

'Right, Harry,' she said, going behind an efficient-looking desk. 'Take a seat and let's go through what we've got so far.'

Libby's mind wandered as Harry and Mel went through menu options, seating arrangements and floral decorations.

'What do you reckon, Lib,' said Harry, 'gold and cream or pink and gold?'

'What?'

'Flowers,' said Harry. 'You're supposed to be here to help. Gold and cream or pink and gold?'

'They both sound a bit naff to me,' said Libby. Melanie giggled.

Harry sighed theatrically. 'All right, O Arbiter of Style. What do you suggest?'

'Where are they coming from?' asked Libby. 'Do you supply them?'

'We can do,' said Mel. 'It depends on how much involvement the client wants.'

'Why not Christmas flowers? White, with holly and mistletoe and fir-coney things. Not too feminine.'

'Oh, get you, ducky,' said Harry. 'Sounds good, though.

What do you think, Mel?'

'Yes, we've done that sort of thing before. I like it better than the obvious stuff.' She turned to Libby. 'Do you want to take charge of the floral arrangements, then?

Libby recoiled in horror. 'Oh, no, thank you,' she said. 'I'm no good at that sort of thing.'

'Poor old dear,' said Harry, patting her arm. 'You've only got to look at her immaculate dress sense, haven't you?'

'Oi,' said Libby.

'No, you take charge, Mel. We might as well let you do the lot, then we haven't got to worry.'

'Do you want our florist to send you pictures of examples?' said Mel, making a note.

'Please, or Pete will go spare, and we can't have him getting his knickers in a knot. Now, can we show Lib the room?'

'Sure.' Mel stood up and led the way out of the office.

The room designated for the celebration of marriages, civil partnerships and, surprisingly, baby welcoming ceremonies, (for the modern atheist, Libby assumed) was just to the right of the imposing front reception hall. Double doors led into what must have once been a formal drawing room, with a large marble fireplace on the left-hand wall and enormous french doors leading on to a balcony, which in turn led on to the imposing front steps.

'For summer weddings,' said Melanie, 'the couple can come straight in from the balcony. Lovely,' she added, looking misty.

'We won't, though,' said Harry, shuddering. 'And anyway, don't we have to see the celebrant first?'

'Just through here,' said Melanie, indicating a little room just outside the double doors on the right. 'Then the celebrant comes in and takes her place –'

'Her?' said Libby.

'Oh, yes. Most of them are, these days,' said Mel.

'Hey, I like the sound of that. Could I do it?' asked Libby.

Mel looked taken aback. 'No idea,' she said.

'Oh, shut up, you old trout,' said Harry. Mel looked even more taken aback.

'It's all right,' Harry assured her sweetly. 'It's our pet name for her.'

Libby shrugged. 'I don't notice it any more,' she said to Mel. 'Sad, isn't it?'

'Anyway, our celebrant is a bloke,' said Harry. 'We've ordered him.'

'Ordered him?' said Libby.

'There's a company who can guide you through this sort of thing and supply sympathetic celebrants and scripts and stuff,' said Harry. 'All we did was find the venue.'

'And that's all right with you, is it, Mel?' asked Libby.

'Oh, yes,' said Mel. 'It's exactly the same as having a wedding planner. Better in fact, because they don't try to interfere with our own arrangements.'

'Oh.' What a lot she didn't know, thought Libby. 'Scripts?'

'Oh, Lib,' said Harry, 'of course. There aren't special words or services written down for CPs. They're not legal.'

'What?'

'No, what I mean is, the ceremony isn't the legal part. The signing of the register is the legal part. So you can design the ceremony yourselves, and this company will send you scripts to help you.'

'Oh,' said Libby again. 'Golly.'

Harry laughed and gave her a hug. 'So you can write in your own part, dear heart. Best Person.'

Libby made a face. 'I'm so old and out of touch.'

'You're not,' said Mel. 'You should see the ages of some the CPs. They've probably been living together for years and years, and finally they can make it legal. We've had several couples in their seventies. Mostly men. The women are usually young or middle-aged.'

'Wow.' Libby was round-eyed. 'And all this just in a year.'

'December 5th 2005,' said Mel.

'And since then you wouldn't believe how many "specialists" have appeared,' said Harry.

'Good job, I'd have thought,' said Libby. 'You've just said it's good to have someone guiding you through the whole thing.'

'But specialist photographers? Ring makers? Tailors? What were they doing before?' Harry made a disgusted sound.

'They were wedding photographers, ringmakers and morning-suit suppliers,' said Mel, with a grin. 'They're all the same people. They have to make themselves appear sympathetic to same sex couples. You've no idea how many of the traditional wedding industry practitioners *aren't* sympathetic.'

'You're not kidding,' said Harry. 'I went to a Wedding Fair in September, and in some places you could cut the atmosphere with a knife.'

'*You* went to a Wedding Fair?' Libby said. 'I don't believe it.'

'Well, I did,' said Harry, colouring. 'Not long after Pete asked me.'

'And I meant to look up civil partnerships as soon as I had my computer, but things sort of put it out of my head,' said Libby, remembering the day in her garden when Harry had told her about the forthcoming wedding.

'They would, seeing as you were out and about solving murders,' said Harry.

Mel's face was a study.

'Harry!' said Libby. 'He doesn't mean it, Mel. He's just making fun of me.'

They completed their tour of the venue with a visit to the garden room, where the reception was to be held.

'Are you having vegetarian food?' asked Libby.

'No. Pete's not veggie, only me, and not many of the guests are. There'll be enough for me to eat.'

Libby stood looking out at the garden, growing dark now, and the view across to a lake in the distance, bare-branched trees creating a lace-like pattern against the sky. What would it feel like to be getting married again, she wondered.

'Won't Pete want James to be Best Person?' she asked in the car on the way home.

'I think we can have as many attendants as we want,' said Harry, 'and you two can be the witnesses. After all, I've got nobody on my side.'

'Nobody?' Libby turned in her seat and looked at him, realising how little she knew of Harry's background except that Peter had met him in the rather exclusive private club where he had been assistant chef.

'Well,' said Harry, shifting uncomfortably, 'not family.'

'Oh?' Libby wanted to know, but sensed that perhaps Harry

didn't want to tell her.

'Pete's got enough for both of us,' said Harry firmly. 'Think of all the relatives I'm going to have!'

'Think of Mad Millie as a mother-in-law,' said Libby. 'What has she said about the wedding?'

'I don't think Pete's told her,' said Harry. 'I don't think she'd take it in.'

'I suppose not,' said Libby. 'Is she coming?'

Harry glanced sideways at her. 'I wish I could say no, but I think Pete wants her there.'

'But she might make trouble,' said Libby, visions of Peter's mother the last time she'd seen her, wild-eyed and quite mad rising before her eyes.

'I know.' Harry nodded and slowed down in front of Number 17. 'I've tried to talk to him. You see if you can have a go.'

'All right,' said Libby, gathering her cape round her and preparing to climb out, 'but I don't see what good I can do. This is where we miss poor old David.'

They were both silent, remembering David, the doctor member of the family who had died so tragically last spring.

'Ben might help,' said Harry, hopefully. 'He's quite sensible for an old –'

'Old?' said Libby.

'Sorry, Lib.' Harry grinned. 'Middle-aged, then.'

'Whippersnapper,' said Libby, and climbed out of the car. 'I'll talk to him. Oh, and what do I wear as Best Person? I haven't got long to find it, have I?'

'What you like, ducky. We're not having themed get ups. Maybe matching ties, that's about it.'

'Golly,' said Libby, trying to picture the flamboyant Harry in a formal suit.

Falling down the step in the dark as she opened the door, Libby noticed the red light winking on the answerphone. Fending off Sidney, who was loudly demanding to be fed, she pressed the button.

'Why don't you ever switch on your mobile?' came the voice of an exasperated Ben. 'Or haven't you even taken it with you?'

Libby remembered turning it off while having lunch in The Swan.

'How about dinner at Harry's tonight,' Ben went on. 'Or can't you face it after your meal there on Wednesday? Give me a ring.'

Libby switched on the lights and let Sidney lead her into the kitchen. After shifting the kettle on to the Rayburn's hotplate and giving Sidney his first tea, she rang Ben.

'I'd love to,' she said. 'In fact, I spent the afternoon with Harry. Are you coming round here first?'

'Is that an invitation?' asked Ben.

'Not that sort of invitation,' said Libby. 'I'd just like to talk to you before we go to the caff.'

Ben groaned. 'Not about this investigation, or whatever it is?'

'No,' said Libby, surprised that she'd actually forgotten about Bella Morleigh and the murder. 'It's about the wedding.'

'Oh.' Ben sounded relieved. 'OK. I'll book a table, if Harry's got one left, of course, and I'll come round about seven, if that's all right?'

Libby rang off and sat down at the kitchen table to wait for the kettle to boil. Now that Ben had reminded her, she wondered whether Fran had come up with anything after their morning's adventures. If she had, she certainly didn't want to share them, thought Libby, reaching an idle hand for the teapot.

With a mug of tea in hand, Libby wandered in to light the fire in the living room, which she did, with the help of Sidney, who insisted on walking through her arms and sticking his bottom in her face. Then, with a little trepidation, she phoned Fran.

'Sorry if I'm intruding,' she said, crossing her fingers, 'but I wondered if there was anything you could tell me about this morning. I know you wanted to think about it on your own.'

Fran sighed. 'Well, yes. I'm not entirely sure what I could see, or feel, but there's something, and I'm trying to make sense of it.'

'Would it help to talk about it?' asked Libby.

'Maybe, but not yet,' said Fran. 'Let me wrestle with it for a bit first.'

'OK,' said Libby. 'Ben and I are going to the Geranium tonight, so tomorrow, maybe?'

'I must do some Christmas shopping tomorrow,' said Fran. 'You haven't done yours, yet, have you?'

'Oh, God, no!' Libby spilt some of her tea. 'What with the panto and the wedding I'd forgotten all about it. Shall we go into Canterbury together? We could do park and ride.'

'Good idea,' said Fran. 'What time?'

After arranging to meet at ten, Libby rang off and finished her tea, before going upstairs to shower and change.

Ben arrived just after seven, while Libby was stoking up the fire, having given Sidney his second tea.

'Pete's right, you know,' said Ben, watching Sidney chase his plate around the kitchen floor. 'Sidney is a walking stomach.'

'He's a fine figure of a cat,' said Libby. 'Do you want a drink?'

'Yes, please,' said Ben, sitting in the armchair. 'So what do you want to talk about?'

Libby told him about her afternoon with Harry at Anderson Place.

'The funny thing was,' she said, tucking her feet up under her on the creaky sofa, 'that he didn't look out of place in his pink shirt and leather trousers and jacket.'

'Like some latter day Regency hero,' said Ben.

'Oh, he'd love that,' laughed Libby. 'But seriously, Ben, he's very worried about Millie.'

'Ah.' Ben sat forward in his seat and looked into the fire. 'Yes.'

'Well, ah, yes, what? Harry thinks Pete wants her there, which is natural, but he's afraid she'll cause trouble.'

'She will,' nodded Ben. 'Think what she was like when she was normal.'

'Has she ever been normal?' asked Libby dubiously. 'I just remember her talking about Peter's "friend", and trying to treat Pete and me as a couple.'

'There you are. She didn't understand then and she won't understand now. It could be really embarrassing.'

'That's what Harry's worried about. Makes you go cold inside, doesn't it?'

'So what's going to happen, then?'

'Well, Harry thought perhaps you could talk to Pete,' said Libby.

'Me? Why would he listen to me?'

'Because he respects you? And you're his older cousin.'

'What about James? He's his brother, the obvious person, surely.'

'Perhaps Harry thinks James is too young.'

Ben laughed. 'James is older than Harry!'

'Oh, you know what I mean,' said Libby, ruffled. 'Anyway, there it is, I've told you. Oh, and it's official, I am to be Best Person, with James, I think.'

'Swank.' Ben leant over and patted her hand. 'Do I get to be chief bridesmaid, then?'

Ben had managed to get a table for nine o'clock, although by the time the previous diners had vacated it, it was nearer half past.

'Sorry,' said Donna. 'You'd think Christmas was just an excuse to eat a lot and get drunk, wouldn't you?'

'I thought it was,' said Ben, pushing Libby's chair in for her. Donna, a staunch member of the local chapel, looked affronted and handed them menus in a marked manner.

Later, while they were drinking their coffee, Harry emerged from the kitchen faintly pink and damp and carrying a bottle of brandy. Sitting himself in one of the empty chairs at their table, he waved at some of the other customers and poured three brandies.

'Here you are, loves,' he said, 'on the house.'

'Heavy night?' said Libby, raising her glass to him.

'Always bloody is, these days.' He looked at Ben. 'She tell you, then?'

'About what?' said Ben, looking cautious.

'Oh, Ben. Yes, of course I did,' said Libby. 'He agrees that it would be a problem.'

'So, are you going to talk to Pete, then?' asked Harry.

'I don't see how I can,' said Ben. 'It's not any of my business, strictly speaking, and I don't want to mess up my relationship with my favourite cousin. I'll volunteer to take charge if her, if you like, and hustle her out if it looks as if she's going to cause trouble.'

'Better than nothing, I suppose,' muttered Harry. 'Who would he take notice of, do you think?'

'You'd know better than we would,' said Libby.

'Oh, I don't know,' said Harry petulantly. 'He goes all upper class and looks down his nose at me if I try and say anything.'

Ben raised an eyebrow. 'Considering his Ma is working class London and his Dad wasn't exactly top drawer I don't know how he manages that.'

'Oh, you know what he's like,' said Harry, and Libby, picturing Peter's patrician nose and floppy fair hair, did know.

'We'll do what we can,' said Libby, 'but we might have to fall back on Ben's suggestion.'

'Oh, well,' said Harry, 'small price to pay, I suppose.'

'*My* small price,' said Ben, 'thank you.'

Harry grinned at him. 'You'll get your reward, darling,' he said. 'And just think, after this we'll actually be related.'

Ben cast his eyes up to the ceiling and Libby sniggered. 'Not sure it works that way,' she said.

'In my book it does.' Harry leant over and poured more brandy. 'Drink up, cousin-in-law.'

'So,' said Ben, as they strolled home a little later, 'what happened this morning with Fran and the theatrical lady?'

'Goodness,' said Libby, 'I'd forgotten all about that. I think Fran came up with something, but she hasn't wanted to share it. We're going Christmas shopping tomorrow, so she'll probably tell me then.'

'She's still scared of them, isn't she?'

'Her moments? Yes, she is.' They turned the corner into Allhallow's Lane. 'She's better at focusing them, now, and she did ask for something to take away, so that she could concentrate on it. That's what the proper psychics do, isn't it?'

'Fran being an improper psychic, eh?' Ben squeezed her arm. 'I wonder how Goodall and Smythe bill her? "Our resident psychic"? "Our investigative medium"?'

'I don't suppose they do,' said Libby, getting out her key. 'I expect they simply tell clients they'll get somebody to look into the property. They must be the very expensive ones, mustn't they?'

'Usually, yes, but occasionally she's had to go to an ordinary street which has a reputation, and on one occasion to a house where it was thought a murder had taken place. She said it hadn't.'

'Was she telling the truth?' asked Libby, opening the door and switching on the light.

'As far as I know.' Ben followed her in. 'And now are we going to talk about something apart from murders and other people's weddings?'

Chapter Six

Bella rang Fran the following morning.

'I'm going to see Aunt Maria's grave,' she said. 'Would you like to come with me?'

As an invitation it left a lot to be desired.

'You know where she's buried, then?'

'Not buried, exactly. I went and asked George at the pub last night, and he said she was cremated, and her ashes had been scattered in the garden at the crematorium.'

'So why do you want to go?' asked Fran, who had no patience with a morbid desire to seek out the remains of human flesh and worship at the graveside. If the spirit was alive, fair enough, but there certainly wasn't anything left in a grave, or ashes.

'I thought I should,' said Bella. 'Don't you think I should?'

'I don't see why,' said Fran, and explained her own feelings. 'Mind you,' she concluded, 'I know mine isn't the popular take.'

'I see what you mean,' said Bella. 'But we've been every year to Andrew's mother's grave, and to look at the tree I planted for my mother and father. It seemed the thing to do.'

'Up to you,' said Fran, 'but I wouldn't get anything from the visit if that's what you were hoping.'

'Well, I was rather,' said Bella, with a nervous laugh.

'I'm still thinking about what we found yesterday,' said Fran. 'Have you had a look through any of those files yet?'

'Yes, but not many. I managed to open the file for the 1920s again, and the one that said "Up to 1920". I didn't know what would be in that one, because Maria wasn't born until 1914, but there were a couple of things listed, so I found the box file.'

'And what was in it?'

'Oh, it was terribly sad. There was a little notebook that I could hardly read with some names and amounts of money beside them, a few leaflets and postcards for The Silver Serenaders and The Alexandrians and a letter from Peter Prince that must have arrived after he died.'

'Oh? May I see them?'

'Of course. Do you want to come here, or shall I come to you?'

'How would you get here?' asked Fran, thinking that although it should be up to Bella to come to her, it wouldn't be the most practical solution.

'Is there a bus?'

'Only into Canterbury, then you have to come out again. I'll tell you what, I'll ask Libby if I can borrow her car, and come to you. I'll have to ring you and let you know when, because we're going Christmas shopping today.'

'Oh, all right, but I have to go home tomorrow. George from the pub is coming in this afternoon to fit a cat flap for me, and the lady next door will carry on feeding Balzac. I hope he learns to use it.'

'All right,' said Fran, 'I'll see if I can come later on today. Otherwise it will have to wait until you come down again.'

'Or I could give you the keys,' suggested Bella. 'If you wanted, of course. I thought you mind find … well, you might–'

'I think it's an excellent idea,' said Fran. 'As long as you don't mind me fossicking around on my own. How will you get the keys to me?'

'I could leave them at the pub? George and his wife were really fond of Aunt Maria, and they seem to want to take care of me, now.' Fran heard a sigh. 'It's quite a novelty, someone wanting to look after me.'

Another black mark for the unknown Andrew, thought Fran.

'Good idea,' said Fran, 'but I'll still try and get over today. Are you ringing from your mobile?'

Having agreed to ring Bella if she managed to find a way of getting to Heronsbourne, Fran switched off the phone and sat down to think. Her eyes went to the photograph propped up on the table.

March Cottage had been a surprise. There was a certain warmth about it, although, as she had said at the time, the upstairs felt as if it had been disinfected. But the outbuilding had been different. Not in itself, but in its contents. Fran had felt all sorts of things swirling around her, so much of it that it was difficult to sort out. She knew without a doubt that the woman in the photograph was Dorinda, she also knew that it hadn't been taken in Nethergate or Heronsbourne. From what Bella had told them of Maria's letter, Dorinda would have been in her late twenties in 1914, so in the photograph she must have been in her late thirties or early forties, judging by the clothes. Where would she have been then? Travelling in South Africa, while Maria and Bertram stayed at home?

Fran stood up with an exclamation of frustration. She could get nothing. The only thing she was going to be able to do was to immerse herself in the contents of that outbuilding.

She phoned Guy and explained the situation.

'I'm really looking forward to spending some time in there, but getting there and back is going to be a problem. I need to get a car. But I'm wary of buying one on my own. I've never done that before.'

'What – never bought a car?' Guy sounded flabbergasted.

'No. When I was married my husband always bought them, and since I've been on my own I haven't been able to afford one. And as far as I can work out from female friends, car salesmen see women coming.'

'That's rather sexist,' laughed Guy.

'But true,' said Fran. 'Especially when it's a woman of my age.'

'So what you're asking is for me to come with you?'

'Would you mind? I can ask all the right questions myself, but I'll be paying cash – blimey, cash! – and I gather you can haggle a bit. I wouldn't be good at that.'

'Of course I'll come with you. When?'

'Not today. Libby and I are going Christmas shopping. Although Bella did want to see me today. Can't see how I could get over there, though, and she's going back tomorrow.'

'How about when I come and pick you up tonight we go there first?' suggested Guy. 'Then I'd be there to give you an excuse to get away.'

'Good idea.' Fran brightened. 'Although I really don't know why I'm putting myself out for her.'

'Neither do I. She isn't paying you, is she?'

'No, of course not,' said Fran. 'All I needed to do was talk to her once, I suppose, because Inspector Connell suggested it. And I haven't felt anything that might have helped him with his murder.'

'So it's just interest,' said Guy.

'Suppose so,' agreed Fran. 'I'll have to think about it. And now I've got to go, or Libby will be here and I won't be ready.'

As Libby drove into Canterbury, Fran told her about her conversations with Bella and Guy.

'Good idea about the car,' said Libby. 'Do you know what you want?'

'Oh, yes,' said Fran, 'I've known for some time. I've been buying all the car magazines for weeks.'

'You dark horse you,' laughed Libby. 'So no help needed there, then. But what about Bella's stuff? Do you want me to come with you?'

'I might. And Guy's got me wondering about why I'm doing it, so I might need a detached bystander.'

'It's got you interested,' said Libby. 'You're beginning to tap into those moments of yours a lot better now, aren't you?'

'I think so,' said Fran. 'I need to concentrate on picking things up from people or objects.'

'Or places. You said you got rather a reaction at the old Alexandria yesterday.'

'Mm, but I think it was from some*one* rather than some*thing*.'

'The body!' said Libby triumphantly.

'The body wasn't there.'

'But it *had* been.'

'Oh, I don't know,' said Fran. 'Let's change the subject.'

By lunchtime they were both exhausted and made for their favourite little back street pub, where the sparkling barman asked after Harry.

'He's fine,' said Libby. 'Getting married.'

'Married?' squeaked the barman.

'Well, Civil Partnership, then. I'm Best Woman.'

'Hmph,' said the barman and slammed her change on the bar.

'That went down well,' said Fran, as they slid onto a bench

75

and stuffed their parcels under the table.

'Known for my tact,' nodded Libby, taking a sip of her alcohol-free lager. 'Yuck. That's awful.'

'You should have had an orange juice or something,' said Fran, taking a large mouthful of white wine.

'You wait until you're the driver,' said Libby grumpily.

'That's just it, I *can't* wait,' said Fran. 'I shall be able to go where I want when I want.'

'Meanwhile, you can borrow Romeo if necessary. But you said Guy's going to take you to see Bella this evening?'

'Yes, because she's going home tomorrow. To Orrible Andrew.'

'Why do you call him that?' Libby looked interested.

'Because he is. We felt it before, didn't we? But I know now. It comes off her in waves. He doesn't like the idea of her having any sort of life of her own, and it's real rebellion, her coming down here, and especially if she refuses to sell. I just hope she stands up to him.'

'Could he be anything to do with the body in the theatre?' asked Libby.

'I don't see how. Bella knew nothing about her family until she got the letter from what's-his-name – Grimshaw. No way Orrible Andrew could have known before she did.'

'Oh, I don't know. Perhaps he intercepted a previous letter.'

'If he had, his reaction would have been the same as it is now, wouldn't it?' Fran reasoned. 'Whoopee – sell it and make money.'

'Oh.' Libby nodded glumly. 'Course it would.' She sat up straight and looked at her friend. 'So, are you interested in Bella's family history, or the murder?'

Fran looked startled. 'I don't know,' she said. 'Both, I think. In fact, there's a link. Just as Connell thought there might be.'

'Have you only just thought of that?'

'Yes. I was suddenly sure.' Fran sat with her fingers to her mouth staring out of the window. 'Oh, Lib, yes. I'm sure.'

On the journey home, Libby tried to get Fran to talk about the certainty of the link between the body in the theatre and Bella's family, but Fran wasn't sure of anything and refused to talk.

'I'll know more tomorrow,' she said, as Libby dropped her outside The Pink Geranium. 'I'll tell you then.'

She was waiting outside for Guy when he arrived to collect her at half-past six.

'No time for dalliance tonight, then?' he said with a grin, as she got in beside him.

'What do you mean?' Fran kept her face down as she fastened her seat belt.

'You didn't invite me in.'

'Sorry.' Fran looked out of the side window.

'Are you making use of me?'

'What?' she looked round quickly.

'It's all right, Fran, don't take the bait so quickly.' He pulled out into the High Street. 'I offered to take you, didn't I?'

'Yes,' said Fran.

'But you don't really want to be beholden to me, do you?'

Fran gave him a startled look.

'See? It's not just you who can see into people's minds,' he said, patting her knee. 'Never mind. Let's go and see Bella.'

March Cottage was positively sparkling inside now. The range in the sitting room was glowing, and Balzac lay stretched out on his back in front of it.

'Thanks for coming,' said Bella. 'Can I get you anything? A drink?'

'No thanks,' said Fran, as Guy opened his mouth. He closed it.

'Well, sit down, then.' Bella indicated the two chairs, and pulled up a straight backed one for herself. 'Here. This is what I found in the box file.'

She handed over a small pile of rather fragile documents. First there was a tiny notebook which contained several names written in a beautiful copper-plate hand, with very small amounts of money written beside them: three and sixpence, two shillings and one and sixpence.

'Piano lessons,' said Fran.

'Really?' said Bella. 'I thought it might be payments to the Serenaders.'

'Too variable, and all the names are female. I think she adjusted her fee according to the circumstances of her customers.'

'But Maria did say the troupe became all female during the war,' said Bella.

'What about the dates?' asked Guy, peering over her shoulder.

'Just says 5th April, and 1st February, things like that,' said Fran. 'No year. But they seem to start in November and finish in April. I would guess that's the year Maria says she ran away from her employers, so 1903 to 1904.'

'Then there's these.' Bella pointed to the poster and postcards, tattered, brown round the edges and age-spotted like ancient hands. The poster advertised the Silver Serenaders on the sands at Nethergate at 11.30, 3 o'clock and 8 o'clock, if wet under the cliff.

'The cliff?' said Bella.

'Where the Alexandria stands now,' said Guy. 'Under the cliff was an area where there were changing rooms and public conveniences. Not then, though, I suppose.'

'No, just a cave-like area in the chalk,' said Fran. 'That's where Bella got her first pitch.'

Guy and Bella stared at her. Fran kept her eyes on the poster and the postcards.

'And these were when she'd formed The Alexandrians, look. Pictures of the performers that were sold around the town and after the performances. Holidaymakers would send them home.'

Guy took one of the sepia tinted postcards, of a group of pierrot-costumed performers looking very seriously into the camera, with the title *The Alexandrians, Nethergate* along the bottom in spidery white print.

'When did she build the theatre?' asked Guy.

'I don't know,' said Fran. 'Bella?'

'Sometime between 1904 and 1914, according to Maria's letter,' said Bella, still looking slightly shell-shocked. 'She was given a pitch, it said, and then bought the freehold.'

'This was before Maria was born, so she wouldn't have known exactly what happened,' said Fran, her hands still on the poster and the remaining postcards. 'The first pitch was below the cliff, but I suppose it became easier to perform on the promenade.' She looked up to stare into the glowing coals in the range. 'I don't know.'

'She was very enterprising for a woman in those days,' said Guy.

'Wasn't she,' said Fran. 'I expect there were a lot of them but we don't get to hear about them. I'd like to know more.'

'So, anything else about her?' asked Bella.

'Nothing at the moment. If I can come and have a look through the other stuff it would help. If you trust me.'

'Of course. I'll leave the keys with George at The Red Lion, like I said.' Bella took the postcards and poster back, looking at them wistfully. 'I wish I knew more.'

'You will,' said Fran, 'in fact you hardly need me. You've got all that lovely information in the shed.'

'I suppose so,' said Bella. 'But Inspector Connell wants to know if there's a connection between the family and the body in the theatre, doesn't he? I couldn't do that.'

'It's not a very old body, so I don't see how there can be,' said Fran. 'If it had been really old, yes, there might have been, except the last thing the building was used for was – what was it – raves?'

'Or a carpet warehouse,' said Bella. 'I don't think anyone's sure.'

'There you are then. Nothing to do with Maria. Or you.'

'But I'm not convinced of that,' she said to Guy, as they drove back towards Nethergate.

'You think she's involved somehow?' Guy glanced sideways at her.

'Not exactly, but there's a link. I'm sure of it. How I can uncover it, I'm not sure. I expect Inspector Connell will do it, though. I suppose it's more a matter of identifying the body before anything else can happen.'

Guy stopped the car at the end of the promenade by the Alexandria, which looked positively eerie in the darkness. The lights strung between the new "vintage" street lamps were lit for Christmas, with the addition of the odd formalised tree or star in lights. Fran shivered.

'Problem?' asked Guy.

'It's a lovely place, but something nasty's attached to it.' Fran pulled her coat tighter round her. 'But wouldn't it be lovely to have live performances here, again? You could have panto in the winter, too.'

'You've got enough to do with this year's panto,' said Guy. 'Don't start thinking about another one.'

'Next year,' said Fran, dreamily.

'Dinner,' said Guy firmly.

Chapter Seven

LIBBY AND BEN WERE invited to supper at Peter and Harry's cottage on Sunday evening, partly, Libby understood, to discuss wedding arrangements. Not having to think about cooking, after a morning in the theatre helping the lighting designer and the set builder who was constructing the beanstalk, she decided to pay Fran a visit.

'So where are we on the investigation now?' she asked, perching herself on the window sill.

'We?' said Fran, raising her eyebrows.

'You, then. You said you'd know more today.'

'A bit. I know Dorinda taught piano lessons the winter after she left her employers, and I know where the original pitch was on the beach at Nethergate. And somehow, there's a connection to this body, but I can't work it out.'

'That's all Connell wanted you to do, isn't it? So there's no real reason for you to carry on, if you don't think you *can* establish the connection.'

'No, and as I said to Bella, she's got all that information at her fingertips now we've found the computer and the files, so she doesn't need me, either.'

'She'd have found that stuff eventually, wouldn't she?' said Libby, pushing the window up and lighting a cigarette.

'You're going to fall out of there one day, you know,' said Fran.

'Don't moan,' said Libby. 'As I said, she'd have found all that stuff. And really Connell only wanted to know if *she* had a connection to the murder, not the family, didn't he?'

'I suppose so. I guess my job's done, really, isn't it?'

'Technically, but you said Bella wants you to go through the rest of the stuff in the shed.'

'I think it's more because she doesn't know how to go about

it than anything else. She wants it all laid out like a story for her.'

'Like the letter from her old auntie.'

'Exactly. I can't blame her. Look at how I wanted to know what had happened in my family.'

Libby nodded. 'Seems to be a problem with old aunties,' she said. 'Look at P.G. Wodehouse.'

'I don't think any of them were involved with murders,' said Fran.

'No, but most of them should have been victims,' grinned Libby. 'Anyway, where do you go from here?'

'Don't you mean where do *we* go from here?'

'Oh, all right, of course I want to be in on it.'

'We go and collect the keys from George at The Red Lion and plough through all the stuff in the shed. If we feel like it.'

'Oh, I expect we will,' said Libby. 'When are you going to look for your car?'

As Guy was expected to take Fran car hunting any moment, Libby took her leave and went to see if the eight-til-late had a suitable bottle of wine to take to with her this evening. Educated by Peter, Harry and old Flo Carpenter, widow of one of the biggest wine buffs in the area, Ahmed supplied a very acceptable bottle of Shiraz, and was proud to show her his special *Jack and the Beanstalk* window display, to which his son and wife were putting the finishing touches before revealing it to the inhabitants of Steeple Martin.

'Oh, Ahmed, that's lovely,' said Libby, touched. 'Where did you get the idea from?'

Ahmed's son proudly showed her a large picture book, from which the display had obviously been copied. The cow looked like the plaster one normally on display in the butcher's, and the beanstalk had a close relationship with a garden hose, but the general effect was magical, and Ahmed had stuck the colourful Oast House posters all round the edges of the window.

'We pull the blackout off tomorrow,' said Ahmed, indicating the blanket tacked to the top of the window frame, hiding the display from public view.

'I think it's wonderful,' said Libby, shaking his hand and bowing politely to Mrs Ahmed and their son. 'I shall give you complimentary tickets.'

'Complimentary?' asked Ahmed.

'Free,' said Libby. 'See you soon.'

She spent the afternoon wrapping the presents she'd bought the day before and Sidney helped by sitting on the wrapping paper. Thoroughly bored by four o'clock, she bundled everything into the cupboard under the stairs, made some tea and sat on the creaky sofa to watch an old film. Sidney, with a chirrup of relief, joined her.

They were both still fast asleep when Ben appeared through the kitchen, having resorted to his private back entrance after failing to gain a response at the front.

'We were supposed to be there at six-thirty,' he said, having woken her, Sleeping Beauty-like, with a kiss.

'Oh, bother.' She sat up, yawning. 'I haven't even changed.'

'You can go as you are,' said Ben.

'In my working clothes? No fear. Peter will be looking smooth in silk, you can bet, and Harry will have his best leather trousers on. How many,' she said, getting slowly to her feet, 'pairs of leather trousers do you suppose he has?'

Ben declined to guess, and offered to feed Sidney while Libby did a quick change. Ten minutes later they were walking down Allhallow's Lane towards the High Street, where Peter and Harry's cottage lay just beyond the Oast House drive.

Peter, as predicted, wore a soft pale pink silk shirt, his fair hair flopping over his high patrician forehead, and Harry wore leather trousers and a slightly darker pink shirt. Libby was glad she'd changed.

'So, how far have we got,' she said, sitting in the collapsing chintz covered armchair she usually favoured.

Peter handed her a whisky. 'You went to Anderson Place,' he said, 'that's about it. I hear you suggested the floral decorations?'

'Don't you like the idea?'

'I do, dear heart, I do. Much better than the naff pink and gold stuff.'

'That's what I said,' said Libby smugly.

'And catering? What about that?' asked Ben.

'Sorted,' said Harry. 'I brought the menus home for Pete to

look at, and he's approved them, so that's about it.'

'How are you getting there?' Libby looked around for her favourite ashtray. Peter supplied it and sat down on the sofa, swinging his legs onto Harry's lap.

'We're hiring a couple of chauffeur driven limos,' said Harry. 'I know they're naff, too, but we thought they'd cope with the whole wedding party. You two, your mum and dad, Susan and James.'

Libby noticed the omission of Millie's name from this list, but forbore to mention it.

'What happens if someone wants to go home early?' asked Ben, no doubt thinking of his father.

'They'll take you and come back. They hang around all evening.'

'Great,' said Libby. 'And what about you two? Are you coming back here?'

'No, we're staying at Anderson Place, then back here for Christmas,' said Peter. 'We'll have a proper honeymoon after the panto. The Caribbean, probably.'

'All right for some,' said Libby.

'You wouldn't enjoy it, you old trout,' said Harry. 'You'd have to take your clothes off.'

'Eh?' said Libby, spluttering over her drink.

'To sunbathe, ducky,' said Peter. 'We'd have to unwrap you like a parcel.'

'Best left to our Ben,' said Harry, waving his glass in the air.

'I'm very pleased to hear it,' said Ben.

Libby, rather red-faced, buried her nose in her drink.

'How did you come to choose Anderson Place?' asked Ben, as Harry seated them round the table.

'It was nearest,' said Peter.

'And Laurence Cooper recommended us,' said Harry.

'Who's he?' asked Libby.

'He *was* the restaurant manager. He's not there any more. I met him at the wholesaler's a couple of times, and he put me on to some good local organic suppliers. He suggested we try the Place when I told him we were looking for a venue. Good bloke.'

'Pity he's left, then,' said Ben.

'It is, but his assistant is very capable and they're still using his old menus. Or rather, his this season's menus. Now,' said Harry, 'shut up while I bring in la zuppe.'

During supper, the conversation turned to the pantomime. Harry was surprisingly laid back about it, considering, as it had left him with most of the work of the upcoming wedding. 'I shall get my own back,' he said, offering more vegetables. 'He can't drag his mind away from it, even though it isn't his baby any more.'

'I know,' said Libby, shooting Peter a malevolent look. 'I wonder sometimes which of us is the director.'

'It's my vision you're mangling,' said Peter, complacently, 'I'm entitled.'

'Who said I was mangling? You didn't say that about *The Hop Pickers*!'

'That was different,' said Peter.

'I'll say,' said Harry under his breath.

'All right, all right, children,' said Ben, 'don't squabble. It's going very well, Pete. Even I'm enjoying it.'

'There you are, you see,' said Harry, 'but I can't get his mind on to anything else. That's why I wanted to have you two over to discuss things. Focus him a bit.'

'Wasn't terribly good timing, was it, Pete?' said Libby, patting his arm.

Peter smiled at her. 'No, it wasn't, and that's my fault entirely. You warned me, Ben, didn't you.'

'I did,' said Ben, 'and don't worry, Hal, I told him he should concentrate on the wedding rather than the panto. After all, he wrote the script during the summer, didn't he? He could have just handed it over to Lib and that would have been that.'

'I know,' sighed Harry, 'but he's just not like that. So I let him get on with it and do all the arrangements myself. Now we need a bit of outside help.'

'What for?' asked Ben and Libby together.

'Clothes.' Harry looked at Libby. 'You asked me what you should wear, and I said we wouldn't wear anything special, but Pete thinks we should. So, what?'

'Oh, God, not those matching shiny frock coats, please,' said Ben.

85

'No?' said Peter.

'You wouldn't!' said Libby, shocked.

'Oh, OK. What then?'

'Why not both choose what you would like best? After all, in a traditional wedding, the groom doesn't know what the bride is wearing until she walks up the aisle,' said Libby.

'This is different. Anyway, the groom always knows the colour scheme, at least, doesn't he?' said Ben.

'Oh. I suppose so. Well, haven't you seen anything you like on any of these websites?'

'I have,' said Peter. 'A black velvet three-quarter-length coat with grey trousers.'

'That sounds good,' said Libby. 'What do you think, Hal?'

'Not sure,' said Harry. 'I like the black velvet, though.'

'How about,' said Ben, as one struck with inspiration, 'both wear black velvet and grey trousers, but design your own coats? And have a trim or waistcoat or something in the same fabric?'

'That's brilliant,' said Libby, looking at him with admiration. 'I didn't know you were so clever.'

'I knew I could rely on my big cousin,' said Peter. 'What d'you reckon, O light of my life?'

'Like it. Can I go over the top?'

'Not too over the top,' Peter with a smile, giving him a hug. 'Now all we have to choose is a fabric.'

'And a tailor,' warned Harry, 'who can do it in two weeks.'

'You don't have to buy made-to-measure,' said Ben. 'All the specialist shops will have ready-mades in all the different styles.'

'Well, this is something you're going to have to do, my love,' said Harry. 'We're going to have to actually go in person.'

Peter shrugged. 'I know.'

'How about,' said Libby, pushing her chair back from the table, 'going online now and finding out where the nearest shop is?'

'Good idea,' said Harry. 'Tomorrow's Monday, and I'm not open, for a change.'

'But I –' began Peter, and was silenced by a howl of protest from the others. 'Oh, all right. Come on then.'

When a list of wedding outfitters had been concocted, dessert offered and eaten, and brandy and coffee supplied in the sitting room, Libby returned to the subject of Anderson Place.

'It's very beautiful,' she said, 'and I remember it being open to the public when the children were small. When did it become a hotel?'

'Not until the late eighties, I believe,' said Peter. 'Laurence Cooper gave us a bit of a potted history, didn't he, Hal?'

'Yes, apparently it had been used as a hospital during the war –'

'Lots of big houses were,' said Libby.

'Don't interrupt,' said Harry. 'Well, the family didn't know what to do with it, and eventually one of the grandsons of the original owner had the idea of a hotel. I don't know how he did it, because they had no money by that time. I think they'd tried giving it to the nation, but the nation wasn't interested.'

'Original owner? That can't be right,' said Libby. 'When was it built?'

'Well, no, not quite right,' said Peter. 'It was a wreck in the early part of the twentieth century, and somebody bought it and restored it to true Victorian grandeur.'

'Should have been Edwardian by that time,' said Ben.

'But the old boy who bought it was a true Victorian gentleman. He renamed it Anderson Place,' said Peter.

'Was that his name?' asked Libby.

'Apparently. I don't think he was famous, or anything. Anyway, that's the story. I don't know what happened to the family.'

'Moved into a semi in Canterbury, probably,' said Ben. 'Wouldn't have been able to afford anything else.'

'Isn't it sad,' said Libby.

'What? Bloated plutocrats being forced out of their palaces?' Harry was indignant.

'Well, yes, in a way.' Libby lit a thoughtful cigarette. 'When they first went to live there it would have been quite normal, and then by the time the war came, the second one, I mean, they would have been broke, with no way of getting rid of this millstone round their necks. How many beautiful buildings have we lost in those circumstances?'

'Several,' said Ben. 'Many of our finest old houses were literally knocked down because of the horrendous taxes and cost of upkeep.'

'Really? What about listed buildings?' asked Peter.

'That only began in 1950,' said Ben. 'Partly a reaction to the war, and partly because we were losing buildings, as I've said. It was the government rapping our knuckles again.'

'Oh, well, we've still got Anderson Place,' said Harry, 'and I'm really glad we're getting married there.'

'So am I,' said Peter. 'Now, get us another drink.'

'So what do you think that was really about?' asked Ben, as he and Libby walked back to Allhallow's Lane.

'Eh?' Libby turned her head to look at him. 'They wanted our advice. They said so.'

'It was hardly world-shattering, though, was it? They could have worked that out themselves.'

'But they weren't, were they? They'd obviously got to an impasse, and needed somebody else to break the deadlock. That's what we were there for. And not before time, otherwise they'd have been going up the aisle in a couple of tablecloths.'

'I suppose so,' said Ben. 'I just hope they're doing the right thing. It's all so sudden.'

'Sudden?' Libby laughed. 'They've been together for nearly seven years, they own a house and a restaurant together. I wouldn't say it was sudden.'

'You know what I mean. They've been pootling along for all this time, then suddenly Peter wants to get married as quickly as possible.'

'I think it was partly the shock he got when he found out Harry had been seduced by the "other side" back in the spring,' said Libby, referring to an unfortunate incident which had been revealed during the murder investigation in which they had all been involved.

'Well, if he thinks being legally bound to each other is going to stop that, he's wrong,' said Ben, taking Libby's key from her hand and unlocking the door.

'That's cynical,' said Libby, 'if true.'

'Harry's much younger than Pete,' said Ben, 'and he might not be completely settled in his sexuality.'

'Oh,' said Libby, going into the kitchen and switching lights on as she went, 'I think he is.' She smiled, remembering Harry's confessions to her. 'I think he is.'

'I just hope so. I have to say I've been put off marriage for life after my experience.' He smiled at Libby. 'And you must have been, too, after Derek's behaviour.'

'Oh, yes, of course,' said Libby dismally, and went to fetch the Scotch.

Chapter Eight

'WHERE DO WE START, then?' asked Libby, as she climbed out of the passenger seat of Fran's smart new car, which Guy had immediately christened the Roller-skate.

'I knew what I wanted,' Fran had told Libby, 'I just wanted him there as back up. He'll have to eat his words when I show him the petrol consumption.'

'It parks really easily,' said Libby now. 'Go on then, where do we start?'

'In the shed, although I want to see if Bella left the letter from Peter Prince in the sitting room. She didn't give it to me with the other stuff and she said she'd found it.' Fran wrestled with the door key they had just picked up from George in the Red Lion. Eventually it gave in and they were able to enter.

'Would this be it?' Libby stopped in her prowl round the sitting room and held up a yellowing envelope with faded writing and a lot of official looking markings.

'Looks like it.' Fran took it and turned it over. 'Yes, this is it.' She sat down in one of the fireside chairs and took the fragile piece of paper from the envelope.

'Nothing much, really,' she said after a moment, 'just how much he misses her and the baby –'

'That would be Aunt Maria,' said Libby.

'– and hoping the theatre is doing well. Oh, and listen to this! "And when I come home, my darling, please will you marry me and give our beloved daughter an honourable name?" Well, well, well.'

'So it was Dorinda who didn't want to get married,' mused Libby.

'I would have guessed as much,' said Fran, 'when you consider what she'd already done by this time.'

'What I still don't understand,' said Libby, 'is why she ran away in the first place.'

'According to Maria, just because she and Peter had an undesirable relationship, she was turned off, she didn't run away.'

'Holiday romance with a Redcoat sort of thing,' said Libby. 'Italian waiter syndrome.'

Fran smiled. 'Exactly, except I'm not sure about that. If it had been, would Peter have stuck by her?'

'I doubt it,' said Libby. 'They don't usually, do they?'

'Don't forget this was 1903. Things were different then.'

'Human nature doesn't change. I would have said the only reason he stuck by her was a) if he was really in love with her, and b) if she was pregnant. Which would have been favourite, in my opinion.'

Fran smoothed the paper in her lap. 'I think he loved her. And Maria was only two when this letter was written.'

Libby shrugged. 'Perhaps she had a miscarriage the first time.'

'Then why did they stay together? She would have been ruined, anyway.'

'Oh, come on, Fran! You're the psychic! For a start, wasn't she earning money by giving piano lessons that winter? You've more or less proved that, haven't you? And then she started the Silver Serenaders. No wonder he stayed with her after that. I'm just surprised that he stuck by her at first.'

'I told you. Love. I think that was genuine. And you're right, she was worth sticking to after that. He was quite a weak sort of person.' Fran stood up. 'Come on, let's go and see what else we can find.'

Fran opened up the shed while Libby made tea. Bella had stocked the cupboards, and even left food in the fridge, so she was obviously intending to come back fairly soon. Balzac came to see what was going on, and Libby gave him some milk.

'Sidney can't drink milk,' she told him, 'but you seem to enjoy it. Just don't get used to it.' Balzac ignored her, so picking up the two mugs, Libby left him to it and went to join Fran.

Over the next few hours, Fran opened all the folders on the computer, and they made a start on the box files. Of the discoveries they made, the most interesting were those referring to Dorinda's management of the Alexandria, which, in its heyday, had rivalled any seaside theatre, attracting some top names long before the glitzy end-of-pier Blackpool-style shows of the sixties. She had even managed to keep the theatre open during the winter, and it was during a sortie up to London to recruit talent for the forthcoming season that she had met Daniel Durbridge.

They also discovered that Dorinda had taken in the young widow of another Silver Serenader, originally a member of Peter's first troupe, Will's Wanderers. This woman and her child shared the second bedroom in March Cottage and looked after Maria when Dorinda was working.

'Well, that answers that question,' said Libby. 'I suppose she was still there when Dorinda went to South Africa.'

'As far as I can see, yes,' said Fran, leafing through the contents of one of the files. 'I don't think she got on with any of the other women at the Alexandria.'

'The performers, you mean? Well, she wouldn't would she? Unless she had been a performer herself.'

'I don't think so. There's a rather odd letter here, returned after Peter died, I think. From her to him. Listen: "I am glad to have dear Phyllis and her little Arthur here. Unlike my Alexandrian ladies, she has no knowledge of those unfortunate events over ten years ago. Dear Algy was too loyal to have mentioned anything to her. How we miss him!" What do you think of that?'

'Algy?'

Fran riffled through a pile of programmes. 'Ted and Algy were a double act with the Silver Serenaders and then The Alexandrians. Algy must have been Phyllis's husband and Arthur's father.'

'Unfortunate events? That means when she went off with Peter, doesn't it?'

'I suppose so, but why is she pleased that Phyllis doesn't know anything about it?'

'Perhaps she was pregnant after all?' Libby leant over and took the letter from Fran's hand. 'Algy was too loyal. Odd wording. I don't get it.'

'There must be something else apart from being turned off

for an inappropriate affair,' said Fran. 'That wouldn't have mattered to the performers, would it? I bet they were always having inappropriate relationships.'

'And who were the Alexandrian ladies?' said Libby. 'Dorinda says they know all about whatever-it-was, and dear Phyllis doesn't. And that's obviously A Good Thing.'

'Wives and girlfriends of the original troupe? They must have been quite old by 1916, though.'

'Perhaps that was all to the good,' said Libby. 'They would be sensible and not compete for attention.'

'But there were hardly any men to compete for,' said Fran.

'Even better. The few still around would be available to the general populace, and not the painted devils.'

'Maybe.' Fran sounded doubtful. 'Anyway, what was it they knew and Phyllis didn't?'

'And why did it matter?'

They sat looking at each other in puzzlement.

'Who were the family Dorinda worked for?' said Libby.

'I can't remember. That was in Aunt Maria's letter, and Bella's kept that.'

'No help there, then,' said Libby.

Fran returned to the letter. 'There's another bit here that's interesting,' she said, 'listen. "Last Thursday to see dear Sir Frederick and Ivy. He keeps very well." Sir Frederick?'

'A patron of the theatre? And why does she only mention him keeping well and not Ivy, whoever Ivy is?'

'Ivy sounds like a maid,' said Fran.

'And she doesn't say "dear Ivy". Everybody else is "dear". Perhaps you're right.'

'We'll come and see if we can find any other reference to them another time,' said Fran. 'I'm tired.'

'OK. Soon, though,' said Libby. 'I'm intrigued.'

They packed everything away in the shed, locked up, and, after washing their mugs and Balzac's saucer, left to return the keys to George.

'Will you tell Inspector Connell what we're doing?' asked Libby, as the Roller-skate bowled along towards Steeple Martin.

'Yes. Simply because all he wanted was a link and I haven't found it, so it'll get him off my back.'

'But you said there was a link,' said Libby.

'I still feel there is, but there's nothing in any of this that provides it, is there?'

'No. I suppose if you found one later you could always let him know then.'

'Except he'd probably accuse me of withholding evidence.'

'And bang you up!' Libby giggled.

'Libby,' sighed Fran.

Fran, however, didn't have to ring Inspector Connell, as he called her five minutes after she'd arrived home.

'No luck, I'm afraid, Inspector,' she said.

'Pity,' he said. 'Have you ever heard of someone called Laurence Cooper?'

'No, who is he?'

'Our body, that's who,' said Inspector Connell. 'Ring a bell?'

'I'm afraid not,' said Fran. 'Have you told Mrs Morleigh?'

'I've called her, but she hasn't rung me back,' said Connell. 'I didn't leave a message with her husband.'

'Oh, well, at least now you can move ahead,' said Fran. 'I'm just going to carry on looking into Mrs Morleigh's family history for her.'

'Let me know if you come across anything interesting,' said Connell.

'Of course,' said Fran, and rang off. She punched in Libby's number straight away.

'They know who the body is,' she said when Libby answered, 'so that lets me off the hook.'

'Who is it, then?'

'Someone called Laurence Cooper –' said Fran, and was cut off by a shriek from Libby.

'Laurence Cooper? Pete and Harry know him! Knew him – he was the one who recommended the Place. He worked there!'

'Really?' Fran sat down rather suddenly. 'Oh, dear.'

'Well, oh dear for him, of course,' said Libby.

'No, I meant – there's the connection.'

'Eh? Connection? Who to?'

'I'm not sure yet,' said Fran slowly, 'but that's it.'

'Can't see it myself,' said Libby, 'but I'll leave you to work on it. I must phone the boys and tell them.'

'Should you tell Inspector Connell?' asked Fran.

'Tell him what? That he recommended his workplace to some friends?'

'I see what you mean. Oh, well,' said Fran, 'you carry on. I'm going to lie down in a darkened room.'

Libby sat on the stairs staring at the phone. How did you announce the death of an acquaintance?

Hoping Harry and Peter were home from their shopping trip, she called their cottage first. Peter answered.

'He's gone to prep up, dear heart,' he said. 'Conscientious to a fault, my Hal.'

'I thought he said he wasn't working today? I just wanted to let you know something,' said Libby, feeling awkward. 'How did your shopping go?'

'Very well, thank you, and he wasn't working during the *day*. He's got a Christmas do tonight. Wanted to let us know what?'

'You know you were telling us about that chap at the Place? Laurence Cooper?'

'Yes,' said Peter.

'Well, he's the body in the theatre,' said Libby.

Chapter Nine

THERE WAS A SHORT silence. 'I don't believe it,' said Peter.

'It's true. Fran just called me. Inspector Connell told her in case it meant anything to her. It didn't, of course.'

'I'll tell Harry. He knew him better than I did. What a godawful thing to happen. Does Fran know how?'

'I don't think so.'

'This is a bit different from the other two, isn't it?'

Correctly interpreting this as the other murder investigations they'd been involved in over the past year, Libby agreed. 'I do come over all Lady Bracknell about it, though.'

'Lady Bracknell? Oh, *The Importance of Being Earnest*, you mean? How?'

'To be involved in one murder, Mr Parker, may be regarded as misfortune, to be involved in two looks like carelessness.'

'Three,' corrected Peter.

'Yes, but I'm not involved in this one. And we didn't get personally involved, either, it was a police matter.'

'Well, I feel a bit personally involved now,' said Peter. 'Especially as our whole wedding is on his recommendation.'

'Well, anyone who has anything to do with Anderson Place could feel like that,' said Libby. 'And anyway, you said he'd left. Did he tell you he was leaving?'

'No, there was no reason why he should. When we confirmed the menu, we were just told his assistant was in charge.'

'You also said they were still using his menus. But he was restaurant manager, not chef.'

'He decided on the menus in consultation with the chef. He was trained himself. Why are you asking all these questions?'

'Habit,' said Libby. 'Anyway, Fran will ask me. And we need to know if Inspector Connell asks.'

'Inspector Connell will already know if he knows who the

body is. Now get off the line, dear heart, so I can call Hal.'

Libby rang Ben, who was duly surprised and said he'd see her that evening, after which she wandered aimlessly into the conservatory and stared at the pristine canvas on her easel.

'It's no good,' she told Sidney, who had come to admire her work in case it got him an extra tea. 'I shall have to talk to Fran again.'

She took the phone into the living room and curled up on the sofa. Giving up his quest, Sidney came too.

'Listen,' she said when Fran answered, 'Peter said that chap never told them he was leaving.' She repeated her conversation with Peter.

'So?' said Fran.

'Well, it sounds as if he just disappeared, doesn't it?' said Libby.

'If he did, then Inspector Connell will know by now.'

'That's what Peter said. By the way, did Inspector Connell tell you how they identified him?'

'Of course not,' said Fran. 'He only wanted to know if it meant anything to me. He won't go around giving out privileged information.'

'Dental records, do you think?'

'How on earth would I know?' Fran sounded exasperated. 'It's nothing to do with us, anyway.'

'Oh, here you go again,' said Libby, exasperated in her turn. 'One minute saying you've found a connection, and the next saying it's nothing to do with us. You were like this all last summer.'

'OK, so I'm ambivalent,' said Fran. 'Half the time I don't know what I can see. I've told you, I don't pick and choose, it's just presented to me.'

'But you're getting better,' said Libby. 'You can focus on something these days, can't you? Like that picture, and the letter.'

'I know.' Fran heaved a sigh. 'But I never seem to get a clear picture. For instance, when you told me Pete and Harry knew this Cooper person, I knew instantly there was a connection of some sort, but to what I haven't a clue.'

'Was it a connection to Pete and Harry? Or to Bella?'

'I've already said, I haven't a clue. Just a – oh, I don't know – a sort of familiarity. Nothing to tell Inspector Connell, as you said.'

'Well, I wish I knew how he was identified,' said Libby, 'and how he was killed. We don't know that, either, do we?'

'Look, Libby, this is nothing to do with us. Honestly, I'd have thought you'd had enough of murders this year. Forget all about it and start concentrating on the pantomime.'

Libby took this in good part, and dutifully took out her script and began making notes. Not that there was anything she could change, now, with opening night only just over three weeks away and the Christmas break between now and then, but there were a few sections which could be tidied up.

She was in the process of tidying up one of these sections between Jack and the Princess that evening at the theatre, when Peter arrived.

'I didn't think you were coming,' she said, after sending Jack and his Princess off to do it again.

'News,' said Peter. 'Tell you later.'

The rehearsal plodded on, the cow sat on the fairy and the beanstalk fell down, but apart from that Libby was reasonably pleased. After brushing down the fairy and consoling the set builders, she returned her attention to Peter.

'So what's this news?'

'I called Harry to tell him about Laurence Cooper, and he already knew!'

Libby's jaw dropped. 'No!'

'Only just, apparently. The chef at Anderson Place rang to tell him. They'd had the police there all afternoon. Everybody questioned. If you want to come back for a drink he'll tell you all about it.'

'At your place or the caff?' asked Libby.

'Oh, home. The do was an early one. They've all gone off to their beds, now.' Peter stood up. 'Shall I get Ben? Is he backstage?'

'Interfering as usual,' grinned Libby. 'Yes, do get him. Wasn't a bad rehearsal, was it?'

'I've seen worse,' said Peter, as he threw a long scarf round his neck and went to find his cousin.

Back at the cottage, Harry, still in his checked trousers, gave them drinks and a plate of hors d'oeuvres left over from tonight's "do."

'Tell all, then,' said Libby, from the chintz chair.

'Well, this bloke Terry, the chef, called me here at about six in a high old state. Apparently, when they told us Laurence wasn't with them any more, it was because he'd just disappeared.'

'Exactly what I said,' Libby said triumphantly.

'He didn't come in one morning, and when no one could get hold of him and he didn't turn up the next day either, someone went round to his flat. He wasn't there, either, and they thought he'd done a runner.'

'Why would he do that?' asked Ben. 'Was he in trouble?'

'Not that anyone knew,' said Harry. 'He didn't seem to be a big spender, didn't gamble, or drink much, lived alone.'

'How long had he been at Anderson Place?' asked Libby.

'Oh, years. It was turned into a hotel first in the eighties, but not like it is now. Laurence went there about ten years ago, I think.'

'No family?'

'Again,' said Harry, 'my mate Terry said he'd never heard of any family, but it was his sister who reported him missing. The police assumed somebody at the Place had told her, but no one there knew she existed.'

'So they didn't need dental records, then,' said Libby. Everyone looked at her. 'Well, I wondered how he'd been identified,' she explained.

'It was sister Dorothy, so Terry says. She came to the Place this afternoon and went into a huddle with the manager.'

'And?'

'And what? That's it. Isn't that enough?'

'I thought there might be a bit more detail,' said Libby, reaching for an hors d'oeuvre.

'No, Lib. Why would there be?' said Ben. 'We're not involved in this one, remember?'

'That's what everyone keeps telling me,' muttered Libby.

'Then everyone's right,' said Ben, sitting on the arm of her chair and patting her shoulder. 'Leave well alone.'

Libby nodded, holding out her glass as Harry approached with a bottle. Looking up, she caught his eye and received a quick wink. Startled, she opened her mouth, but an almost imperceptible shake of his head made her keep quiet.

When she and Ben left half an hour later, he whispered, 'Ring you,' in her ear as he kissed her goodnight. She puzzled over this all the way home, and even in bed Ben complained that she wasn't concentrating.

'Sorry,' she said, sliding her hand downwards, 'my teacher always used to say that.'

'Well,' said Ben, slightly breathlessly, 'I hope you didn't respond in the same way.'

The following morning she couldn't settle. She didn't dare ring the cottage in case Peter, as he so frequently did, was working at home, and she had no idea what time Harry would get to The Pink Geranium. When he finally rang at eleven o'clock, she nearly jumped down his throat.

'All right, all right, knickers and knots, dearie,' he said.

'I know, but the suspense is killing me,' said Libby plaintively.

'Well, if you're a good girl and eat up all your greens, you can come here for lunch. There won't be many in, and we can have a good old goss.'

'But what about Fran? She might see me,' said Libby, thinking of Fran's flat above The Pink Geranium.

'Has she been telling you to leave it alone, too?' asked Harry. 'Oh, well, in that case we'll have to hide you under a table. Don't be daft, Lib. If she sees you, so what. Come around twelve. I'll finish prepping up, then Donna can do most of it.'

Libby filled in the remaining hour by doing some unaccustomed housework, and so surprised Sidney that he left home without the usual detour round the food bowl. Feeling dusty but righteous, Libby washed her hands, attacked her hair with some hairpins and lost the battle, slung her cape and a scarf round her shoulders and set off for the caff.

Harry was still in the kitchen when she arrived, but Donna sat her on the sofa in the window with a glass of wine as she had been instructed.

'Are you exhausted yet?' Libby asked. 'Have you had any

help?'

'Oh, yes,' said Donna, 'Harry's got a couple of lads in the kitchen and one of them helps out waiting in the evening as and when. And he never expects me to be here if we open at odd times.'

'No? That's good,' said Libby. 'You like working for him, then?'

Donna smiled. 'Wouldn't work anywhere else.'

'Where did you work before? Were you always in catering?'

'I worked up at the Place,' said Donna.

'Anderson Place?' gasped Libby. 'Does Harry know?'

'Of course he knows.' Donna looked surprised. 'He had to ask them for a reference. Oh, and he told me about old man Cooper, too. Sad, that.'

'Old man Cooper?' Somehow, Libby had thought of Laurence Cooper as a young man.

'Dear Larry,' said Harry, coming up behind Donna. 'Off you go, poppet. You're in charge.'

He sat down next to Libby as Donna went back to the kitchen.

'I didn't know Donna worked at the Place,' said Libby accusingly.

'Why on earth should you?' said Harry.

'Um – I don't know.' Libby took a sheepish sip of her wine. 'I didn't know Laurence Cooper was old, either.'

'He isn't – wasn't. About 60, I suppose.'

'Old to Donna, then,' said Libby.

'She was only 16 when she started there, so he would have seemed old to her.'

'Why did she leave there to come here?'

'Firstly, I suppose, she lives in the village, and second, she would never have been able to progress up the ladder as quickly.'

'And she has here?'

'Don't be daft, Lib. She practically runs this place. She wanted to become a fully-fledged restaurant manager, which is what Laurence was. She'd never have taken over from him, would she?'

'She would now,' said Libby.

'Not even now. His assistant has been deputy RM for at least five years, so he automatically steps into Laurence's shoes.'

'Did he hate him?' Libby's eyes lit up.

'No, Lib, he loved him.' Harry fixed her with a basilisk stare.

'Oh.' Abashed, Libby once more resorted to her wine.

'Look, I wanted to talk to you about this, but you'll have to let me tell it in my own way, without interruptions. Do you want to stay here, or come through to the back?'

'What, the garden? Too bloody cold.'

'Not the garden, fathead. The staff room.'

'Oh, the cupboard? Is there room for two?' asked Libby.

'Nasty, nasty.' Harry stood up. 'We'll go and have a chat, then you can come back out here and have whatever we've got left over in the kitchen.'

'Ooh, thanks a bundle,' said Libby, following him, nevertheless.

The staff room, or cupboard, was a small, window-less room at the back of the kitchen, with a table, four chairs, a sink and a kettle. Harry made himself a cup of coffee and sat down next to Libby.

'Now,' he said, 'I know they've all said leave it alone because it's nothing to do with you, but I have a very good reason for wanting to know a bit more about this.'

'Go on,' said Libby. 'Is this to do with the assistant?'

'Clever clogs. Yes, it is.' Harry drank some coffee. 'As you no doubt gathered from my subtle statement just now, said assistant is gay and a mate of mine.'

'Like Terry, the chef?'

'Not at all like Terry the chef. I only met him through Laurence, and as far as I can tell he's as straight as a telegraph pole, and about as thick. Good chef, though. No, I met Laurence through Danny.'

'Danny being his assistant?' Libby was on the edge of being confused. 'But I thought you said you met him at the wholesalers?'

'I did, often. But I first met him with Danny.'

'Where?'

Harry went faintly pink. 'In a club.'

'A gay club? Down here?'

'In London.'

'Does Pete go there too?'

'No.' Harry was a much brighter pink, now. 'It's just an occasional jaunt on my own. To catch up with old mates. That sort of thing.'

'Oh, right.' Libby was dubious. 'And Danny is an old mate?'

'We'd met a couple of times because we both lived down here. Then he introduced me to Laurence. He was completely smitten, even though he's so much younger.'

'How old is Danny?'

'About the same age as me,' said Harry. 'A really good bloke, and someone to talk to down here in the back of beyond when I feel the need.'

'I thought you talked to me?' Libby bristled.

'I do, lambkin, but you can't get away from it, you're female.'

'Hmm,' said Libby.

'So, what I'm coming to is – guess who's the chief suspect?'

'Danny?' Libby's eyebrows disappeared into her hairline. 'But why?'

'Always look for the nearest and dearest, don't they?' said Harry, leaning back in his chair.

'But how did they know? The police, I mean. He lived alone, didn't he?'

'Technically, yes, but Danny stayed over most of the time.'

'So why didn't he report him missing? Oh, don't tell me – they'd had a row.'

'On the button. A humdinger, according to Danny. And mostly our fault.'

'*Your* fault? How?'

'Our Civil Partnership. They were both involved in ours, Laurence had even suggested Anderson Place. And it gave Danny ideas.'

'Oh, dear. He wanted to do it and Laurence didn't?'

'Exactly.' Harry rocked back on his chair. 'No idea why. Danny said all Laurence would say was he was too old.'

'I can understand that,' nodded Libby. 'Sensible man, in my opinion. Look how silly Derek was with that Marion over half his age. Or should it be under?'

Harry shrugged. 'Well, whether you agree or disagree, that was the root cause of the fight. And then Laurence just disappeared. Danny thought he'd gone off to sulk, but after a while got worried. That was when he phoned sister Dorothy.'

'Why didn't he tell the management?'

'They didn't know about the relationship. Wouldn't have approved, according to Danny. So he phoned sister Dorothy, who didn't approve either, but at least knew about them. So she reported it to the police. And the rest you know.'

'So why didn't you tell us all this last night?' asked Libby.

'I'll give you three guesses,' said Harry, looking up at the ceiling.

'Pete. He doesn't know you knew them.'

'Oh, he knew I knew them, but he assumed, like you, that I'd met them through wholesalers and being in the same business locally.'

'So he didn't know about the club in town?'

'No. Still doesn't.' Harry let his chair crash back on to four legs. 'Anyway, you see the problem? Danny is in the frame for this murder. So he needs your help.'

'*My* help? What on earth can I do?' said Libby, looking interested, nevertheless.

'Well, Fran's help, I suppose, and your nosiness. Go on, you always said playing detectives was my idea. I'm putting my money where my mouth is.'

Libby stared into her empty wineglass. It was tempting.

'Yes, but when we tried to find things out about the last two murders it was because we were involved personally and knew things to start off with. This time we're completely outside, and we can hardly ask Inspector Connell for any more information.' She thought for a moment. 'Although, he did ask Fran in the first place ...'

'Exactly.' Harry picked up her glass and refilled it from a bottle next to the kettle.

'But that was because he thought she might connect the body to Bella Morleigh,' said Libby.

'No, it was because he wanted to find out if Fran could feel anything at all about the body. He suggested Bella should contact Fran because he was being sneaky.'

'Can I talk to Fran about this?' asked Libby. 'I'm not sure what she'll say, because she's in one of her ambivalent phases, but she did say she felt a connection as soon as I told her you knew him. A familiarity was how she described it.'

'There you are then,' said Harry. 'You've got to take it on.'

'And what do I say to Ben and Pete?'

'You've been asked to look into it,' said Harry loftily. 'Come on and I'll give you some grub. Oh – meant to tell you, someone asked if you were my mother the other day.' He giggled his way back through the kitchen leaving Libby to grind her teeth in his wake.

Chapter Ten

AFTER LUNCH, LIBBY LEFT The Pink Geranium and knocked on the door of Fran's flat. She heard the window go up.

'Oh, it's you,' said Fran's head. 'Hang on, I'll come down.'

'I've got someone with me, though,' she said, leading the way back up the stairs. 'So keep quiet.'

Libby opened her mouth in indignation and shut it again when she saw Inspector Connell getting politely to his feet.

'Mrs Sarjeant,' he said.

'Hello,' said Libby, and went to perch on her usual window sill.

'Inspector Connell was just filling me in on the details about the – er – the body,' said Fran. I bet he was, thought Libby, looking at Fran's tall, voluptuous figure and sleek dark hair. Why can't she see how attractive she is?

'Well, that's about it, actually, Mrs Castle,' he said, remaining on his feet. 'If you should come up with anything, you won't forget to let us – me – know, will you? Anything at all.'

'Of course not,' said Fran. 'I'll see you out.'

'Cor, that was a bit of luck,' said Libby, who, by the time Fran had returned had pushed up the window again and lit a cigarette.

'It was? Why?' Fran came back in and sat down.

'You'll never guess,' said Libby, and recounted all that Harry had told her before lunch.

Fran sat in silence after Libby had finished.

'Well, say something,' said Libby, climbing down from her windowsill.

'That was the connection I saw, wasn't it?' said Fran.

'Must have been. All a bit surprising really. What a coincidence.'

'I hate coincidences. What are the odds? Really, I mean? Of me getting involved with a body as a result of Connell, and then the same body turning out to be a friend of Harry's, with another friend of his as chief suspect?'

'The biggest coincidence in my book is that you and I have been personally involved in two murder cases this year and now Harry is as well. That's far more coincidental than the Inspector Connell Bella Morleigh connection.'

Fran sighed. 'You're right. But I still don't trust coincidences. There's a link somewhere, I know there is. I just can't see it yet.'

'So do we look into it?' Libby leant forward.

'I suppose so. But I'll have to tell Connell what you've told me.'

'Well that doesn't matter, he knows all that already. Just get his blessing.'

'I think I've got that already, haven't I?'

'Oh, please get in touch, Mrs Castle. Anything, anything at all.' Libby grinned. 'I should say you have!'

'I don't know how I look into it, though. What do you suggest?'

'Try and speak to this Danny? Look at Laurence's flat? Speak to sister Dorothy?'

'We'd never get near his flat,' said Fran. 'Ask Harry if he can introduce us to Danny.'

'Unless they've got him in jug,' said Libby.

'Try and be serious, Lib,' said Fran, standing up. 'Shall we go down and ask him now? If he's still there?'

'OK, down the back way,' said Libby.

From the courtyard, they could see Harry in the kitchen. He waved, and a moment later came out wiping his hands on a paper towel.

'Will you introduce us to Danny?' said Libby, before anyone else had a chance to speak.

'Yes,' said Harry, looking surprised. 'You're going to help, then, Fran?'

'I don't have much of a choice,' said Fran, with another sigh. 'Even without you, it would be nagging away at me. When could we speak to him?'

'I don't know. I'll try calling his mobile, but if he's still talking to the police we might not be able to get hold of him.'

'Why don't you ask your friend Terry the chef?' said Libby. 'He's the one who told you about it in the first place, so he'd probably have up to date info.'

'All right, but it'll have to be after I've finished here. I'll come up and tell you. Will you still be there, Lib?'

'If you're not too long and Fran can put up with me,' said Libby.

Harry appeared, however, within twenty minutes.

'They've let Danny go for the moment, apparently,' he said, throwing himself into a chair, 'but he's not to leave town.'

'Where is he?' said Libby.

'He's got one of the staff accommodation places in the grounds, so he's there, I think. He's not working. The management don't quite know what to do for the best, Terry says.'

'Who are the management?' said Fran.

'I don't know.' Harry shook his head. 'I don't even know who owns it.'

'Haven't you got a formal letter from them about the wedding?' asked Libby. 'You must have. That would have all the directors and info on it, wouldn't it?'

'Yes, I have. It's at home. I'll have to see if I can sneak it out without Pete realising what I'm doing.'

'Why does it have to be a secret from Pete?' asked Fran. 'I've been asked to look into it. He can't have any objection to it, even if he did tell Lib to leave it alone.'

'Very true, O wise one,' said Harry, standing up. 'I'll go home and look for it. Is it important?'

'I think so,' said Fran slowly, 'but first, what are we doing about Danny?'

'I'll try ringing him when I get back home and as soon as I've got anything to report, I'll ring you both.'

'Can't do anything tonight, though,' said Libby. 'We're rehearsing again.'

'Bloody panto,' said Harry. 'Always getting in the way.'

After he'd gone, Libby picked up her cape, scarf and basket and wrapped herself up. 'I bet he is cursing the panto, really,'

108

she said. 'He was quite jokey about it the other evening, but Pete's left all the Civil Partnership stuff to him because he can't think of anything else but flippin' Jack and his flippin' beanstalk.'

'It's yours, now, anyway,' said Fran following Libby down the stairs. 'You're the director.'

'I know, I know. I keep trying to tell him, but he was the same with *The Hop Pickers,* wasn't he?' She opened the front door. 'See you tonight, but probably speak to you before then if Harry phones.'

'If he does,' said Fran.

'He will,' said Libby confidently. 'This is his idea, after all!'

It was dark by the time he rang, though, and Libby had lit the fire in the sitting room, drawn the curtains and made tea.

'He says he doesn't want to go out anywhere, and at first didn't want to talk to anyone,' said Harry, 'but I persuaded him that Fran wasn't just anyone and would be able to help.'

'What about me?' said Libby.

'It's Fran who might be able to find something out, isn't it? Not you.'

'I don't know about that,' said Libby. 'Anyway, I shall go too, shan't I?'

'I expect so,' said Harry. 'No keeping you away.'

'So when can we see him?'

'Tomorrow morning, if that's all right? I want to come too, so I said ten o'clock, then I can be back here by about eleven-thirty for lunch time.'

'That won't give us long,' said Libby.

'I'll go in my car, then and you two can go in one of yours. Then if Fran hasn't finished I can leave before you.'

'Oh, OK. Have you spoken to Fran?'

'No, I thought you'd be madly jealous if I did that. Shall I say you'll pick her up?'

'I expect she'd prefer to go in her Roller-skate, so she can pick me up. She thinks she's a safer driver than me.'

'She's probably right,' said Harry. 'See you in the morning.'

At rehearsal later that evening, Fran confirmed that she would most certainly prefer to take her own car, if only because it was still a novelty to drive it.

'I'm scared though, you know, Lib,' she confessed quietly, while sitting in the auditorium with Libby watching the chorus being put through their paces by the musical director, who was proving efficient if a little inclined to make them all sing higher than they wanted.

'What of?' asked Libby. 'Not of Danny?'

'No, just the whole thing. I really thought it was all behind me after the business with Aunt Eleanor's death.'

Libby looked at her with sympathy.

'It can be, you know,' she said. 'You don't have to do this. I just get over-enthusiastic. Just tell Harry and Bella you don't want to continue.'

'They'd be disappointed,' said Fran. 'And Danny really needs help, if what Harry says is true.'

'And Bella doesn't?' asked Libby. 'Well, no, I suppose she doesn't. She can find everything about her family on that computer and she's got her inheritance, so she doesn't need you.'

'But she does. There's something there, too, but I haven't got to the bottom of it. Could just be that I think she's got a lousy husband, of course.'

Libby giggled. 'Join the club, Bella,' she said.

Chapter Eleven

THE NEXT MORNING FRAN drove the Roller-skate decorously behind Harry's car to where the main drive to Anderson Place divided and swept round to a stable yard.

'This is it,' said Harry, 'although we have to walk to get to the cottage.'

'Oh, he doesn't live here, then?' said Libby, looking round at the stables, which were obvious conversions.

'Only senior staff and some guest rooms here,' said Harry. 'Come on. We go through here.'

They tramped along a pathway which became less manicured as they went on, until they came to a pair of semi-detached redbrick Victorian cottages.

'Here we are,' said Harry, and went up to the dark green front door, which was opened before he could knock.

'Hi, Dan,' said Harry, and enfolded the slight dark young man before them in a bear hug.

'This is Fran,' he said, disentangling himself, 'and this is Libby. I think they might be able to help, as I told you. Well, Fran, might. I don't know about Lib.'

Libby glared, before stepping forward and holding out her hand. 'Hi, Danny,' she said. 'I'm so sorry.'

'So am I,' said Fran, coming up behind her.

'Thanks,' said Danny in a rather high and unsteady voice. 'Please come in.'

They followed him into a small, untidy sitting room, obviously furnished with discarded items from the main house. He sat down and waved a hand towards a small sofa. Harry took one look and sat on the floor.

'So what's happened, Dan?' he said. 'The police don't think you had anything to do with it, now?'

'I don't know.' Danny took a deep breath. 'I don't know why

111

they wanted to question me in the first place.'

'Because you were the closest to him,' said Fran, 'and they always look there first. Don't they Libby?'

'Yes,' said Libby, not knowing, but willing.

Danny nodded, leant back in his chair and let out a sigh.

'How did they know you were closest to him?' asked Fran. 'Harry said no one here knew you were a couple.'

'Management didn't, but a few of the blokes did. Terry knew,' he said, looking at Harry, 'and Dorothy knew. Didn't approve, but she knew. It had caused a split between her and Larry, although I don't think they'd been very close before.'

'How old is Dorothy?' asked Libby.

Danny looked surprised. 'I don't know. Older than Larry. Late sixties? Early seventies?'

'Well, that explains it,' said Libby. 'Large age gap between brother and sister and she's of the generation that maybe wouldn't understand about gay couples. I bet she didn't approve of civil partnerships and women vicars.'

Harry and Fran looked scandalised, but Danny smiled slightly. 'You're dead right,' he said. 'Mind you, Larry wasn't that keen on civil partnerships, either.'

'So Harry said,' said Fran quickly, trying to regain control of the conversation before Libby took it over completely. 'And Harry blames himself for your row.'

'That's daft, Hal,' said Danny, putting out a hand to Harry. 'It wasn't civil partnerships in general so much as ours. He just didn't want it.'

'The same as people not wanting to get married,' said Libby.

'Exactly,' said Danny, smiling at her again. 'I think there must have been something in his past that put him off, although he never told me.'

'Could he have been married?' asked Fran. 'Had he only come out recently?'

'Not that recently,' said Danny, 'we'd been together, what – three years, Hal? – he wasn't new on the scene then. He never said much about his past life, though. I met Dorothy because he wanted me to, but neither of us wanted to meet again.'

'But you went to her when he disappeared?' said Harry.

Danny shrugged. 'I didn't know what to do. Management

didn't seem too bothered, although I don't know why. He was very good at his job and he never stepped over the line. I thought it would seem a bit odd if *I* reported him missing, so I went to Dorothy. Phoned her, rather.'

'Did she come here?' asked Libby.

'Not until after he was found.' Danny swallowed. 'She had to identify him. Poor soul.' Whether he referred to Dorothy or Laurence wasn't clear.

'So she called the police to report him missing. I'm surprised they took it seriously,' said Fran, 'after all, he was single, living alone and didn't see his sister regularly.'

'I think it was because someone thought about the body,' said Danny, 'otherwise they wouldn't have done.'

'Had you been to his flat? After he disappeared, I mean,' said Fran.

'Oh, yes. I had a key. I lived there most of the time. I – I don't feel at home here.' Danny lowered his head, and Libby felt sympathetic tears spring to her eyes.

'So the police would have found your prints and DNA all over the place?' said Fran.

'Well, of course they would,' snapped Libby. 'He's just said he more or less lived there.'

Fran pursed her lips.

'But they wouldn't have known who it belonged to unless they had Danny on file,' said Harry.

'Oh, Dorothy told them all about me,' said Danny, without bitterness. 'She told them I had called her and all about what she called our "association".'

'Hmph,' said Libby.

'So they came and asked you about it,' said Fran. 'What makes you think they suspect you?'

'Their attitude,' said Danny, sitting up straight. 'It was so bloody obvious. The only thing they couldn't seem to fit in was the timing. We had our row over three weeks ago, and they don't think he's been dead that long.'

'Golly,' said Libby, wrinkling her nose.

'But just because you had your row three weeks ago doesn't mean you couldn't have killed him *after* that time, does it?' said Fran.

The other three stared at her in horror.

'Well, it doesn't, does it?' she said. 'So you must have a pretty solid alibi for the last two weeks.'

'I do,' said Danny, surprisingly. 'I was away.'

'Away?' chorused Harry, Fran and Libby.

'After we'd had our row, I took some annual leave. That was why I didn't realise he'd gone missing at first. I was just as huffy as he was, so I went off to my parents.'

'Where?' said Libby.

'Durham,' said Danny.

'You haven't got an accent,' was all Libby could think of to say.

'They moved there when I was sixteen,' said Danny. 'I love it. And I couldn't nip home in a couple of hours to commit a murder, could I?'

Fran looked at Harry in exasperation. 'So he doesn't really need our help, does he? He's got a perfectly good alibi.'

'I didn't know that,' said Harry. 'I just wanted to help.'

'I know, Hal,' said Danny, squeezing his hand. 'And I'm truly grateful. The police won't stop trying to break my alibi, anyway, so all help gratefully received. But Harry says you're a psychic.' He turned to Fran. 'Can't you help find his murderer?'

'She is,' said Libby.

'No, I'm not,' said Fran.

'The inspector in charge of the investigation put the woman who found the body in touch with her,' explained Libby, 'to see if she had any connection with the case.'

'And has she?' asked Danny.

Libby opened her mouth and Fran shut her up with a look.

'I can't see how,' said Fran. 'We've gone through her family background and there aren't any Coopers as far as we know, but it could be unconnected with her family.'

'It could be anything, couldn't it?' said Danny, looking more animated. 'A lover – or, no, not that –'

'It could be,' said Harry, 'if she had a lover who thought she was carrying on with Laurence.'

'Oh, come on, Harry,' said Libby. 'She knew nothing about the body.'

'Did she see it?' asked Harry.

'Well, of course she saw it.' Fran shuddered. 'Although she wouldn't have been able to identify it at the time.'

'Anyway,' said Libby, 'if that woman has ever had a lover I'll be a hat stand.'

Fran and Harry murmured agreement.

'Are you going to try and find out?' asked Danny, after a moment.

'She won't be able to help herself, will you Fran?' said Libby.

'Not if you've got anything to do with it,' said Harry.

'I could help,' said Danny tentatively. 'I mean, it would give me something to do and make me feel a bit less useless, and I know as much as anyone except Dorothy about him.'

'You said he never said much about his past life,' said Fran.

'No, but there were a few things. And maybe Dorothy would talk to you. She was a bit nicer to me after – after –'

'I don't think she would,' said Fran, 'but perhaps we'll keep her in reserve.'

'Well,' said Harry, standing up, 'I don't know if you two want to stay on, but I've got to get back.'

'Shall we go, Danny?' asked Libby. 'Would you prefer us to come back another time?'

Fran frowned, but Danny nodded.

'Could you come back?' he said. 'I'll think about everything he ever told me, and look out his letters. That would help, wouldn't it?' He turned to Fran.

'Possibly,' she said, 'but don't hold out too much hope. I might not find anything.'

Looking far better than when they had arrived, Danny saw them to the door. 'I might even go back to work,' he said, 'if they let me.'

'Might they not?' asked Libby. 'Why?'

'Because of the relationship angle, I think. And they weren't too keen on having an employee questioned by the police.'

'If they try to sack you because of that you could sue them,' said Libby, bristling.

Danny smiled bleakly. 'I suppose I could. But management aren't actually too bad. Old Jonathan's all right.'

'Jonathan?' said Fran.

'Jonathan Walker,' said Danny. 'He's a descendant of the chap who originally built this place.'

'Anderson?' said Libby.

'So it's stayed in the family,' said Fran thoughtfully.

'Only just, I think,' said Danny. 'They nearly lost it. It was a hospital or something during the war. Or a school.'

'Like Tyne Hall,' said Libby to Fran.

'Tyne Hall?' asked Danny.

'A place we went to last summer,' said Fran. 'It's falling down now, but that was a hospital during the war, too.'

'I expect this would have fallen down, too,' said Danny, 'but old Jonathan decided to turn it into a hotel.'

'How did he afford it, I wonder?' mused Libby.

'No idea, but whatever he did, it worked,' said Danny.

'Is all this public knowledge?' asked Fran.

Danny shrugged. 'I think so. Larry seemed to know all about it, anyway.'

When they'd left Danny to go and ask if he could go back to work, Fran and Libby set off down the drive in the Roller-skate.

'What do you think?' asked Libby, after they'd negotiated the turn out of the gates.

'I don't know,' said Fran. 'I want to find out more about Laurence Cooper, and Danny's the only link.'

'You think he's got some connection to Bella's family, then? Or to Bella herself?'

'I wish I knew,' said Fran with a sigh. 'There's a feeling sort of buzzing around the back of my head like tinnitus, but I can't put my finger on it.'

'Danny didn't do it, though, did he?' said Libby.

'As far as I can tell, no,' said Fran, 'but I don't really know anything, do I?'

'Let's go back and sleuth through the documents some more,' suggested Libby. 'We might come up with a Cooper somewhere along the line.'

'Or a Walker,' said Fran.

'Walker?'

'The owner of Anderson Place,' said Fran. 'I've got a feeling about him.'

Chapter Twelve

'Do you know anything about Anderson Place?' asked Libby, as she accepted a glass of red wine from Flo Carpenter in her little house just off the High Street the same afternoon.

'Where our Peter and Harry are gettin' 'itched?' Flo sat down with a thump and lit a cigarette. 'Not much. Horspital during the war, like Tyne Hall. Could'a been a school.'

'Do you know who owns it?'

'No,' said Flo. 'Don't think it was ever sold, so in the same family, I expect.'

'You didn't know the family?'

'Me?' Flo let out a screech of laughter. 'Go on with you, gal. How would I know? My Frank weren't gentry any more'n I am. We used ter get a few of 'em in the pub during the war, but we wasn't welcome in the pub. You know about the locals and the hop pickers, doncher?'

'Yes, daggers drawn, weren't they?' said Libby. 'But some of the Anderson Place people came down here?'

'Nurses and doctors and some of the patients. I don't know whether any of the family were there then.'

'Oh, well, it was worth a try,' said Libby. 'How are you and Lenny getting on?'

'Not so bad,' said Flo, leaning back with a smug expression on her face. 'Good job we didn't get together when we was younger, though. We'd'a scratched each other's eyes out.'

'Really?' said Libby.

'Oh, yers. We was never suited in the early days. I told yer before. Now, though, it's different. I tells him what to do, and he does it.'

Libby laughed. 'Where is he now?'

'Off up to Hetty's. Greg's not so good, you know. Oh, course you know. How *is* Ben?'

Libby coloured. 'Fine, thank you.'

'See, I told you he needed a good woman of his own age.'

'Actually, you said a good *solid* woman of his own age,' said Libby.

'There you are, then. I was right, wasn't I?' said Flo.

Libby saw fit to leave this part of the conversation out when she reported to Fran.

'Have you looked it up on the internet?' asked Fran. 'It's bound to have a website, and probably a page about its history.'

'Oh, of course,' said Libby. 'Why didn't I think of that?'

'Because you're not used to having a computer yet. Don't worry about it. Ring me when you've looked it up.'

'Why don't you come over and we can look it up together,' suggested Libby. 'Then, if there's anything else you want to look up, you can.'

'All right,' said Fran, after a pause. 'I suppose it makes sense.'

'You can eat here if you like, as we've got rehearsal this evening,' offered Libby.

'No, it's OK. I've got a casserole in the oven already,' said Fran.

'How organised,' said Libby gloomily. 'All right, just come over for a cuppa.'

'I'll be there in about fifteen minutes,' said Fran, and rang off.

Libby lit the fire in the sitting room and switched on her computer, then put Anderson Place in to the search engine. Sure enough, it did have a website, and yes, it had a history page. She clicked on it and was still immersed when Fran knocked at the door.

'Look at this,' she said, drawing up another chair to the table.

'"Anderson Place,"' she read, '"was re-built in 1904 by Sir Frederick Anderson. He moved in with his wife and family, and the house has remained occupied by descendants of the family up to the present day. During the war, it was turned into a military hospital and the family moved to the gatehouse and one of the lodges on the estate. A great deal of damage was done to the house at this time, and after the war, Sir Frederick's eldest grandson, William, began to try and repair the devastation.'

'"It wasn't until Jonathan Walker, Sir Frederick's great-grandson, had the idea of turning the house into a country hotel in the 1980s that the fortunes of Anderson Place began to turn. A series of open air concerts and festivals in the grounds began to make enough money to finance the venture, as did the hiring of both house and grounds for cinema and television filming."' There followed a list of the prestigious films and television series in which Anderson Place had appeared.

'"The house and grounds are still used as a film location, and concerts are still held in the natural amphitheatre, but it is as an hotel and wedding venue that Anderson Place is known throughout south eastern England."'

'Well, that doesn't tell us much,' said Libby getting up to go and make the tea.

'I suppose William Anderson must have had a daughter as Jonathan's surname is Walker,' said Fran.

'It doesn't actually say how many of his family he moved in with, does it?' said Libby from the kitchen.

'It says wife and family. Do you suppose Ivy was the wife?'

'Must have been,' said Libby. 'It was Sir Frederick and Ivy that Dorinda says she went to see in that letter. At the Place, I suppose.'

'It doesn't feel right.' Fran shook her head. 'Ivy doesn't feel right.'

'Well, it doesn't seem to have a link to Laurence, anyway. He just worked there.'

'He could still be a relative. Anderson was the old man's name and Walker is the great-grandson's name. There could be a Cooper in there, as well.'

'You're convinced, are you?' Libby came in with two mugs. 'That Laurence is an Anderson? And so is Bella? I don't get that at all, or why you should think so.'

'Neither do I,' said Fran. 'I'm just sure there's a link.'

'Well, Bella fell over Laurence's body, that's a fairly substantial link,' said Libby.

'Do you think that's all it is?' asked Fran, going to the armchair by the fire. 'And I'm connecting things just to prove something?'

'Not consciously,' said Libby, settling on the creaky sofa,

'and after all, we did find a mention of Sir Frederick and Ivy in Maria's stuff, and he had Anderson Place re-built, so there is a sort of connection.'

'Yes, but only because Laurence worked there. That's probably all there is.'

'What about Danny?'

'What about him?'

'He wants to find out who killed Laurence.'

'But I don't think Bella had anything to do with it. I can't quite see why I'm bashing my head against a brick wall, can you?'

Libby regarded her thoughtfully. 'No, but then, I never can. It's your little synapses going hell for leather that make these connections, isn't it? There must be some reason you're trying to find things out. Why don't we go and sleuth among the papers again, like I said?'

'I suppose it wouldn't hurt.' Fran gave a tired smile. 'For historical interest, if nothing else.'

'Better phone Bella and let her know, then,' said Libby. 'Shall we go tomorrow?'

'Haven't you got anything else to do?' laughed Fran. 'Christmas? Panto? Finding an outfit for the wedding?'

'Oh, I've done most of the shopping and I'm getting a supermarket delivery a few days before Christmas. Nothing I can do about the panto now, and I've ordered an outfit for the wedding from an online shop.' Libby looked smug.

'Really? That's adventurous of you.'

'Not really. A shop I used to know in the north east, near Newcastle, have now got a website. Smashing clothes, they all fit me and they're my style. You know, like you were saying the other day. A bit sort of ethnic-ey. I'll give you the name, but they aren't quite tailored enough for you.' Libby looked her friend up and down.

'Oh.' Fran frowned. 'Am I really boring?'

'Of course not,' said Libby. 'And Guy doesn't think so, does he?'

'I don't know,' said Fran. 'I suppose not.'

'Well, you're not as conservative as you were when you first came down,' said Libby. 'You wear jeans and stuff now. You used to be all navy blue and court shoes.'

'And what's wrong with that?'

Libby frowned. 'Just different, I suppose. Not very – er –'

'Not very you,' finished Fran, with a smile. 'Now I'm a bit more you.'

'Yes, well.' Libby looked embarrassed. 'Getting back to Bella and Laurence.'

'I'll do a little more research on Maria's papers for Bella and if anything occurs to me about Laurence, all well and good,' said Fran, 'but I don't see that there's anything else I should be doing.'

'Not even for Danny? You wanted to see him.'

'Because Harry asked me to. Not my idea. If Danny comes up with anything, I'll see what happens.'

Libby looked at her from under her eyebrows. 'Hmm,' she said.

'Right, I'm off, then. Not much point in me coming round, was there? You could have read all that to me over the phone.' Fran stood up and reached for her coat.

'I thought you might want to research further and I don't know how,' said Libby. 'You could have said no.'

Fran stopped with one arm in a sleeve. 'Are we having a row?' she said.

Libby stuck her chin up. 'Yes,' she said.

Fran continues putting on her coat. 'I don't expect it will be the last,' she said with a sigh. 'See you at rehearsal.'

Libby glowered at her and went to open the front door.

'Cheer up, Lib. You'll still be in on anything I do find out.' Fran gave her a kiss on the cheek and set off down Allhallow's Lane in the dark.

And what about what *I* find out? thought Libby, as she shut the door. She went and collected the tea mugs and stood staring at the computer screen, which was now dark. Putting the mugs down, she pressed a key and the history of Anderson Place reappeared. Where could she go from there?

She typed William Anderson into the search engine, but nothing relevant appeared. Jonathan Walker, however, produced a few items, but they all related to Anderson Place or hotels, and occasionally to the use of the Place in a film or television series. Laurence Cooper produced nothing. Following some obscure train of thought, she typed in Andrew Morleigh, and was surprised when he came up as a partner in a company of financial advisors with several branches in London and within the M25 envelope. So not exactly poor, then. Switching off the computer, Libby took the mugs through to the kitchen and rang Ben.

'I just feel so pushed aside,' she said, after explaining what had happened. 'We've been the ones who welcomed Fran down here and found her somewhere to live, and now she's got all this money she doesn't need us any more. And she wouldn't even be here if it wasn't us. And if it wasn't for me, she wouldn't even been buying Coastguard Cottage. She wouldn't even know about it.'

'All right, Lib, all right,' said Ben in a soothing voice. 'I'm sure if she thought you felt like that she'd be horrified. We were all thrilled for her when she came into the money, weren't we? You're not jealous, are you?'

'Of course not,' said Libby, squashing a horrible little flutter in her stomach which acknowledged that this was probably not the truth. 'I just feel sidelined.'

'Because she doesn't feel she should be investigating any more *you* feel sidelined? I don't get that.'

Libby frowned. 'I can't explain it. I feel she's in charge, and – well, I suppose I don't like it.'

Ben chuckled. 'You're in charge at the theatre, aren't you? You can give her hell tonight and make yourself feel better.'

Libby laughed reluctantly. 'As if I would,' she said. 'I'm being pathetic, aren't I?'

'I didn't say that,' said Ben. 'Go on. I'll see you later. And forget about Bella and Laurence and Danny. Concentrate on *Jack and the Beanstalk* and the wicked Baron.'

'All right, wicked Baron,' said Libby. 'I can't wait.'

Chapter Thirteen

THE DANCERS WERE DEMONSTRATING that Happy Days Were Here Again all over the stage in unitards and leg warmers that Libby thought had gone out with Irene Cara. The rehearsal pianist, who was also the musical director, was shouting at them, as was the choreographer. The dancers were, apparently, taking notice of neither.

'How did the meeting with Danny go?'

Libby swung round to face Peter.

'Eh?'

'Harry told me.' He grinned and chucked her under the chin. 'Can't keep anything from me, the silly boy. Are you going to help?'

'That's debatable,' said Libby, throwing her cape onto the back of one of the seats.

'Surely you're not losing interest?' Peter unwound his scarf and bent a sardonic gaze on her.

'No, of course not.' Libby was indignant. 'But I think Fran is.'

Peter raised his eyebrows. 'Dear, dear. Fed up with us, is she?'

'What makes you say that?' asked Libby, although remembering Peter's attitude when Fran first came among them, she thought she knew.

'Oh, I don't know.' Peter shrugged. 'But she won't be in Steeple Martin for much longer, will she?'

'She'll only be in Nethergate.' Now, illogically, Libby wanted to stand up for Fran.

'And apart from last summer's little escapade, how often do you go to Nethergate?'

'When I need to see Guy. And Ben's taken me to The Sloop.'

'Once? And how often will Fran need to come here?'

'Whenever she wants to see us – me. And I'll go there.'

'Not the same as living within walking distance, is it?' said Peter, sitting down and propping his long legs on the back of the seats in front. 'Can't pop out for a drink together.'

Libby sent him a fulminating look and stomped off to the stage.

'Can we start, please?' she said to the choreographer, who gave her a look of weary gratitude.

'Beginners, then, please,' yelled Libby. 'Fairy Queen? Are you there?'

The Fairy Queen appeared stage right in confusion and a flurry of draperies, and peered short-sightedly into the auditorium. Libby wished for the umpteenth time she'd stuck to her guns with Peter and insisted on playing the part herself.

'OK,' she said. 'Off you go. Chorus positions, please, and remember, don't move.'

'But we haven't got the gauze yet, Libby,' said one plaintive voice. 'It doesn't matter.'

'If you get into the habit of not moving now it won't come so hard when the gauze is in place with an audience out front,' said Libby patiently. 'Tabs, please.'

The curtains were closed between the Fairy Queen and the chorus, and opened slowly as the opening monologue was delivered, somewhat hesitantly. The chorus, discovered outside Dame Trot's house, stood in sulky positions and scratched noses, heads and bottoms. Mostly their own. Libby sighed.

The rehearsal wound its weary way to the end of the first scene and Libby went to the front to give notes. She knew there wasn't a lot of point at this stage, but there were one or two habits she had to correct. None of these, she was forced to admit, belonged to Fran.

Finally, at just after ten o'clock, she called a halt.

'Pub?' said Fran, as Libby climbed onto the stage to talk to the crew.

Tempted to say "Don't we always?" Libby swallowed and smiled. 'See you there,' she said.

'Unusually diplomatic,' murmured Peter in her ear.

'Oh, shut up,' said Libby, and went over to the construction team who were sucking their collective teeth over the state of the beanstalk.

Leaving them soothed, and with the promise that they would lock up when they left, Libby joined Ben at the auditorium doors.

'Pub?' he said.

'I said I'd see Fran there,' said Libby.

'Ah. Forgiven her, have you?' Ben held open the glass doors and then went out into the winter air.

'Pete thinks the same as me,' said Libby.

'He was always prejudiced against her, you know that,' said Ben. 'I think you should both give her a chance. Her life has changed dramatically since she moved down here, and I expect it's quite hard for her to come to terms with that, without having someone else's problems to deal with, too.'

Libby tucked her arm through his as they reached the bottom of the theatre drive. 'Especially as looking in to a family whose existence was never known must bring it all back, being so similar to her own experience.'

'That's my girl,' said Ben, and kissed her cheek. 'Let her find her feet.'

'Pete says she won't bother to keep up with us once she's moved to Nethergate,' said Libby, as they reached the pub.

'Rubbish,' said Ben, pushing the door open. 'Now, go on, make your peace.'

Fran behaved as if nothing had happened, so Libby was able to do the same, and when Fran asked if she would like to go to March Cottage the following morning, agreed quickly.

'I thought we'd give it one more shot and look for references to Anderson Place,' said Fran, 'which was what you wanted to do, wasn't it?'

'Well, yes, but not if you don't think it's worth it,' said Libby, generously.

'I think it will be,' said Fran, with a smile, 'but I'm not sure just how.'

'There,' said Ben, as he and Libby walked back to Allhallow's Lane. 'All patched up.'

'Well, it wasn't really a row,' said Libby.

'It wasn't at all a row on Fran's part,' said Ben. 'It was you feeling, as you said, sidelined.'

Libby nodded. 'I still do, a bit, but I know it's not really Fran's fault. I shall be determinedly bright and cheery in the morning.'

'Not too much or she'll wonder what's wrong with you,' said Ben, giving her a squeeze and opening the front door of Number 17. 'In you go, and get Sidney out of the way before he tries to trip me up again.'

Libby walked round to The Pink Geranium in the morning and found Fran washing the windows of the Roller-skate.

'You've only had it five minutes,' said Libby, watching admiringly.

'It's winter,' said Fran. 'The windows were filthy.'

Libby thought fleetingly of Romeo's besmirched windows. 'As long as we can see our way to Heronsbourne,' she said.

'Beautifully,' said Fran with a grin. 'Hop in.'

'Will you still come and see us when you've moved to Nethergate?' asked Libby as they bowled along the road past Steeple Mount.

Fran gave her a quick, surprised look. 'Of course I will. Why on earth wouldn't I?'

'It won't be like living round the corner.'

'We've only lived round the corner from each other for the last few months.'

'We've only *known* each other for the last few months.' Libby turned and smiled at her friend. 'But it's made such a difference to me.'

'It's made more than a difference to me, you know that,' said Fran, 'and I'd hope we would never lose that friendship. Anyway, you can have your Steeple Martin life back, now, and I'll take over Nethergate. If we want a drink when we see each other, we've both got spare rooms.'

'That's true.' Libby gave sigh of relief. 'I feel better now.'

'Good.' Fran slid a sideways look at her. 'Now we can concentrate on Laurence and Danny.'

'And Bella?'

'Well, her, too, but it's not actually anything to do with her, is it?'

'She's the catalyst. None of this would have happened

126

without her.'

'Laurence would still have been killed, and Harry would still have got in touch with us.' Fran turned into Pedlar's Row and drew up outside March Cottage.

'That's true, too,' said Libby, much struck. 'But we wouldn't have known about old Sir Fred, would we?'

'By now we would,' said Fran, getting out of the car. 'We looked it up yesterday, didn't we?'

'Oh, yes. I'm getting muddled.'

'Come on, then,' said Fran, 'let's go and get the keys from the pub.'

George was pleased to see them and asked after Bella.

'Nice lady,' he said. 'Reckon she'll move down here permanent, like?'

'No idea,' said Libby, hoisting herself onto a bar stool and settling down for a chat. 'She's got children at school in London–'

'Has she?' George looked surprised.

'Doing A and O levels,' nodded Libby. 'She won't want to leave them.'

'What about her husband, then?' said George.

'Well –' said Libby.

'Libby, are you coming?' said Fran. 'We don't want to be all day.'

'OK, Fran, you go ahead. I'll follow,' said Libby.

Fran shook her head and left with the keys.

'Right,' continued Libby, resting her elbows on the bar. 'Her husband. We don't think they get on. I don't think he wants her to move down here.'

'Oh, that's a shame,' said George, propping a foot up on a shelf behind the counter. 'She'd fit in here real well. Nice quiet bunch the folks here are. And I wouldn't want to see March Cottage go to any of them weekenders.'

'I think that's what it will be, for the time being at least. I don't think Bella will sell it, but she'll only be able to get down now and then.'

'That's all right, then. We can keep an eye on it for her. She's not like a proper weekender, is she?' George shook his head. 'And she's got kids. Somehow I didn't think of her with youngsters.'

'No, me neither. She looks –' Libby stopped.

'Yeah.' George grinned. 'I know what you mean. I thought she might be a young grannie, though.'

'Oh, dear,' said Libby. 'Aren't we awful? I'd better go.' She slid off her stool. 'See you later, George.'

Fran was already in the outbuilding with the computer and the heater switched on.

'Everything isn't catalogued here, you know,' she said as Libby came in. 'There's loads more stuff in the box files than there is on the computer. We'd better go through it.'

'Why is that, do you think?' said Libby, unwinding her scarf and shrugging off her cape.

'It's mainly from the early days. Maria wasn't born then, so I suppose she didn't bother. Afterwards there's a lot of detail about the costumes and the different shows. And both of them were members of something called the Concert Artistes' Association.'

'Really?' Libby leant over Fran's shoulder and peered at the screen. 'I know a bit about them. They've got a building in Bedford Street in London.'

'Oh, yes, I vaguely remember. I think I went there once for a meeting with someone about cruise ships.'

'What were you going to do? I didn't think you sang,' said Libby, looking at Fran in surprise.

'Thanks,' said Fran. 'What is it I do in the panto? Croak?'

'That's not proper singing,' said Libby. 'If you're a production singer on a cruise ship you have to be a proper singer.'

'I wasn't going to be a production singer,' said Fran. 'Somebody wanted to put on small cast plays rather than the musical shows they do. It didn't work out.'

'Oh, pity,' said Libby. 'Still, you might have been sea sick.'

Fran looked at Libby and shook her head. 'What an outlook you've got,' she said.

'Always look on the bright side,' said Libby, and began humming.

'Come on then, get those box files out,' said Fran, pushing back her chair.

There were several box files holding material before 1914, as Fran had said.

'What I can't understand,' said Libby as she blew dust off one of them and sneezed, 'is why Bella only found those bits and pieces she showed you the other night.'

'There's only one folder on the computer labelled "up to 1920s",' said Fran, 'and that box file's over here. The others aren't labelled. I think Maria just stuffed everything else she found in there in any old order.'

'Oh, good,' groaned Libby. 'That means we've got to go through the lot?'

'What I think,' said Fran, sitting on the floor surrounded by box files, 'is that Maria filtered out those few leaflets for the Silver Serenaders, the notebook and the letter referring to Sir Fred because they were things she knew about. She just left the rest alone.'

'Why didn't she throw them all out?' Libby looked at the files in disgust.

'Whether it meant anything to her or not, it all belonged to her parents,' said Fran, 'and she was obviously a hoarder.'

'Only in this,' said Libby. 'Those bedrooms in the cottage are as clean as a whistle.'

'Her history meant a lot to her,' said Fran, opening a file. 'Come on, let's get on with it.'

It soon became apparent why Maria had only catalogued the few items they had already seen. Most of the rest were of little interest to anyone but a social historian. Receipts for material, for sewing, for boots and mending, letters of engagement and a few postcards from artistes enquiring about the next season, or just enquiring after Dorinda and Peter's health. The only thing Fran found remotely interesting was the correspondence between Dorinda and the council, first negotiating for her "pitch", and subsequently for the land on which she built the Alexandria. To her disappointment, there were no original plans or correspondence with builders, but the appearance of a programme for the Alexandria dated 1912 indicated that it was in existence by then.

'Well,' said Libby eventually, brushing dust and cobwebs off her face, 'there's nothing here.'

'What about the newspapers?' asked Fran, indicating a file they had put aside.

'Oh, no,' said Libby, 'we can't go through all of those.'

'Not now, maybe, but perhaps we could take them home and go through them?'

'We?' Libby glowered. 'You can. I'm not. I've got other things to do at home.'

'You're the one who wanted to become an investigator.'

Libby glowered some more. 'Oh, all right,' she said. 'But Bella might not want to let us take them away.'

'I'll ring her now,' said Fran, scrambling to her feet.

'Right,' said Libby, following her example. She began to put the files back on the shelves and stopped when she heard Fran speak.

'Well?' she said, when Fran switched off.

'She says that's fine, she knows we'll look after them, and had we found out anything more. You heard me tell her all about Laurence.'

'And?'

'She didn't know anything about him, but we didn't expect her to, did we?'

'When's she next coming down?'

'She wasn't sure. She sounded very dithery.'

'That's Orrible Andrew getting to her,' said Libby. 'And now it's nearly Christmas she won't be able to get down here at all, bet you.'

Fran nodded and sighed. 'Oh, well, let's take this lot out to the car.'

After getting rid of Balzac, who had followed them in and gone to sleep by the heater, they turned off the computer, lights and heater and locked up.

George offered them a drink when they took the keys back, but Fran said sensibly she was driving and they ought to get back home. Libby pulled a face and, waving to George, followed Fran back to the car.

'Sorry if you wanted to stay,' said Fran, as she drove back towards Steeple Martin, 'but I want to get on with those papers. I've got a feeling we might find something in them.'

'Something about the building works? Would they print

planning applications like they do today?'

'I don't know, but I didn't mean that. There must be a reason for Dorinda to have kept all those papers.'

'They might fall to pieces,' said Libby. 'They should be preserved in a museum.'

'I expect they are, somewhere,' said Fran. 'Newspaper archives have copies of everything, don't they? Local and national papers.'

'Oh, yes,' said Libby, looking wise.

'Anyway, we'll go through them and see if anything turns up,' said Fran.

'What exactly are we looking for?'

'Anything relevant. Anything about Dorinda, or Peter, or Sir Frederick or – what were they called? The family?'

'Oh, heavens,' said Libby. 'I can't remember.'

They both thought for a moment, until Fran turned into Allhallow's Lane and pulled up outside Number 17.

'Here, you take half of them,' she said leaning over and retrieving the file from the back seat.

'Thanks,' said Libby, looking with disfavour on the yellowing bundle she was given.

'They weren't Andersons, were they?' said Fran.

'Who? The family? No. Bella would have noticed that.'

'Of course she would. I wonder what the connection is.' Fran stared out through the windscreen as if she might find the answer in the Manor woods before her.

'People they met and made friends with?' suggested Libby. 'They were here from 1904, and Peter was probably here with the other troupe before then. They must have known a lot of people.'

'But not titled people. They wouldn't have mixed with theatricals.'

'What about stage door johnnies?' Libby turned excitedly to her friend. 'I bet that's it! Sir Fred and Ivy – well that would be it, wouldn't it? A friend of Dorinda's perhaps, someone who'd been in The Serenaders or The Alexandrians, maybe went on into the chorus at one of the London theatres – and Sir Fred married her! It was always happening.'

Fran looked interested. 'It certainly could be. So nothing to do with Dorinda and the family at all?'

'Oh.' Libby's face fell. 'Yes, of course. Oh, bugger.'

'But you're right, Lib,' said Fran, 'it is by far the most likely and obvious explanation. I don't know why we didn't think of it before.'

'Because we were too busy looking for connections,' said Libby. 'That'll teach us.'

'Go and find me some more connections to shoot down.' Fran grinned. 'And I'll see you tonight.'

Chapter Fourteen

LIBBY WAS TRYING TO keep awake over the brittle copies of the newspapers when her phone rang.

'Lib?'

'Harry. What's up?'

'Danny just called. I don't know how important this is to you, or Fran, or – well, the fact is, the police have just been back on to Danny.'

'Go on.'

'Dorothy's dead.'

'Huh? Dorothy?'

'The sister.'

'Oh! Dorothy. Good God.' Libby sat down suddenly on the sofa.

'As far as Danny can make out, the police went back to talk to her and found her dead in her house.'

'Murdered?'

'It looks like it.'

'Have they arrested Danny?'

'No, but she lives a long way away, and I suppose they've been keeping tabs on him, so he couldn't have got there without them knowing.'

'Where does she live?'

'I don't know, do I?' said Harry testily.

'Sorry.' Libby thought for a moment. 'Have you told Fran?'

'No. You can tell her. Much as I like her, I don't always find her sympathetic. She makes me feel as though she can see right through me.'

'Really?' Surprised at this further evidence of her friends' attitudes towards Fran, Libby felt obliged to defend her. 'She can't, you know. I wish she could sometimes, but she's as full of insecurities as we all are. More, actually.' She thought of Guy.

'I know,' said Harry, sounding uncomfortable, 'and I really like her, otherwise I wouldn't be happy to have her upstairs, would I? And if she could find anything out for Danny it'd be great.'

'Right,' said Libby. 'I'll tell her, and see what she says. Although I don't see how it helps.'

Harry sighed. 'Neither do I. Bugger, isn't it?'

After Harry had rung off, Libby punched in Fran's number.

'We have a development,' she announced.

'In the papers?'

'No,' said Libby, and explained.

'Hello?' she said, after a prolonged period of silence. 'Fran?'

'Do we know who their parents were?' Fran said finally.

'What?'

'Laurence and Dorothy. Who were their parents?'

'How on earth am I supposed to know?' demanded Libby. 'Or Danny, come to that.'

'Can we ask him? And how was she murdered? And where did she live?'

'Oh, good lord, Fran! How on earth can we find all that out? Danny won't know – well, I suppose he might know about the parents, but not about anything else. You're the best person to find out, with your connection to Inspector Connell.'

'I can't ask him.'

'Of course you can!' said Libby in exasperation. 'The last thing he said to you in my hearing was, "You won't forget to let me know, will you? Anything at all." Now, from your silence just now, I guess you must have had a bit of a moment when I told you about Dorothy. So, tell him.'

Fran was quiet again. Eventually, Libby heard her sigh. 'I suppose so. I feel the parents are important. Perhaps Laurence's mother was an Anderson?'

'That would have come out by now, Fran. A Walker, perhaps? No, that would have come out, too.'

'You're right. I'll call the Inspector. I'll let you know what he says.'

After Fran had rung off, Libby sat for a long time gazing into the fire, until Sidney reminded her of the time. She cast a look of dislike at the papers still spread out over the table in the window next to the computer and went to make a cup of tea and put something in the oven. Sidney was given his afternoon tea after which he took an evening constitutional round the garden. Libby watched his ghost-like shape through the conservatory windows.

Something was wrong. Fran was not herself, although Libby wasn't quite sure what Fran's real self was, their association having been forged during a series of quite abnormal events. Ben was right, Fran's life had changed completely since they'd met, far more than Libby's had, and maybe it was difficult for her to come to terms with it. Perhaps it was becoming involved with a murder investigation as an outsider. It did make one feel rather like a voyeur, Libby decided, which wasn't a pleasant feeling. Was that how Fran felt?

In the little flat over The Pink Geranium, Fran was feeling exactly like that. And more. She was experiencing a horrid, stomach churning certainty that somehow Bella was concerned in the murder. No, that wasn't quite right, she thought, pacing up and down the small living room. Not concerned, exactly, but affected by it.

Which, of course, was ridiculous. Of course she was affected by it – Bella had found the body, in premises she now owned. But Fran felt sure there was more to it than that. When Libby had told her about Laurence Cooper's sister's death, she had experienced the same black suffocation that had overcome her when she heard about her own aunt's death, and that of the second murder victim in that case, not to mention when she had gone to see the Alexandria, which indicated that this, too, was murder. And therefore, a legitimate reason to ring Inspector Connell.

And that was the other problem. Fran was aware of a guilty thrill of excitement at having an excuse to ring Inspector Connell. The thought of someone's murder being an excuse to speak to someone to whom you were, however unwillingly, attracted, made her feel physically sick. Not only that, Guy and she were, in most people's eyes – certainly his – an "item". This was not only slightly perverted, but unfaithful, if you had always been a one-man woman as Fran had. Not that she and Guy had even slept together, let alone given each other any sort of commitment, as Fran was as wary of middle-aged romantic

135

entanglements as Libby had been only a few months ago. In fact, it still astonished her that she should be in this position.

She knew, too, that her new friends, particularly Libby, Peter and the lovely Harry were finding her difficult. Never good at giving much of herself, except when she was playing a part in her former life as a professional actor, she didn't know what to do about this. Libby would have sat down and poured her heart out, not that anyone had much difficulty in seeing what was in Libby's heart, as it was usually on her sleeve.

Her phone rang. Fran fished it out of her handbag.

'Mrs Castle? Connell here.'

Fran's heart went down in a lift. Why didn't she check who was calling before answering? The simple answer was if she hadn't got her glasses on she wouldn't be able to see the screen.

'Hello, Inspector,' she said.

'I probably shouldn't be telling you this, but in case it – er – strikes any chords with you, our victim's sister has been found murdered.'

'How?' asked Fran, just managing to bite back the words "I know".

'How?' Connell sounded surprised. 'Hit on the head, as far as we know.'

'Where?'

'At her home. Look, Mrs Castle, do you know something about this?'

Fran paused, collecting her thoughts. 'I was going to call you,' she said finally. 'Apparently, my landlord knew the first victim.'

'You should have told me,' said Connell accusingly.

'Not well, only as a business acquaintance,' said Fran, crossing her fingers. 'But he knows Danny rather better.'

'Danny?'

'I don't know his surname,' said Fran.

'Danny Lee,' growled Connell.

'Ah,' said Fran.

'So what else do you know?' Connell's tone was now glacial.

'Danny told Harry – that's my landlord – that Dorothy had been found dead. He didn't know any more than that. Danny hasn't anyone else to talk to, that's why he told Harry, as a

136

fellow restaurateur.'

'Chef at The Pink Geranium, isn't he?'

'*Owner* of The Pink Geranium,' corrected Fran.

'So, why were you going to call me, Mrs Castle?'

'Because I thought Dorothy had been murdered, Inspector.'

'Thought, or felt?'

'Felt.'

'But we know that anyway. Nothing else?'

'No.' Fran hesitated. 'I can't find anything linking Laurence Cooper to Mrs Morleigh or her family, either, I'm afraid, or to Anderson Place.'

'He worked there,' said Connell sharply, 'of course he's connected to the place.'

'Other than that,' said Fran, wondering if she'd said too much.

'You think there's some other connection?'

'No – I just said – I can't *find* a connection.'

'But you think there is one?'

Now Fran knew she'd said too much. 'I don't know,' she said honestly. 'I'm not a magician, Inspector. I can only tell you what I feel, or see.'

'Right.' He was silent for so long Fran wondered if she'd been cut off. 'Is there anything else you'd like to know, Mrs Castle? Anything you think might help you feel, or see, something?'

Fran sat down in surprise. 'Oh. Well, what was Dorothy's surname? Was she a Cooper?'

'No, she was a widow. Name of Buller.'

'Where did she live?'

'Yorkshire. Near Richmond.'

'And where did the Coopers live as children?'

'I've no idea!' said Connell. 'Is it relevant?'

'I don't know, but I think it might be. Had anything been taken from her house?'

'Yes, it had been ransacked. We don't have any idea what has been taken. The only one who could have told us was her brother. She had no children.'

'Neither did he. How sad,' said Fran.

'According to her neighbours – and to Danny Lee, as a

matter of fact – she was a right old –' Connell paused, 'well, not a particularly pleasant person, shall we say.'

'Yes.' Fran knew that. Somehow.

'So, anything else?'

'Not without something more concrete,' said Fran.

'Concrete? What do you mean?'

'Oh, I like to see places and people,' said Fran vaguely.

Inspector Connell was silent again. Then, 'Would it help if you saw Laurence's flat and Dorothy's house?'

Fran was so taken aback she couldn't say a word.

'Mrs Castle?'

'Well – yes,' she said finally.

'If I could arrange it, when would you be free?'

'I'm rehearsing a pantomime,' she said, 'so evenings are a bit difficult.'

'Richmond's a long way away,' he said.

'Yes, that's how you know Danny had nothing to do with Dorothy.'

'Quite. When don't you rehearse?'

'Friday,' said Fran.

'We could go to Richmond on Friday, then.'

'We?'

'I could hardly allow you to go on your own.' Connell was at his most forbidding, reminding Fran of when she first met him.

'No,' she said, feeling breathless.

'I'll get back to you as soon as I can,' he said briskly, 'oh, and Mrs Castle – don't go telling the world and its wife about this, will you?'

'No,' she said, crossing her fingers again. Just Libby and Harry.

It was while she was eating baked beans on toast on her lap and watching the news that Connell called back.

'I can take you to see Cooper's flat tomorrow,' he said, 'and we've an appointment set up with Richmond CID on Friday at two.'

'Oh.' Fran felt her heart go up a gear. 'Two in the afternoon?'

He sighed. 'Yes, Mrs Castle. I'll pick you up tomorrow morning at nine-thirty, if that's all right, and we can make arrangements about Friday.'

'Fine.' Fran cleared her throat. 'I'll see you then.'

She took her tray into the kitchen and stood staring into the sink. Now she really did feel sick. She was excited about two days with Inspector Connell, all because two people had met their deaths by violence. How low could you go?

Chapter Fifteen

LIBBY WAS BESIDE HERSELF with excitement at the news.

'Just think,' she said, 'All tomorrow morning and all day Friday with him!'

'That isn't the point,' said Fran severely. 'The point is, I might be able to find something out about Laurence's life.'

'Of course,' said Libby, 'but you can't deny you're just a little bit excited about Connell.'

'I know,' said Fran. 'Isn't it awful?'

Libby looked concerned. 'I knew that's how you were feeling,' she said. 'I feel a bit like it myself. Ghoulish. Almost like slowing down on a motorway to look at an accident.'

Fran shuddered. 'I can't do that. I have to look the other way.'

'Difficult when you're driving.'

'It's all bloody difficult,' said Fran. 'Come on, madam director, what are we doing tonight?'

The rehearsal of act two went slightly better than the previous night's act one, and Libby called a halt just before ten o'clock.

'I'll give the pub a miss tonight if you don't mind, Lib,' said Fran. 'I've got a heavy two days in front of me.'

'Don't forget you don't need to be at rehearsal tomorrow,' Libby reminded her. 'It's chorus and dancers only.'

'Oh, bother,' said Fran. 'I had forgotten. Connell and I could have done both visits in one day.'

'What, Laurence's flat in the morning and straight on up to Richmond? That's an even longer day.'

'Yes, but then again, it only *wastes* one day.'

'And you wouldn't have to feel guilty for more than one day,' said Libby with a smile.

Fran laughed. 'I'll see if he can arrange it, but I doubt it. I'll let you know how things turn out.'

'So what are you going to do tomorrow?' asked Ben, when Libby told him about the latest developments as they walked back to Allhallow's Lane.

'Carry on going through those old papers, I suppose,' said Libby. 'I don't know what I'm expected to find, though.'

'Why don't you come up to the Manor and give me a hand?' said Ben. 'I'm turning the estate office into an office for me, and Mum wants to start putting up the decorations. You know they have the party this weekend.'

'I know,' said Libby, 'what I don't know is who comes? I mean, it used to be for all the farm workers and tenants, didn't it? Who is it now?'

'All the retired farm workers, of course! And their families. Flo, and some of the other hop pickers who stayed down here.'

'So they'll all eventually die out, then?'

'Yes, but so will Mum and Dad,' said Ben. 'I don't think I shall be expected to carry on the tradition.'

'Will Millie go this year?'

'I shouldn't think so. Susan's going, which is very brave of her.'

'Do Peter and James go?'

'Of course. And Harry. Have you never been?'

'This is only my second Christmas in the village,' said Libby, 'and I didn't really know your family last year.'

'Well, you do this year,' said Ben, 'intimately. So this year you'll be there, won't you?'

'Love to,' said Libby, 'and yes, I'll come up and help your Mum with the decorations. I can't see that I'm going to find anything in those papers.'

'If Fran thinks you will, I expect you will,' said Ben, 'but you need a break from all this detection.'

'If you're being sarcastic,' said Libby, 'let me tell you it's bloody hard work, investigating. And a bit emotional, too.'

'I know. But forget it for now and come and be emotional with me.' Ben took the door keys from her hand and unlocked the door of number 17.

The following morning, Libby felt a surge of Christmas expectation as she walked up the drive leading to both The

Manor and the Oast House Theatre. Ben's mother Hetty had already draped the two small fir trees outside the front door with lights and a large holly bough had been positioned across the lintel. A banner across the front of the theatre announced *Jack and the Beanstalk*, and two small silver trees stood either side of the glass doors to the foyer. It all felt extremely seasonal.

'All we want is snow,' Libby muttered to herself as she knocked on the front door of the Manor.

Hetty was pleased to see her in a forthright and down-to-earth manner. She had Libby up a ladder hanging ornaments on the huge tree in the hall before Libby could protest that she really wasn't terribly keen on heights.

'Mum,' said Ben, coming into the hall, 'you should have asked me to go up that ladder.'

'You weren't here,' said Hetty, and handed him a box of ornaments. 'You go up, then. Libby can come and help me in the library.'

Libby climbed thankfully down and followed Hetty into the library, where various pieces of greenery, tinsel and crepe paper lay over all available surfaces. Hetty produced treacly coffee in large mugs and showed Libby what she wanted done.

'Did you know anything about Anderson Place in the past, Hetty?' asked Libby as they worked.

'Useter see some of them in the village in the war,' said Hetty.

'What, the patients, or the staff?'

'Staff, mainly. They wasn't bad to 'em, you know, the family.'

'Oh, you mean the owners' staff, not the hospital staff.'

'Both. Some o' the walkin' wounded come down.' Hetty sniffed. 'And the nurses and such. They wasn't always supposed to, but they did.'

'Did you know any of them?' asked Libby, sticking a piece of fir tree behind a portrait of a disgruntled-looking Wilde ancestor.

'One girl, Edith, she'd been there from the beginnin' of the war. Worked for Mrs Nemone as a scullery maid. 'Ad 'er own room, she did, at first, before the army took over the Place. Not often that happened.'

'What, a room of her own?'

'Yes. They all 'ad to share in them days. Well, so did Edith when they moved to the Lodge.'

'So, who was Mrs Nemone? A relation of Sir Frederick?'

'Not sure. She was old in the war, but kind to Edie. There was someone else livin' in the Dower House, another relative, I s'pose. They was good to the staff they kept. Course, most of 'em went off to the war, but they kept one of the gardeners – Potter, I think 'is name was – and a gamekeeper, although all the ground was dug up for veggies. Not much call for pheasants. They useter give the girls time off for the pictures in Canterbury if there was one on, and the dance in the 'all 'ere, like. Not that we went o' course.'

This was a long speech for Hetty, and Libby was impressed, particularly as Hetty had stopped making paper chains and was staring into the fireplace.

'Did Edith stay round here after the war?'

'Went off to join the RAF just after we left in 1943. Never saw 'er again.' Hetty looked down and resumed cutting strips of crepe paper.

'Did you ever hear anybody talk about a Nemone family when you were a boy?' Libby asked Ben over lunch in the Manor kitchen.

'Nemone? Spelt how?' said Ben.

'I don't know,' said Libby. 'Your mum pronounced it "Nemonney".'

'No,' said Ben slowly, 'but I do remember a very old lady with a strange Christian name sounding a bit like that.'

'Where did she live?' asked Libby eagerly.

'I've no idea,' said Ben. 'She used to come and see my grandmother occasionally, I think. I hardly remember, but I know she seemed very old.'

'Nemone.' Libby brooded over the name. 'Do you know, I think it *is* an old-fashioned girl's Christian name. So old Mrs Nemone was probably Mrs Nemone Something. Living in the Lodge at the Place. With another relative whose name we don't know in the Dower House.' Libby shook her head. 'No nearer then.'

'Why so interested in the Place anyway?' asked Ben.

143

'Laurence didn't die there, he only worked there.'

'Because in the letters we found at Bella's there is mention of visiting Sir Frederick and Ivy at Anderson Place. Fran is sure there's a connection.'

'They could have been anyone,' said Ben. 'Someone the old girl knew from London, or anything.'

'I know. I suggested Ivy was a performer who married a title. They were always doing that, weren't they?'

'Good point,' Ben nodded. 'P.G. Wodehouse had loads of them, didn't he?'

'And aunts,' said Libby, 'but yes, and when he started writing it was that sort of era. I bet I'm right.'

'Mum,' said Ben, as Hetty came into the room, 'do you remember Mrs Nemone coming to visit grandmother when I was little?'

Hetty shook her head. 'I don't remember any of 'em,' she said. 'I was always outside workin', wasn't I?' She collected a tin of polish and a duster and left the room again.

'She's still bitter about having to come down here and take over from my grandparents, you know,' said Ben, 'and knowing the full story now, I don't blame her.'

'Neither do I,' agreed Libby. 'Brave woman, your mother.'

Ben looked at her sideways. 'She never liked my ex-wife, you know.'

Libby felt the blush creeping up her neck. 'Oh,' she said.

They sat in silence until Libby jumped up and said. 'I think I should go and see if she needs any more help,' and disappeared summarily from the room.

Hetty was polishing bookshelves in the library before training paper chains and greenery along them. Libby started handing up chains and drawing pins.

'Nemone wasn't her family name,' said Hetty suddenly. 'Wasn't Anderson, either, although that other one, up at the Dower House, she was an Anderson.'

'Did they move back into the Place after the army left?' asked Libby.

'Think so, although old Nemone might not have. Too old, see. There were youngsters, too. Well, they weren't youngsters exactly, but Nemone's children, I think. I can't rightly remember. We wasn't in the same circles, even if old mother Wilde was.'

'Might Greg remember?' asked Libby hesitantly.

'Might, I s'pose. You're not to go worryin' 'im unless I'm there, though.' Hetty looked down at her. 'When you goin' to move in 'ere with our Ben?'

Libby's breath left her body in a whoosh and she had the strangest sensation of having been whopped over the head with a cricket bat.

'Oh, no mind, duck,' said Hetty, going back to her bookshelves. 'Just thought it'd be easier for you.'

Libby reported this remarkable conversation to Ben as he walked home with her later that afternoon.

He laughed. 'You can't put much over on my mother, can you?' he said. 'Do you want to?'

'Want to what?' asked Libby warily. 'Put one over on her?'

'No, stupid. Move in to The Manor.'

Libby took a deep breath. 'Well, if you don't mind, I'd rather not,' she said.

'OK,' said Ben easily, and tucked her hand through his arm.

Later, while she pushed an eclectic mix of vegetables round a wok and Ben was looking through some of the old newspapers, she returned to the subject.

'I'm not being rude, you know,' she said.

'Mmm? Rude? About what?' said Ben, without looking up.

'Moving into The Manor.'

He looked up now. 'I know you're not.'

'It's just that – well, I'd sort of feel it wasn't mine and I couldn't do what I wanted.'

'It's all right, Lib,' he said, standing up and coming into the kitchen. 'I understand perfectly. And after all, we do have quite a nice arrangement as we are, don't we?'

'As long as you don't mind having to go home in the mornings,' said Libby.

'But I don't have to, do I? I can hang around, if I want to.' He laughed at her face. 'It's all right, Lib, I wouldn't. But that's exactly what I mean. We've both got our own space this way. We're one of those LAT relationships.'

'What? LAT?'

'Living apart together,' explained Ben. 'It's now a recognised phenomenon. Haven't you heard of it?'

Libby frowned. 'Yes, I think I have. Not the name, but the situation. I remember reading an article in a magazine years ago by a woman who married her husband and lived down the street from him. So it's quite normal, now, is it?'

'Absolutely,' said Ben. 'Keeps the mystery in the relationship, doesn't it?' He turned away to collect cutlery and Libby scowled at his back. 'Especially as you get older and more selfish.'

Libby sighed and piled stir fried vegetables on to rice. 'Hmm,' she said.

Chapter Sixteen

FRAN WAS WATCHING FROM the living room window when she saw a car pull up on the opposite side of the street. Grasping her handbag, she stood poised until she saw Inspector Connell emerge from the rear. Squashing a feeling of disappointment that there would be a third person with them, she ran down the stairs and was shutting the door as he arrived in front of her.

'Prompt, Mrs Castle,' he said.

'Mustn't waste police time,' said Fran, as he took her elbow and piloted her across the street.

'Constable Maiden, Mrs Castle,' he said, as he showed her into the back seat and climbed in beside her.

'Ma'am,' said Constable Maiden keeping his eyes on the road ahead.

'Good morning, constable,' said Fran.

Their journey took them on the Nethergate road, past Steeple Mount and eventually turned on to a newly tarmacked road that Fran recognised.

'This is where Jim Butler lives,' she said, breaking the silence that had lasted almost all the way.

'Who?' Connell turned to look at her.

'Someone who used to own my cottage,' said Fran. 'He lives in that big bungalow down there. He built this estate, I think.'

Connell nodded, but the car swung left to the other end of the road, which Fran now noticed was called Canongate Drive, to where stood three small blocks of flats. The car stopped, and Constable Maiden got out and held the door for Fran.

'Thanks,' she said smiling into a pair of bright blue eyes under a mop of the reddest hair she could ever remember seeing.

'Ma'am,' he said again, but with a broad grin this time.

Inspector Connell was holding open a door to the middle block, an air of impatience surrounding him like a cloak.

'Sorry,' said Fran, hurrying forward.

There was no lift, and the three of them climbed two flights of stairs to the first floor, where Connell opened the door to number 3, taking off a blue-and-white police tape. Fran took a deep breath as a familiar wave of blackness washed over her.

'Mrs Castle?' Connell took her arm and bent towards her.

'I – I'm all right.' Fran opened her eyes and stood up straight. 'I don't know why that happened.'

'Well, come inside and let's see if we can find out.' Connell held the door wide for her to precede him into the flat.

Shaking off the remnants of the blackness, Fran looked round the tiny hall. Apart from three doors, it was completely featureless. Connell indicated the door in front of them, which stood half open, and they went into the living room. Large windows opened on to a Juliet balcony and two sofas were positioned to make the most of the distant view of the sea. A large shelving unit stood against one wall, and Fran went straight to it.

'We've been through it,' said Connell. Fran nodded.

'May I?' she said.

'Go ahead', said Connell.

Constable Maiden stood by the door and Connell prowled round behind her as she looked through the few books and ornaments on the shelves and then opened the cupboards at the bottom. After ten minutes she turned round and shook her head. 'Nothing,' she said.

'Try the bedroom,' said Connell, and led the way back into the hall.

There had been no attempt at decoration in the bedroom either, although there was evidence here of Danny's presence. Two sorts of cologne and two toothbrushes in the bathroom confirmed this, but nothing emerged to reinforce Fran's reaction when they arrived. They went back into the living room.

'Did you find his passport or birth certificate?' asked Fran, sitting on one of the sofas.

'No,' said Connell, looking surprised. 'He must have had them, mustn't he?'

'How long had he been here?'

Connell shrugged. 'Several years.'

'Address book? Would that have had a previous address?'

'We found an old address book, but no current addresses in it. No one from round here.'

'So he didn't come from round here originally?'

'He might have done. There was nothing to indicate where he came from. Which is one of the reasons we wanted to talk to his sister again.'

'Didn't she say anything when she was first told about his death?'

'Nothing about their history. She came down here, as you know,' said Connell, 'but she was understandably upset, so we sent her home again and said we'd need to talk to her again. But someone got there first.'

Fran thought. 'Mobile phone?' she asked.

'None found. And we've looked at the landline records. Nothing there except a local taxi firm.'

'And you've checked with them?'

Connell gave her a scornful look.

'Well? Any local trips?'

'From The Red Lion in Heronsbourne and Anderson Place.'

'The Red Lion?' Fran sat up straight. 'That was Mrs Morleigh's aunt's local.'

'What?' Connell stared. 'But she must have been ninety!'

'But she still went in there regularly. The landlord looked out for her, and it was he and his wife who got her into hospital when she was ill.'

Connell sat down on the other sofa and leant forward. 'Is this relevant?'

'I don't know,' said Fran honestly, 'but it could be, couldn't it? I mean, it's not a link to Mrs Morleigh, but it is to her aunt.'

'I can't see what it means, though,' said Connell. 'They could just be drinkers in a local pub. No reason for them to know one another at all.'

'And maybe Laurence didn't drink in there regularly, anyway. Only one trip?'

'I don't know about that,' said Connell. 'We only checked the recent calls, so the taxi firm only checked recent trips.'

'Should we check with George at The Red Lion?' asked Fran.

Connell looked as though he was about to question her use of pronoun, but after a moment stood up and nodded. 'Nothing else here?' he said.

Fran shook her head, although she was aware of something lurking at the back of her mind. But it was too formless to describe, so she filed it away to think about later.

Constable Maiden held the front door open for her, and Connell replaced the police tape. She felt a brief resurgence of the black suffocation and lurched towards the stairs.

'Careful,' said Connell, reaching out to steady her.

'Something happened here,' said Fran, turning to look up at him. 'Out here on the landing.'

Constable Maiden made a stifled sound in his throat and Fran glared at him.

'But we've established he was killed at the old theatre,' said Connell.

Fran shook her head. 'I don't know what it means,' she said.

They proceeded down the stairs and back to the car in silence, when Connell took out his phone and made a call, walking away so that Fran couldn't hear.

'They'll get SOCO back to the hallway,' he said, coming back to the car. 'OK, Maiden. The Red Lion in Heronsbourne.'

It was strange to be here without Libby, thought Fran, as Connell and she went into the bar, leaving Maiden in the car.

'Hello, young lady,' said George, coming forward with a smile. 'Brought yer boyfriend this time?'

'Inspector Connell, Nethergate CID,' said Connell holding up his identification while Fran blushed furiously.

'Sorry, I'm sure,' said George, unabashed. 'Can I get you anything, or are you on duty?'

'I want to know if you recognise this man,' said Connell taking a photograph in a clear bag from an inside pocket. Fran craned to see. 'Taken at work, by the look of it,' Connell told her, as George studied it.

'Larry,' said George. 'Used to come in now and then, sometimes with another chap, younger. Worked up at the Place. Why, what's he done?'

'Got himself murdered,' said Connell and watched as George turned pale.

'No.' George swallowed. 'Fuck. Sorry, missus.'

'Wasn't it in the papers?' asked Fran.

'No identity and we've only just got hold of this from the Place,' said Connell. 'So, can you tell us anything about him?'

George subsided onto a stool. 'Nothing to tell,' he said. 'Used to chat a bit. Always had a cab back home. Sensible drinker.'

'What time did he come in usually?' asked Fran. Connell frowned at her.

'All different,' said George. 'Depended on his time off, he said. Sometimes earlyish. Round about seven thirty.'

'So he would have known Aunt Maria?'

George looked surprised. 'Not to say known, no, but they was often here at the same time. He asked after her when she went to hospital.'

Fran turned triumphantly to Connell. 'There,' she said.

He looked bewildered, but game. 'Right, Mr –?'

'Felton. George Felton.'

'We might need to talk to you again, Mr Felton. Thank you for your help.'

George nodded and whispered to Fran as Connell went to the door, 'What's it all about?'

'Tell you later,' Fran whispered back, and followed Connell out of the pub.

'So he knew Mrs Morleigh's aunt,' he said, as Maiden started the car. 'Where does that get us?'

'It's a link,' said Fran. 'And it means he knew when she died.'

'And?'

'He could have known Bella was to inherit everything. George said Maria used to say she was leaving everything to a niece she'd never met.'

'I still don't see what it had to do with him.' Connell frowned down at his hands.

'Not yet,' said Fran. 'Something will turn up.'

'Thank you for that, Mrs Micawber,' said Connell. Fran turned and smiled delightedly at him.

'You're human,' she said.

Another stifled snort emanated from Constable Maiden, and

Connell scowled.

'Only just,' he said.

Fran phoned Libby just as she was putting the dishes in the sink.

'Glad I caught you,' she said. 'I didn't phone earlier because I was thinking.'

'Did it hurt?' said Libby. 'Sorry, sorry. Didn't mean that. How did it go?'

Fran told her, gratified by Libby's exclamations and gasps of astonishment.

'I need to get all this straight in my head, but you're going to rehearsal now, and I'm off to Richmond in the morning, so I don't know when we'll get the chance to talk about it.'

'When you get back from Richmond?' suggested Libby.

'I don't know what time I'll get back,' said Fran. 'Our appointment with CID is at two, so we might not be finished until late afternoon.'

'And then you might have to have a meal,' said Libby.

'I doubt it,' said Fran. 'Not if we have a chaperone like we did today.'

'Really?'

'Oh, yes. A nice boy called Maiden. Red hair and freckles. He was very amused by the whole proceedings.'

'Do you remember that DC when Murray came here to question you? He was gobsmacked, especially when Murray seemed to believe you.'

'Well, Maiden obviously thought Connell had lost his marbles,' said Fran, laughing in spite of herself. 'Especially when he ordered an examination of the hallway at the flats.'

'That's really interesting, actually,' said Libby.

'What is?' said Ben, coming into the kitchen.

'Oh, Fran, I'm sorry, I'm rambling on and I'm supposed to be at the theatre.' Libby waved at Ben. 'I shouldn't be too late. Shall I ring you when I've finished?'

'How late?' asked Fran. 'Any chance of popping in here on your way home – or to the pub?'

'Yes, of course, good idea,' said Libby. 'I'll get the rehearsal over as quickly as I can.'

'You don't mind if I go and see her, do you?' Libby asked

Ben as they walked to the theatre. 'She obviously needs to talk.'

'No, of course not. I'll go and have a drink, and if you haven't appeared by closing time I'll come and get you.' He smiled at her. 'Independence, that's what we've got.'

Libby, with a rueful smile, nodded.

The chorus and dancers pranced unenthusiastically through their routines, causing both musical director and choreographer to tear their hair out, quite literally in the case of the choreographer, who pulled at his curly locks in a distracted fashion throughout. Eventually Libby, who couldn't see any improvement in the last hour and a half decided to call it a day.

'When the principals are there, and it's in front of an audience it'll be fine, you'll see,' she said, crossing her fingers behind her back. The chorus looked a bit more cheerful, and the musical director and choreographer glared at one another and stalked off to their respective cars. Ben reappeared from backstage and grinned.

'Tact personified,' he said. 'Want to have a look at the rejuvenated beanstalk?'

After approving the beanstalk, and casting an apprehensive eye over the giant's legs, Libby left Ben and his backstage cohorts to lock up, and hurried down the drive towards the High Street and The Pink Geranium.

Fran let her in and produced a bottle of wine as she took off her cape.

'Come on, then,' said Libby, perching herself on the window sill and opening it a crack. 'Tell all.'

Fran went back over the events of the morning, including the surprising revelation that Laurence knew Aunt Maria.

'And this worries you?' asked Libby, blowing smoke through the window. 'I must say, I agree with Connell. I can't see the relevance.'

'He was found in the Alexandria and he knew Maria. Isn't that relevant?'

'Yes,' said Libby slowly. 'I suppose it is.'

'Why was he there? He knew she was dead, didn't he?'

'Did he arrange to meet someone there?' said Libby. Her hand flew to her mouth. 'Oh, God, not Bella?'

'I'm afraid that makes sense, doesn't it?' said Fran, looking miserable, 'but I just can't believe in it. Bella didn't kill him. She'd never even heard of him.'

'And come to think of it,' said Libby, sliding down from the window sill, 'how would he know about Bella? No one but the solicitor knew about her, and even he had a struggle to find her. All Laurence could have known was that Maria had a niece.'

'But why, anyway? You can't exactly steal a derelict theatre,' said Fran.

'What about that hallway?' asked Libby, taking a sip of wine.

'Oh, I don't know,' said Fran with a sigh. 'It was Aunt Eleanor all over again. Something happened there, but I don't know what. It was something to do with all this, I'm sure, although I suppose it could be an argument between the other tenants, but I don't think so. The police are convinced that Laurence was killed where he was found, and they don't make mistakes about that sort of thing, do they?'

'I don't think so,' said Libby. 'It's one of the first things they know these days, isn't it? Not like the old days.'

Fran raised her eyebrows. 'What do you know about the old days?'

'In detective stories, I mean,' explained Libby. 'Weren't they always bundling bodies into boots and dumping them elsewhere?'

'Possibly,' said Fran, amused. 'I didn't read many.'

'Well, anyway,' said Libby, 'they wouldn't have made a mistake this time.'

'No, so it's something else that happened on that landing,' said Fran.

'And won't we look fools if it's someone clobbering a door to door salesman,' said Libby.

'No, *we* won't,' said Fran. '*I* will. But it isn't. I can't explain it, but I'm sure it's something to do with Laurence.' She held out the bottle to top up Libby's glass. 'And tomorrow I've got to try and find out where he came from.'

'Do you think Dorothy's house will have some sort of clue?'

'If whoever killed her hasn't removed it,' said Fran, 'but then, whoever killed her might not have known what they were looking for.'

'Do you?' asked Libby.

Fran sighed. 'I haven't the faintest idea,' she said.

Chapter Seventeen

INSPECTOR CONNELL ARRIVED IN an altogether sportier-looking car at seven o'clock the following morning, wearing altogether more casual clothes. Fran, wearing her navy coat over tailored trousers and a roll necked sweater, felt quite drab beside him.

'No Constable Maiden this morning?' she asked, as he held the passenger door open for her.

'Can't be spared for a whole day.' He got in beside her and reached round for his seat belt.

'And you can?'

He turned to look at her. 'It's in my interest, but only semi-official,' he said. 'Like Murray did, I'm treating you more or less as an expert witness, but I don't want anyone looking too closely.'

'I thought you said other police forces had used psychics?'

'They have, but in much the same way as I'm – er – as I've asked you to help.'

'As you're using me,' said Fran with a smile. She noticed his neck go slightly pink.

'Anyway, today, we're on our own,' he said, turning right on to the main road to Canterbury, 'and it's a hell of a long drive.'

'Yes,' said Fran. 'It must be all of six hours.'

'That's a conservative estimate,' he said. 'I've allowed seven hours, so hopefully we'll arrive in time to grab a sandwich before our appointment.'

'And if we need to stop on the way?' asked Fran.

'Just ask,' he said shortly, and put his foot down.

He had the radio on quietly, and every now and then a local traffic update would come through. Happily, they came up against no difficulties until they got to the Heathrow area of the M25, which, as Fran knew, was always a traffic black spot.

However, the M1 was moving at a reasonable speed and they were soon past Luton.

'How are you enjoying living in Steeple Martin?' he asked suddenly.

'Very much,' replied Fran, slightly startled. 'How did you know I hadn't been there long?'

'DCI Murray. Said you'd only just moved down when I met you.'

'That's right. But it's only temporary.'

He turned his head briefly to look at her. 'Oh?'

'I'm hoping to move into my cottage in Nethergate after Christmas,' she said. 'I mentioned it yesterday, I'm sure.'

'Oh, yes.' He pulled out to overtake a lorry. 'Where in Nethergate?'

'Harbour Street,' said Fran.

He looked sideways at her, and surprised her with a grin that made her feel quite breathless. 'I wasn't really paying attention yesterday,' he said.

'Too intent on Laurence Cooper's flat,' she said.

'Quite. So recap for me. What did you say about your cottage yesterday?'

Fran explained about the builder Jim Butler having bought Coastguard Cottage from her family, and how he'd built the estate on which Laurence Cooper's flat stood.

'Did Laurence rent it, or had he bought it?' she asked, finally.

'Rented it. Some speculator owns the whole block. He says references were taken from Cooper and he's never defaulted on the rent.'

'Did he still have the references?'

'No, which makes me suspicious,' said Connell. 'Not necessarily about Cooper, but about the landlord. I think we're going to have to put someone in to have a look at his books.'

'Could he have a motive?'

'Who, the landlord? I can't see why, can you? He never saw any of his tenants and had never met Cooper.'

'So what do you think about it all?' asked Fran. 'Personally, I mean.'

'I don't know what to think. Forensics tell us he was killed where he was found, yet why on earth should he be there? There were no keys or documents on him, and it was only through sister Dorothy reporting him missing we found him. We were having no luck with dental records, but that doesn't surprise me.'

'Oh? Why? I thought that was a favourite method of identification,' said Fran.

'If everyone went regularly to their dentist, yes,' said Connell, 'but with so few National Health dentists now and the cost of dental treatment, people don't go any more.'

'That's true,' said Fran. 'I haven't been for years, and I can't even remember who my last dentist was. I suppose I ought to register down here, now.'

'If you can afford it,' said Connell grimly. 'Dentistry's an absolute scandal these days.'

'And they lecture one so, don't they?' said Fran. 'Shake their heads at you as though you're a recalcitrant child.'

He grinned. 'Dead right,' he said. 'So there we are. No dental records. Oh, we might have found them in time, but he certainly hadn't visited a dentist in the last six years.'

'What else, then? Why did you tell Mrs Morleigh to speak to me?'

'Because she had no idea about her family who left the theatre, and I wondered if Cooper had anything to do with them, as I couldn't think of any other reason for him to have been there.'

'Couldn't he have been forced in there by someone trying to mug him? Who then went too far?'

'Possible, but how would they have got in? The door hadn't been forced.'

'What?' said Fran. 'I didn't know that.'

'I'm surprised Mrs Morleigh didn't tell you.'

'How could anyone have got hold of keys? She'd only just been given them by the solicitor.'

'We don't know. We're tracing everyone who rented the place over the last twenty years or so, but as the last people to use it were holding illegal raves they're staying well out of sight.'

'They must have got the keys from somewhere,' said Fran,

turning to look at him.

He shrugged. 'Sure, but for all we know, each succeeding tenant changed the locks. There could have been any number of keys around.'

'Was there no chain and padlock? Any other security measure?'

'The main doors were boarded up and secured, but the side door, where you saw me the other day was a Yale and an old-fashioned sash lock.'

'What's a sash lock?'

'One that has an old-fashioned key.'

'Oh.' Fran turned back to the windscreen which showed an uninspiring view of rain swept vehicles. 'So, not a mugging because the murderer had keys.'

'Or Cooper did.'

'Oh, yes, of course. That's why you hoped to find a link to Mrs Morleigh's family.'

'If there had been a link, it might have explained the keys, but as I've said, there could be dozens of sets of keys in circulation around Nethergate and the area.' He sent her a brief smile. 'No, what I want from you now is just who he was and why he was there.'

'Oh, is *that* all,' said Fran, smiling back. 'And if I can't find it?'

'We'll carry on with dull old police routine until something turns up.'

Fran requested a comfort stop as they got near to Sheffield, and suggested buying sandwiches in case they didn't have time when they arrived in Richmond. They ate them in the car park, unable to see out of the windows through the dirty curtain of rain.

They just made it to Richmond in time to meet a disgruntled detective sergeant in a wet raincoat outside a small terraced cottage in a pleasant, cobbled lane. What Fran could see of Richmond, she liked.

Connell introduced them both and once more Fran ducked under blue police tape.

'SOCOs finished?' asked Connell as they went into the tiny front room.

'Yeah,' said the DS, whose name was Fitch. 'Bloody mess, it was, pardon the pun.'

Fran stared at the chair by the fireplace. Her stomach swooped and she swallowed hard. DS Fitch nodded.

'Yes, that's where they found the old girl,' he said. 'Tied to the arms she was, then bashed over the head.'

'I've read the report, thank you, Sergeant,' said Connell.

'I was telling the lady, sir,' said Fitch defensively.

'Thank you, Sergeant,' said Fran, and moved away to look at the shelves in the alcoves. Taking a deep breath, she moved her hands over the small ornaments that Dorothy had obviously liked to collect. Nothing was coming through.

'Papers?' asked Connell.

'Bills and stuff in a cupboard in the kitchen, sir.'

'Passport? Birth certificate?'

'No passport, sir. Birth certificate with the parents' death certificates in a dressing table drawer.'

'Where are they now?'

'At the station, sir. Well, over at HQ.' Fitch looked over at Fran, who was now looking through a pile of magazines. Connell frowned and shook his head.

'Was there anything else in the dressing table drawer?' asked Fran suddenly.

'Some old photos, I think. Nothing much.'

'Are they still here? Or are they with the birth certificates?'

Fitch looked nonplussed. 'Here, I think,' he said.

Connell turned and went into the hall. 'Come on, then,' he said over his shoulder to Fran.

The biggest of the two bedrooms held a large old-fashioned wooden bed, so high that a step had been provided to climb into it, a dressing table and a carved wardrobe. Fran went straight to the dressing table, where she found a very old box of loose powder, a venerable comb and a lot of dust. Opening the middle drawer, she found several faded black and white photographs and an envelope, inside which was a lock of brown hair. This brought tears to her eyes and a lump to her throat, although she had no idea whose it was, or what connection it had to sister Dorothy.

Picking up the photographs, she went to sit on the bed.

Connell came and sat next to her.

'What are they?' he asked.

Fran shook her head. 'I don't know. A lot of people from the forties and fifties by the look of them.' She showed him the blurry images of children posed in gardens and adults at the seaside. 'I wonder where these were.'

'Nethergate, do you think?' he said.

'I don't think so.' She looked through a few more and stopped, her breath catching in her throat.

'What?' He was watching her intently.

'This one –' she held out a picture '– it's Anderson Place.'

The black and white photograph showed a much more overgrown building standing in untidy gardens. But posing against the wall in the foreground stood the two children in the other photographs, obviously Dorothy and Laurence.

Connell looked puzzled. 'Why would they be there?' he asked. 'I suppose it is the two Cooper children?'

'Oh, yes, it's them.' Fran stroked a finger over the photograph. 'But why, I wonder? The house wasn't open to the public in those days, was it? It had been a military hospital during the war.'

'Looks like some kind of notice there, look,' said Connell taking it from her and peering closely.

'Pity it isn't clearer,' said Fran, and carried on looking through the photographs.

'We'll get it scanned and let the boys have a go at it,' said Connell, standing up. 'Do you want to see anything else?'

'I'd like to have a quick look round up here,' said Fran.

'I'll be downstairs with Fitch, then,' he said.

When she heard his footsteps going down the stairs, she went to the wardrobe and opened the door. A few dispirited garments hung there, polyester blouses and pleated skirts, but nothing that gave any clue to Dorothy as a person. Fran shut the door and went into the room next door. Immediately, she felt something. 'Laurence,' she muttered to herself.

The room contained only a single bed, a small wardrobe and a bedside table. A few male items of clothing hung in the wardrobe, although nothing of the kind Fran felt sure Laurence would have worn. In the bedside table drawer she found another photograph, this time on its face, of two young men, arms slung carelessly about each other's shoulders, and by the clothing, taken sometime in the sixties.

'Before or after it was made legal?' murmured Fran. She put the photograph, along with the others from the dressing table, into her bag and went downstairs. Here, the sense of Laurence wasn't as strong as it had been in his room, but there was a sense of someone else. A very strong feeling of anger – and fear. Mainly fear, thought Fran, as she stood in the little sitting room with her eyes closed, ignoring the two men staring at her.

'What did he tie her with?' she asked, opening her eyes suddenly.

'Er –' Fitch was floundering.

Connell looked at him contemptuously. 'Picture wire,' he said. 'It was in the report. From those pictures.' He nodded towards two blank spaces on the walls. Fran went over and ran her hands over the spaces. She didn't know if she would get anything from them, but she had to try. She was new at this, and every situation would be a testing ground. Nothing came through except more fear and confusion. Nothing at all from Dorothy. She went back to the chair and went to touch the back, but pulled her hand back quickly.

'What is it?' said Connell.

Fran smiled at him wryly. 'Squeamishness,' she said.

He smiled back. 'Come on, then,' he said. 'If you've finished here, we'll go over to HQ and see what they've got.'

Fitch, even more disgruntled than when they arrived, locked the door, checked the tape and said they could follow him to HQ. Fran and Connell shook the rain off and set off after him.

The DCI in charge of the murder enquiry was pleasant but wary. They were shown the evidence bags, and allowed to take out the birth and death certificates.

'Father, Colin Cooper – what's that? Army?' said Fran, peering. 'Mother, Shirley Cooper, housewife. And these are their death certificates.'

'And this one.' Connell held it out. 'You'll love this.'

Fran took it and gasped. 'Laurence Cooper! But what on earth is his birth certificate doing here? He'd have needed it himself.'

'Is it Laurence's, though?' said Connell, pointing. 'Look at the Christian name.'

'Earnest,' said Fran. 'But it is Earnest Laurence, look. Maybe he preferred Laurence.'

'It's the right date, anyway,' said Connell. 'I think we have to assume it's his. Born in 1946.'

Fran picked up another evidence bag and hastily put it down again.

'The picture wire?' said Connell, picking it up. 'What beats me is how whoever it was had time to take down the pictures and take off the wire. How come she didn't make a run for it?'

'Perhaps he'd already bashed her over the head?'

'Then why would he need to tie her up?'

Fran shrugged and they stared at each other, perplexed.

'Weapon?' said Connell, turning to the DCI, who shook his head. 'Any chance of a copy of the landline records?'

After half an hour in the canteen with some indifferent coffee and a small packet of bourbons, they were on their way home with the phone records and other information Connell had requested and been grudgingly given. Fran opened her bag to take out the photographs.

'What the hell are you doing with those?'

She looked up. 'Shouldn't I have taken them?'

Connell gave an exasperated sigh. 'No, you shouldn't. For God's sake woman, this is a murder investigation.'

Fran bristled. 'I'm aware of that,' she said, 'and may I remind you that you asked me here, not the other way round. *I'm* helping *you*. I have no personal interest in this case.'

'Not much we can do about it now, anyway,' muttered Connell, and swore as a lorry overtook them, throwing a swimming pool's worth of rain at the windscreen.

Fran put them back in her bag. 'I'll look at them at home tonight and send them back tomorrow,' she said.

'I'll come and collect them tomorrow,' corrected Connell. '*If* you don't mind.'

For the rest of the journey, except for a stop at services near Luton, they were silent. Fran peered ahead into the darkness and tried to quell a deep sense of disappointment.

Chapter Eighteen

LIBBY AND SIDNEY PUT up the Christmas decorations on Friday. When she had lived in the big Edwardian house on the other side of Canterbury, Libby refused to put them up until the last possible minute, telling the children it devalued the essence of Christmas. But now she wanted to keep Christmas going as long as possible, having decided that anticipation was the best part of it all.

Sidney was a great help, naturally, especially when Libby brought in the tree she had dragged home from the Manor estate after Ben had helped her cut it down. Feeling virtuous, as she had only taken the top of a healthy tree, she stuck it in a large tub of earth and sand and stood it on an apple crate covered in crepe paper in the corner behind the armchair. If anyone sat at the table in the window the tree would have their eye out, but it looked good. Sidney immediately jumped up on to the table and began to select baubles.

After half an hour of vigorous table tennis, Libby gave up and shut him in the conservatory. After retrieving the baubles Sidney had knocked into various corners of the room, she hung them on the tree and switched on the lights. Just garish enough, she told herself, as she stood back and gave it the once over. Then the cut out felt stockings were pinned to the mantelpiece and the effect was complete. Sidney was allowed in to give his opinion, and after tapping the baubles he could reach and finding them intransigent, he turned his back and began to wash.

Libby contemplated lighting the fire to complete the picture, but decided it was too early. In fact, it was only lunchtime, and the rest of the day stretched ahead without even a rehearsal to look forward to. Wondering if there was anything she could do for Peter and Harry, whose wedding was now only a week away, or for Hetty, who would be busy organising the Christmas Party, she phoned them both, and discovered that nothing was outstanding.

'You can come and have bowl of soup with me, though,' said Harry. 'I haven't got a "do" on this lunchtime and I'm bored. Pete's in London.'

'OK, that'd be nice,' said Libby. 'Ben's doing estate business with his dad, and his mum obviously didn't want me getting under her feet while she organises the party.'

'Oh, yes, the great party. I'm doing some little bits and pieces for it.'

'When will you have time?'

'I'm here in the kitchen most of the weekend, course I'll have time,' said Harry. 'Now, are you coming down or what?'

Libby gathered up her cloak, a scarf and her basket and said goodbye to Sidney. The air was damply cool, the sky a muddy grey and puddles lay down the middle of Allhallow's Lane in the tyre ruts. Once in the High Street, though, lights twinkled in shops and on Christmas trees glimpsed through cottage windows. In many of those windows were the professional-looking posters for *Jack and the Beanstalk*, and Ahmed's display in the eight-til-late looked wonderful.

In The Pink Geranium Harry had a tasteful tree decorated with dried chillies, raffia and other natural ingredients, and artistically arranged bunches of holly, ivy and mistletoe hung from the ceiling and wall lights.

'Aren't they an environmental health hazard?' asked Libby, unwrapping her cloak.

'If they are, no one's told me,' said Harry cheerfully. 'Lentil soup, honeychile?'

'Yes, please,' said Libby, sitting on the sofa in the window. 'And can I still smoke in here?'

'Only if no one else is in here. And after July next year, never,' said Harry, going into the kitchen. 'Want a glass of wine? I've got some red open.'

Libby told him the latest developments in Fran's investigations. 'I don't feel part of this one,' she said. 'Connell asked Fran to look into it but didn't want me around, and now he's actually offered to take Fran to all these places, she's official. And probably can't discuss them with me.'

'I thought you said she told you all about yesterday's shenanigans?'

'Well, yes, she did,' admitted Libby reluctantly, 'but I don't expect she was supposed to.'

'And she still wants you to help, doesn't she?'

'Only like a – a – oh, I don't know. Like a research assistant. I'm expected to go through all these old newspapers, and I haven't got a clue what I'm looking for.' She sighed and took a sip of wine. 'It's got nothing to do with Laurence Cooper, anyway. It's all Bella Morleigh's family history.'

'I thought,' said Harry, helping himself to one of Libby's cigarettes, 'the dashing Inspector Connell thought there *was* a connection. That's why he asked Fran to do her voodoo that she does so well.'

'That was the idea, but there's no connection at all, as far as I can see. So Fran's just looking into Bella's family for interest's sake. Bella isn't even down here, so I don't know why we're bothering.'

'Don't, then. Bother, I mean.' Harry stood up. 'But I bet those old newspapers are fascinating. I wonder why the old auntie kept them?'

'Fran thinks there must be something of value in them. Can't see it myself.'

'I'll have a look through if you like,' said Harry. 'And now I'm going to get the soup, so sit yourself down at the table like a good girl.'

'When would you have the time to look through old newspapers?' asked Libby, when they were seated with bowls of lentil soup and hunks of fresh bread.

'After work. I need to relax sometimes by doing something totally different.' Harry sipped wine reflectively. 'And at the moment as soon as I finish work, the wedding takes over. It would be good to do something else.'

Libby shook her head. 'I still say you won't have time. And the wedding's next weekend, isn't it? Maybe after Christmas. Pete'll get all caught up in the panto and the caff'll go quiet.'

'I thought it would all be over by then,' said Harry.

'Not Bella's family investigations. The murder might be. I don't know anything about that, and they might have a suspect

166

already.'

– 'Fran would have told you.'

'Hmm. Well, they've ruled out Danny, anyway.'

'Do you know that definitely?'

'He certainly didn't murder sister Dorothy,' said Libby.

'That's a comfort,' said Harry.

After the soup, Harry brought out a large piece of banana bread, some of which had played quite a part in Libby's unwise investigations into the death of Fran's aunt last summer.

'How about I come back with you and have a quick look at some of those papers?' he suggested. 'I haven't got any prepping up to do until later, and Pete's off doing something or other today.'

'You're really keen on those old papers, aren't you?' said Libby, licking crumbs off her fingers. 'Yeah, come back if you like.'

A brisk wind had sprung up while they were eating lunch, and it whipped Harry's blond spiky hair into even wilder spikes, and tangled his pink scarf with Libby's multi-coloured one. 'Cold,' he muttered, thrusting his hands deeper into his jacket pockets.

'Should have worn something warmer,' said Libby, tucking her arm through his.

'I only have to walk about fifty yards to work in the mornings,' said Harry. 'I didn't think I'd be going on a hike into the past with a batty old woman.'

'Your idea,' said Libby, unsympathetically.

Libby lit the fire in the front room while Harry put the kettle on the Rayburn. Sidney rolled on his back in appreciation.

'These them, then?' Harry picked up the pile of newspapers from beside the computer on the table in the window.

'That's them,' said Libby. 'Ben and I have been through some. Maria wasn't born until 1914, so we didn't think it was worth looking before then.'

'These aren't even in date order,' said Harry, with a frown.

'They weren't when we found them,' said Libby, going into the kitchen to make the tea. 'Not something I've found the time or energy to do.'

'I will,' said Harry. 'Let me take them home with me. I can

spend a nice mindless half hour in the evenings doing this. Just the sort of thing that appeals to my sense of order.'

'I didn't know you had one,' said Libby, bringing teapot, mugs and milk on a tray. 'Although, come to think of it, you are very organised in the caff.'

'And at home. When did you ever see Peter tidy anything away? Or make tea?'

'Never, I suppose,' said Libby, 'but I always expect him to be organised, being a journo and all that.'

'Take it from me, he isn't,' said Harry. 'And who, pray tell, organised the bloody wedding that was all his idea?'

'That's true,' said Libby. 'You're full of surprises, you know that?'

Harry winked. 'Not 'arf,' he said.

He had gone by the time Ben arrived from the other end of Allhallow's Lane, coat collar turned up and nose slightly red.

'Harry's going to look through those old papers for me,' said Libby, hanging up his coat. 'He says he needs a bit of relaxation.'

'Too right he does,' said Ben, rubbing his hands in front of the fire. 'He does far too much, that lad. Pete runs him ragged.'

'Oh, he doesn't,' protested Libby, 'at least, not on purpose.'

'Not on purpose, no,' said Ben, 'but Pete has all the ideas and Harry has to carry them out.'

'The wedding,' nodded Libby.

'Yes, the wedding, also the caff, the cottage –'

'How do you mean, the cottage? I thought that was already Pete's?'

'When Millie gutted the kitchen at Steeple Farm Pete was going to let all that lovely stuff go to a firm of house clearers, or the skip. It was Harry who stepped in to rescue it.'

'I didn't know,' said Libby.

'And Pete was supposed to be an active partner in The Pink Geranium, but what have you seen him do?'

'Well, he waits on tables, sometimes.'

'More often just sits in the corner reading the paper.'

'You're not being very nice to your cousin,' said Libby reprovingly.

'I adore my cousin Pete, and in a crisis I would always turn to him. He's clever, generous and kind, but thoughtless. If you point these things out to him it's like kicking a puppy.'

'He doesn't realise?' said Libby, pouring tea.

'Not at all. Has the ideas, and then when they come to fruition, thinks it's all down to him.'

'Well, in a way it is,' said Libby, curling up on the creaky sofa. 'Harry would never have suggested the caff, would he? Or getting partnered.'

'True, O queen,' said Ben. 'Nevertheless, our Hal does all the work. What he wants to be doing with going through old newspapers I can't think.'

'That's just what I said,' agreed Libby. 'Must be mad.'

'So, do you expect to hear from Fran tonight?' asked Ben, idly stroking Sidney with a foot.

'No idea. It's a long way to Richmond. She and Connell might go for a meal on the way home.'

'You think so? I wouldn't have thought he would let personal life in while he's working.'

'It's hardly personal, is it? You have to eat.' Libby frowned. 'I just hope Fran doesn't get carried away with him. Guy's been sitting so patiently on the sidelines.'

'Look, Lib, you can't dictate people's love lives. If Fran doesn't like Guy as much as she likes Connell, although I can't see why, either, she's under no obligation to him, is she?'

'I know that,' said Libby, 'I'm not stupid. When Derek went off with his floosie it was no use people saying how stupid he was, he was convinced she was the love of his life.'

'There you are then,' said Ben, 'and anyway, has she actually said she likes Connell better than Guy?'

'No-o,' admitted Libby. 'I just get that feeling.'

'Well, I'd leave her to sort out her feelings, without you interfering,' said Ben. 'You're not that good at sorting your own out, after all.'

'Gee thanks,' said Libby.

Fran's spirits got lower and lower the nearer they got to Steeple Martin. Eventually, plucking up courage, she cleared her throat and asked Connell to stop at a service station.

'I need milk, you see,' she said, 'and the eight-til-late will be closed when I get home.'

'I'm sorry,' he said gruffly. 'What about food? Do you need a supermarket?'

'No, I've got eggs and things,' she said. 'I'll be all right until tomorrow.'

'Would you like to stop for a meal?' Fran got the impression that the words were forced out of him. 'I should have thought of it before.'

'No, please don't worry,' she said. 'I've got food at home.'

He turned a quick smile on her. 'Ah, but I haven't,' he said. 'Take pity on me and keep me company.'

Fran was glad of the darkness in the car as she blushed. 'OK,' she said. 'That would be nice.'

It wasn't until they were drawing up in the car park of a country pub that Fran realised with a jolt that she didn't know if he was married. There had naturally been no reason for anyone to have provided this information, and although one or two people had said they thought he was interested, that didn't mean he was available.

The pub provided basic and unremarkable food, for which Connell apologised. 'I should have gone somewhere I knew,' he said, providing her with the gin and tonic she'd asked for.

'But that would have meant going on further,' said Fran.

He nodded. 'And you must be hungry. All we've had all day is that sandwich.'

'And biscuits at HQ,' reminded Fran.

'Very sustaining,' he said, with a grin. 'So tell me, now we're well away from the place, any ideas?'

Fran thought about it. 'All I can come up with is a connection to Anderson Place, which, as you said, is obvious as he worked there. But there is another connection, I'm sure. Those photographs of him and Dorothy when they were children. Why were they there?'

Connell shook his head and poked at his indifferent meat pie. 'No connection to Mrs Morleigh's family, then?'

'Not that I can find at the moment,' said Fran. 'But don't forget, I'm certainly not infallible, and I haven't investigated this sort of thing before.'

'You did with your aunt's death,' said Connell.

'Only because it was forced on me,' said Fran, feeling rather uncomfortable.

'But you've investigated other things,' persisted Connell.

'Nothing like this,' said Fran.

'I gather you turned up one or two murders for Goodall and Smythe.' He sent her a sly grin.

'But not solving them. They'd just occurred, that's all.' Fran frowned at him. 'And how did you know?'

'I had to check you out, I'm afraid,' he said. 'No,' he added hastily as she opened her mouth, 'don't get upset. We always have to do it. You could have been a fraud.'

'I still could be,' said Fran grumpily.

'I don't think so.' He pushed his plate away. 'Well, I wish I could say that was a great meal, but I can't. Sorry.'

Fran smiled. 'Don't worry. It was better than the plain omelette I would have had at home.'

'And better than my beer and cheese. I don't even know if I've got any bread.' He laughed. 'You can tell I live on my own, can't you?'

Well, that answers that question, Fran thought, watching him as he paid the waitress. And should it matter to me, anyway?

'I'll buy you a decent meal to make up for it,' he said as he held the passenger door for her. 'If you're free, of course.'

'I don't know when you're going to ask me,' said Fran, puzzled.

'I meant – if you're able to accept an invitation.' He didn't look at her, and swung the car back on to the slip road for the motorway.

'Oh,' said Fran, and then didn't know what to say. Disappointed earlier that he had made no move towards her, she was now uncomfortable because he had. She glanced quickly sideways at his dark profile and thought again how like a romantic hero he was. What the hell he saw in her she just couldn't think. To her embarrassment, he turned his head and caught her looking at him.

'Problem?' he said with a smile.

'No,' she said. 'Just wondering what makes you tick.'

'Work,' he said, looking back at the road. 'Nothing else.'

'Nothing?' said Fran, dying to ask if he had a family.

'No time for anything else,' he said.

When they finally drew up outside The Pink Geranium, he got out and held the door for her.

'So,' he said, 'dinner some time?' He saw her hesitation. 'As a thank you for all your help,' he added.

'I haven't really done anything,' said Fran.

'You have, you know. You've established a previous connection between Laurence and Anderson Place and got us looking at whatever went on outside his flat. That could be important.'

'But not proved a connection between him and Mrs Morleigh's family,' said Fran.

'Well, that was always a long shot,' he smiled. 'Can't win 'em all.'

'May I keep hold of the photographs?' asked Fran, pausing in the act of putting her key in the door.

'Let me know when you've finished with them,' he said. 'And if you find anything of course.'

She smiled gratefully. He wasn't going to push for a dinner date, then, or demand the return of the photographs. 'I'll call you,' she said. 'And thank you for the opportunity to see Dorothy's – house. It was very kind.'

'Not kind at all. I needed to see it, too. Thanks again.' He gave her a mock salute and got back into his car, pulling away without another glance. Fran felt slightly let down.

'You really are a silly cow,' she told herself out loud as she climbed the stairs to the flat. 'First you fancy him, then you're disappointed when he ignores you, and when he does look interested you take fright. Then, blow me down,' she said, as she switched on lights, 'you're cross because he takes the hint.' She sighed heavily and went to see if she had any gin left. As she poured the last into a glass, she realised she needed to do some larder restocking before Christmas, especially as she hoped some of her friends would be able to come for Christmas drinks. And Lucy was bringing Rachel and Tom down at some point, after grumbling that her mother wouldn't be in London to cook Christmas dinner. Fran had pointed out gently that she had a new life now and would be spending the day with friends. In fact Hetty had extended a gracious invitation to the Manor,

172

where she would be joined by Libby, Ben, two of Libby's children, Peter and Harry, Flo and Lenny and James. Ben's sister Susan had opted to spend her day helping at the local hospital, at which decision everyone seemed relieved.

She sat down in the front room and took out the photographs. The one of Laurence taken in the sixties gave her nothing, although she would have given anything to find out who the other man was. The Anderson Place pictures, however, were tickling away at the corners of her mind, and she was sure they had some kind of significance. She sat back and thought. There must be someone she could ask. Danny hadn't been there long enough, but what about the woman Libby had met with Harry? How long had she been there?

Fran downed the last of her gin and gathered up the photographs. Tomorrow she would phone Libby and ask for her help.

Chapter Nineteen

'THE PARTY'S ON SUNDAY,' said Libby, when Fran phoned her on Saturday morning. 'Are you going to come?'

'I didn't know I was invited,' said Fran.

'Oh, I don't think that matters. It's a bit of a free for all, as far as I can understand. Come with me. The family will all be busy with the tenants so I'll need company. And think of all those children!'

'Do you need help with them?' asked Fran nervously.

'I don't think so. I hope not,' said Libby. 'Anyway, what did you call me about? Certainly not the party.'

'I thought you might want to know what happened yesterday.'

'Well, yes, but not if you're not supposed to tell me.'

'Inspector Connell didn't say I shouldn't,' said Fran. 'Anyway, I want your help.'

'My help?' Libby was puzzled, if gratified.

'I'll have to tell you all about yesterday first, so I can explain,' said Fran. 'Do you want to come over? Or shall I come to you?'

'Come over for lunch,' said Libby. 'Only bread and cheese sort of lunch, but Ben's busy putting up trestle tables at the Manor, so I shall be on my own.'

Fran agreed, offering to bring a bottle of wine with her. Libby made a half-hearted attempt to tidy the sitting room and kitchen, lit the fire and was writing her last few Christmas cards when Fran arrived. They settled either side of the fireplace with Sidney between them, and Fran told Libby about her visit to Richmond.

'So what do you want my help for?' asked Libby. 'I'm not psychic. I can't see things that aren't there.'

'I want to talk to someone who might remember that era.'

'Well, I don't,' said Libby, slightly affronted.

'No, I didn't mean that. I thought you might have some sort of idea about who to ask. You've lived in this area longer than I have.'

'But not that long. We moved to Kent when the children were small.'

'But you still know more people here than I do. What about Hetty? Or Flo?'

'I've asked them both already,' said Libby. 'I thought I told you about that?'

Fran shook her head.

'Well, Hetty remembers a kitchen maid called – um, Edith, I think, and an old lady coming to call from the Place, but nothing else, and Flo knew nothing at all.'

'Who was the old lady?' asked Fran.

'I don't know. Hetty didn't either, and although Ben remembers her a bit he hasn't got a clue. So that gets us no further.'

'Would she have been Jonathan – what's his name? – Walker? His mother?'

'If she was very old back in the early fifties I wouldn't have thought so. He was described as "old" Jonathan, wasn't he? He'd have to be positively ancient if she was his mother.' Libby stared into the fire. 'I tell you what, though. How about asking him?'

'How?' said Fran. 'He's the owner. He probably doesn't even live there. Anyway, he's the boss of the Place. I doubt we'd get near him.'

'It's a good idea, though, isn't it?' said Libby. 'Who could we ask about him?'

'Danny? Or what about that woman you met up there with Harry?'

'Mel,' said Libby. 'I suppose so, but Danny would be preferable. He'd know why we wanted to speak to the old man.'

'Let's ring him, then,' said Fran. 'Did you say they've let him go back to work?'

'I think so. Have we got his number?'

'I have,' said Fran, digging out her mobile. 'Here. If he's working it'll go straight to voice mail, won't it?'

'But at least he'll know. I'm sure it's Jonathan you need to speak to.'

'Although even he might not know. They could have just been loitering outside the walls, couldn't they?'

'I haven't seen the photographs, so I don't know,' said Libby.

'Here.' Once more, Fran scrabbled in her bag and drew out an envelope, which she emptied onto the table at her elbow. 'There,' she said.

Libby looked through the photographs. 'I can't really work out where they are,' she said. 'That looks like the front of the Place, but it's all different, now.'

'That's what's so difficult,' said Fran. 'Are they there because they belong there? Or trespassing? Or actually outside?'

'If they belonged there, Laurence wouldn't have been working for them now, would he?'

'Well, he might have been. If, say, his parents had worked there, he might have been given a job when it was turned into a hotel.'

'Oh, yes. That's true.' Libby looked thoughtful. 'Wouldn't Danny have known that, though?'

'Damn. Yes, of course he would.' Fran sat back in the chair. 'We haven't got much further forward, have we?'

'Oh, I don't know. We're going to try and speak to old Jonathan, aren't we? That's progress. Go on, ring Danny and I'll open the wine.'

Fran left a message for Danny to call her as soon as he was free and Libby came back with the wine.

'And now tell me all about Inspector Connell,' she said, handing Fran a glass.

'Tell what?' said Fran, looking innocent.

'Oh, come on. You know what I mean. Did he take you for a meal?'

'Yes, but only because it was late and we both needed to eat. Nowhere flash.'

'He needn't have done.'

'No.' Fran looked down into her glass.

'Come on, there's more, isn't there?'

'He sort of asked me out again.' Fran wouldn't look up.

'What do you mean "sort of"? He either did or he didn't.'

'He offered to take me out for a proper meal to make up for the crap one.'

'So?' Libby stared at her friend intently.

'I – um – didn't really answer.' Fran looked up. 'It was weird. We had a bit of a spat in the car because I'd brought the photographs away and I shouldn't have done, then we didn't speak until we got to Kent. And I was disappointed because he hadn't – er –'

'Made a pass?'

'Shown interest. Then when he did I got scared, and when he didn't pursue it I was disappointed again.'

'Freaked you out, did it?' Libby grinned. 'Is it because you really fancy him, or is it just because he *has* shown interest?'

Fran stared at her. 'Oh, Lib, I don't know. I'm so unused to this.'

'You've had Guy since the summer. You can't be *that* unused to it.' Libby failed to keep an accusing note out of her voice.

'I know,' said Fran. 'And that's the other thing. Connell actually asked me if I was free to accept invitations. He knows I've been seeing Guy.'

Libby stayed quiet. This was where Fran started to work out her own love life.

'I know you think I shouldn't see anyone else now I'm seeing Guy, but we haven't exactly been love's young dream, have we?'

'Whose fault is that? Guy's been champing at the bit since you met.'

Fran looked flustered as colour seeped up her neck. 'Yes, but you know how confused I've been over that,' she said.

'Worse than I was,' said Libby. 'Middle-aged confusion.'

'You're not kidding,' said Fran. 'I still can't understand how anyone remotely attractive could like anyone boring and middle-aged like me. No one ever has before. I'm just not that sort.'

'Neither was I,' said Libby, 'and let's face it, I'm shorter and fatter than you. What Ben sees in me I can't think. But I've now accepted that he does love me, and I'm batty about him, and I can relax. But if you don't really, really fancy either of them, don't prolong it just because it's flattering.'

Fran stared at Libby with her mouth open. 'Good lord, is that what I'm doing?'

Libby shrugged. 'I don't know. I do know that you felt ambivalent about Guy at first because you couldn't believe it was happening, and I'd felt like that myself, but what I wonder now is, has Connell's attention convinced you that you are attractive, so you can play them off.'

'Libby!' Fran looked outraged. 'How dare you. You really can't believe that of me.'

'I wouldn't have done, no, but I think it might have had that effect on me if Ben and I hadn't – er – cemented our relationship, so to speak.'

Fran was silent. Libby got up to fetch the wine bottle and put a pan of soup on the Rayburn. Her own complicated feelings about middle-aged relationships were resurfacing uncomfortably with this analysis and she had to take a deep breath and remind herself that Ben had said he loved her, and done nothing to disprove that, quite the reverse. But she understood totally Fran's slightly panicky, exhilarated feelings, her unwillingness to take anything at face value. She took the bottle back into the sitting room.

'I do understand, Fran,' she said, topping up their glasses. 'Go out with Connell if you want to. Perhaps it would be better if you did. At least you'd know if he really is interested.'

'That's all very well,' said Fran with a rueful smile, 'but I can hardly ring him up and ask him, can I?'

'You could,' said Libby, 'but I don't suppose you would. But isn't he coming round to get the photographs?'

'I think so,' said Fran, looking unsure.

'Well, there you are, then,' said Libby. 'Give him the right signals, then if he asks you again you can say yes. Then you'll know.'

'But he's younger than I am,' wailed Fran.

'Oh, stuff. My only encounter pre-Ben was with someone twenty years younger than me.' Libby gazed at the ceiling. 'I was stunned.'

'Blimey!' said Fran. 'Who was that?'

'Oh, no one you'd know,' said Libby, colouring faintly. 'But

I can't quite believe it even now.'

'I suppose if you can do it, I can,' said Fran, 'but you're much more outgoing than I am.'

'I don't think being outgoing has anything to do with it.' Libby poked the fire into a more satisfying blaze. 'Ben had to ramraid his way past my defences.'

'He's too laid back to do that,' said Fran, amused.

'A subtle ramraid,' said Libby, with a grin. 'Now, how about my nice home-made soup?'

'So who do you think Connell suspects for these murders?' asked Libby, after they'd seated themselves at the kitchen table.

'I suppose it was Danny, originally, and Bella.'

'And now?'

'Not Danny, because he couldn't have killed Dorothy.'

'But he could have killed Laurence and someone else killed Dorothy.'

'Why?' Fran asked. 'That really is far-fetched, Lib.'

'Yes, it is, isn't it. So where does he go from here?'

'They're doing more forensics on the landing outside Laurence's flat, although what he expects to get from that I can't think. And he's intent on finding the motive for the killings to give him a lead. That's where I come in. But I haven't actually been any help.'

'You have. You've pointed him to a connection to Anderson Place. That must have something to do with it, surely?'

'I feel it has,' said Fran, 'but nothing that would stand up in court, as they say. I would have dismissed it before Dorothy died –'

'No, you didn't,' interrupted Libby.

'Yes, but I could have done. But once she was murdered, there must be something that the killer wanted either concealed or found. Can't work out which.'

'He wanted to find something and then conceal it, you mean,' said Libby.

'That's what I mean,' agreed Fran. 'So who could it be?'

'Bella.' Libby offered more soup. 'It's her theatre and she found the body.'

'It's not Bella. But she's connected, somehow.'

'To Laurence or to Anderson Place? Or Dorothy?'

Fran shrugged. 'Both, I think.'

'Well, what other suspects are there?'

'I haven't got a clue. I can hardly ask, can I?'

'You could. When Connell comes to collect those pictures.'

'He won't tell me.'

'Try. Meanwhile, we could find out for ourselves.'

'What?' Fran put down her spoon. 'What on earth for?'

'To find the murderer, of course,' said Libby, looking away.

'Libby, we are not Miss Marples and we have no personal interest in this case whatsoever. It's not up to us.'

'What about poor Danny?'

'He's off the hook now, so he doesn't need us.' Fran pushed away her bowl. 'That was gorgeous, thank you.'

'More? Or some cheese?'

'Cheese would be lovely, thanks,' said Fran.

Libby brought stilton and more bread to the table. 'I must do some Christmas stocking up,' she said.

'I was thinking of that, too,' said Fran. 'I need more gin.'

Libby laughed. 'Get the essentials right,' she said.

After lunch, Libby returned to the subject of suspects.

'Do you suppose there were rivals for Laurence's hand? Or Danny's.'

'More likely to be Danny's,' said Fran. 'He's younger. But if that's the case, I'm sure the police have found them.'

'What about money? Did he have any?'

'He didn't live very well if his flat is anything to go by, but perhaps he just didn't care about belongings.'

'What about his clothes?' Libby lit a cigarette.

Fran looked bewildered. 'His clothes?'

'Were they expensive?'

'How would I know?'

Libby sighed an exasperated sigh. 'Were they Marks and Sparks, supermarket or designer?'

'No idea,' said Fran. 'Oxfam, probably.'

'Nah, not Laurence.' Libby shook her head. 'Think how Pete and Harry go on about my Oxfam look.'

'True.' Fran laughed and leant back in her chair. 'Not Oxfam, then.'

'What we need to do is talk to young Danny again,' said

Libby, flicking ash into the fire. 'I wish he'd hurry up and ring back.'

'Yes, but he's supposed to be telling us about old Jonathan,' said Fran.

'We're not restricted to one subject, are we? We can ask him about Laurence's finances and other friends.'

Fran's phone rang.

'I bet that's him now,' said Libby, leaning forward.

But it wasn't.

'Oh, Inspector Connell,' said Fran, and Libby was intrigued to see her go very slightly pink. 'No, I'm having lunch with Mrs Sarjeant. Yes, I can be home by then. Goodbye.'

'What?' said Libby. 'He's coming round? Did he ask you to lunch?'

'He asked if I was at home,' said Fran patiently, 'and I said I could be home by four. That's all.'

'Oho! The end of the working day. That could be significant,' said Libby, her eyes sparkling.

'Oh, rubbish. Detectives don't have those sort of working days. They work all hours. Remember Murray?'

'He just wanted to get away from Mrs Murray,' said Libby. 'I wonder if she's dragging him along to the panto?'

'I bet she is,' said Fran with a grin, 'and she'll come up afterwards and claim undying friendship with you. That's what you get for being a celebrity.'

'Only inside the Oast House Theatre,' said Libby, with an answering grin. 'Go on, then, you'd better get off to meet your aspiring swain.'

'He isn't,' said Fran frowning at her, 'and it's only half-past two. Can't I stay a bit longer? Danny might ring.'

'Good thinking,' said Libby, standing up. 'Come on then, we'll do the washing up.'

'Thanks a lot,' groaned Fran.

Her phone rang again just as they came back into the sitting room.

'Danny,' said Fran. 'How are you?'

Chapter Twenty

'WELL?' SAID LIBBY, WHEN Fran switched off her phone.

'If we go up tomorrow, old Jonathan will be there. Danny says he always wanders round talking to guests and staff, so it shouldn't be difficult. And he says we can talk to him, Danny, too.'

'But it's the party tomorrow,' said Libby.

'Not in the morning, is it? Have you got to help with anything?'

'I don't think so,' said Libby. 'I'd better ask Ben. I wouldn't like to upset his Mum.'

'Well, I can always go on my own,' said Fran.

'Than you'll only ask about those old photographs,' said Libby. 'I need to be there.'

But Ben absolved her from all responsibility for the party, so they arranged to meet at The Pink Geranium at ten o'clock the following morning.

'My car,' said Fran.

'Of course,' said Libby. 'Romeo isn't up to the job.'

Fran flushed. 'I didn't mean that. I'm still excited by being a car owner.'

Libby grinned. 'I know, and I'm grateful,' she said. 'Off you go, now. Give my love to Inspector Connell.'

'Libby!'

'Oh – and find out what his Christian name is. Can't go on calling him Connell, can you?'

Fran frowned at her and set off down Allhallow's Lane. Libby grinned again and went back inside Number 17. Sidney had jumped up into Fran's abandoned armchair and the fire crackled pleasantly as she spread herself out on the sofa, avoiding the creak, and settled down to think about suspects.

Fran was right, of course, it was nothing to do with them.

Nothing to do with her, specifically, because Fran had been asked by the police to look into certain aspects of the case. But Libby was just an interested bystander, and she had to remind herself of her own expressed views that she hated books where the protagonist was always falling over bodies and had access to all sorts of information denied to the police. Now she was doing her damnedest to become exactly that person.

'Well,' she told Sidney, 'we do know a few things they don't know. We know that Bella's grandmother knew the original owners of the Place.'

But, she reflected, that didn't actually have any relevance to Laurence's murder. Unless Laurence turned out to be a long lost relative who should have been left the theatre, of course. Libby sat up straight to think this one through. But he couldn't be, could he. Dorinda had Aunt Maria and Bella's father Bertram, and as Maria had no children and Bertram only one, that was a non-starter.

Perhaps, she thought, he was a descendant of the original owners of the Place, old Sir Frederick and Ivy. But then Jonathan would know, and surely he would have told the police.

Libby closed her eyes. The police would find the murderer. They always did, and usually without any help from gifted amateurs. She slept.

Inspector Connell arrived promptly at four o'clock. Fran indicated the sofa and took the armchair herself.

'So what have you found out from the photographs?' He leant back, looking relaxed.

'Nothing, really.' She wondered whether to tell him about the proposed visit to old Jonathan, and decided against it. 'I'd like to know who the other person is in the picture of Laurence as a young man, and just for interest's sake, where the holiday pictures were taken, but there's nothing that gives me a clue about who could have killed him – or Dorothy.'

'Well, it was an outside chance. If you have any flashes of inspiration you know where to find me. And so far forensics haven't found anything on the landing.'

'Are there no suspects?' Fran asked bravely. 'Any friends? People jealous of his relationship with Danny?'

He smiled. 'I shouldn't tell you anything, but of course there were people in both those categories. They're all in the clear, though. Mostly clubbing friends of Danny's and work friends of Laurence's. All alibis check out. That's why we're stumped.'

'And why you've asked me,' said Fran.

'Yes, although we did ask you right at the beginning.'

'Only to talk to Mrs Morleigh.'

'Because it was the only link we had.'

'And there isn't one,' said Fran.

'It seems not.'

'I'll give Mrs Morleigh a bit more help with her family research, but then I'm out of it,' said Fran. 'It's nothing to do with me.' She stood up. 'Would you like some tea?'

His face brightened. 'Yes, please. Very kind.'

'So, are you going to come out for that meal with me?' he asked when she came back to the sitting room with two mugs.

Fran took a deep breath. 'I'm not sure,' she said. 'Sorry to sound so pathetic.'

He nodded and put his mug down. 'Just as a thank you for all your help,' he said. 'I do understand, you know.'

Fran let out her breath. 'Thank you,' she said. 'I – er – didn't know if I was being – um – presumptuous. If you know what I mean.'

He grinned at her. 'You weren't. But the elegant Mr Wolfe got there before me, didn't he?'

Fran felt herself going fiery red. 'Well,' she managed to gasp, 'I – er – oh, lord.'

'I'm sorry, Fran.' Ian Connell leant over and patted her arm. 'I can call you Fran, can't I? You're a very attractive woman, as I'm sure you know, and you can't blame me for trying.'

'No.' Fran swallowed and stared hard at her mug.

'I'd better be going, then,' he said.

'Oh, please finish your tea,' said Fran, looking up.

'Thanks,' he said. 'And thanks for all your help.'

'I haven't really done much,' said Fran. She chewed her lip for a moment, then looked back at him. 'I suppose I couldn't keep a couple of the photographs? I was going to try and find out where they were taken.'

He shrugged. 'You might as well hang on to the lot for the

time being,' he said. 'I know I said I'd come and get them today, but to be honest –' he paused.

It was an excuse, Fran thought. And I should be flattered.

'I can't see what good they'll do up in Richmond,' he continued, 'especially as they appear to have been taken down here.'

'What about the birth certificates?' asked Fran. 'Have they traced the parents?'

'They've got their certificates,' he said, looking puzzled.

'No, I mean have they traced the parents' parents? Laurence's grandparents?'

'No, of course not. They wouldn't be alive, and what relevance would it have?'

'It could have. You wanted me to find out about Mrs Morleigh and a possible connection. That connection could be in the past. Not just Mrs Morleigh's past.'

Connell sat forward. 'That's a bloody good idea,' he said. 'Why didn't I think of that?'

Fran laughed. 'Because it isn't normal police procedure?'

'Neither's using a psychic,' he grinned back. 'I'd better get going. I'll get hold of the SIO in Richmond and see if he can set some young DC on to tracing those records.'

'If not, I could try,' said Fran. 'If you gave me the details, of course.'

'I'm sure we'll be able to do it,' he said, and stood up. 'Our name opens doors, you might say.' He picked up his mug and finished the last of the tea. 'I'll be in touch.'

Fran followed him downstairs. 'I'll let you know if I come up with anything,' she said.

He turned at the front door and held out his hand. 'And I don't mind if you call me Ian,' he said. 'Inspector Connell seems so formal.'

'You're a formal sort of person,' said Fran, thinking back to the first time she'd seen him, a glowering presence at a murder site.

'I'm breaking out, now,' he said.

And that's that, thought Fran, as she watched him drive away. She turned and went upstairs to get ready for her evening with Guy, and was conscious of a distinct sense of relief.

*　*　*

Ben and Libby dined at The Pink Geranium that evening and Libby told Ben of her conclusions about the case. Harry came and joined them when he finished in the kitchen and gave his opinion on the matter.

'I think Danny's OK now he isn't under suspicion,' he said, 'but still obviously upset. I hope next weekend doesn't get to him too much.'

'God, yes,' said Libby. 'That's going to be really hard for him, isn't it? Perhaps he could have the day off?'

'What, with Laurence gone? No chance, love.' Harry delved into Libby's basket. 'Come out the back and give me one of your fags.'

'Bit cold out there, isn't it?' said Ben.

'Very,' said Libby, getting up to follow Harry into the kitchen. 'Coming?'

'Even the staff-room has to be smoke-free now the law's come in.' Harry leant against the wall. 'Bloody nuisance.'

'Not for your health, though,' said Ben.

'Don't start,' said Libby.

'So, who dunnit, then?' said Harry. 'A passing tramp?'

'One day there'll be a murder where it really *is* done by a passing tramp,' said Libby, 'and everybody will be so surprised he'll get away with it.'

'How well did you know Laurence?' asked Ben.

'Not terribly well. I knew Danny better. Good bloke, though.'

'Did he ever talk about the Place?' said Libby.

'Well of course he bloody did! I told you, it was his idea we had the partnership there.'

'But did he say any more about it? Did it mean anything to him?'

'What do you mean? Mean anything? He worked there.'

'I know,' said Libby, 'but did he say he wished he owned it or anything?'

Harry stared at her. 'What are you on?' he said. 'Of course he didn't.'

'Oh, OK,' sighed Libby. 'Just a thought.'

'What did you mean about Laurence wanting to own the

186

Place?' asked Ben as they walked slowly home half an hour later.

'I told you about those photographs Fran thinks are Dorothy and Laurence taken outside the Place?'

'Yes.'

'Well, suppose they were children of servants, or something? Who felt they should have had a stake in the place?'

'You've been reading too many novels,' said Ben, and wrapped an arm round her. 'Now, come on. Tomorrow we go all feudal ourselves and I've got to get up early.'

'And I'm meeting Fran at ten, so I mustn't be late either. You're sure you don't need me at The Manor in the morning?'

'No, you'd get in the way. Just turn up at two looking regal.'

'And you're sure it's OK to bring Fran with me?'

'Of course. Unless she's seeing Guy tomorrow.'

'Why? Couldn't he come?'

'Well, he's not village, is he?'

'Neither's Fran, not really,' said Libby, as they stopped outside Number 17.

'But she is living here temporarily, and she's coming as your guest,' said Ben, avoiding Sidney as he tripped down the step after Libby.

'OK,' said Libby. 'Now, do you want a nightcap, or do you want to go straight to bed?'

'Mrs Sarjeant, the things you say!' said Ben.

Chapter Twenty-one

'WHAT ARE WE GOING to do once we get inside?' hissed Libby as she and Fran walked up the steps to the front entrance of Anderson Place on the Sunday morning.

'Find the bar,' said Fran.

'We can't drink at this hour in the morning!' said Libby.

'Coffee,' said Fran. 'It says open to non-residents.'

'Oh.' Libby lifted her chin and put her shoulders back. 'Here goes.'

However, there was no need to find the bar. As they crossed the entrance hall somewhat nervously, Melanie Phelps appeared, today attired in sober black and grey, her startling hair toned down to an almost normal auburn.

'It's Harry's friend, isn't it?' she said, approaching with her hand held out.

'Libby Sarjeant, yes,' said Libby, shaking the hand. 'And this is Fran Castle. Fran, this is the lady who's organising Pete and Harry's wedding.' She glanced at Melanie. 'Civil Partnership, I mean.'

'Melanie Phelps,' said Melanie, turning to Fran. 'And we don't mind calling them weddings. That's what they are, really, isn't it?'

'Of course,' said Fran, looking slightly nonplussed, Libby thought.

'Are you here on Harry's behalf?' asked Melanie.

'Not exactly,' said Libby, feeling her cheeks go warm. 'We were – er – hoping we might see old – um – sorry, Jonathan.'

'Jonathan Walker?'

'Yes. He's the owner of the Place, isn't he?'

'Yes, he is.' Melanie's eyes narrowed. 'What for?'

Libby's heart thumped in her chest.

'We want to ask him if he recognises these children,' said

Fran, whipping the photograph of Dorothy and Laurence out of her bag.

'That's taken from the front, isn't it?' Melanie looked up and smiled. 'Well, I don't know if he'll recognise them, but he'll be delighted to see it. He loves anything to do with the history of this place.' She cast her eyes to heaven. 'Sorry, no pun intended. We do it all the time.' She turned and beckoned them to follow her down the same corridor as before. She stopped at a pair of double doors standing partially open and knocked.

'Couple of visitors for you, Sir Jonathan,' she said, and ushered them inside.

'Sir Jonathan?' whispered Libby to Fran.

The man seated in the red and gold upholstered armchair before the large marble fireplace stood up. Tall and well built, his hair was completely white, but still plentiful, as were his large moustache and eyebrows, which he now raised.

'Thank you, Mel,' he said, coming forward.

'Libby Sarjeant –'

'With a J,' put in Libby.

'And Fran Castle,' continued Melanie. 'This is Sir Jonathan Walker, ladies. They've something to show you. Would you like coffee?'

'We'd love some, wouldn't we?' said Sir Jonathan, smiling on Libby and Fran in turn. 'Thanks Mel. Now come over here and sit down.'

Libby, feeling as though the wind had been completely knocked out of her sails, followed Fran to where Sir Jonathan indicated they should sit on a small sofa. Fran gave her a quick grimace and then smiled at their host.

'It's very kind of you to see us,' she said, 'we didn't want to bother you, just to ask you if you recognised this photograph.' She handed it over, and they watched the old man's face light up.

'Why, that's taken from the old ha-ha,' he said, 'before the car park and drive were there.'

'Do you recognise the children, sir?' asked Libby.

He peered more closely, then shook his head. 'I don't think so,' he said. 'Should I?'

'Was the house open to the public in those days?' asked

Fran.

'When was it taken?' asked Sir Jonathan, turning the photograph over.

'In the early fifties, we think,' said Libby. 'Can you see the sign just behind them? We wondered if that was anything to do with the military occupation?'

'Oh, yes, I see.' He peered again. 'It could be. I can't read it, and I'm afraid I wouldn't have been around much then. I was in my late teens. Either still at school, or officer training. I used to come home for visits, of course. They were back in the house by then.'

'Your parents?' asked Libby.

'The family. My mother, my Uncle William and my grandmother.' He looked again at the photograph. 'Now let me see. Who did you say they were?'

'We didn't but we think it's Dorothy and Laurence Cooper,' said Fran.

He looked up. 'Cooper?'

'Yes, Sir Jonathan.'

'You mean – *our* Laurence Cooper?'

'It was found with his sister's things,' said Fran. 'There are quite a lot of photographs of them as children, and most of them–' she crossed her fingers '– seem to be taken around here.'

'With his sister's things, you say? Was she – was she all right? She came here, you know.'

'I'm afraid she died,' said Libby, wondering why the old man didn't know.

He sat looking at the photograph for a long time. Fran and Libby looked at each other and remained silent until Melanie followed her knock into the room with a tray of coffee cups and a cafetière.

'Here you are,' she said cheerfully.

'Thank you, Mel,' said Sir Jonathan, sitting up straight and clearing his throat. 'I'll pour.'

Melanie left the room with a frowning sidelong look at Libby, and Sir Jonathan pushed down the plunger on the cafetière.

'There is something I remember, now,' he said slowly. 'I should have remembered it before, when the police came.'

'What was that, Sir Jonathan?' said Libby.

'Perhaps there was no reason for you to remember it,' said Fran.

'Of course, that's it,' said Sir Jonathan, giving her a grateful look. He handed coffee cups and offered milk and sugar, then got up and went to a glass-fronted bookcase in the corner.

'Just after we'd moved back into the main house I remember mother and grandmother being in a great taking because someone had come to visit. Well – barged his way in, apparently. We had no staff to speak of then, of course, just after the war, and Uncle William was away, so they'd had to deal with him themselves.' He opened the bookcase and looked through the bottom shelf. 'Here we are. Mother's letters.'

He came back to his armchair and began looking through a pile of fragile-looking papers. *It all comes down to old letters*, thought Libby, *things always seem to be rooted in the past*.

'Yes, I think this must be it.' He smiled as he read. 'Listen. "A most unpleasant man," she writes, "Grandmother and I had to take up your father's old golf clubs and brandish them wildly. He had two small children with him, and we were worried we would frighten the little mites, especially as they didn't appear to be very happy." Then she goes on to something else, but I'm sure there was more.' He shuffled through a few more pages. 'Ah, here it is. I must have written asking about the incident, because this is a different letter. "The man who came to see us was someone we had known many years before, my dear, when I was a young girl. I cannot now recall his name." Oh.' He turned the paper over. 'That seems to be all.' He looked up. 'Do you think Laurence was one of those two children and that man his father?'

'It seems likely,' said Libby.

'And could I ask you what your interest is?'

Wondering why he hadn't asked before, Libby looked at Fran helplessly. But her friend was equal to it.

'Laurence was found in some property belonging to a friend of ours,' she said. 'We also found references to Anderson Place in some documents left her by her aunt.'

'I see,' said Sir Jonathan. 'How exciting. And this aunt. When did she die? Or rather, when did she live?'

'She was born in 1914, and the letter mentioning Sir Frederick was dated 1916.'

Sir Jonathan sat very still. 'Sir Frederick?' he said at last. 'And who was the letter from?'

Libby and Fran looked at one another.

'The aunt's mother,' said Libby. 'Our friend's grandmother.'

Sir Jonathan sat back in his chair and stared into the fire. Libby and Fran sipped at their coffee.

'Sir Frederick,' he said eventually, 'was my great grandfather. He was the Anderson of Anderson Place. He renamed it.'

Libby didn't say she'd already found that out.

'So who was this lady who mentioned Sir Frederick in a letter? Obviously a lady living nearby?'

'In – er – Heronsbourne,' said Fran.

'Heronsbourne? That's near Nethergate, isn't it?'

Fran nodded. 'Don't remember any connections over that way, but then, it was a long time before I was born, of course. And what's the connection with Laurence?'

'He was found in our friend's property.'

Sir Jonathan frowned. 'I can see that there is a sort of link, but I'm damned if I can see what,' he said, looking irritable. 'What were he and his father doing here in the fifties? And why hadn't he told me he'd been here before?'

'Perhaps he didn't remember,' said Libby. 'He must have been very young.'

'It's all very odd,' said Sir Jonathan and finished the rest of his coffee at a gulp. 'I wish my mother was still alive. She'd have known all the answers.'

'Please don't worry about it,' said Fran, 'we just wanted to throw a little light on the matter for our friend, as he was found on her property.'

'Nasty for her.' Sir Jonathan stood up. 'Now, I'm awfully afraid you'll have to excuse me, ladies. I have to go and do my rounds of the bar and restaurant. I always do on a Sunday, you know.'

'Of course,' said Fran, standing and putting her cup back on the tray. 'It was extremely good of you to see us.'

'I didn't have much choice, did I?' he said wryly, and Libby felt her face flame. 'Oh, don't be embarrassed my dear,' he said hastily. 'Melanie knew I'd be interested. And Laurence was a much-valued employee. I am appalled at what happened to him.'

'He was a friend of another friend of ours, too,' said Libby.

'Really? How sad for you all. And what a coincidence.'

'It was rather,' said Libby, trying to avoid knocking over the delicate table as she skirted round it. She stopped in front of a portrait by the door. 'Is that one of your relatives, Sir Jonathan?'

'My Uncle William,' he said. 'A bachelor all his life, which is why the property came to me.'

'Do you still live at the Place?' asked Fran, as they walked together down the corridor towards the front door.

'Yes, I have a private apartment.' He stopped in the hall. 'And this is where I must say goodbye.' He shook hands with them both. 'You will let me know if you find out anything more about –' he waved his hands in the air '– all this?'

They assured him they would. He turned towards the bar and then stopped.

'If you're interested in the family,' he said, 'that is Sir Frederick's daughter, my grandmother.' He pointed at another portrait near the front door. 'Goodbye, ladies.'

Libby and Fran went over to have a look. The woman, a little sad-faced, wore a typical Edwardian high-necked dress with leg-of-mutton sleeves, her brown hair dressed a la mode, full at the sides and high on top. Libby sighed.

'So flattering,' she said. 'I wish I could wear my hair like that.'

'You need rats and a maid,' said Fran.

'Rats?' Libby looked horrified.

'They were tied round the head to pad out the hair.' Fran grinned at her. 'Not real rats.'

'Oh.' Libby returned to the picture. 'She looks nice.'

'Yes,' said Fran, 'but we'd better go if you want to change before we go to the party.'

Libby sighed again. 'Oh, all right.' She turned to leave, cast one last look at the painting and stopped.

'Fran,' she said, 'look.'

'What?'

'The name under the painting.'

The discreet gold plaque attached to the frame read: Mrs Nemone Shepherd.

Chapter Twenty-two

'SHEPHERD?' SAID FRAN. 'THAT'S the name we couldn't remember. The family Dorinda worked for.'

'Exactly,' said Libby, returning to the painting. 'Pity we didn't see this before Sir Jonathan disappeared into the bar.'

'It would have confused him even more,' said Fran, 'and I must say, I'm a bit confused myself. I'm going to have to sit and think about this.'

'Me too,' muttered Libby, following Fran out of the door and down the steps.

'Why can't we go and have another look through Bella's stuff tomorrow?' she asked, as they got into Fran's car. 'This could be a breakthrough.'

'I think I'll have to let Bella know first,' said Fran, putting the car into gear and pulling away across the forecourt. 'But you're right. We'll have to have another look.'

'Are you going to tell Inspector – oh, sorry, Ian – about this?'

'What's there to tell? We've discovered that the grandmother of the present owner of Anderson Place used to employ Bella's grandmother? How on earth could that have any bearing on Laurence Cooper?'

'Suppose you're right,' said Libby. 'Shame though.' She was quiet until they drove down the hill into Steeple Martin. 'But what was he doing there in that photograph? That's what we went to find out. And we didn't.'

'Sir Jonathan read us those bits out of his mother's letters,' said Fran. 'We were very lucky. I'm surprised he didn't just brush us off or throw us out.'

'Mel wouldn't have taken us to see him if she'd thought that,' said Libby. 'He's obviously very interested in the history of the house and family.'

'Well, we might have a lot more to tell him, soon,' said Fran.

'I have a feeling this is all going to get more complicated, and he'll have a right to know.'

Libby looked at her in silence. Fran drove into Allhallow's Lane and pulled up on to the little green opposite Libby's house.

'Are you being psychic again?' said Libby, turning to face her.

'What? No.' Fran tapped the steering wheel.

'Yes, you are. You're doing it more and more often. How do you know this is going to get more and more complicated?'

'Well, it's obvious, isn't it?' Fran continued to stare out of the windscreen.

'Not to me it isn't. All I can see is a lack of suspects for the murder, Laurence's, anyway, I don't know about Dorothy's.'

'Yes, well, I think there might be more to it.' Fran cleared her throat. 'Now, go on, get out. I want to go home and change, too.'

Libby watched her drive back down Allhallow's Lane and went indoors to placate Sidney and change into something suitable for a feudal Christmas party.

The Manor looked even more like something on the front of a Christmas card to Libby as she walked up the drive. A little over to her right stood the converted Oast House which was the theatre, with its large billboard and banner advertising *Jack and the Beanstalk* flanked by two enormous trees from the estate garlanded in multi-coloured lights, which had joined the two silver ones by the glass doors. The two trees standing either side of the Manor's impressive front door and the bough across the lintel had been supplemented by an equally impressive garland. Libby pushed tentatively and the door opened.

Inside, Ben was putting parcels under the tree in the hall and Hetty could be seen through the door to the right in full bustle mode. Ben came forward and kissed her.

'Glad you're early,' he said, 'you can go and help Ma. She's getting into a state.'

'I thought your mother never got into states?'

'No, she doesn't normally. I'm not sure what's wrong, unless it's Dad. He's not too well again, although he laughs it off and calls himself a creaking gate.'

'I'll go and see what I can do. I'll tell her what we found out at the Place this morning.'

'Aren't you going to tell me?'

'Yes, if you want to come with me. Otherwise I'll tell you later.'

After that, Libby had no time to call her own. Hetty barked out orders, Libby obeyed them and eventually, Peter and Harry turned up to help. Ben was everywhere and at some point saw him usher Fran into the library. The tenants and their children ate voraciously and ran wild in the old ballroom and Libby served up glass after glass of punch. Finally, she grabbed Peter as he passed languidly by, and forced him to take over while she went outside for a reviving cigarette.

'Old Het still don't like us smokin' indoors, then.' An old man sitting on the wall by the kitchen garden waved a pipe at her.

'No,' said Libby, as she lit her cigarette, 'although she used to smoke herself, I believe.'

'Sure 'er did,' said the old man. 'I remember 'er in the war.'

'Do you?' Libby went to sit beside him. 'So did you come and see the play about the family that we put on in the new theatre?'

'O' course I did. My daughter would'a made me go, anyway.' He laughed wheezily. 'Good it were. You did it, didn't yer?'

'Um, yes,' said Libby. 'So were you a picker or a home dweller?'

'Home dwellers we was,' said the old man. 'Me mam worked up at the 'ospital.'

'The hospital? In Canterbury?'

'No, up the Place. Fer the soldiers.'

Libby held her breath. This couldn't be true. 'Your mum wasn't Edith, was she?'

'Edith? No, 'er was Lil. Lil 'Edges afore she were married. Arnold, after, like me.'

'So did she know all the people up there?' asked Libby.

'Whatjer mean? People? All soldiers, they was.'

'Yes, but I meant the people who owned the house. They were in The Dower House, I think.'

'Oh, ah. Old Anderson's widder. But my old mum didn't 'ave nothin' to do with her.'

'Oh.' Libby was disappointed.

'Whatjer want to know for? Goin' to do another play about 'em?' Mr Arnold laughed again and coughed.

'Maybe,' said Libby. 'I'd better go in or they'll be after me.'

'That 'Et's a right one, ain't she?' marvelled Mr Arnold, as Libby left him sitting on his wall.

Much later, sitting with her feet up in the library surveying the wreckage of the Christmas tea, Libby was able to tell Fran about the conversation.

'Well, we guessed that, didn't we?' said Fran. 'Sir Frederick's widow still living in The Dower House – she must have been very old, though. And why was the Shepherd woman there, too?'

'I don't know, but Hetty remembers her. She told me about Mrs Nemone when I asked her about the Place the other day. When she told me about Edith the scullery maid. I assumed she was the owner.'

Ben came in with whisky and glasses on a tray.

'Ma says take it easy now, and she'll clear up later,' he said handing them each a glass.

'Oh, yeah? Who does she think she's kidding?' said Libby, adding water to her glass. 'Are you sure you wouldn't prefer gin, Fran?'

'Oh, damn, I forgot. Sorry, Fran,' said Ben.

'No, it's fine, I often have the odd whisky.' Fran smiled and raised her glass to them. 'Here's to a successful party.'

'And a happy Christmas,' said Ben.

'Anyway, we'll help her with the clearing up in a minute,' said Libby. 'I was just telling Fran about my conversation with old Mr Arnold this afternoon.'

'You haven't told me yet about your visit to the Place this morning,' said Ben, sitting on the edge of the club fender. 'Start with that.'

Libby and Fran brought him up to date between them.

'So Mrs Nemone Shepherd used to employ Bella's grandma, and lived at the Place with old Sir Fred and his missus, whom we presume is what's-her-name, Ivy.'

'That what it looks like,' said Libby.

'So what's it all got to do with Laurence Cooper?'

'Sod all, as far as I can see,' said Libby.

Fran looked at the ceiling.

'Come on,' said Libby, poking her with a foot. 'What are you thinking?'

'Nemone Shepherd was Sir Frederick's daughter, wasn't she?'

'That's what Old Jonathan said. Unless she was his daughter-in-law.'

'Shepherd, Lib,' said Ben, patting her on the hand. 'Couldn't be.'

'Oh, no, she'd be Anderson then, wouldn't she?'

'But we never hear of Ivy as Mrs – or rather, Lady – Anderson. Just Ivy,' said Fran.

'We've only heard of her once anyway,' said Libby. 'In Dorinda's letter. Perhaps she is just a maid.'

'Could she be Laurence's grandmother, or something? If she was a maid?' asked Ben.

The two women looked at him with surprised admiration.

'Bloody hell!' said Libby. 'Of course.'

'So his Dad took him there when he was little to visit grannie? That makes sense.' Ben looked pleased with himself.

'Close,' said Fran. 'Very close.'

'What do you mean, close? It's inspired,' said Libby indignantly. 'That's why Dorinda goes to visit her. They both worked for Mrs Shepherd.'

'Why doesn't she say that in the letter, then? Why does she say she visits *Sir Frederick* and Ivy, and not *Mrs Shepherd* and Ivy?'

Libby glared at her in silence.

'Well, I shall leave you to fight it out,' said Ben, standing up. 'I'm going to start clearing up in the ballroom. Those little monsters have wrecked it.'

'OK, I'll start in here, then,' said Libby. 'This is a room you use after all. When did you last use the ballroom?'

'I'll give you a hand,' said Fran. 'Then you can carry on moaning at me.'

'I wasn't moaning.' Libby stood up. 'I just thought Ben had

cracked it.'

'There's still no connection to Bella, though.'

'Not directly, no.' Libby began to stack plates. 'Did you phone her?'

'Not yet. I'll try this evening. Do you still want to go over there again?'

'Yes, of course. It's bugging me, now. I wonder if Harry's had any luck with those old newspapers?'

'I don't suppose he's had time, what with the wedding and everything,' said Fran, rolling up the sleeves of her sweater.

'I don't think he's got much to do for that, now,' said Libby. 'It's just all these Christmas specials he's doing.'

'He was here this afternoon.'

'Still is, I expect. He's not opening tonight, or tomorrow.'

'Or Friday or Saturday.' Fran grinned across the table. 'I don't know how he's tearing himself away!'

'For the love of a good man,' said Libby. 'I'll go and get a tray.'

An hour later most of the rooms had been cleared and the second load of dishes loaded into the dishwasher. Hetty and Greg, their family and friends sat around the large kitchen table looking tired but happy.

'Thanks, everybody,' said Hetty. 'Good party.'

'Do the tenants really enjoy it?' asked Harry.

'They expect it, I don't know about enjoy it,' said Greg, who was looking frailer and more tired than Libby had ever seen him. 'It's part of Christmas, and they would fight tooth and nail to keep it.'

'Ben'll have to take it over soon,' said Hetty. 'I'm too old.'

They all looked at her.

'OK, Mum,' said Ben, and everyone looked away again.

Fran stood up. 'Thank you so much for inviting me,' she said. 'I've enjoyed it, even if the tenants didn't, but I must be off, now.'

'Thanks for gettin' stuck in, gel,' said Hetty, also standing.

'Don't get up,' said Fran, 'I can see myself out.'

'Yer all right, gel,' said Flo, pushing herself to her feet. 'Lenny an' me are going now. We'll walk down the drive with you. Too dark to go on your own.'

Flo, Lenny and Fran all said goodbye and went out into the crisp evening air.

'Not cold enough fer Christmas,' grumbled Lenny, turning up his coat collar.

'Cold enough fer me, you old fool,' said Flo, slipping her arm through his. 'You warm enough in that Harry's flat, gel?'

'Oh, yes, thanks,' said Fran. 'I miss a fire, though.'

'I got an electric one. Couldn't be bothered with coal, but I like to look at it,' said Flo. 'You and young Libby got any further with yer investigations?'

'Well,' said Fran, assuming that Libby had told Flo at least the basics, 'we know that our friend Bella's grandmother worked for someone who lived at Anderson Place, although she wasn't the owner.'

'And what's that got to do with the price of eggs?'

'I don't really know,' said Fran, laughing.

'Well, don't you let that Inspector feller talk you into doin' 'is dirty work for 'im,' said Lenny. 'You just remember what you and young Libby have got yerselves into before. Murder, indeed.'

Chapter Twenty-three

'CAN I HAVE A word, Lib?'

Libby turned at Harry's voice. Hetty had packed them all off to the library and Ben was sorting out drinks.

'What's up?' she said.

'I found something in one of those old papers.'

'You mean you've actually had time to look through them? My God!' Libby patted the arm of her chair. 'What is it?'

'It was a little report about a stolen necklace. I don't know whether it's got anything to do with your new mate, but it mentioned Sir Frederick Anderson, so I thought it might.'

'Necklace? What did it say? Did it mention anyone else?'

'Just that a Mr Shepherd had reported the theft of a necklace belonging to his wife who was the daughter of Sir Fred.'

'Really?' Libby frowned. 'Did you notice the date?'

'It's on the paper. 1903, I think.'

'Which month?'

'Oh, gawd, Lib, I don't know.' Harry made a face.

'Can I come and get it?'

'Whenever. Pete and I are going home in a bit. I'm bloody knackered.'

'I bet you are.' Libby patted his arm. 'It's all a bit much, really, isn't it? Have you got anything else to do before next weekend?'

'I don't think so. That Mel's amazing. She does everything.'

'At a price,' said Libby.

'Yeah, well, rather she does it than us, and we can afford it.' Harry stood up. 'You'll pop in on your way home, will you?'

'If that's all right,' said Libby. 'Thanks, Harry.'

She relayed this news to Ben when he brought her a whisky.

'We won't stay long, will we?' he said.

'No, of course not, they need to relax, but you don't have to come at all.'

'Oh,' said Ben, looking put out. 'Don't you want me to come home with you, then?'

'Don't be daft. I was just saying I could pop in and you could go on home. You might want a chat with your Mum and Dad before you go.'

'OK.' Ben brightened. 'I'll see they're OK, then follow you down.'

Peter let her in, glass in hand, and waved her towards the sitting room, where Harry lay on the sofa, an arm across his eyes.

'What's up?' said Libby, sitting in her favourite sagging chair.

'Poor sod's bollocksed,' said Peter, lifting Harry's feet and replacing them on his own lap as he sat down. 'I've made him do too much. Thank God he's cut down this week.'

Libby pursed her lips.

'And don't,' said Peter, pointing a finger at her, 'say I told you so.'

'I wasn't going to,' said Libby, who was.

'Newspaper,' said Harry, lifting his arm. 'Top one on the pile.'

Libby looked round and saw the pile of newspapers on the dining table. She went over and spread the top one out. Immediately, the little headline leapt out at her.

"Diamond Necklace Stolen from the daughter of Sir Frederick Anderson" it read.

'If you want a drink while you're reading that you can help yourself,' said Peter. 'I'm not disturbing my boy now I've got him to relax.'

'OK, thanks,' said Libby, and poured herself a whisky from the selection on the slightly battered chiffonier. Taking the paper back to her chair, she began to read.

"A diamond necklace belonging to Mrs Earnest Shepherd has been reported stolen from the house which the family, including Sir Frederick Anderson, Mrs Shepherd's father, have taken for the season. We do not believe any of the good people of Nethergate are suspected of this heinous crime."

'Which means,' said Libby, after reading this aloud, 'they

thought it was one of the servants.'

'And your mate's grandma worked for them, didn't she?' said Harry.

'Do you think it was her?' Libby was shocked. 'But she was a governess.'

'Didn't she run off with a pierrot or something?'

'Yes, but we know that she went to see Sir Frederick years later, and she wouldn't have done that if she'd stolen the necklace, would she?'

'What you need is another piece in a later edition of the paper telling you what the outcome was,' said Peter.

'Or something else in Aunt Maria's documents,' said Libby. 'Fran's going to ask if we can go through them again.'

Ben arrived to collect her and walk her home, and she left Peter with the admonition not to get up and to look after Harry.

'Peter's finally realised Harry's been doing too much,' she said, tucking her arm through Ben's. 'I hope he doesn't forget as soon as things are back to normal.'

'He won't,' said Ben. 'Why are we stopping here?'

'I want to speak to Fran,' said Libby, ringing the doorbell. 'I won't be a minute.'

Fran opened the door cautiously and looked surprised to see her visitors.

'Come up,' she said opening the door wider.

'We won't stop,' said Libby, 'but I've just seen a piece in one of those newspapers Harry was looking at. It says a diamond necklace was stolen from Mrs Shepherd and they think it was the servants.'

'It didn't exactly say that,' said Ben.

'Near enough. Anyway, Harry hasn't found a follow up and he won't have time now, so we've brought the papers away.' She indicated the large plastic bag Ben carried. 'But I think we need to go through Aunt Maria's stuff and see if there's any reference to it.'

'I was going to phone Bella tonight anyway, so I'll tell her we need to go over again this week. Tomorrow?'

'Fine. Ring me when you've spoken to her.' Libby gave Fran a kiss on the cheek. 'Bye.'

'Bye,' said Fran, looking surprised.

'What was that for?' asked Ben, as they walked away.

'What?'

'The kiss. You two don't usually. Everyone else does, but you don't.'

Libby thought. 'Right from the start she's seemed a bit remote – aloof, even. Shy, really, and as I've got to know her better, I've realised that's all it is. But she's never seemed the kissy sort, not like us luvvies.'

'You speak for yourself,' said Ben. 'I'm no luvvy. And she was a professional, like you.'

'Not a louche old tart like me, though,' said Libby, grinning.

'That's true.' Ben gave her arm a squeeze. 'Lucky for me, though.'

Fran was also surprised as she went back up the stairs to the flat. Over the months in which she had known Libby, she'd loosened up considerably, she admitted that to herself, but Libby had seemed to know and respect the barriers between Fran and the outside world. Not, she thought, that she minded that Libby had kissed her. She was rather pleased.

She sat down by the table in the window and stared out at the dark High Street. The shop windows, alight with Christmas sparkle, were reflected in damp pavements as wavering columns of gold, and she could just see the twinkling fairy lights in the baskets of holly hanging outside the pub. She sighed with pleasure, remembering the shabby top floor flat in London she had abandoned to come here.

She picked up her phone and found Bella's number in the address book.

'Oh, Fran.' Fran heard a door closing. 'What can I do for you? Have you found anything out?'

'Well, yes, we have. Quite surprising things, actually.' Fran related the findings of the previous week, finishing with the theft of the necklace. 'Aunt Maria didn't mention anything about that, did she?'

'Well, no, but she wasn't born until 1914, she wouldn't have known about it.'

'But she's catalogued everything from when Dorinda first met Peter Prince, hasn't she? So there must be some mention of it somewhere, if it's relevant.'

'I don't see how it can be. She was turned off in 1903 because of her relationship with Peter. Look, do what you want. If you want to go through the stuff again, please do. I'm not going to be able to come down for a while yet.'

'Why not?' Fran was sure she knew, but she wanted Bella to admit it.

'Andrew doesn't like me going down. He says I'm neglecting the family.'

'Does he still want you to sell?'

Fran heard the sigh. 'Oh, yes. He can't see why I should want to live in such a god-forsaken place, or why I want to turn the theatre into a going concern. He says it would cost too much money. The site would be a worth a fortune, apparently.'

Fran was quiet for a moment. 'Would it cost more than you could afford?'

'I don't know quite what the full value of the estate is, yet,' said Bella. 'I don't suppose there's a lot there.'

'Well, Libby and I will carry on for a bit, just in case anything we find throws any light on Laurence's murder. As we now know there's a link between the two families, we might be lucky.'

'That will only make Andrew even angrier,' said Bella. 'He's furious about a murder having happened on our doorstep, as he puts it. He's desperate for me to sell the Alexandria.'

'You can't until probate's granted, can you?' said Fran. 'Or while there's a police investigation going on.'

'No, and you should have heard him shouting at the policeman who came up here to interview us.' Fran heard the suppressed shudder. Bella was having a hard time.

'Why did he want to interview you both?'

'He wanted to know if Andrew had any contact with Laurence before I went to see the solicitor. How on earth he could have I don't know, but I suppose they had to check.'

'Exactly,' said Fran. 'If you'd never heard of Dorinda and Maria until you met Robert Grimshaw, how could Andrew have done?'

'Well, anyway, all he'll say now is he wishes we'd never heard of the theatre or the cottage, so I expect I will have to sell up. If you go over this week, would you check that Balzac is all right? I feel so guilty about that cat.'

'Of course,' said Fran. 'If you like, when I move into my cottage in Nethergate, I'll take him over for you. Unless you want to take him up to London?'

'Oh, no,' said Bella quickly. 'Andrew wouldn't like it.'

Andrew wouldn't like the Crown Jewels done up in gold paper, thought Fran as she rang off. What Bella was doing staying with him she couldn't fathom. Although the children were presumably enough to keep her there, and she wouldn't want to upset the apple-cart so near to Christmas.

Fran had a dream that night. She was standing in the doorway of Laurence Cooper's flat watching a fight. Two men struggled at the top of the stairs, one obviously drunk, the other sober but frightened. As Fran watched, the drunk fell against the door opposite, which sprung open, and he fell inside. The other man, with a quick look over his shoulder, ran down the stairs. Neither of the men was Laurence Cooper, but who they were, she had no idea.

Chapter Twenty-four

Nethergate, Summer 1903

'LADIES AND GENTLEMEN, DON'T forget the name – Will's
Wanderers, next performance three o'clock on the sands, if wet,
under the pier.'

Will Beddowes swept off his pointed hat and bowed to the
circle of his audience. Peter Prince took the box from Algy who
was 'bottling' through the crowd and made his way over to
where a pretty girl in grey stood with three older women who
were obviously in service. The young woman dropped a coin
into the box and smiled.

'Thank you, pretty lady,' said Peter, with a bow. 'Are there
any more at home like you?'

'Oh, any number sir,' said Dorinda. 'Every home should
have one.'

The other three women nudged each other and giggled.

'Be still my beating heart,' said Peter. 'She speaks.'

'I have to, sir, to earn my living,' said Dorinda.

'And so beautifully,' said Peter, trying to lead her away from
her companions, who, however, stuck close behind them. 'Do
you mean to tell me what you do?'

'I am a governess, sir.'

'Peter.' Will's voice came from the promenade above them.
'Bring that bottle.'

Peter glanced up, then back at Dorinda. 'Will you come and
watch our next performance –' he noticed the other three
women. '– ladies?'

'I 'ave me work to do, young feller,' said the oldest. 'Can't
stand around 'ere wastin' time.'

'Ellen?' said Dorinda, turning to one of the others.

'I reckon we've got an hour or so before the missus and Sir

Freddie gets back,' said Ellen. 'You goin' to stay, Ivy?'

'Not 'alf.' The youngest of the three winked flirtatiously at two more of Will's Wanderers who had appeared behind Peter. 'Makes a change to see some real men, don't it, miss?'

Dorinda laughed. 'Ivy, behave.' She turned to Peter and smiled. 'Yes, sir, we'll come and watch your performance for a while.'

'If you can't stay to watch all of it, we perform again at seven o'clock,' said Peter, 'You could come back to watch the rest.'

One of the older Pierrots took Peter's arm. 'Come along, lad. You won't be performing at all if you don't get off quick.'

'And Will don't like it if we're not all there by the quarter, and you don't want to be out of a job this early in the season,' said the other.

'I'm coming,' said Peter. 'I shall look for you then.' He kissed his hand to Dorinda and followed the other two men up to the promenade.

'You stayin' 'ere, then, Ellen?' said the older woman.

'Better keep an eye on these two young things, May,' said Ellen with a laugh and a nudge. 'Missus won't be back before 'alf past four for little Julia's tea.'

'And I'd better be back by then for Sir Freddie I s'pose,' said Ivy.

'I reckon you're more of a nursemaid than Ellen 'ere, young Ivy,' said May.

'Oh, Sir Freddie's not so bad,' said Ivy. 'E's a lively old gent for all 'e's in that bath chair.

'I reckon 'e fancies you, Ivy,' said Ellen.

'Ellen!' said Dorinda. 'You shouldn't say such things.'

Ivy laughed. ''S all right, Miss. 'E does. Leastways, 'e's always tryin' to 'ave a feel.'

'Ivy!' said Dorinda, aghast.

'You watch your mouth, young Ivy,' said Ellen. ''Tain't proper to talk like that.'

'Sir Freddie ain't very proper, 'imself,' said Ivy, giggling.

'No more'n the guvnor,' said May, folding her arms and drawing in her substantial chins.

'Mr Shepherd?' said Dorinda. 'What do you mean?'

'You want to watch 'im, Miss,' May said with a hortatory

nod. 'We've lost more'n a couple of maids because of 'im.'

'I don't know what you mean. Was their work not up to standard? Weren't they suitable?'

The other three laughed.

'Oh, they was suitable, all right,' said Ellen. 'Too suitable. Missus 'ad to turn 'em off 'afore it was too late.'

'I still don't know what you mean,' said Dorinda, continuing to look bewildered.

'Gawd, girls, what an innercent,' said May. 'Ain't 'e ever bothered you, Miss?'

'I've hardly see him,' said Dorinda. 'Don't forget I was only at the London house for a week before we removed here.'

'Well, you just keep out of his way when 'e comes down at the weekend, Miss,' said Ellen. ''E likes 'em young and pretty, and you've got a touch of class, so 'e's bound to try it on with you.'

Dorinda's mouth gaped. 'You can't mean …?'

'Oh come on, Miss,' said Ivy. 'You must 'ave 'ad the odd run in with men in your other 'ouseholds?'

'I haven't been anywhere else,' said Dorinda. 'I was an assistant mistress at a School for Young Ladies – the same one Mrs Shepherd attended as a girl.'

'Ah.' Ivy looked at her thoughtfully. 'So you don't know much about men, then?'

'Ivy,' said May, with a warning nudge.

'Oh, come on, May. Poor girl needs to 'ave 'er eyes opened, don't she? 'Specially now that young bottler's taken such an interest.'

'Bottler?' said Dorinda.

'That young chap 'oo was so interested in you just now, Miss,' said Ellen. ''E carried round the bottle to collect the money.'

'But he was carrying a box,' said Dorinda looking puzzled.

Ellen shrugged. 'It's always called a bottle,' she said. 'And you want to watch them Pierrots, too. They're none of 'em no better than they should be. Only after one thing, like all men.'

May nodded. 'She's right, Miss. Now, Ivy, 'ere, she can look after 'erself.'

'Not 'alf,' said Ivy. 'But you don't know nothing, do you,

Miss? I reckon you need puttin' right.'

'Perhaps I'd better not watch the performance, then,' said Dorinda, nervously.

'Oh, you'll be all right,' said Ivy. 'Tell you what, though, we'll go back 'ome now, and sneak out fer the seven o'clock performance, shall we? Then you won't 'ave to rush off at the end.'

'I can't come out at night,' said Dorinda, looking appalled. 'Whatever would Mrs Shepherd say?'

'She won't know,' said Ivy. 'Come on. Let's get off 'ome.'

Chapter Twenty-five

Balzac was pleased to see them when they arrived at March Cottage the following morning. Fran went round to see the neighbour who was feeding him and explained that Bella wouldn't be coming down until after Christmas.

'And so,' she said with a sigh, reporting the conversation to Libby, 'I'm going to have to take him back to the flat with me. I can't blame the poor woman for going away for Christmas, after all, but she could have told Bella before now.'

'I wouldn't like to have a cat on our main road,' said Libby. 'You'd better let him come home with me.'

'Sidney won't like it,' said Fran.

'I know he won't, but he'll have to lump it. Now let's get on with looking through this stuff, then I'll see if there's a cat basket somewhere.'

Balzac accompanied them into the outbuilding and attempted to help at the computer. Libby scooped him up and put him down by the heater, then began to go through the box files while Fran searched the folders on the computer.

'I don't know what I'm looking for,' said Fran with a frown. 'Most of this is a list of contents for each file.'

'Nothing about diamond necklaces, then?' said Libby.

'No, but there's something here about a letter to Julia. Or maybe from Julia. Wasn't there a Julia in Aunt Maria's letter?'

'Was there?' Libby looked up. 'It was all a bit confusing, if you ask me. What date is the letter? Which file should I look in?'

'1920 to 1925. There's no date next to the letter.'

Libby found the right file and began scrabbling through it.

'Ah!' she said finally. 'Look at this!'

Fran got down on the floor with her and peered over her shoulder.

'There are two letters here in the same envelope,' said Libby, 'one from Julia and one – obviously from Dorinda – back to her.'

'What's the address?'

'March Cottage – oh, I see. Anderson Place. There.' They looked at each other.

'That proves something, then,' said Fran, taking the letter from Julia. 'But, look. This is the reply, not the other way round.'

Together they pored over the two letters.

"My dear Dorinda," Julia's letter read. "I was pleased to receive the news of your theatre and of Maria and little Bertram. I am so glad you felt as you did about my last. Mother and I were very worried, and as I said, she would never have told me had not the unfortunate circumstances demanded it. However, rest assured we made no mention of you. Ivy wishes to be remembered to you and we all wish you well."

Fran picked up Dorinda's reply and read it out loud.

"Dear Julia," it began. "Thank you for being so concerned about us, and for your discretion. Please assure your mother I bear her no ill will, for she is kindness itself. I send my best wishes to you and Ivy, whom I would be pleased to welcome at the Alexandria."

'Well,' said Libby. 'Now what?'

'Isn't there a first letter from Julia? There must be.' Fran began looking through the file.

'Something happened to Julia and her mother that Dorinda needed to know,' said Libby. 'They wrote to tell her, she wrote back and that is Julia's reply. And Julia hadn't known about it before.'

'So presumably it was something that happened when she was a child.' Fran sat back on her heels. 'Dorinda running off with Peter?'

'But by this time he's been dead for eight years,' said Libby. 'What could have happened that would concern him?'

'Unless it's something to do with Bertram. His father was a bit of a rogue. Didn't he go back to his wife, or something?'

'We need to read Aunt Maria's letter again,' said Libby, scrambling to her feet. 'Where is it?'

'Bella's got it.' Fran stood up. 'What about the diamond necklace? Could that be it? Was Dorinda accused of stealing it?'

Libby stared at her. 'Oh, yes! But she can't actually have taken it, or they wouldn't be concerned about her. And she would have gone to prison, wouldn't she?'

'Unless it was covered up. Perhaps that was why she was turned off, not because she ran off with Peter.'

'Perhaps she ran *to* him, rather than *with* him,' said Libby, warming to the idea.

Fran perched on the edge of the computer desk, frowning. 'It doesn't feel right, somehow,' she said. 'We're nearly there, but not quite.'

'And what about Sir Fred and Ivy? Dorinda has been to visit them at the Place before Bertram was born, hasn't she?'

'For upper-middle-class Edwardians they must have been very broadminded,' said Fran. 'Not minding about children born out of wedlock.'

'Perhaps they didn't know she wasn't married,' said Libby.

'They'd have known about Bertram,' said Fran. 'Anyway, that isn't the point. It's what could have been revealed about Dorinda that was dangerous or embarrassing to her that we need to know.'

'But absolutely nothing to do with murder,' said Libby. 'Shall I take a couple of these files back home with me to look through? There must be more we could find.'

'Why not,' said Fran. 'We'll take a couple each – the earlier ones, I think. And perhaps you could look through the newspapers again?'

'OK.' Libby began shovelling papers back into the file. 'There's no real hurry, though, is there? We're only doing this for interest's sake now, not to help a murder enquiry.'

Fran shrugged. 'Suppose so. I wish I could get rid of this feeling that there's a connection, though.'

On the way home, Libby sat in the back of Fran's car trying to keep Balzac from crawling under the clutch pedal, an area which seemed to hold a fascination for him. Fran related her dream.

'And you're sure it wasn't Laurence?'

'In my dream I was sure,' said Fran. 'I haven't a clue who he was. Who either of them were. Should I tell Ian?'

'He might know himself by now,' said Libby, 'if they sent the forensics people in.'

'I'll tell him, anyway,' said Fran. 'Oh, for goodness' sake, get that cat off my neck.'

She phoned Inspector Connell as soon as she got back to the flat.

'I'm not sure I should tell you,' he said, when she'd told him about her dream, 'but you're quite right. Apparently, traces were found which we were able to link to a neighbour, who'd had a row – he says – with an unknown man he saw coming out of Laurence's flat.'

'And nobody had asked him about this before?' Fran was incredulous.

'He hasn't been there before,' said Connell. 'He's some kind of commercial traveller.'

'That sounds a bit outdated,' said Fran, laughing. 'Does he sell nylons?'

'I don't know what he sells,' said Connell, sounding faintly put out. Fran sighed. No sense of humour.

'So, now he's been questioned, what about this other man?' she asked.

'The description doesn't match anyone with a connection to the case so far, and there's no DNA match from the traces found.'

'So, back to square one?'

'Not quite.' Fran heard what she thought might be excitement in Connell's voice. 'We have a very good description, and this chap Brown's coming in to do a photofit. We can show it to everyone and there's a good chance someone will recognise it. We'll also send it up to Richmond to see if anyone up there recognises it.'

'Oh, yes, of course.' Fran thought about it. 'I could have a go, too.'

There was a pause. 'You could,' said Connell slowly.

'You don't want me to?'

'Er –'

'Loyalty. That's what it is, isn't it? You think I might recognise someone and not tell you who it is.'

'How did you know?' Connell sounded surprised.

'It wasn't difficult.'

'Of course.' Connell was grudging. 'What I don't know is why you wouldn't tell me.'

'You think it might be misplaced loyalty. I might have a feeling that whoever it may be hasn't got a connection to the murder so I won't tell you.'

Another pause. 'I think that could be it.'

'If I promise to tell you whatever I see or feel, will you let me have a look at it? After all, I don't want a murderer to go free.'

'All right,' he said. 'I'll call you when we've got something.'

Fran rang off and punched in Libby's number. She was sometime answering, and when she did, sounded out of breath.

'Did I interrupt something?' asked Fran.

'Yes – a cat fight,' said Libby.

'Oh, dear. Perhaps I'd better have home after all,' said Fran.

'Oh, early days yet,' said Libby, 'but please call Bella and tell her soon. This really isn't our problem.'

'I will. As soon as I've told you about Connell's news.'

When she'd finished, Libby said, 'And you've had more thoughts about it since he told you all this?'

'How did you know that?' said Fran.

'I guessed.' Libby sounded triumphant. 'I'm getting to know your methods, Holmes. Connell's told you about Mr Smith –'

'Brown,' said Fran.

'Brown, then, and it's all become clearer in your mind. Am I right?'

'Sort of. I've got to sort it out, but I think so,' said Fran. 'Not that I've got any idea who the other man is.'

'Well, you phone Bella and then sit down and think about it. I'm going to try a bit more cat mediation and then I've got panto stuff to do before tonight. See you later.'

Libby rang off and looked down at Balzac who sat looking cowed by the door.

'Come on, stupid,' she said. 'I won't hurt you, and neither will Sidney.' She held out a hand for him to sniff, and he allowed her to stroke his head. 'Let's light the fire, shall we? You'll like that.'

From behind the kitchen door came an indignant yowl. 'All right, all right,' she said. 'I'll come and light your fire, too.'

She lit the heater in the conservatory for Sidney and shut him in there with a treat of tinned tuna, then lit the fire in the front room with a similar treat for Balzac, who deigned to be pleased. She felt very guilty about Sidney, but promised herself that she would make it up to him as soon as Balzac moved on.

Fran called back to say that Bella was very worried about the cat and would try and get down to pick him up before Christmas, but she didn't know what she was going to do with him.

'Oh, for goodness' sake,' said Libby. 'Tell her not to bother. I'm sure I can cope until you move to Coastguard Cottage.'

'Which might be sooner than you think,' said Fran. 'I just had the solicitor on the phone. Because of Christmas they want to exchange contracts and complete the sale by the end of this week.'

'Blimey!' Libby sat down suddenly. 'Bet you can't believe it, can you?'

'No, it is a bit sudden,' said Fran. 'I can't really organise moving in before the weekend, but as soon as Christmas is over and I can hire a van, I can go. So Balzac can come with me.'

'Well, you won't have much time to go looking into murders or Bella's history, will you?' said Libby. 'Perhaps we'd better put it all on hold. After all, we've got the wedding at the weekend, and Christmas, then New Year and the panto. Too much to do.'

'Maybe,' said Fran, sounding doubtful, 'but if Connell calls me I shall go and look at the photofit, whatever else I don't do.'

'What about packing up the London flat?'

'All done,' said Fran. 'And Dahlia's got the key already for her cousin's daughter who's taking over, so she'll oversee the removal people taking it all out. I'll have to organise that as soon as I can, won't I?'

'Could you be in before New Year?'

'If I can get a firm to do it then, yes,' said Fran. 'Wow. I can't believe it.'

'Neither can I,' said Libby, 'when I think how long probate usually takes. I can't believe it was this quick.'

'Because probate was granted years ago on Uncle Frank's will,' explained Fran, 'so I didn't have to wait for anything. And then there was the trust fund, too. That came through quickly.'

'Lucky rich person,' grunted Libby.

'I know.' Fran sounded guilty.

'Hey, I'm only jealous,' said Libby. 'Cheer up. It's not your fault.'

'No.' Fran said. 'Perhaps I'd better have Balzac here at the flat after all. It won't be for long.'

'Oh, you can't uproot the poor old thing again,' said Libby. 'He's only just got here. He'd have to move again today, then again next week. No, leave him. We'll cope.'

Although, she thought, what with cats, panto, wedding and murders, she wasn't sure just *how* she would cope. 'Let's hope,' she said to Balzac, 'that nothing else happens.'

Chapter Twenty-six

LIBBY TRIED TO INTEGRATE the two cats at intervals during the afternoon with little success, then, after a quick meal of bread and soup, shut them in their respective rooms and went to the theatre.

The lights and heating were on and Peter emerged from the lighting box at the top of the spiral staircase.

'Finished your investigations?' he said.

'For the time being,' said Libby. 'But I've got a lodger cat.'

'I bet Sid the stomach doesn't like that,' said Peter, descending gracefully.

'At the moment, no, but it won't last. Fran looks as though she's moving in to her cottage just after Christmas, and she'll take him with her.' She unwound her cape. 'Is the lighting plot OK?'

'You'll need to sit down with them and make sure they've got all the cues,' said Peter. 'No need until after the holidays.'

'You won't be here, then.'

'Who said I won't? We're not having our honeymoon until after the panto – I told you.'

'Hmm,' said Libby.

The set looked wonderful. Dame Trot's cottage stood at the back of the stage with real straw stapled to the roof (and treated with fire retardant to meet the Health and Safety regulations), a wishing well stood to one side and all was surrounded by a mass of brightly coloured vegetation. Someone was up a ladder attending to the giant beanstalk which was to be lowered from the flies, someone else wandered around with a pot of paint and a brush and the wardrobe mistress stood in the middle of the stage with an armful of costumes and a harassed expression. Libby felt herself settle into the atmosphere as if into a comfortable chair.

After the cow and the Fairy had had their third tussle of the evening due to an unfortunate confluence of wand, wings and udders, she was feeling slightly less comfortable. Then the chorus got the giggles and tripped up the Princess, who landed on her bottom and howled. Libby stomped to the edge of the stage.

'How many more rehearsals have we got?' she demanded. 'And when do we go up?'

There were subdued mutterings and much shuffling of feet.

'You might think this is boring and doesn't matter, but this is a working theatre that a lot of people have put effort into. Also, the public pay money for their tickets and it isn't right to short-change them with an indifferent performance. We're in competition with a lot of other pantomimes in the district, some large and some small, and I want this to be the best. So shape up–' Libby just about stopped herself saying "or ship out" because that would be a disaster. She took a deep breath.

'Right, I'm going to the pub and we'll start again tomorrow. Don't forget you've got a week off between Christmas and New Year, then it's tech, dress and performance. Think about it.'

'That's telling 'em, lovey,' said Harry from behind her left shoulder.

Libby scowled. 'Yes, but I hate doing it. This is a hobby, it's supposed to be fun. You can't sack people or tell them off too much, they'll just walk, and quite right too.'

'On the other hand,' said Peter, coming up on her other side, 'what you said about the public is true. Even after one show, we, and the theatre, got ourselves a reputation, and people are going to expect a professional standard from us. The odd rocket up the jacksie is definitely required.'

'Thanks, guys,' said Libby. 'I'll buy you a drink.'

But before this happy end could be achieved, one more problem was added to Libby's store. As she completed her round of backstage, saying goodnight and checking the back doors, a flustered Fairy Queen appeared before her, wringing her hands.

'Libby, can I talk to you?' she said.

Libby's heart sank. 'What's up, Edna?' she said, as calmly as she could.

'I don't think I can carry on with this,' said Edna, now wringing the edges of her cardigan.

'With?' said Libby.

'The play – I mean the panto.' Edna's breath was coming in gasps now, and her cheeks had turned an alarming mottled puce.

'Are you all right?' Libby put out a hand, but Edna shook her head.

'No, I'm fine. Just a touch of blood pressure,' said Edna. 'But it seems to be having a – well, a – an unfortunate effect on me.'

'You mean it's making you ill?'

Edna looked embarrassed. 'Sort of, and I'm getting clumsier than ever. And I keep forgetting the words, and –' she stopped, obviously thinking she'd gone far enough.

Libby maintained a calm exterior. 'Don't worry Edna. At least you told me before the show. That would have been awful, wouldn't it? If it had made you so ill you couldn't go on?'

Edna nodded gratefully. 'I just don't want to let you down,' she said, 'and I know I would have done.'

Patting her gently and helping her into her coat, Libby saw her off the premises and then walked slowly down the drive. By the time she'd reached the pub, she'd made up her mind.

'Edna's leaving,' she said without preamble to Peter, Harry, Ben and Fran, who sat round a table waiting for her.

The reaction was much as expected, horror, worry and the inevitable conclusion to which she had come herself.

'So you'll be the Fairy Queen, then?' said Peter, handing her a glass.

'Yes. I can't see any other way round it, and I more or less know the words.'

'That costume will swamp you,' said Fran. 'Edna's at least a foot taller than you.'

'My extra foot round the middle will take it up,' said Libby, with a grin.

'So, yet another problem,' said Fran. 'You'll have to leave all the files and papers, Lib. You just won't have time.'

Libby nodded. 'I know.' She sighed. 'And I was really looking forward to getting to the bottom of it all.'

'We might still,' said Fran. 'I told you, I'll go and look at the photofit, and I've got a couple of files I can look through this week.'

'What photofit?' asked Peter.

'Shouldn't you be packing?' said Harry.

'Which files?' said Ben.

Fran made a wry face at Libby. 'There's hardly anything to pack, some of Bella's files from the cottage, and a photofit of a possible villain.'

'Wow,' said Harry admiringly. 'You two do know how to live.'

Spotting the wardrobe mistress on the other side of the bar, Libby went over to tell her about possible alterations to the Fairy Queen costume. The wardrobe mistress looked as though she might burst into tears.

'Will she be all right?' asked Fran.

'As the Fairy Queen? Of course she will,' said Ben.

'It was a part she'd made her own in her old society,' said Peter. 'I first met her when she was a fairy.'

Harry snorted.

'She'll be far better than poor old Edna,' said Ben.

'She wanted to do it in the first place,' said Peter, 'but I vetoed it. I'm not sure about directors being in things.'

'They do it in films,' said Harry.

'But they have first Assistant Directors and second Assistant Directors and continuity people,' said Peter.

'None of which we have,' said Fran. 'But it's virtually all done now, so all Libby's got to do is slot herself in.'

'And make sure she knows the words,' said Ben, smiling as Libby returned gloomily to the group.

'That went down well,' she said, seating herself beside Ben with a thump. 'You'd think I'd done it on purpose.'

'Are you sure you didn't?' said Peter.

'What?' Libby looked indignant. 'I've been nursing that woman along like my own mother. I had nothing to do with her leaving.'

'It was the cow.' Harry nodded sagaciously.

'And the wings,' said Fran.

'And the udders,' said Ben.

'And the Princess,' said Libby. 'I just hope it doesn't throw them all completely.'

'Will you put in extra rehearsals?' asked Ben.

'No, of course not,' said Libby. 'We've got tomorrow and Thursday this week, then a break until Thursday week, that'll be enough.'

'I just hope everything else is sorted before we start the run,' said Fran.

'Everything else?' Harry raised his eyebrows.

'You know. What we were talking about before.'

'Oh, your move? And the photofit?'

Fran nodded.

'And the murder, she means,' said Libby shrewdly.

Fran coloured and a collective sigh went up from the men.

'And I agree with her.' Libby lifted her chin.

'Here we go again,' said Peter.

Later, as she and Ben walked slowly home to Allhallow's Lane, she justified herself.

'Fran was actually asked into this by the police,' she said.

'She was asked to look into Bella's history,' said Ben, 'and I bet that was only because Ian Connell fancied her.'

'Yes, I thought that,' said Libby, 'but nevertheless, she was asked. It wasn't us getting involved like misguided –'

'– Miss Marples,' Ben finished for her.

'Well, yes.'

'Then there was Harry's friend Danny and neither of you could resist it, could you?'

'Harry asked,' said Libby, taking her key from the pocket of her cape.

'Too many coincidences,' said Ben.

'Can't help that,' said Libby, leading the way in and stopping Balzac from escaping through the front door. 'This is Balzac.'

Ben made the appropriate noises and Balzac slunk away to sit in front of the fire.

'Coincidences happen in real life,' said Libby, 'but if you read them in a book you don't believe them. I mean, look at me and Fran and Coastguard Cottage. Who'd believe that, yet it was all perfectly logical. Nethergate was a popular seaside resort in the fifties and sixties, so it wasn't unusual that both of us should have spent family holidays there.' She had taken off her cape and put the kettle on the hob. 'Do you want tea?'

'No, I want whisky,' said Ben, stretching out on the creaky sofa. 'And where's Sidney?'

'In the conservatory, sulking,' said Libby. 'I daren't put Balzac in there because he might damage the paintings. Sidney doesn't bother with them.'

She fetched the whisky and glasses and put them on the side table. 'Anyway, now I've just got to concentrate on the panto, the wedding and Christmas. There's no way I can help Fran, or Bella, come to that, until the New Year.'

'Famous last words,' said Ben, and raised his glass.

The following morning Libby received a phone call from the wardrobe mistress to tell her that Edna had taken her fairy costume home with her, so could Libby please collect it from her. Groaning, Libby agreed and still muttering to herself, looked up Edna's number.

'Oh, dear, I'm sorry, Libby, I didn't think,' said Edna, sounding even more flustered than she had the previous evening.

'When can I come and collect it, then?' asked Libby.

'Oh dear,' said Edna again, 'I'm afraid I'm in the shop this morning – well, almost, if you know what I mean. I'm just on my way.'

'Shop?'

'I work in the animal shelter shop on Tuesday and Thursday mornings.' Edna gave a little giggle. 'Keeps me out of mischief.'

'Er, yes,' said Libby, making a face. 'Where is it? Or shall I call round this afternoon? It's fairly urgent, you see. We need to make alterations.'

'Alterations? Oh, I see, for someone else. Oh dear, Libby, I do feel bad about this.'

'No need,' said Libby brightly, 'I'm going to do it myself, so we'll have to make the costume wider and shorter.'

Edna gave another nervous giggle. 'Oh, well, dear, that's all right then, isn't it? Come round this afternoon – anytime after three. I'll have the kettle on.'

'Lovely,' said Libby, through gritted teeth. 'And where is it you live?'

'I'm staying with my brother at the moment, dear, he had a bit of an accident, so I'm looking after him.'

'Yes, that's lovely, but *where*?'

'Oh, didn't I say? On the outskirts of Nethergate, dear. Canongate Drive. I don't suppose you know it, do you?'

Libby frowned. For some reason, Canongate Drive rang a bell, but for the life of her she couldn't think why.

'Oh, look, dear, it's such a long way for you to come,' Edna rushed on, 'why don't I drop it off at the theatre?'

'No, no, Edna, I couldn't think of putting you to all that trouble,' said Libby, suddenly remembering. 'I do know where it is. Just give me the full address and I'll pop round this afternoon.'

For what Libby had remembered was that Canongate Drive was where old Jim Butler lived. And that, Fran had told her, was also where Laurence Cooper had lived.

Chapter Twenty-seven

'ONE MORE COINCIDENCE,' SHE told Ben on the phone. 'I tried to call Fran to ask her where the flat was, but she's either got her mobile switched off or gone out without it.'

'You're both as bad as each other,' said Ben. 'Would you like me to come with you?'

'If you like,' said Libby.

'Don't sound so enthusiastic. I just thought we might pop in and see old Jim at the same time.'

'Oh, I'd like that,' said Libby. 'But I should really be learning my lines.'

'I thought you said you knew them.'

'I do – sort of, but it's different knowing them as the director and then having to stand up on stage and do them. And I need to know my cues properly.'

'Look, I tell you what. I'll come and pick you up, we can go and have a pub lunch, pop in and see Jim, then go and see Edna. Then we'll come home and I'll go through your lines with you.'

'Sounds like a packed programme,' said Libby.

'Why are you so keen to go and see Edna, anyway?' asked Ben half an hour later, as they drove towards Nethergate. 'You wouldn't be able to see Cooper's flat.'

'I know.' Libby frowned. 'I'm just nosy, that's all.'

Ben looked sideways at her and grinned. 'I know. We *all* know.'

'Oh, all right. But at least I admit it.' Libby looked at him and grinned. 'And I've got results from being nosy, haven't I?'

'Maybe. But then, Fran's got results from being psychic.'

'Which she says she isn't.'

'And the police would have got there anyway,' said Ben, glancing to his right as they passed Steeple Mount and Libby shivered, remembering the Black Mass that had been held there at Tyne Hall a few months ago.

They stopped at a pub not far from Canongate Drive and had indifferent sandwiches, lager for Libby and coffee for Ben, then went straight to see Jim Butler in his big bungalow overlooking Nethergate Bay. He came alone to the front door, and Libby looked round anxiously.

Jim smiled. 'Old Lady's gettin' too lazy to see who's comin',' he said, 'but she's still here.'

Sure enough, Lady pushed herself to her feet and waddled over to Libby as she went to the large sofa.

After refusing offers of tea and coffee, Ben explained that they were calling on someone at the other end of Canongate Drive.

'Nasty new flats down there,' said Jim. 'Not big enough to swing a cat.'

'So I've heard,' said Libby.

'And that bloke got himself murdered down at the old Alexandria? He lived in one of them.'

'Yes,' said Libby. 'My friend Fran told me. You remember Fran?'

'Course I do.' Jim grinned. 'Fine lookin' woman. Did you find anything out about that old cottage?'

'Yes, we did, thanks, Jim,' said Ben, 'and Fran's moving in next week.'

'No! Well, would you believe it.' Jim stood up and went to a sideboard. 'I looked this out after I saw you before. If young Fran's going to have the cottage, she might like this.'

He handed Libby a photograph and an old leaflet, badly colour printed, advertising Coastguard Cottage along with two or three others. The photograph was of Coastguard Cottage with a family standing outside, the paraphernalia of a 1950s summer holiday around them.

'Who are these people?' asked Libby. 'This must have been when I was going to the cottage.'

'I dunno, Libby love. I think we was going to put the picture on the leaflet, but never got around to it. I expect that was when it was sold.'

'Well, Fran will love this,' said Libby. 'Thank you so much.'

They left Jim and drove to the other end of Canongate Drive

where Edna was waiting for them in her brother's flat.

'It's quite inconvenient, really,' she told them, as she settled them in dralon-covered armchairs either side of an electric fire. There's only the one bedroom, you see, so I'm sleeping on the sofa.'

'Where's your brother now?' asked Libby.

'Having a rest,' said Edna. 'He's really shocked after his little accident, especially what happened the other day.'

'Why? What accident?'

Edna looked embarrassed. 'He was – um – questioned by the police.'

Ben and Libby tried not to look at each other. 'Oh dear,' said Libby weakly.

'Oh, it wasn't anything he'd done,' said Edna. 'More what he hadn't done.'

'That wasn't the accident, though, was it?' said Ben.

'No.' Edna blushed. 'It was after that.'

Thoroughly confused, Libby shook her head. 'Sorry, Edna, I'm not sure I understand.'

'It doesn't matter, Edna,' said Ben, shooting Libby a warning look. 'Have you got the costume?'

'Oh, yes, of course,' she said, 'it's right here in this bag, but wouldn't you like tea? I've got some lovely home-made cake.'

'That would be lovely, Edna, thank you,' said Libby, 'if we're not putting you to any trouble.'

'Oh, no, no trouble at all,' said Edna, clearly delighted. 'I don't get much company down here, you see. I really want to go home to Steeple Martin, but – well, my brother –'

'Yes, of course,' said Ben.

Edna smiled gratefully and disappeared into what was obviously the kitchen.

'Are you thinking what I'm thinking?' said Libby softly.

Ben groaned. 'Yes, it crossed my mind,' he said.

'It's got to be him, hasn't it?'

'Not necessarily,' said Ben, leaning forward. 'I expect the police questioned a lot of people in these flats. We don't even know if it's the same block, do we?'

'I could ask,' said Libby.

'I wouldn't if I were you,' said Ben and sat up quickly as

Edna returned with a laden tray.

'Sorry about the mugs,' she said, 'But you know, it's all my brother's stuff.'

'I have mugs at home,' said Libby, accepting one. 'So what happened to your brother? Was he questioned about the murder? The victim lived in one of these flats, didn't he? I suppose the police questioned everyone.'

'Oh!' Edna's hand flew to her mouth. 'How did you know?'

'About the murder?' Libby helped herself to a slice of cake. 'Everyone knows, don't they? It was in the papers and on TV.'

'But about him living here?'

Libby felt the colour rising up her neck and looked at Ben for help.

'He was a friend of a friend of ours,' he said. 'He worked at Anderson Place, where Peter and Harry are having their Civil Partnership celebration next Saturday.'

'Oh, yes.' Edna's colour was heightened again, and Libby could feel disapproval radiating from her. 'Well, yes, that was what it was. You see, my brother was away from home – he travels in stationery, you know – and when he came back, he found out that all the neighbours had been questioned because of Mr Cooper living here, so he thought he ought to tell the police about this – er, argument.'

'Argument?' said Libby, trying not to show any excitement.

'Apparently,' said Edna, warming to her story, 'it was the very day poor Mr Cooper's body was found. My brother was coming home just as this man came out of the flat opposite.'

'Opposite? Opposite this flat?'

Edna nodded. 'That's right. Well, my brother knew that Mr Cooper would normally be out at that time and asked if he was all right, thinking, you know, that he must at home ill.'

'Mmmm?' said Libby, with a mouthful of cake.

'And this man just pushed my brother out of the way and went down the stairs. Made him fall against the door and bang his head actually. Well, the next day he went away to the West Country and that was that.'

'So when did he have his accident? Not when he banged his head?' said Ben.

'No,' said Edna, blushing yet again. 'It was after the police came to talk to him. He – er – he was rather upset.' She looked up to see Ben and Libby staring at her. 'He fell on the stairs.'

'I hope he wasn't too badly hurt?' said Libby.

'Oh, no. A bit of a bang on the head and a sprained ankle.' Edna picked up the teapot. 'More tea?'

Fifteen minutes later, Ben and Libby escaped with the fairy costume.

'A drunk,' said Libby, staring at the doorway of Laurence Cooper's flat. 'I bet he wouldn't have challenged the murderer otherwise.'

'Aren't you assuming a lot?' said Ben, giving her a gentle push towards the stairs.

'It has to be,' said Libby. 'Edna's brother is going to do a photofit. They wouldn't ask him to do that if they didn't think it was the murderer. And,' she said, turning to Ben triumphantly as they emerged into the open air, 'what about that for a coincidence, then?'

'Now that I agree about,' said Ben, unlocking the door, 'but it doesn't get your investigation any further, does it?'

'It's not my investigation,' said Libby, 'it's a police investigation. Fran's just helping.'

Producing her mobile with an expressive scowl at Ben, she punched in Fran's number as they pulled away from the block of flats.

'Hi, it's me,' she said. 'Where are you?'

'At the Swan with Guy,' came the crackly reply. 'Why?'

'She's at The Swan with Guy,' said Libby to Ben. 'Can we …?'

'Don't interrupt them,' said Ben. 'Leave it.'

'Why, where are you?' said Fran. 'I heard that. If you're here, come and join us.'

'See,' said Libby, putting her mobile away. 'Let's go.'

'I thought we were going home to do your words,' said Ben with a sigh, nevertheless turning the car towards Nethergate.

'Oh, I'll be all right,' said Libby. 'I won't do anything but concentrate on panto for the rest of the week.'

'And the wedding.'

'Oh, yes, and the wedding. And Bel and Ad are coming Sunday.' She turned to him with a smile. 'It was lovely of your mum to ask us all to the Manor. Even Fran.'

'Don't say "even Fran" like that,' he laughed.

'Well, what I meant was, Hetty doesn't know Fran that well.'

'But Fran's your friend –'

'And yours.'

'Yes, I know, and she's on her own down here. My mum remembers what that was like.'

'She's lovely, your mum.'

'I know.' Ben took a hand off the wheel and squeezed Libby's thigh. 'So are you.'

Libby snorted with laughter.

'Oh, thanks,' said Ben indignantly, removing his hand.

'Not you.' Libby wiped her eyes. 'I just remembered what she said.'

'Edna? What did she say?'

'He *travels* in *stationery*,' said Libby, and whooped again.

Guy and Fran were sitting by the fire in The Swan with the remains of lunch around them. Libby wrinkled her nose.

'Service is going down in here,' she said.

'They don't get the staff in the winter,' said Guy. 'What'll you have?'

'I'll get them,' said Ben, 'while Libby fills you in on what we've been doing.'

'Coincidence,' said Fran, when Libby had finished.

'But not helpful?'

'I can't see how it would be,' said Fran. 'Ian's already told me about him. Knowing it's Edna's brother doesn't make any difference.'

'Poor Edna,' said Libby. 'I know she was widowed some years ago, but to have to spend Christmas on your drunken brother's sofa is the outside of enough.'

'How do you know he's drunken?' asked Guy.

'Libby's making assumptions again,' said Ben.

'He came home and challenged a stranger who pushed past him. He fell and banged his head. Then, after he was questioned by the police, he fell down the stairs. Sounds like a drunk to me.'

Fran nodded. 'It looked like that to me,' she said.

They all looked at her and she blushed. 'In my dream,' she

said.

'And you've still no idea who the other man is?' said Libby.

'No.' Fran looked out of the window at the wintry sea and Libby frowned.

'Well, I hate to break it up, folks,' said Guy, standing up, 'but I've got to get back to the shop. There's a slow rush on, it being Christmas.'

'We'll just finish our drinks then we'll be on our way,' said Ben. 'What about you, Fran?'

'Oh, I'm going to do one or two things in the cottage,' said Fran. 'I know I shouldn't really, but I've got a key, and we're doing all the legal stuff on Thursday, so I might as well.'

'Oh, that reminds me,' said Libby, searching in her basket. 'Here. Jim looked this out and asked us to give it to you.'

She handed over the leaflet and the photograph. Fran was delighted. 'I shall frame the photograph,' she said.

'Here,' said Guy, 'let me. That's what I do.'

They all left The Swan together, Fran and Guy walking off towards the shop and Coastguard Cottage, and Libby and Ben to retrieve Ben's car from the car park.

'Are they going to make it?' asked Libby watching her friends disappearing into Guy's shop.

'Don't know,' said Ben. 'I hope so. Nothing's certain, is it?'

Libby looked across at him, a worried expression on her face. 'Isn't it?'

He grinned and started the engine. 'Except us,' he said.

Chapter Twenty-eight

FRAN SAT ON THE window sill in Coastguard Cottage and looked out at the sea. This was the view Libby had been painting for several years now, based on the memory of a painting she owned in her childhood, and the view Fran herself remembered from holidays spent here with her mother and her Uncle Frank. Now it was hers, or would be on Thursday, and she was conscious of a contentment she had never previously experienced. She hoped her children would enjoy coming here, although not too often. That could be a problem with the grandchildren, as Lucy might well decide it would be a good idea to off-load her children for a fortnight with granny by the sea. Fran smiled at the darkening sea. No way was she going to let that happen. Lucy would have to learn that she had a life of her own.

Meanwhile, she wanted to focus on something that had come in to her head when they had been discussing Edna's brother and the stranger. She was only just getting used to attempting to control what her family had always called her "moments". When working for Goodall and Smythe she just allowed things to come into her mind and reported on those that seemed relevant, not really believing in any of it. Now, she was seeing that they could be put to work, as they had been by accident last spring and, more usefully, in the summer. She closed her eyes and concentrated.

It was the stranger, she realised. A large man, with a lot of fairish hair. Or maybe grey hair, and wearing a fawn raincoat, the sort that used to be known as a trench coat. She couldn't see him clearly, but she was also aware of Bella somewhere in the picture, and of an overwhelming sense of danger. Her eyes snapped open.

It was almost dark now, and Fran stood up stiffly. Time to go back to Steeple Martin, and time to think about what danger to Bella meant.

As she drove, she tried to make sense of the picture in her head. With a shock of surprise, she realised she had never seen a picture of Laurence Cooper, and wondered briefly if he was the stranger, but instinctively knew he wasn't. So the stranger, the murderer, posed a threat to Bella. Why? He had left Cooper's body in the old Alexandria; was it something to do with that? Something connected the Andersons from the Place to the Cooper family, and there was an implicit connection, too, to Bella's grandmother Dorinda. There must be something that linked them all together. Suddenly, a name popped into her head: "Earnest." Earnest? Fran dipped her headlights as she drove into Steeple Martin's High Street and looked for a place to park as near as possible to The Pink Geranium and the flat.

She was climbing the stairs when it came to her. On his birth certificate, Laurence Cooper's first name had been given as Earnest. Now why was that significant? Was that the name of the stranger, too? Was there a link between these two?

Thoughtfully, she took off her coat and went to put the kettle on. They couldn't be brothers, she concluded, as Dorothy had been Laurence's only sibling. So what other link could there be? Something connected to the past, to Bella's ancestors and the Anderson family? She sat down and put her head in her hands. This was getting her nowhere. Time to forget it and think about something else entirely. She lifted her head and looked straight at the script of *Jack and the Beanstalk*. Well, that was certainly something else entirely.

Later, Libby called the entire company together before starting the rehearsal and informed them of the change in casting. She was uncomfortably aware of the general approval of her involuntary takeover, which made her feel even sorrier for Edna.

'We must get her out of there,' she said to Ben, when they had a ten-minute coffee break. 'She must be so lonely. I bet she loved doing this panto.'

'Then why did she back out?' said Ben. 'She didn't have to. She wouldn't have been that bad.'

'Oh, she was pretty bad,' said Libby, 'but I was minimising

the effect. She would have been much happier as an old villager in the chorus. I wonder who she was particularly friendly with?'

But no one in the cast appeared to have been on those sort of terms with Edna, although one of the chorus members volunteered having seen her in company with some of the ladies who sold programmes and sweets, and someone else said she lived in Maltby Close.

'Flo,' said Ben and Libby together.

'I'll go and see her tomorrow,' said Ben, 'you've got enough to do.'

But Libby wasn't about to let him go alone, and informed him over breakfast at Number 17 that she had already called Flo and Lenny, and they were invited to coffee at ten-thirty. Ben groaned and gave in, and Libby took her toast into the sitting room, where she sat down and called Fran.

'You didn't say anything last night,' she began, 'but there was something on your mind, wasn't there?'

'Yes.' Fran sighed. Libby was getting to know her too well. 'Something to do with Bella, danger and Earnest.'

'Earnest? As in Importance of?'

'Well, not that one in particular, but the name, yes.'

'And Bella's in danger? From Earnest?'

'I don't know. I just got this impression of this big man in a trench coat and Bella being in danger. And after that, the name Earnest. Then I remembered that Earnest was Laurence Cooper's first name.'

'Well, she's not in any danger from him, is she?'

'No, but because of him, perhaps.'

'Is he an Anderson?'

'He could be,' said Fran slowly, 'or maybe I'm just coming at it from the wrong angle. After all, I'm not very experienced at all this, am I? I don't really know what I'm looking for. It's more waiting for inspiration to strike, and it could be totally irrelevant.'

'Shall we go up to the Place and see if we can see old Jonathan again?'

'When, exactly? It's going to be frantically busy up there the week before Christmas, and I bet you haven't finished your wrapping yet.'

'Hmm,' said Libby, thinking hard. 'I bet there's something Harry will need to check for Saturday. I could do that.'

'Libby, you've got the panto to sort out, too,' said Fran. 'Leave it.'

'Oh, all right,' said Libby grumpily. 'But you're to tell me straight away if you think of anything else.'

'Yes, yes,' said Fran. 'Of course I will. Now I've got to get on with packing boxes ready for next week.'

Lenny opened the door to Ben and Libby later in the morning. Flo welcomed them in with a steaming cafetiere in one hand and a cigarette in the other. 'They'll never stop me,' she said to Ben in answer to his questioning look. 'Young Libby's a different matter.'

Young Libby looked sideways at Ben and cleared her throat.

'So what's the problem, then?' said Flo, when they were settled. 'Edna Morrison?'

'Well, yes,' said Libby, and explained.

Flo snorted. 'That brother,' she said. 'More trouble than 'e's worth.'

'Oh, you do know them, then?' said Libby with relief.

'I've known Edna since 'op pickin'. She's younger than me, o' course, but I knew her then. That Eric was always a nuisance.'

'Is he a drunk?' asked Ben. 'That's what Libby thinks.'

'Oh, yes. She's gone over there to make sure he don't go off on another bender. 'Ow he keeps his job, I don't know.' Flo sniffed and poured coffee. 'She ought to come back 'ome fer Christmas. They're all having dinner together in Amy's house, you know.'

'Amy?' asked Ben.

'The warden. They have a lovely time,' said Flo. 'Course, I got me family, 'aven't I?' She reached across and patted Lenny's arm. Lenny smirked.

'So she has got friends, then?' said Libby. 'I was worried about her.'

'And she's worried about her brother,' said Flo. 'Mind you, she could always bring him back here. She's got a spare room.'

'What a good idea!' Libby turned to Ben. 'I'm sure it's her brother that's made her give up the panto. If she brought him back here, she could come back into it.'

'Not as the Fairy?' Ben was aghast.

'No, she wouldn't want to,' said Libby. 'But in the chorus. Like I said last night.'

'You could ask, I suppose,' said Ben doubtfully, 'but I don't see how you can suggest she bring her brother here. It's nothing to do with you.'

'Flo could,' said Lenny. 'Couldn't you, gal?'

Flo nodded. 'Course. I'll give 'er a ring when you've gone. Let you know later.'

'Thanks, Flo,' said Libby, looking as though she would really rather Flo phoned now. 'I feel really bad about her being stuck down there.'

'She still does the shop,' said Lenny. 'In Steeple Mount.'

'Oh, the animal rescue place? Yes, she mentioned that,' said Libby. 'I'm glad she's got something in her life except her brother. And she shouldn't be sleeping on a sofa at her age.'

Flo gave her an old-fashioned look. 'Course not, gal,' she said.

It was after Libby had spent an hour at the theatre with Ben sorting out a lighting problem and reluctantly returned home to finish wrapping Christmas presents that Flo called.

'Difficult, gal,' she said after a discreet cough. 'She wanted to bring 'im up 'ere first off but 'e wouldn't come.'

'But all he's got is a sprained ankle and a bump on the head,' said Libby. 'Surely he could be left, now.'

'I told yer, she don't want 'im goin' on a bender. Says she'll think about it and try and make 'im see sense.'

'Did you tell her about coming into the chorus?'

'Course I did. Sounded pleased.'

'Well, that's all we can do, I suppose,' said Libby. 'At least she knows she's got friends.'

By now, the afternoon was drawing in and Libby had had enough of wrapping. It was nearly all done now, thanks to Balzac being a less interfering cat than Sidney, who had, in fact, finally been released from seclusion in the conservatory and sat glaring at the interloper from the back of the sofa. Libby lit the fire, put the kettle on the Rayburn and took a couple of the newspapers and files to the table in the window, pushing the laptop aside.

She found nothing relevant in either of the newspapers. The files contained mainly postcards, leaflets and the odd letter, some of which were almost undecipherable. Until she found one which looked like a receipt, which read "In respect of goods received the sum of Fifty Pounds. Albert Cooper." The date was September 1904.

Libby sat back in her chair and stared out of the window. Goods? The diamond necklace? And 1904? Surely the news item about the necklace had been 1903? But Cooper. Laurence's grandfather? At least here was a link between Dorinda and Laurence, even if there was no link to the Andersons.

She rang Fran, who said she would be round immediately. Libby decided she was probably fed up with packing boxes.

By the time Fran arrived, Libby had drawn the curtains, stoked up the fire and made a fresh pot of tea.

'This is nice,' said Fran holding out her hands to the blaze. 'Just think, this time next week I could be lighting my own fire.'

'Yes, but you won't be able to pop round here at the drop of a hat,' said Libby. 'And moving in the week between Christmas and New Year won't be much fun.'

'I don't care when it is. Having my own home is just about the best Christmas present I could have.' Fran moved to the table. 'So, where's this receipt, then?'

'Here.' Libby handed it over. 'I'll get the tea.'

When she came back into the sitting room with two mugs, she found Fran sitting at the table holding the piece of paper in her hand, her head bowed.

'Fran?' she said.

Fran looked up. 'I'm learning,' she said.

'How?' Libby perched on the arm of the armchair.

'I tried to focus properly on the piece of paper and let my mind go blank. You know I've told you most things just appear in my head as if I've known them all along?'

Libby nodded.

'Well, I've realised that if I concentrate, I can do it to order. Sometimes, anyway.'

'OK,' said Libby, 'but don't keep me in suspense. What can you see?'

'I can't "see" anything, but I know that this is a receipt given to Dorinda for something very important, something that upset her.'

'The diamond necklace?'

'No, it's something to do with a person.'

'But it says "goods",' said Libby.

Fran shook her head. 'I'm going to ask Ian about the birth certificate they found in Dorothy's house. That's where I found out that his name was Earnest.'

'Do you think Albert's name will be on his certificate?'

'This is dated 1904. He's hardly likely to have been Laurence's father in 1946, is he?'

'I did think that,' agreed Libby. 'I thought grandfather.'

'Yes, that makes sense. I just thought perhaps we could look up Laurence's father and go from there.'

'Will you ring Connell now?' said Libby.

Fran looked at her watch. 'Isn't it a bit late?'

'Policemen don't keep office hours, do they?'

Fran took out her mobile.

Libby went over to the sofa, where Sidney still loomed on the back, while Balzac sat under the armchair.

Fran was put straight through to Inspector Connell, to her surprise.

'We're ahead of you,' he said, 'although I don't know where it's got us.'

'What do you mean, you're ahead of us?' said Fran. 'You've looked up the parents on the birth certificate?'

'Yes. Hang on a minute.' She heard him shuffling papers. 'Here we are. Father, Colin Cooper, mother Shirley.'

'Yes, we knew that, we saw it in Richmond, but did you go back any further?'

'What for? The murder wasn't done by a ghost.'

'No, but you were looking for a connection to Bella Morleigh. If Laurence's grandfather had known Bella's grandmother, perhaps that's the connection.'

'And you think they did?'

'Oh, I *know* they did,' said Fran.

'How?'

'Libby found a receipt made out to Dorinda by an Albert

Cooper.'

There was a moment's silence.

'How do you know Albert Cooper is anything to do with Laurence? Cooper's a very common name.' Connell sounded irritable.

'Isn't it worth checking?' asked Fran. 'Have you got any other leads.'

'Several,' said Connell sharply. 'But yes, I'll get someone to check it. Not that it'll get us any further.'

'Colin Cooper,' Fran told Libby when she'd finished the call. 'He was Laurence's father, and he was in the army. I told you that before. Ian's going to look up his parents.'

'Blimey!' said Libby. 'You *have* got influence. I wonder how long that'll take?'

Fran stood up and went to the armchair, scooping Balzac from underneath it on to her lap. 'No idea,' she said. 'And I'm getting very fed up with the whole thing. I've a good mind to tell Bella we can't find anything else and wash my hands of it.'

Libby nodded. 'You've done what you were asked to do. We could just relax and forget it.'

Fran raised an eyebrow. 'Oh yes?' she said. 'That's what you were doing this afternoon, is it? Once you've got your teeth into something you never let go.'

Libby felt herself going pink. 'Oh, all right, I'm nosy. And it is interesting, you've got to admit.'

'I know, but I'd just as soon forget it now. Except when things pop into my head like they did yesterday. But perhaps I could learn to suppress them, just as I'm learning to focus on them?'

Libby looked doubtful. 'I don't know. I don't think you'd have that much control.'

'Maybe you're right.'

'Well, let's forget it now,' said Libby. 'We've got panto, moving, wedding – all sorts. Unless something else turns up, we needn't even think about it.'

Chapter Twenty-nine

THE THURSDAY NIGHT REHEARSAL was the last before Christmas, and Libby had persuaded Peter, who was the nominal licensee, to open the bar. To her surprise, one of the first people to arrive was Edna.

'I'm so pleased to see you,' said Libby, going forward to take her hand. 'Did you persuade your brother to come and stay with you after all?'

'Yes, I did,' said Edna, 'and I'm so grateful you suggested it.'

'Well, it was Flo and Lenny, really,' said Libby. 'And will you come into the chorus?'

'I'd love to, if you're sure you don't mind.' Edna was quite pink in the face, although not the alarming colour she had been when Libby last spoke to her. 'I was really finding the Fairy too much, you know, but I did love being part of it all.'

That's great,' said Libby. 'I'm sure we'll be able to find you a costume.'

She watched as Edna moved across to join some of the other members of the cast, who were obviously happy to see her.

'There,' said Ben, coming up behind her. 'You've done your good deed. Pleased?'

'Yes, very.' Libby turned and planted a kiss on his cheek. 'And now we'd better get started.'

The rehearsal went as well as could be expected, after which Libby gritted her teeth and stood everyone a round of drinks, and Christmas cards were exchanged. Edna went off happily to Maltby Close, the rest of the cast and crew dispersed and Peter invited Ben, Libby and Fran back to have a last "single" drink with him and Harry.

'Do I have to do anything special?' Libby asked, as she accepted a glass of champagne. 'On the day, I mean.'

Harry gave her a look. 'Apart from holding the rings and the speech, you mean?'

'Speech?' Libby's voice rose in a screech. 'You never said anything about a speech!'

'Stop it, Hal,' said Peter, giving his beloved a poke in the ribs. 'He's winding you up, Lib. Unless you'd like to do a speech, of course.'

Libby glowered at them both and took a reviving swallow of champagne.

'We go in and talk to the registrar first,' said Harry, 'then you're all called in. You come and stand just behind us to the right and hand over the jewellery when commanded.'

'And that's all?'

'And that's all. Nothing mawkish.'

'No words of abiding love, then?' said Ben.

Peter made a face. 'No.'

'Tell you what, though,' said Harry. 'We'd like Lib to come here and go with us in the car.'

Ben and Libby looked at one another, surprised.

'Really?' said Libby.

'In case we forget something or turn chicken,' said Peter, grinning at Harry.

'OK,' said Libby, pleased. 'But I'll get a taxi. I'm not walking the streets of Steeple Martin in my finery.'

'I'll drop you off,' said Ben, amused. 'It means you'll have to get ready earlier than you intended, though.'

'I can manage that,' said Libby. 'Thanks for asking me.'

'Best woman's got to be good for something,' said Harry.

Ben and Libby saw Fran to her door. 'I phoned Bella this evening,' she said, 'to bring her up to date.'

'Did you tell her about Edna's brother?' asked Libby.

'Of course, as it looks as though he might be able to identify the murderer.'

'If it *is* the murderer,' said Libby.

'Oh, it is,' said Fran. 'Quite definitely.'

'And you said there wasn't any more we could do?'

'Yes,' said Fran. 'I don't think she minded. She said she'd be down in the New Year and would collect everything from us then.'

Ben and Libby walked slowly back to Allhallow's Lane.

'What are you going to do tomorrow?' asked Ben, as Libby went to put the kettle on the Rayburn.

'I'm waiting in for my supermarket delivery, then I'm having my hair done. Then I suppose I'll do whatever I can to get things ready for the kids arriving on Sunday.'

'You won't want me around, then,' said Ben. 'What about tomorrow evening?'

'I hadn't planned anything,' said Libby, carrying two mugs through to the sitting room.

'Come up to The Manor and I'll cook you supper.'

'Won't you be in Hetty's way?'

'Not if we eat later than six,' grinned Ben. 'She'll be in front of the TV by then.'

'All right,' said Libby. 'I'd like that. Will you see me home afterwards?'

'Try and stop me,' said Ben, removing the mug from her hand.

Ben had cooked a very respectable beef in red wine casserole for Friday evening's supper, which they ate in the kitchen. Hetty looked in from time to time, to Libby's amusement.

'She still can't understand why you won't move in,' said Ben after the third little visit.

'It's not going to help if she keeps coming in to keep an eye on us, is it?' said Libby.

'She's hoping to persuade you with her chumminess,' said Ben, with a grin.

'Oh, is that what it is,' said Libby, grinning back. 'Well, she's not going to persuade me. I like my little house.'

'Would you move in with me if I bought a house of my own?' Ben sent her a considering look.

'I hadn't thought about it,' said Libby in surprise. 'I thought you moved back here to take over the management of the estate.'

'I did. Once I'd given up the business it seemed like a good idea. Dad isn't fit enough and Mum's getting on. But they don't necessarily need me in the house, do they?'

'Well, no.' Libby looked thoughtful. 'But my house isn't big enough …'

'I didn't say anything about moving in with you, did I? Although I seem to be there more than here at the moment.'

'And it's working, isn't it?' said Libby. 'If it ain't broke –'

'I know, I know,' said Ben, standing up. 'Pud?'

Saturday morning found Libby unexpectedly nervous. 'Why?' said Ben, as he poured tea at the kitchen table, fending off Balzac and Sidney, who had tacitly agreed to ignore one another in peace.

'I don't know,' said Libby. 'I just don't want to do anything wrong and spoil it for them.'

'You've only got to hand them the rings,' said Ben. 'Now, drink your tea and go and have your bath. I'm going home to get m'lady's transport.'

Dressed in her new wedding outfit, her hair pinned up as the hairdresser had shown her, Libby surveyed herself in the landing mirror. It didn't look like her, she decided, although the slimming effect of the dress was quite pleasing. Ben, coming up the stairs behind her, was obviously impressed.

'Everyone will think you're the bride,' he said, kissing the back of her neck.

'Oh, God, don't!' Libby turned to face him, nearly tipping them both down the stairs. 'I'm not going to upstage them, am I?'

Ben laughed. 'I doubt if you could upstage Harry,' he said. 'Come on, time to get round there and soothe the savage beasts.'

'I thought it was breasts,' said Libby.

'Not in this case,' said Ben, handing her bag. She took it and wrinkled her nose. 'Why couldn't I use my basket?' she said.

'Doesn't go with the outfit. Stop complaining,' said Ben, holding the front door open and stopping escaping cats with a foot.

The atmosphere in Peter and Harry's cottage was surprisingly calm. They were both dressed and offered Libby a glass of champagne as soon as she set foot inside the door.

'Only one, though,' said Peter. 'We don't want to be smashed before we get there.'

'So is there anything for me to do?' asked Libby, taking a grateful sip.

'Keep us calm,' said Harry, with a grin. 'Or should it be the

243

other way round?'

'Probably,' said Libby. 'I don't know why *I'm* nervous, though.'

'Fear of the unknown,' said Peter. 'Civil partnerships aren't exactly the norm, yet, are they?'

'Maybe.' Libby looked into her glass. 'I'm very proud to be part of yours.'

She received a kiss on each cheek for this statement, and the emotional level went up a notch or two.

'Quick, have a fag,' said Harry, offering a packet. 'No outbursts yet.'

'I'm trying to give up,' said Libby, taking one, nevertheless. 'I'm down to one or two a day, now.'

'Good girl,' said Peter, 'but not today. Wait until after Christmas.'

The car arrived shortly afterwards, and Libby sat in front with the driver. She was surprised at how many villagers waved at their procession through the High Street, and reflected that prejudice seemed to be far less rampant than it had been only a few years ago. Peter and Harry had fallen silent, and peering over her shoulder, she smiled to see them holding hands and gazing at each other.

Most of the guests were waiting on the steps of Anderson Place as they drew up. Libby felt like a handmaiden to royalty as she followed Peter and Harry into the reception hall and watched them go into the ante-room with the celebrant, a small, round man with a jolly, smiling face, who looked as though he'd be more at home in a red suit with white whiskers. The guests crowded round her.

'They look very calm,' said Fran, resplendent in peacock blue.

'They are. Much calmer than I am,' said Libby. 'I don't know why they needed me at all.'

'Have you got the rings?' asked Ben.

'Here.' Libby patted her small bag. 'I hope I don't drop them.'

But there were no disasters. Peter and Harry emerged from the ante-room, and, according to their wishes, the guests took their places in the large room Libby had seen before, then the celebrant led them in, with Libby following behind. She stood to Harry's right as the service began, surreptitiously feeling inside her bag for the rings and a tissue. Which, she discovered, as she sat down next to Ben after handing over the rings, was just as well, as the script which the couple had settled on with their celebrant was intensely moving. Both tall and blond, their black coats and grey trousers emphasising their height and physiques, they made an impressive picture, and at the end, when Peter kissed Harry's hand and then his cheek, the room was filled with a fluttering of sighs and sniffs, before the spontaneous applause broke out.

Libby and James left their seats to stand beside the table where the register was signed, and added their signatures under a positive lightning storm of camera flashes. Then it was off to the garden room under the watchful eye of Melanie, who Libby saw had attended the ceremony in formal black, not a trace of unusual colour in her hair. She winked as Libby passed her.

'What do you think of the floral decorations?' she whispered.

'Just right,' said Libby. 'Thanks for all your trouble.'

'It's my job,' said Melanie, 'but these two are just dreams, aren't they? What a waste for the female population.'

'Oh, yes. But they make great friends.'

'I can see that,' said Mel. 'Now you'd better hurry, or you'll miss the receiving line.' She made to go, then turned back. 'Oh, and Sir Jonathan's going to look in. He said he'd found something that might interest you.'

'Oh, how kind of him,' said Libby. 'Did he say when?'

'No, just that he'd be in sometime. He doesn't want to intrude.'

'I'm sure Pete and Hal will be delighted to see him,' said Libby, and followed the crowd towards the garden room.

The champagne flowed, the buffet, overseen by a rather subdued Danny, was decimated rather more quickly than anyone had anticipated, and the speeches were short and witty. Peter and Harry paid tribute to their friends and families, or family, Libby supposed, as none of Harry's were there, and she was surprised and pleased to see Peter's mother, mad Millie, sitting between James and Hetty. Looking bewildered, it had to be said, but there, nevertheless.

When Harry turned towards her, Libby's heart turned over. He held out a hand towards her, and Ben gave her a hefty push in the back. 'Go on,' he whispered. 'They want you up there.'

She shuffled awkwardly towards them and was swept into a bear hug by Harry, while Peter kissed her cheek.

'This is our bridesmaid, everybody,' said Harry, 'or Best Person. I'm not sure which, and despite an unfortunate tendency to get involved in other people's business, she's been here for both of us for a long time. So we'd like you to accept this, Lib.'

Peter handed her a beautifully wrapped package, and Libby's throat went tight. She managed a croaky 'Thank you', kissed them both, and amid loud applause, staggered back to Ben.

'Open it, then,' said Fran, appearing by her side.

Inside, the package contained the most beautiful silver necklace Libby had ever seen, set with a large oval cornelian.

'And look, Lib, matching earrings.' Fran stroked the silver. 'How beautiful is that.'

Libby once again had recourse to her tissues and had to be revived with more champagne, brought by Danny.

'By the way,' he whispered, leaning over her shoulder and flicking a glance towards Fran. 'Do you know anyone by the name of Durbridge?'

'Durbridge?' Libby searched her slightly fuzzied memory banks. 'I'm sure I do.' She turned to Fran. 'Do we know a Durbridge?'

Fran's expression sharpened. 'Durbridge? Why?'

Danny stood up straight looking self-conscious. 'Laurence was talking about someone called Durbridge a few days before he – went missing. I've only just remembered. Is it important? Should I tell the police?'

'Yes, do,' said Fran slowly. 'Don't be surprised if they don't take much notice, but tell them anyway. Thanks, Danny.'

'Durbridge?' whispered Libby. 'Why do I know the name?'

'Bella's maiden name, remember? Now why would Laurence know that? Even George at The Red Lion didn't know Bella's name, so how did Laurence know it?'

Libby looked up at her in bemusement. 'I thought we were going to let it lie?'

'Yes, but if this is a clue to the murder ...' Fran's voice

trailed off.

'And you think it is.' Libby stood up. 'I forgot to tell you, Sir Jonathan's going to pop in. He's got something to tell us – or show us, Mel said.'

'Really.' Fran's eyes had gone blank. Luckily, at that moment Guy came over and put his head on one side quizzically.

'And where exactly have you gone now, Mrs Castle?' he said, and Fran snapped back to normal.

Libby had gone on to water by the time Sir Jonathan put in an appearance. He went straight to the happy couple and obviously delighted them by his attention, before surveying the room for Fran and Libby. Libby waved and began to make her way across the garden room.

'Mrs Sarjeant,' he said, 'may I say how charming you're looking.'

'You may, Sir Jonathan,' she twinkled up at him.

'And Mrs Castle.' He turned as Fran came up behind them. 'You were interested in the portraits, weren't you? Did you like the one of my grandmother?'

'She was very beautiful, but rather sad,' said Libby.

'Well observed, Mrs Sarjeant.' Sir Jonathan patted her arm. 'Well, there's another you might like to see upstairs in my suite. It might interest you, I don't know.'

'Who is it?' asked Libby.

'Sir Frederick and his wife,' said Sir Jonathan. 'Would you like to see it?'

'We'd love to,' said Fran. 'When would you like us to come?'

'If you can slip away, we could pop up there now?'

Libby and Fran looked at each other.

'Great,' said Libby.

They excused themselves to Ben and Guy, who both looked resigned, and followed Sir Jonathan out of the room. He led them into a gilded lift cage which took them to the third floor, and then into a large comfortable room which, thought Libby, would have wonderful view in the daylight.

'There,' said Sir Jonathan, leading them to a small painting hanging over a pretty bureau.

It was an uncharacteristic Edwardian painting, of two heads and shoulders, not the traditional one-seated one-standing pose. The gentleman, who looked a lot like Sir Jonathan, was positioned just behind his much younger wife. Libby frowned and looked at Fran, who was transfixed.

'The diamond necklace,' she breathed.

'Oh, yes,' said Sir Jonathan from behind. 'Still in the family. It passed to my mother.'

'And that's Ivy,' said Fran.

'Yes.' He sounded surprised. 'His second wife.'

'Ah.' Fran nodded. 'So Nemone – your grandmother – was the daughter of his first marriage? And she married a Shepherd?'

'Yes, that's right,' said Sir Jonathan. 'Earnest Shepherd.'

Chapter Thirty

'EARNEST!' SAID LIBBY, TURNING to Fran.

'Yes, that was his name.' Sir Jonathan frowned.

'It was also Laurence Cooper's name,' said Fran.

'Really?' Sir Jonathan looked as though he wanted to say "So?" thought Libby.

'I suppose there's no chance there might be a family connection?' said Fran.

'Good Lord, no!' said Sir Jonathan. 'Earnest and Nemone had three children, William, Frederick and Julia. Unless –' he broke off, frowning.

'Unless?' prompted Libby.

'There was another child born – hmm – out of wedlock.'

Fran nodded. 'Yes,' she said. 'Laurence's father.'

'We know Laurence's father was Colin Cooper,' said Libby.

'Do you?' said Sir Jonathan.

'Yes, it's on Laurence's birth certificate,' said Libby.

'So where does Albert come in?' said Fran with a smile.

'Albert? Oh, Albert.' Libby frowned.

'Who's Albert?' asked Sir Jonathan, sitting down with a bemused expression on his face.

'We don't actually know yet,' said Fran, 'but as soon as we do, we'll let you know everything.'

'What?' said Libby.

'Laurence's father,' repeated Fran, 'and who Albert is.'

'Laurence's grandfather?' hazarded Libby.

'I don't think so,' said Fran.

Sir Jonathan was sitting with his mouth open looking from one to the other.

'The necklace,' said Fran, turning to him. 'Are there any stories about it?'

He shook his head. 'Not that I know of. I believe there was

some concern when it was given to Ivy, as my grandmother had it before then.'

'I suppose her mother left it to her?' said Libby.

Sir Jonathan nodded. 'But from what my mother told me, Nemone never liked it much. She said it suited Ivy much better.'

They all looked at the portrait above the bureau. Ivy positively sparkled, and Libby agreed that the necklace suited her far better than the sad-looking woman in the other portrait.

'So, when it was stolen, it was obviously recovered,' said Fran.

'I didn't know it had been stolen?' Sir Jonathan sat up straight looking startled.

'We found an old press cutting dated 1903,' said Libby. 'It was reported to the police.'

'I know nothing about that,' said Sir Jonathan, 'and Sir Frederick and Ivy weren't married until the following year.' He got to his feet. 'If you find out any more, I would be most grateful if you'd let me know.'

Fran was silent as they returned to the garden room. Libby glanced at her a couple of times, but said nothing.

'Where have you been?' demanded Harry, as they walked in.

'Looking at a picture with old Sir Jonathan,' said Libby. 'Did you miss us?'

'I thought you were supposed to be attending to our every whim,' said Harry, throwing an arm round Peter's shoulders. 'Isn't she, Pete?'

'What is your whim, then?' asked Libby.

'Oh, I don't know – a bath of asses' milk, or possibly just another glass of champagne.' Harry held out his glass.

Libby took the glass from his hand. 'Your wish is my command, O master,' she said.

'So what's it all about, then?' she asked Fran as together they made their way to the drinks table, where a white-coated waiter ceremoniously poured more champagne.

Fran shook her head. 'Not here. I've got to think about something. And to be honest, it's more deduction than psychic mumbo-jumbo. Have a think yourself.'

Libby scowled. 'I can't think,' she said. 'And I'm sure we weren't going to do this any more.'

'Hmm,' said Fran. 'But I think we'd better.'

Libby stared at her. 'That sounds ominous,' she said.

'I think it could be.' Fran took a deep breath. 'Now come on, let's enjoy ourselves.'

The local band who had been booked to play during the evening had turned up by this time, and there was no more opportunity for private conversation. By eleven o'clock everyone was winding down and Peter and Harry were seen off to their suite by a cheering crowd, after which the guests trickled out in sporadic bursts.

Fran, Guy, Libby and Ben squeezed into the hired car and set off for Steeple Martin. For a while they discussed the wedding, the ceremony and reception, until Libby said: 'How are you getting back to Nethergate, Guy?'

Ben, sitting in the front next to the driver, turned round and glowered at her.

'I'm not,' said Guy, amusement sounding in his voice. 'I'm booked in at the pub.'

'Oh,' said Libby. 'Well, would you all like to come in for a nightcap?'

'Love to,' said Guy. 'Fran?'

'Yes, thanks, Lib,' said Fran, although to Libby's ears it sounded as though Fran wasn't actually taking much notice of what was going on.

'So,' said Guy after the drinks had been poured. 'What investigations did you two get up to so inappropriately?'

Libby flushed. Fran appeared unmoved.

'It wasn't our fault,' said Libby. 'Sir Jonathan's the owner of Anderson Place and he wanted to show us something.'

'Connected with Laurence Cooper's death?' said Guy.

'No,' said Libby.

'Yes,' said Fran. They all looked at her.

'Really?' said Libby.

'Oh, yes,' said Fran, and shut her mouth firmly.

Before she went to sleep, Libby tried to work out why the portrait could have anything to do with Laurence's death. It was beginning to look likely that Albert Cooper might have been Laurence's grandfather, in which case there might have been a connection with Dorinda, but not with Anderson Place. Then again, there was the Importance of Being Earnest …

Christmas Eve went by for Libby in a storm of activity. Bel and Ad arrived, final presents were wrapped and put under the tree, Sidney and Balzac came to a reluctant truce and sat back to back in front of the fire and there were several panic-stricken sorties to the eight-til-late for essential forgotten items such as tins of sweets which would remain uneaten until Easter.

'Mum,' said Bel with amusement after the latest of these purchases, 'we're not even here tomorrow. We're going to Ben's.'

'There's the rest of the holiday,' said Libby defensively. 'Even if you're not here.'

'We're not going until the day after Boxing Day,' said Ad, peering through a curly fringe from his place on the floor, 'if I can stand sleeping with these cats, that is.'

'I'll shut them in the conservatory,' said Libby. 'They're getting on better now.'

Ben arrived at supper time to whisk Libby off to the pub. She persuaded him to eat first, then they collected Fran and crammed themselves into the bar.

'Any more thoughts?' Libby shouted at Fran over the hubbub.

'Oh, yes,' said Fran. 'But I can't talk about it now.'

'Oh? Why not?'

'I'm not prepared to shout it for all to hear,' said Fran snappily.

'Oh.' Libby felt colour creeping into her cheeks. 'Sorry.'

'Hello, gals,' said a voice, and they looked round to find Lenny piloting Flo towards them.

'Thought I'd find you 'ere,' said Flo, as they found her a seat at their crowded table. Lenny began pushing through the crowd to get to Ben at the bar. 'Something to tell you.'

'Oh? What's that?' Libby leant nearer in order to hear. Flo didn't want to shout, either.

'That Eric. Seems his flat was broken into.'

'No!' Libby looked at Fran.

'I was afraid of that,' she said.

Chapter Thirty-one

'YOU WERE?' LIBBY STARED, mouth open.

'He saw the murderer, didn't he?' Fran looked down at the table, fiddled with a beer mat.

'Oh, God, yes.' Libby's hand flew to her mouth. 'So the murderer thought he would be there?'

'Looks like it, doesn't it?'

'So why 'asn't 'e been back before?' asked Flo, squinting through the smoke of her cigarette.

'Because he's only just found out that Eric's been asked to do a photofit,' said Fran.

'And how has he found out?' asked Libby.

Fran looked uncomfortable. 'I don't know,' she said.

'You do,' said Libby. 'You're just not going to tell us.'

'I might be totally wrong, so I'm not going to say anything in case I am. You could probably work it out yourself, anyway. I told you the other day, it's deduction more than psychic revelations.'

Libby looked puzzled, Flo confused and Fran unhappy. Ben and Lenny arrived back at the table carrying the drinks between them. Lenny had managed to spill his down his front, and Flo tutted at him.

'Silly old fool,' she said.

'What's up with you lot?' asked Ben, looking round at the three solemn faces. 'It's Christmas Eve.'

'Eric's flat's been broken into,' said Libby.

'Oh.'

'Thinkin' 'e'd be there, o' course,' said Flo. 'You know more about it than me, but I reckon it's someone who you've told, one of you.' She looked at Fran and Libby. 'That's right, isn't it, young Fran?'

Fran nodded.

253

'What?' said Libby, aghast. 'But who? I haven't told anybody.'

'We've discussed it between us,' said Ben, 'and all of us sitting round this table know. I expect Fran's told Guy, too.'

'Yes,' said Fran.

'So it could be anyone we've spoken to in the last couple of days,' said Libby, 'but I haven't told anyone else about it, honestly.'

'Don't forget Edna,' said Flo. 'She knows. And she wouldn't think anythink of talking about it to all 'er mates. At the shop, fer instance, or in the Close.'

'Oh!' Libby looked at Ben and Fran. 'Of course! She could have told anyone, couldn't she?'

'But nobody in Maltby Close is connected with Laurence,' said Ben.

'How do we know?' said Libby.

'No, he's right,' said Fran.

'What about the shop? Do we know anything about her friends there?'

'It's in Steeple Mount,' said Flo with a sniff. 'Course we don't.'

'Ian Connell will ask all these questions,' said Fran. 'I don't think we need to worry about it.'

'But it could be our fault,' wailed Libby.

Fran shook her head. There was a short silence.

'Well, come on, everyone,' said Ben, 'cheer up. It's the best night of the year.' He lifted his glass. 'Cheers!'

Somehow, but with an effort, the subject was changed and the atmosphere lifted. By the end of the evening, when an impromptu carol concert broke out, they were all in considerably better spirits.

Ben and Libby left Fran at the door of her flat.

'Don't worry about it,' said Libby, as she kissed her friend on the cheek. 'We can't do anything over the holiday, anyway.'

'I know,' said Fran. 'I feel uncomfortable about it, though.'

'Forget it,' said Ben, giving her a kiss on the other cheek. 'Just look forward to tomorrow. Presents under the tree, turkey, Christmas pud – the works. And us, too!'

There had been some discussion between Ben and Libby as

to whether he would stay at Number 17 that night with Libby's children in residence. Libby was dubious, but Ben said he wanted to wake up with her on Christmas morning, and promised to be very quiet and leave early. As Belinda and Adam hadn't yet returned from their night out in Canterbury, where they had met up with some old schoolfriends, no problems were incurred, so it was with some concern that Ben woke suddenly an hour later to find Libby sitting bolt upright in bed whispering 'Oh, my God!'

'What? What's happened?' he muttered.

'I know who it is,' said Libby shakily. 'Oh, my God. I know who it is. No wonder Fran was so miserable.'

'Who, then?' said Ben, now thoroughly awake.

'No.' Libby lay down again. 'I'm not saying anything until I've talked to Fran. As she said earlier, I could be wrong, and I'd hate to have accused the wrong person.'

Frustrated, Ben, too, lay down again and tried to go back to sleep, mentally cursing all murderers and his beloved's insatiable curiosity.

He left early in the morning, stepping carefully over Adam's body on the sitting room floor, to go and help with preparations at The Manor. Libby came downstairs and sat in the kitchen with the cats and a cup of tea, brooding over the night's revelations, or, at least, what she thought of as the night's revelations. The more she thought about it, the more likely her theory appeared, although the finer details still escaped her. Finally, at eight o'clock, she could bear it no longer and phoned Fran. She was unsurprised when Fran answered immediately, sounding wide awake.

'You've worked it out, haven't you?' said Fran.

'I think so,' said Libby warily, 'although it doesn't seem very likely.'

'Inevitable, though,' said Fran. 'Tell me what you think.'

Libby told her.

'I think so, yes,' said Fran with one of her doom-laden sighs. 'I've just called Ian. I think he'd more or less come to the same conclusion.'

'What's he going to do?' asked Libby. 'It's Christmas Day.'

'I don't know. There isn't much evidence, and they can

hardly get old Eric in to do his photofit today, so I suspect he'll leave it at least until tomorrow.'

Libby heaved a sigh of her own. 'And we still don't know all the connections, do we? I suppose Ian didn't say anything about Colin Cooper's birth certificate?'

'No. I don't suppose it was urgent enough to do anything quickly. And I suppose it wasn't, really.'

'No. I still want to know, though.'

'I think I know,' said Fran, slowly.

'You what? And you haven't told me?'

'It's only guesswork,' said Fran.

'Not entirely, I bet,' said Libby.

'I think I saw something.'

'As in "saw",' said Libby.

'Yes. Like the attack on the landing, although I think that was misleading.'

'True, though.'

'Yes. But this time – well, I think Albert Cooper was Colin Cooper's adoptive father.'

'The receipt!' gasped Libby.

'Yes. I think he "bought" Colin –'

'From Dorinda!' Libby finished for her. 'So Colin was really Dorinda's son! But by who? Whom?'

'Dorinda was dismissed from the Shepherd household, wasn't she?' said Fran. 'Why?'

'I can't remember,' said Libby, frowning in concentration and pushing Sidney off the table.

'Remember the piece in the paper about the diamond necklace, and we couldn't find another report saying it had been recovered?'

'Well, it obviously was,' said Libby, 'because Ivy's wearing it in the portrait, and Jonathan told us Nemone didn't much care for it. Don't know why, though. It looked beautiful.'

'Don't you think it could have been a set-up?' said Fran. 'Dorinda dismissed for stealing the necklace when in fact it was something quite different?'

'She was pregnant?'

'At a guess.'

'By Peter?' Libby snorted. 'I've just realised how ridiculous that sounds, knowing our Peter.'

'I don't think so. Just think about Laurence's attachment to Anderson Place, and those pictures.'

'So, Colin took him there when he was young. What does that prove?'

'And do you remember those letters? Jonathan's letters from his Mum? About the unwelcome visitor? And the ones we found from Dorinda and Julia?'

'Remind me.'

'Julia said her mother, that would have been Nemone Shepherd, wouldn't have told unless – what was the phrase? – the circumstances hadn't demanded it. Something like that. And Dorinda said please don't blame Mrs Shepherd, she'd been kindness itself.'

'Yes – and that was about a visitor, too! Wasn't it?' said Libby.

'I think so. So what have we got? You see, I told you it was deduction rather than my dubious psychic powers.'

'Hang on,' said Libby, hearing sounds of movement from the sitting room. 'Ad's alive. I'll work it out and call you back.'

'I'll be seeing you in a couple of hours,' said Fran, 'don't bother to ring.'

'I don't think we can talk about this at The Manor,' said Libby. 'Tell you what, I'll pop round to you half an hour before we're expected up there and we can go together.'

'What about Bel and Ad?'

'They can go on their own. They know the way.'

Libby found Belinda sitting on Adam in the sitting room and wished her children Merry Christmas. After a pleasurable half an hour exchanging family presents, she sent them to get showered and dressed while she cooked breakfast. Adam, predictably taking longer than Belinda, then complained that his egg was hard.

'Tough,' said Libby appropriately. 'Now you two can clear away while I get ready, then I'm going over to Fran's for half an hour. I'll see you both at The Manor at twelve sharp. OK?'

'Happy Christmas!' she said, as Fran opened her door an hour later.

'You'll have to excuse the mess,' said Fran as she led the

way up into her living room, which was filled with boxes. 'I didn't realise I'd brought this much down with me.'

'You didn't at first,' said Libby, 'you've just added to it as time's gone by. And you had to clear out the London flat, didn't you? Have you got someone to move you?'

'It was easy,' said Fran. 'No one wants to move in Christmas week apparently, so those removal companies that are working haven't got much on.'

'Good.' Libby perched at the window as usual. 'Can I have a fag? I'm hardly having any, now, but it is Christmas.'

'Course you can,' said Fran, 'and you can have a glass of fizz, if you like, too.'

'Blimey! That's pushing the boat out,' said Libby.

When they were both settled with glasses, Libby returned to the subject of Dorinda.

'That visitor was the same visitor that Julia told Jonathan about, wasn't it?' she said. 'And it must have been Colin.'

'So, work it out. Why did he keep visiting the Shepherds?'

'I wouldn't call twice "keep visiting",' said Libby, 'but you're right. There must have been some reason …'

'He found out about his real parentage,' said Fran, watching Libby as a teacher might watch a favourite pupil.

'Oh, bugger,' said Libby. 'Earnest.'

'I think so. It all makes sense. Dorinda is thrown out, and the necklace used as an excuse. I would guess Shepherd raped her, probably because she refused him. There's no mention of him at Anderson Place, so I expect Sir Fred took Nemone and the children with him. Nemone would have known about the rape, and maybe she helped Dorinda with money.'

'Kindness itself,' repeated Libby.

'Exactly.

'So what's Ivy all about then?'

'It looks as though Sir Fred married Ivy. Perhaps she and Dorinda were friends. We don't know. We'll never know any of this unless we can find proof.'

'So Laurence was actually Earnest Shepherd's grandson. No wonder he was so attached to Anderson Place. He must have thought he had a stake in it.' Libby stubbed out her cigarette.

'So did Colin. I don't suppose he realised it was nothing to do with the Shepherds. The grandchildren inherited because they were Sir Fred's.'

'But none of this makes any sense of Laurence's murder. He wasn't killed by any of the Shepherds,' said Libby.

'No, but you've worked that out for yourself.'

'I know, but not *why*,' said Libby.

'Oh, come on, Lib. Money.'

'Hmm. Yes. Horrible.' Libby drank the last of her champagne and slid off the window sill. 'Come on, then. Let's forget it and have a lovely day. Your Inspector Connell will be on it quickly enough.'

Chapter Thirty-two

THE MANOR WAS LIKE everybody's vision of an old-fashioned Victorian Christmas. Libby and Fran had already seen the tree and a lot of the decorations, but Hetty had excelled herself now, and every inch of the downstairs appeared to be weighed down with holly, mistletoe, ivy and candles. The large family sitting room had a traditional Yule log burning in the enormous hearth and a smaller Christmas Tree stood in the corner surrounded by presents. Fran and Libby added theirs to the pile and kissed everyone. Belinda and Adam were already ensconced on one of the sofas clutching glasses, Ben's father Gregory sat upright and smiling in his chair by the fire and Ben himself wandered about with a napkin-wrapped bottle.

At twelve-thirty a horn sounded outside. Rushing to the window, they saw Peter and Harry waving from the front seats of a beautiful old Morgan sports car.

'Wow!' said Ben and Adam together, and dashed out to greet the newcomers.

'So, what do you think of our wedding present, girls and boys?' said Harry, emerging into the sitting room and divesting himself of tweed coat and cap.

'Love the costume,' said Libby.

'Wedding present?' asked Fran.

'From Pete,' said Harry. 'Gorgeous, isn't it? Course, we'll both use it, so it's for both of us, really.'

More champagne was poured, Hetty decreed that present giving should begin and thereafter, Christmas Day proceeded as do most Christmas Days all over England. Lunch was much later than Hetty had anticipated, but the more convivial and jovial for that. Guy, having spent the morning and early afternoon with his mother and Sophie, arrived to pick Fran up, but was pressed to stay, and the evening progressed into a game playing marathon, with charades the top favourite.

Fran and Libby volunteered to make turkey and ham sandwiches during the evening, with a few salad ones for Harry. In the comparative quiet of the kitchen Fran gave a pleasurable sigh.

'This is what Christmas is supposed to be like,' she said.

'If you're not a bah, humbug type,' said Libby.

'Well, I'm not.'

'Where are your kids?' asked Libby, beginning to slice Hetty's home made bread.

'Lucy's with her kids at their other grandparents. The ex is elsewhere, I gather. Jeremy's still in New York and Chrissie's husband Bruce doesn't approve of me. They're spending Christmas somewhere warm.'

'Did they send you presents?' asked Libby curiously.

'Oh, yes.' Fran was chopping lettuce and tomatoes. 'Rachel and Tom make their mother send me a present, because if she doesn't, they think I won't send them any, Jeremy is always extravagant and phoned me this morning, and Chrissie sent me a lovely lavender bath set.'

'Eh?' Libby looked up. 'Bath mat?'

'Talcum powder, bathcubes and soap.' Fran looked up and grinned. 'She is desperately trying to change me into a suitably blue-rinsed matron to fit in with dear Bruce's executive job and lifestyle.'

'You?' Libby laughed. 'Blimey, she doesn't know you very well, does she?'

'No,' Fran said.

'Oh, God, sorry, Fran. That was tactless.'

'No, it was truthful,' said Fran, now buttering massive slices of bread. 'I neglected my kids when they were little because I was concentrating on my career. My mother knew them better than I did for a long time. And look where it got me? A grotty rented flat in London and no future.'

'That's not true, now, is it?' said Libby, tearing lumps off the turkey. 'You've got your lovely cottage, a nice car – and a boyfriend.'

'Boyfriend? Is that what Guy is? Aren't we a bit old for boyfriends?'

'Oh, all right, then, whatever. Not partner, though. You don't live together.'

'No, and I don't want to,' said Fran. 'Now I've got Coastguard Cottage I want to savour it all to myself for a bit.'

'No Lucy and the kids, then?' said Libby wickedly.

Fran laughed. 'Definitely not!' she said. 'They're welcome to come for the odd weekend, but that's it.'

'What about the others?'

'Jeremy will come when he's next over, but that's different. And I can't see Bruce wanting to come. They might come for a flying visit, I suppose.'

'Is he that bad?' said Libby.

'Actually, although I know we're not supposed to be talking about this today, but he's exactly as I imagine Orrible Andrew to be.'

'Oh.' They both stopped working and looked at each other. Then Libby picked up the sliced ham and began to assemble the sandwiches. 'It is him, isn't it?' she said finally.

'Who else can it be?' said Fran. 'He must have intercepted a call from Laurence to Bella and decided that he would come between them and the money from the site. And then he went to the flat and found out about Dorothy.'

'Where does Dorothy come in?'

'I suppose Laurence must have told him Dorothy was also due part of the money. Something like that. So he had to kill her, too.'

'Birth certificate, too. Bet he looked for that and couldn't find it, so thought it must be at Dorothy's.'

'And Eric's flat is the clincher. As you said, who else could it possibly be? Bella's known everything we've done all the way through, and would have told Andrew.'

'Although I thought she was getting a bit stronger,' said Fran. 'She seemed quite determined to come and live in March Cottage and do up the Alexandria.'

'This is why you felt she was in danger from Andrew?'

'I suppose so.' Fran had her uncomfortable face on now. 'Although I'm not sure of any of this. It's pure speculation.'

'But you said Connell had come to the same conclusion,' said Libby, frowning as she tried to cut through a tower of sandwiches.

'More or less. He was very cagey, though. I suppose he would be, wouldn't he. I haven't exactly impressed him with my infallible insights.'

'Well, nothing we can do right now,' said Libby. 'Could we perhaps give Bella a ring tomorrow? Or the day after?'

'It might be rather inappropriate if her husband's just been arrested,' said Fran. 'Perhaps we just ought to take the files and the newspapers back and leave it at that.'

'She'll want to know about Laurence and the family, though, won't she? After all, they're – or they were – cousins.'

'If Andrew worked it out, she could.'

'But Andrew didn't work it out, did he? Laurence told him.'

'Yes.' Fran looked thoughtful again.

'Hoy, you two! How long are those sandwiches going to be?' Harry appeared in the doorway. 'I said you should have let me make them.'

'No work for the newly-weds,' said Libby. 'You can help carry in, though.'

Fran and Libby had no more opportunity to talk about their suspicions that evening, and eventually, the party broke up and they all went their separate ways.

'Do you think Guy will stay with Fran tonight?' Libby asked Ben, as they strolled down the Manor drive behind Belinda and Adam, who professed to have had one of the best Christmases ever, to Hetty's unsuccessfully concealed delight.

'I don't know and I don't want to know,' said Ben. 'Don't be such a nosy old cow.'

'She says she doesn't want to live with anyone once she's moved in to Coastguard Cottage.'

'Well, of course she doesn't,' said Ben. 'You don't want to live with me, do you? You want Number 17 all to yourself.'

'Mmm.' Libby thought about it. 'But with Guy literally just down the road, won't it be a temptation? For him to stay over, I mean.'

'More for him than her. He could get a bit too presumptuous.'

'She doesn't feel the same about him as I feel about you,' said Libby.

'Really?' Ben gave her shoulders a squeeze.

'Well, she hasn't had the practice.' Libby poked him in the ribs. 'Anyway, I'm a sucker.'

Boxing Day was spent quietly. Libby invited Fran – and Guy, as he still appeared to be around – to a buffet lunch of traditional cold meats and pickles, which Belinda and Adam said they enjoyed more than Christmas dinner itself. Before Fran and Guy arrived, she collected all the material they had taken from Bella's cottage and piled it into the conservatory.

Fran spotted it as she was helping clear away after lunch.

'Shall we take it back tomorrow?' she asked, pausing with an armful of dirty plates.

'If you want to,' said Libby. 'Did you phone her?'

'No, I felt awkward,' said Fran. 'I know it's not my fault if her husband killed somebody, but I shall feel responsible. After all, we did point Ian in the direction of Laurence's father and his connection with Bella, didn't we?'

'Didn't *you*, you mean,' said Libby, plunging her arms into the sink. 'And are we going to try and find out if we're right about Colin being Dorinda's?'

'I don't think we can,' said Fran, 'not unless we go through all that stuff in the files page by page. And I still don't think we'd find anything conclusive. She obviously didn't keep a diary, did she?'

Libby sighed. 'No. So that's that. Unless Bella finds anything later and lets us know.'

'She may want to wash her hands of the whole thing,' said Fran. 'I think I would if I was her.'

'So,' said Libby, after a pause. 'How come Guy's here today?'

'You invited him,' said Fran in surprise.

'Because he was there when I phoned,' said Libby.

'He spent the night on the sofa,' said Fran, blushing.

'On your sofa?' Libby's voice rose. 'Impossible.'

'That's what he said,' said Fran.

Libby turned round, folding soapy arms. 'Come on, Fran. Tell all.'

Fran's colour deepened. 'He couldn't drive home, could he?

After all that drink Hetty kept giving us. So I offered him the sofa. He could hardly go to the pub at that time of night, they'd closed.'

'Is that all?'

'Yes.' Fran looked her friend straight in the eye. 'He didn't sleep with me, Lib. I was tempted, believe me, but when it came to the crunch I was just too scared.'

'Mm.' Libby turned back to the sink. 'You'll have to get over it sometime unless you want to dwindle into an old maid.'

'I couldn't be that, could I? I've already had kids.'

'You know what I mean,' said Libby. 'Just think, no sex for the rest of your life.'

'I've done without it for the last few years, and I'm no spring chicken,' said Fran, bending her face to the plate she was drying so that Libby couldn't see her expression. 'I don't see why I shouldn't go on like that.'

Libby looked severely over her shoulder. 'Oh, yeah?' she said.

Opting to take Romeo the Renault the following morning as there was more room for the bulky files and newspapers, Libby picked Fran up and immediately enquired about Guy's whereabouts.

'If you noticed,' said Fran, buckling herself in to the slightly unsteady passenger seat, 'he didn't drink more than a glass of wine yesterday, so he drove home. He was spending the evening with his mother.'

'I didn't know he had a mother,' said Libby, pulling out into the High Street with an alarming jerk.

'She's quite old,' said Fran. 'He and Sophie had lunch with her on Christmas Day.'

'Is she in a home?' asked Libby, thinking of The Laurels, where Fran's aunt had died last summer.

'No, she lives alone. Quite independent, apparently.'

'Is he going to take you to meet her?'

'I don't know,' said Fran testily. 'Just leave it, Libby.'

Libby pulled a face and concentrated on driving.

March Cottage was cold, and the room at the back even colder. Libby put on the heater while Fran turned on the computer.

'Why are you doing that?' asked Libby. 'I thought we were only coming to put the stuff back?'

'Just wanted to update the folders on the computer to clarify it for Bella, whenever she wants to look at it. Easier than going through all that stuff.'

They carried all the folders and newspapers back inside and began to put them back in date order.

'Hey! Look!' said Libby suddenly, as she opened a folder to check the date it started.

'What?'

'Why didn't we see this before?' Libby held out a letter written in a spidery, brownish ink on thin paper.

Fran came over to look.

'My God,' she whispered, as she read it. 'It's from Ivy.'

Libby was reading over her shoulder. 'And if only we'd found it first.'

Fran frowned up at her. 'Why didn't we?'

'I don't know, do I?' Libby shrugged. 'We didn't look in this folder.'

'Why didn't we?'

'Because – oh, for goodness' sake, I don't remember! You tell me.'

Fran returned to the folder. 'Look. It's out of order. There's more leaflets here, and a cutting advertising piano lessons. They're dated before this letter.'

They looked at each other in silence.

'Perhaps Bella's been down,' suggested Libby. 'Without telling us. Perhaps she wanted to get away from Orrible Andrew.'

'She told me she couldn't get away until after Christmas,' said Fran.

'Well –' Libby frowned in concentration, 'perhaps he came down –' She stopped as the thought struck them both at the same time.

'Oh, God,' said Fran, as the door opened.

Chapter Thirty-three

'OH, IT'S YOU,' SAID Libby weakly.

'Who did you think it would be?' Bella came in and perched on the counter by the side of the computer.

'No one,' said Fran, 'it's just that we didn't expect you.' She peered into Bella's face. 'Are you all right?'

'Fine, thank you,' said Bella, pulling off her gloves. 'Did you both have a nice Christmas?'

'Yes, thanks. Did you? Oh …' Libby looked nervously at Fran.

'Yes, well, as good as can be expected,' said Bella, with a slight smile. 'You know.'

'Yes.' Fran put the letter back into the folder. 'I was going to ring you today. We brought all the stuff back. I don't think there's anything more we can tell you.'

Bella sighed. 'Oh, well, never mind. I thought about it all over Christmas and talked it over with Andrew.'

Libby and Fran exchanged a furtive look.

'I think he's right, actually. I wouldn't really know what to do with the Alexandria, so I'm going to ask Mr Grimshaw to go ahead with the sale of the site after all. I don't feel the same really, after that man was found there.'

'We found out who he was,' said Libby gently.

'I know. Laurence Cooper. You told me.'

Fran glanced at Libby. 'No, what Libby means – and I was going to break it to you more gently – is that Laurence was actually your cousin.'

'My –' Bella's face was completely blank.

'Shall I go and make some tea?' asked Libby, scrambling to her feet. 'It must be a shock.'

'No, no.' Bella seemed to pull herself together. 'Please – tell me.'

267

Fran embarked on the story of Laurence Cooper, his father Colin, and the receipt for fifty pounds. Libby filled in all the extra details, including Anderson Place, the diamond necklace and finally, Ivy.

'And this is the letter we've just found,' said Fran, holding it out.

'Could you – could you read it?' Bella was pale, and Libby hovered from one foot to the other wondering whether to make a dash for the kitchen and a glass of water, or simply position herself to catch her if she fell.

'Here goes, then,' said Fran, and adjusted her reading glasses.

'"Dorinda dear, it was good of you to let us all know how you go on. You know dear, my old Sir Freddie is as good as his word and we are to be married next month. How we would like you to be with us, but I daresay you wouldn't like it. May and Ellen still don't like it much, either, but we're all going off to the new place together, so that's all right. Mrs S and Julia will come too, and the boys in the holidays of course, and Sir Freddie's having it done up lovely and calling it Anderson Place. And I shall be Lady Ivy! Fancy that, dear.

'"We was so sorry about the little boy. It must have hurt you terrible to have to give him away, although he was such a reminder of that terrible time, dear. Mrs S wishes she could have done more, I know, and won't have Mr S's name mentioned. Well, you can hardly blame her, can you. No blame at all to you, though, dear. And to tell everyone you took my necklace. He was no good, dear. No good at all.

'"May says to tell you she knows Albert Cooper and his wife and they are good people. Your little boy won't want for nothing.

'"Keep in touch won't you, dear, and let us know if we can help you and Peter in any way.

'"With love from all here, your affectionate Lady Ivy!!!"'

Fran looked up to see Bella swaying in her chair. Libby leapt forward and put a steadying hand on her shoulder.

'Shall I go and make that tea?' asked Libby.

'I'd rather have a drink,' said Bella, in a strangled voice.

'Let's go into the cottage, then,' said Fran. 'Have you got

anything to drink in there?'

'Let's go to the pub,' said Bella. 'I don't want to be here.'

Fran looked at Libby. 'All right,' she said. 'Come on, Lib, let's lock up here.'

Five minutes later they were walking up the road to the pub. George welcomed them delightedly from behind some dangling tinsel and flashing lights.

'Going to move in then, are you?' he asked Bella, as he put a double whisky in front of her.

'I don't think so,' she said.

'Oh.' George looked disappointed. 'Not even as a weekend cottage? We'd keep an eye on it for you?'

'No.' Libby could have sworn Bella looked frightened. Fran was staring at her intently.

'What about tonight?' Libby said. 'Were you going to stay here tonight?'

Bella swallowed some whisky. 'Yes. Yes, I was. I – I suppose I still can.'

'Shall I pop back and light the fire? Warm it up for you?' said Libby.

'No – I'll be fine, thank you, Libby.' Bella sat up straight on her bar stool. 'It was a bit of a shock that's all. To find out that there was a connection after all. That it was true.'

'Well, that's what we wanted to find out, wasn't it?' said Fran. 'That's why Inspector Connell asked me to help.'

'Yes.' Bella looked close to tears. 'And now it's all over.'

'You've still got the cottage,' said Libby. 'I bet your kids would love to come down here during the holidays.' Might take their minds off their father, she thought.

Bella just shook her head. 'Thanks all the same,' she said and finished her whisky. 'I'd better get back there. I'll switch on the storage heaters and light the fire. Then I'll be warm enough.' She slid down from her bar stool.

'What did you come down for today?' asked Fran.

Bella looked startled. 'I told you,' she said. 'I'm going to see Mr Grimshaw and sort out the sale.'

'Couldn't you have done that over the phone?'

'Fran!' said Libby in a scandalized undertone.

'Yes, I could,' said Bella wearily, 'but I wanted to sort a few things out before people come tramping all over the cottage.'

'Of course,' said Fran. 'Well, if you need any help, just call us.'

'No, thanks, Fran. You've done enough.' Bella lifted a vague hand. 'Bye.'

'I didn't like the way she said that,' said Libby. 'You were only doing what she asked you to.'

'She's scared,' said Fran, taking out her mobile.

'Was she trying to get away from Andrew?' said Libby. 'Who are you calling?'

'Ian.' Fran punched in the number.

'We should have gone with her,' said Libby, sliding inelegantly off her bar stool.

'I don't think we could have done anything up against Andrew, do you?' said Fran. 'Oh, Ian, yes, I'm sorry to call you so late, but I think this is an emergency.' She wandered off towards the door, still talking, while Libby fidgeted by the bar.

'We should go after her.'

'Ian was already on it,' said Fran. 'Andrew left home just after she did.'

'They've been following him, then?' Libby's eyes were wide.

'Yes. They knew we were there.'

'They watched us?' Libby sounded outraged.

'Only because they were watching the cottage waiting for Andrew to arrive. Come on, Lib, you know how it works.'

'Yes. So what happens now?'

'We wait,' said Fran.

'Here?'

'In case Bella needs us.'

'Oh.'

'Ian sounded a bit put out.'

'Wouldn't they move us on?' said Libby. 'If they're expecting trouble, I mean.'

'They might. I think Ian wanted us to go home.'

'I think that's very sensible,' said Libby, making for the door. 'Bella's got the police. She doesn't need us.'

'I think she does,' said a new voice.

Libby stopped short as Ian Connell appeared in the doorway.

'Can we go to her?' asked Fran.

'I'll take you,' said Connell.

They found Bella sitting in the front room of March Cottage wrapped in a blanket and accompanied by a female police officer. Libby looked over her shoulder nervously, as if expecting Andrew to appear wielding a blunt instrument.

'What happened?' Fran asked Connell.

Bella looked up and held out a hand. 'Please – let me talk to Fran.' Her voice sounded rusty.

Connell nodded and indicated that the police officer should step out of the way. Libby and Fran took chairs either side of Bella and Fran took her hand. Libby noticed from the corner of her eye the police officer taking a notebook out of her pocket.

'Did Andrew come?' Fran asked in a gentle voice.

Bella nodded.

'I said we should have gone after her,' muttered Libby. Fran shook her head.

'Go on.'

'I'm so sorry, Fran.'

'Sorry?' Libby looked at Fran.

'So am I,' said Fran. 'I didn't see Andrew until it was too late.'

Bella sighed. 'It was all my fault.'

'No it wasn't,' said Libby. 'Andrew –'

'Shut up, Libby,' said Fran.

Bella shook her head. 'Andrew only wanted to help,' she said.

'Help?'

'I've never been any good at doing things on my own, and I ended up telling him everything. He's always annoyed me, taking things over, never letting me do what I want, but in the end I told him.'

'About the cottage and the Alexandria,' nodded Libby. 'We know.'

'No,' said Bella, leaning forward. 'About Laurence Cooper. I killed him.'

271

Chapter Thirty-four

'SO THAT'S WHY SHE wanted you to find out about the family?' said Ben later. At Libby's request, he had driven over to pick up the two shell-shocked women from March Cottage and bring them back to number 17. Guy, Peter and Harry had all arrived carrying various aids to recovery such as champagne and whisky. Libby opted for whisky, saying this was hardly an occasion for celebration.

'Yes,' said Fran. 'Apparently, Laurence rang her the day after her first visit to March Cottage and said he was Dorinda's grandson and should have inherited half the estate. Bella said she didn't believe him, there was no mention of him in her aunt's letter, but he said he had proof.'

'And did he?' asked Peter.

'If he did, Bella didn't see it. She agreed to go down and meet him at the Alexandria, where he said he would show her the proof.'

'And she hit him over the head? Just like that?' Guy looked incredulous.

'According to Bella, who wanted to tell us everything because, she said, she felt so guilty about using us, he wanted to go and see the solicitor with her and got very aggressive. It was self-defence. She picked up something heavy – she wasn't sure what and hit him with it.'

'What did she do with the weapon?' asked Harry.

'Dropped it in one of the flowerbeds on the promenade. She was wearing gloves. I think the police found it – I can't remember.'

'So why bring you into it? And what about Dorothy? That was premeditated.' Ben topped up their glasses.

'She went home and confessed all to Andrew. It was he who went to Laurence's flat. Connell was furious with the London policeman who went to interview Bella and Andrew, although how he could have put two and two together I don't know.' Libby shivered.

'And it was Andrew who went up to Richmond,' said Fran. 'Meanwhile, he said Bella ought to take up Connell's suggestion about me looking into her family in case there was some proof about Laurence being Maria's brother. He said it would point to her.'

'Well, it would have done,' said Libby, 'except we never actually found concrete proof of it. But there was enough for us to realise Andrew was the only one who could have broken into Eric's flat, because he and Bella were the only ones connected to the case who knew about the photofit.'

'I can't believe that little mouse Bella was a killer,' said Ben, shaking his head.

'It really was accidental,' said Fran, 'but after she'd told Andrew he terrified her into doing whatever he said, and once he'd deliberately killed Dorothy, she was scared that he would turn on her, too.'

'Those poor children,' said Libby. 'What will happen to them?'

'Children?' asked Harry.

'Amanda and Anthony, GCSEs and A levels respectively. I can't bear to think of them.'

'Well, don't start. Or you'll be inviting them down here to keep an eye on them,' said Ben.

'Why did Andrew follow Bella down here?' asked Peter.

'She ran away from him, although why the silly bugger didn't realise he would follow her I can't think,' said Libby.

'I think she was going to go to the police,' said Fran. 'But the police got to her, just in time. Andrew was hammering on the door when they arrived. He went mad, apparently.'

'We didn't see that bit,' said Libby, 'we were in the pub.'

'It was nice of Ian to let her see us, wasn't it?' said Fran. 'He could have just hauled her off to the station.'

Guy gave her a sideways look.

'So that's that, then, is it?' said Harry. 'I can tell Danny all about it?'

'Yes, and Connell says we can tell old Jonathan. Poor old

Laurence. His father must have brought him up to think he had a stake in Anderson Place and the Alexandria,' said Libby.

'So why didn't he make a move earlier?' asked Peter.

'Apparently he waited until Maria died because his father had tried it on with her and with Jonathan's mother and got nowhere. I suppose he thought Bella would be a softer touch.' Fran sighed. 'What a mess.'

'Well, it's over now,' said Guy. 'All you've got to worry about is moving in to your lovely cottage.'

'And the panto,' said Libby.

'Oh, yes,' said Guy, pulling a face, 'the panto.'

'Just what we need,' said Ben. 'Cheer us all up.'

'I wasn't un-cheerful,' said Harry, flinging an arm round Peter. 'I've just got married.'

'Exactly,' said Libby. 'So let's drink to that.'

They all lifted their glasses. 'Peter and Harry,' they chorused.

'And *Jack And The Beanstalk*,' said Libby.

'And Coastguard Cottage,' said Guy.

Fran smiled. 'And no more murders.'

First Chapter of *Murder by the Sea*

THEY DID BOAT TRIPS around the bay. George took the *Dolphin* chugging round the uninhabited island in the centre every other day and Bert took the *Sparkler* to the little cove round the point. The next day they changed over. Tourists asked them if they didn't get bored doing the same thing all summer from Easter to September, but they just shrugged and smiled. The sea was always different, they said, the people were always different and the weather – well, the weather could be even more different. Sometimes they couldn't go out for a week; one year they hadn't gone out for the whole of August. Then they would sit in the Blue Anchor by the jetty, drinking tea and smoking, until the government forced them outside, where Mavis supplied them with a cheap canvas gazebo and an environmentally unfriendly heater.

But this year the weather was good. This year the regulars came back with smiles on their faces and the odd present of a bottle of whisky, which George and Bert would share on board the *Dolphin* or the *Sparkler* when the tourists went back to their hotels and apartments.

This year, too, there were the other visitors. Dark, olive-skinned, wary-looking, who worked in the hotel kitchens, cleaned the lavatories and worked on the farms outside the town. The tourists, for the most part, ignored them; the hoteliers and café owners despised them and paid them as little as they could get away with. The rest of the town's residents were divided in opinion. Those, like Mrs Battersby and Miss Davis, who complained bitterly to anyone who would listen and to a lot more who would not, that these people should not be allowed and should be sent back to their own countries, and those whose determinedly liberal attitude drove them to be fiercely defensive on the immigrants' behalf.

There were those, of course, who viewed both sides with amusement and detachment. George and Bert, and their friend Jane

Maurice, who worked for the local paper, were among them. Jane would go down to the Blue Anchor and chat to George and Bert, and occasionally go out on the *Dolphin* or the *Sparkler* and help them entertain their passengers.

Which was what she was doing one day in July at the beginning of the school holidays. It was George's turn to go round the island, and, due to the unusually calm sea, the *Dolphin* was packed with families, nice middle-class families who preferred a traditional British seaside holiday to the dubious delights of sun, sea and Malibu, with unbearable temperatures and incomprehensible currency. Those families who, had they chosen to fly to the sun, would not have dreamt of looking for English bars, breakfasts and nice cups of tea, but who were secretly pleased that these essential delights did not have to be foregone.

It was Jane who spotted it. Something had been washed up, or dumped, on the far side of the island, but what made her look harder was its position, well above even the waterline from the high equinoctial tides.

'George, what's that?'

George squinted through his cigarette smoke, keeping one hand on the wheel while pushing Jane out of the way with the other. Then he reached for the radio.

'What's going on down there?' Libby Sarjeant peered round her easel in the window of her friend Fran's cottage.

'Hmm?' Fran wandered in from the kitchen with an enamel jug full of flowers.

'Down at the end by The Sloop.' Libby stood up and leaned out of the open window. 'There's a police car and – what's a blue and yellow car?'

'Eh?' Fran came forward and leaned over Libby's shoulder. 'Oh – Coastguard, I think.'

'I didn't hear the lifeboat, did you?'

'No, but they don't always send up a flare, you know. Anyway, perhaps the lifeboat hasn't gone out.' Fran turned away from the window and looked round for somewhere to put the jug. 'Much as I love my fireplace,' she said, 'I wish it had a mantelpiece.'

Libby turned round. 'Instead of a bloody great wooden lintel? I know which I'd prefer.'

'I just need somewhere to put my flowers.' Fran sighed and put the jug on the hearth. 'I also need some more furniture.'

'Ooh, look!' said Libby suddenly. 'The lifeboat *had* gone out. It's on its way back.'

Abruptly the window went dark.

'Oh, dear,' said Libby and Fran together as the ambulance passed the cottage.

'Shall we go and have a look?' said Libby, wiping a brush on a piece of rag.

'Libby!' Fran looked shocked. 'Don't be such a ghoul. Anyway, we wouldn't be allowed to get near the place.'

'We could go to The Sloop for lunch?' suggested Libby hopefully.

'The Sloop will be cordoned off.'

'The Blue Anchor?'

'No, Libby! Really, you're incorrigible.' Fran went back towards the kitchen. 'If you're going to behave like this, I shan't let you paint from my window any more.'

Libby grinned and turned back to the easel, knowing this was an empty threat. She'd been painting pictures of this view for years without having been inside. Both she and Fran had owned pictures of this view as children, and now Fran actually lived here.

'How's Guy?' she asked now, considering where to position the next blob of white cloud.

'OK, I think.'

'You think? Don't you know?'

'I'm still trying to keep him at arm's length,' said Fran, and held up the kettle. 'Tea? Coffee?'

'Tea, please. But why?'

'Why am I keeping Guy at arm's length? I told you before I moved here. If I wasn't careful he'd have moved in within a week, and I want time on my own.'

'You can't really feel much for him, then.' Libby stabbed at her painting.

'Hello, pot? Who are you calling black?'

'Ben and I are – what's it called – Living Together Apart. Or something. We've got our own spaces'

'Well, so have Guy and I.'

'But you never see him.'

'I do, so.' Fran put a pretty bone china mug on the windowsill in front of Libby. 'Almost every day. And he's been very helpful with things like tap washers and radiators.'

'Taking advantage,' said Libby, with a sniff.

'Not at all. He notices things when he's round here and offers to put them right.'

Libby swung round to face her friend. 'And are you still keeping him at arm's length in the bedroom?'

'Libby!' Fran's colour rose and she turned away.

'Look, we've had conversations like this in the past, and I know how difficult it all is, but for goodness sake! You've known him for a year, now, and I can't believe he's still hanging on in there. He's still an attractive man, and you're no spring chicken, pardon the cliché.'

'Well, thanks.' Fran sat down in the armchair beside the inglenook fireplace.

'Oh, you know me,' shrugged Libby, with a sigh. 'Speaks me mind.'

'I had noticed.' Fran stared down into her coffee mug. 'As it happens, he *has* got past the bedroom door. No –' she held up a hand to stop Libby, 'I'm not saying anything else. We respect each other's space. He'd still like to be round here every night, but I really do want to savour this experience on my own for a bit.' She looked round the room with a smile. 'It's just like a fairy tale. I still can't quite believe it.'

Libby regarded her with an indulgent expression. 'Well, I'm glad to hear it,' she said. 'You deserve your cottage, and you deserve Guy. Mind you, I don't know how you kept it from me.'

'We don't live round the corner from each other any more, that's why, and Guy lives almost next door.'

Guy Wolfe lived above his small art gallery and shop a few yards along Harbour Street from Fran's Coastguard Cottage.

'He might know what's going on by The Sloop,' said Libby, turning to peer out of the window again. 'The ambulance is still there.'

Fran sighed. 'Drink your tea, and we'll go and see if Guy knows anything,' she said. 'You'll never settle otherwise.'

Libby smiled broadly. 'How well you know me,' she said.

In the event, it was Guy who came to them.

'I was going to take you both to The Sloop for lunch,' he said, after kissing Fran lightly on the cheek, 'but it looks as though it'll have to be The Swan.'

'That'll be lovely, thank you,' said Fran.

'Do you know what's happening?' asked Libby.

'Not sure, but an ambulance arrived as I was walking here, so whatever it is, it's serious.'

'We saw it,' said Libby. 'I'll go and wash my hands.'

'Look, the *Dolphin*'s come in,' said Guy as they left the cottage. They walked over to the sea wall and leaned over. Sure enough, the *Dolphin* was gently rocking at its mooring outside The Sloop while the passengers trooped off, watched over by a couple of yellow jacketed policemen.

'Perhaps that was it,' said Libby, 'an over-boarder.'

'Perhaps.' Guy frowned. 'I hope not.'

A passenger from the *Dolphin* broke away from the others and spoke to one of the policemen. Libby peered round Fran and tried to see what was happening.

'What's she doing?' she said.

'How do we know?' said Fran, exasperated. 'Come on Lib. We're going to The Swan.'

'I'm with the *Nethergate Mercury*,' said Jane. 'Can you tell me anything?'

The policeman looked her up and down. 'If you've just got off the boat, miss, you know more about it than I do.'

'Can I write it up for my paper?'

The policeman frowned. 'Don't know about that,' he said.

'Do you need me any more, then?' Jane had visions of bylines in the nationals and wanted to get to her phone.

'All passengers over there, miss. Names and addresses.'

Jane sighed and went over to the group of passengers huddled round George, who was holding forth in aggrieved tones to another, harassed-looking policeman. Under cover of the argument, which seemed to centre on George's rights as a citizen being undermined, she dragged her daily paper out of her shoulder bag, looked up the number of the news desk and punched it in to her mobile phone. Several other people were on their phones, so her quiet conversation didn't appear out of the ordinary, neither did her second one to her own paper, which had been put to bed earlier in the day. Her excited news editor promised to try and halt production until they could get in a stop press report and Jane, satisfied, put her phone away and moved up to hear what was being said by George and his policeman.

Fifteen minutes later, she and George were sitting outside The Blue Anchor with large mugs of coffee, supplemented, in George's case, with a generous tot of Mavis's whisky.

'Treatin' me like a suspect,' huffed George, lighting a cigarette with his ancient Zippo.

'No, they weren't, George,' said Jane. 'They had to get down exactly what happened, didn't they? And they talked to me as well.'

'Hmph,' said George as Jane's phone rang.

Her news editor said that he had wangled half an hour for her put in a full report, so could she do so now? Jane filled in what she could, and being an honest girl, told him which national newspaper she had rung.

'No bloody scoop, then, is it?' grumbled the news editor.

'More local people will see the *Mercury* tomorrow, though,' comforted Jane, 'and I can also do an in-depth follow up, can't I? I know the area.'

'If you can think of an angle, yes.'

'Anyway, it'll have been on the local news before then, won't it? Radio Kent will have got it, and so will Kent and Coast.'

'I know, I know,' sighed the news editor. 'Gets harder and harder for the poor newspaperman.'

'Who do you think it was, George?' said Jane, returning to the table.

'How do I bloody know? Couldn't see its face, could I? Wouldn't be a local. More sense 'n to go gallivantin' on Dragon Island.'

'Looked as though it'd been dumped, though.'

'Hmph,' said George again.

'I wish I could find out.'

'Course you do, you're a bloody reporter ain't you? Police'll give a statement, won't they?'

'I suppose so.' Jane sighed. 'They won't give much away. I wonder who'll be in charge of the investigation.'

'That there Connell, it'll be. If 'tis murder, anyhow.'

'Inspector Connell? He's scary.'

'Nah. That woman was scary.'

'What woman?'

'The one what 'e got involved in that murder last winter. The body in the ole Alexandria.'

Jane looked along the bay to where The Alexandria Theatre stood on the promenade, now surrounded by scaffolding.

'Weren't there two women? Oh –' Jane pointed a finger. 'You mean that psychic, don't you?'

'Lives along 'ere, she does.'

Jane looked surprised. 'Does she?'

'Didn't you find that out when you was coverin' the story?' George looked sly.

'I didn't cover it,' said Jane. 'Bob did.'

'Ah, the boss. Stands to reason. Anyway, she moved in round about that time, far as I remember. Coastguard Cottage, 'er lives.'

'Does she, now,' said Jane, looking thoughtful.

'Look, now.' George pointed. 'Ain't got it all to yerself, now, 'ave you?'

A TV van was moving slowly along Harbour Street. Jane sighed.

'It must be serious,' said Fran, as they watched the Kent and Coast Television van stop by The Blue Anchor.

'Not necessarily,' said Libby, evincing a cynical view of local reportage.

'They were quick, weren't they,' said Guy, wiping his soup plate with the last of his bread.

'Media wire,' said Libby knowledgably. 'A reporter must have got on to it straight away.'

'It'll be on the local news tonight, then,' said Fran.

'Probably on the local radio news now,' said Guy. 'Shall we go back to mine and see if we can find out?'

'No, thanks,' said Fran quickly, as Libby opened her mouth eagerly. 'Libby will have to finish her painting, or clear things away, anyway.'

'OK.' Guy shrugged. 'Will you be around this evening, Libby?'

'No.' Libby sighed. 'Peter wants a production meeting.' Libby and her friend Peter Parker helped run The Oast House Theatre, owned by Peter's family, in their home village of Steeple Martin.

'For what?'

'The next panto, would you believe?' Libby sighed again. 'I've written it this year, but I want to be in it, not direct.'

'Is it mutually exclusive?' Guy regarded her with bright brown eyes full of amusement. 'Would you be struck off if you did both?'

'It's too difficult to do both, to be honest. Anyway, I don't want to strain my poor brain any more than I have to, and directing's such a responsibility.'

'Are you going to do it again, Fran?' Guy looked over at Fran, whose serene gaze was fixed on the horizon, her dark hair framing her face like a latter day – and slightly mature – Madonna.

'No.' Fran looked back at him. 'I don't learn lines as well as I used to, and it's one thing turning out every night if you live round the corner, and quite another with a twenty minute drive each way.'

'Shame,' said Libby. 'I'll miss you.'

'I said I'd help, Lib. Props, or something. As long as I don't have to be there all the time.'

Guy was looking pleased. 'So you'll be here more often,' he said.

'More often than what?" asked Fran, looking surprised. 'I'm here all the time at the moment.'

'I meant more often than if you had been doing the panto,' said Guy, with a cornered expression.

'Ah,' said Libby and Fran together.

'Come on, then,' said Fran. 'Let's go back and see how that picture's coming along.'